MAFIA TARGET

THE KINGS OF ITALY

BOOK 4

MILA FINELLI

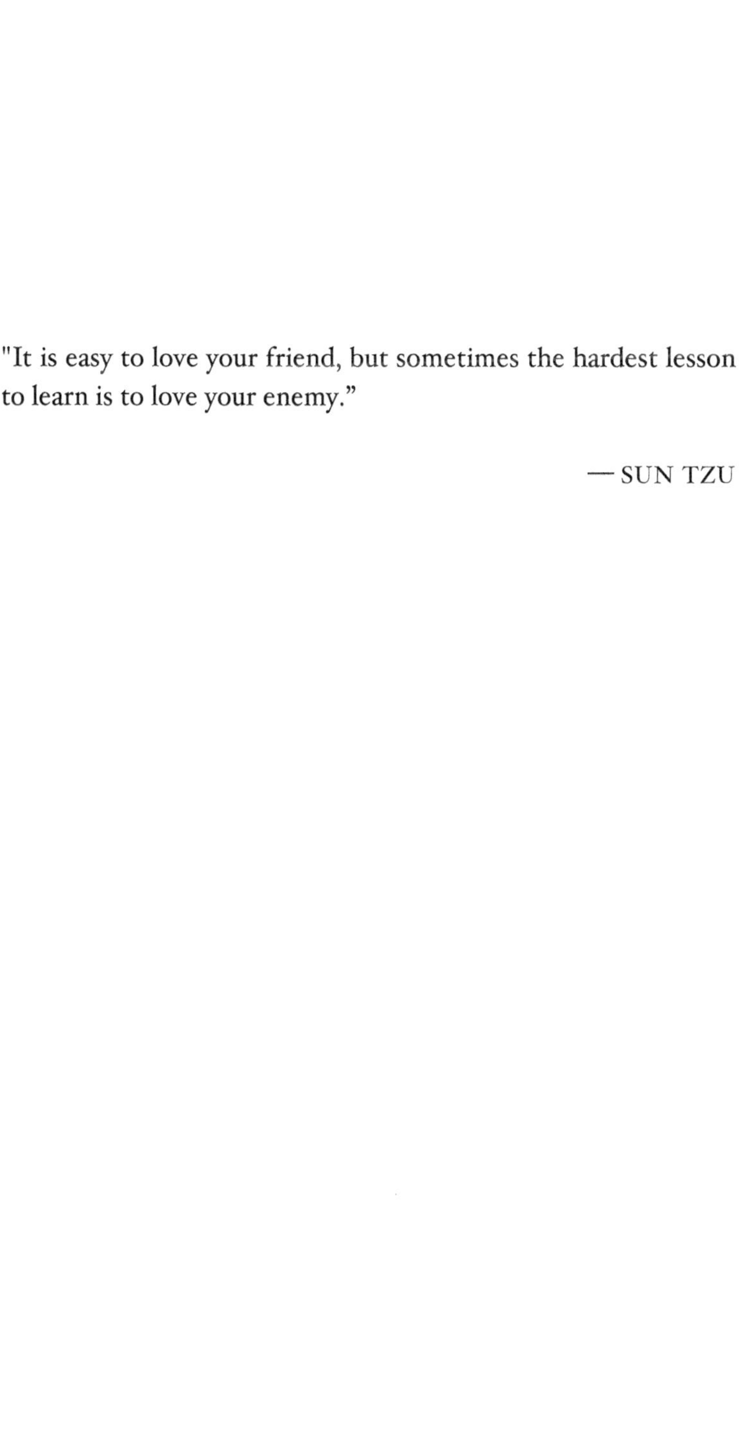

"It is easy to love your friend, but sometimes the hardest lesson
to learn is to love your enemy."

— SUN TZU

CHAPTER ONE

Alessio

A Siderno rooftop on a warm September afternoon

The Calabrian sun beat down on the roof, hot and unrelenting. Familiar.

I was in position early. The view from up here allowed me to see the whole street. I slipped a slice of fresh fig into my mouth and slowly chewed.

Most of my time was spent alone, waiting. I didn't mind. I didn't play nice with others. This was one of the many reasons the army and I had parted ways.

I pulled on the brim of my baseball cap, keeping to the shadows. There was a slight wind out of the east today, but nothing I needed to worry about. I could almost do this job in my sleep.

Killing was the one thing I excelled at, and the Italian Army had rewarded me for it. I served for eight years, the most decorated sniper in the 1st Bersaglieri Regiment. We saw combat in Afghanistan, Syria, Iraq, and other places I wasn't at liberty to divulge.

When I left the service, people wanted me to keep killing for them. I liked this better. It allowed me to travel and keep my own schedule. And I made a fuck lot of money.

After the number of kills climbed beyond fifty, I lost track. It wasn't important. Until my hands started to shake and my eyesight failed, this was my purpose. *No one is better at it.*

My phone rang. I looked at the display. Normally I wouldn't answer while on a job, but there were a few pieces still unknown today. This might be one of them.

I tapped the glass. "Pronto."

"Everything is in place," said Vito D'Agostino, the brother and consigliere to a Napoli mafia don. "Our man on the inside said we're a go in forty-five minutes."

I checked my watch. One o'clock exactly. I set my timer to begin a countdown. "Va bene."

"As soon as it's done we'll wire your assistant the remaining half of the money."

This was standard, but unnecessary. I never failed. "Of course."

"This could get ugly once word gets out."

Vito had mentioned this before. I didn't care. There was a reason no one could find me unless I allowed them. "Don't worry. I'll forget our association just as soon as I'm paid."

"Good." Vito hung up.

I didn't care about repercussions. To me, this was just a job. The reasons why, or what the target had done to deserve death, didn't matter to me. I was collecting a paycheck for services rendered.

Once I fired the shot, I would stow my rifle and head for the Ducati waiting at the base of the stairs. Minutes later I would jump into a car and drive into the mountains. Then I would disappear for a few weeks at one of my many homes around Europe.

The weather in the French countryside was particularly nice this time of year.

Thinking of wine and cheese, I carefully unpacked my rifle from its case. It was the same type used by the British Special Forces, the L115A4 Long Range Rifle. Portable and concealable, the weapon has excellent low light and daylight optics, a double turn telescopic sight, and a suppressor to reduce the flash and noise. And it had never let me down.

I unpacked it methodically, each piece in the same order. I never deviated. The others in my unit had called me superstitious, but they were superstitious, too. Many Italians were, but snipers even more so.

With my rifle assembled, I approached the edge of the building. I kept low, a dark dot on a random rooftop. I sat with my rifle and case by my feet. The roof's temperature was nearly unbearable on my skin, but I forced myself to wait it out. I'd endured worse.

Soon my body adjusted and I maintained my slow and steady breathing. Twenty minutes. My target would be well guarded. I examined the address across the street, where the wife's doctor worked. They would undoubtedly pull the car directly out front and try to hurry inside.

I needed to be quick.

I loaded the rifle. These bullets were low drag, heavier, and specially made for me by a man in Berlin. I found them more accurate than the kind I used in the military.

Ten minutes.

I flexed my fingers. Re-tied my shoelaces. Verified the wind and distance. Adjusted my sight. There was no room for error.

By the time the line of cars pulled around the corner and began to slow, I was already in position. I had the second car in my scope, as this was undoubtedly the one carrying my target.

I rubbed the gold cornicello charm around my neck for luck, then put the tip of my finger on the trigger.

The first car advanced down the street, but the second car, the one I was tracking, came to an abrupt halt farther up the block. The third car stopped behind it. I held my breath. Had they spotted me?

Impossible. There had to be another reason.

I checked the first car to make sure. He definitely wasn't in there. I shifted back to the second car. The door opened and I saw a well-dressed man emerge. Minchia! I hadn't expected this.

Before I could pull the trigger, a larger man blocked my angle.

Porca di puttana. Then the target helped a woman out of the car. I didn't have a clear kill shot. The entire group walked to the gelato shop, disappearing inside.

I shifted my shoulders and made some quick calculations, then adjusted my scope for the new distance. I would need to kill him when he emerged from the shop. Waiting, I forced my heartbeat to slow, my breath to even out.

Then I saw him.

The most gorgeous man I'd ever seen stepped into my view, and it was like being struck by lightning. *Colpo di fulmine.*

A thunderbolt.

My breath left my lungs in a rush as I studied him. Tall and thin, with bright blue eyes and dark hair. Young, maybe nineteen or twenty. His jaw was a work of art, his face absolute perfection. He hadn't shaved today and that scruff was sexy as fuck.

I followed him as he moved, needing to make sure I wasn't hallucinating. His blue shirt was tailored to fit perfectly, the color matching his eyes. His jeans clung to his long legs like the fabric had been made expressly for him. No man outside of a Milan runway had the right to look this good.

Did he work for my target?

He laughed at something that was said and I stared, mesmerized. Dio, that smile. It could melt ice caps.

I was attracted to both men and women, but I'd never felt a flicker of interest for anyone while on a job before now. Why this man? I watched a few more seconds, hoping for answers.

Then I noticed my pulse was hammering in my ears. Cristo, I needed to focus and calm down.

I jerked the sight away from the beautiful man to watch the storefront. As I waited, I tried to regulate my breathing. I hadn't been this rattled before. It was a bad sign.

Basta. I would be fine. I once stayed awake for three days, lying in wait to successfully kill a Taliban leader. I could do this.

In and out . . . in and out. I counted my breaths and willed my muscles to relax.

But in the end it all happened too fast. I hadn't planned for gelato or colpo di fulmine. I rushed my shot.

And I missed.

CHAPTER TWO

Alessio

Four years later
Málaga, Spain

I didn't want to be here.

In fact, I wanted nothing to do with this man or his family. He was the cause of the only blunder of my career, a shameful secret that only few knew.

I watched from the shadows as he strode along the dark street. He was using a different name now, as he did in every city he visited, but I would know that face anywhere. He'd grown bigger, more handsome. His jaw more angular. I felt the same jolt of awareness and attraction as I did four years ago.

Cazzo, it was like a cruel joke.

Earlier this week I received the call I had been dreading.

"I need you to drop everything and go to Málaga," Don D'Agostino ordered.

I swallowed a sigh. "This is for the son, I assume. Vito warned me."

"He's using the name Javier Martín. I have an image of him in the Málaga airport five days ago."

He'd caused me to miss on that Siderno street. And now they wanted me to hunt him down and kill him? "No."

Don D'Agostino snarled on the other end, "Do you honestly think to refuse me?"

"You can't expect me to—"

"What I expect is for you to do anything I fucking ask. You failed in your last job for me, and with one call I can let Ravazzani know who shot him and almost killed his pregnant wife. Is this what you want?"

"If I kill his son, he will hunt me down like a dog."

"That is not my problem."

Fucking mafioso. I never should've accepted the job to kill Fausto Ravazzani in the first place.

Giulio Ravazzani turned the corner and I followed at a distance. It hadn't taken long to track him down once I arrived yesterday. Now it was a matter of opportunity, of finding the right place and the right time.

I liked to observe my targets. Learn their routines. I didn't like to rush it, if at all possible.

This was no hardship with Giulio. He was gorgeous, his movements fluid. I could see the outline of a gun beneath his jacket. Smart of him, considering the number of enemies his family has accumulated over the years. He hadn't shaved for a few days, the whiskers on his jaw not quite a beard but a sexy scruff.

It's a shame I have to kill him.

Pulling a baseball cap onto his head, he entered a large building. What was he doing?

I slunk toward the side, keeping out of sight. There was a fire escape leading up to a higher floor. If I could reach the windows, I should be able to sneak inside.

Jumping, I grabbed onto the iron bar and lifted myself up. Then I climbed the fire escape. The first window I tried was painted shut, but the next one opened. I slipped in.

The old wood floor was dusty, like no one had been up here in years. My steps were careful, silent. I bent down and edged toward the sound of voices.

I spotted a group of men on the ground floor. Giulio was standing beside a table, one white rectangular package in front of him.

They were speaking in English.

"Despite what our mutual contacts are telling me, this can't be better than the product we already import," a man wearing alligator boots said, nearly sneering at Giulio.

"If you don't believe me," Giulio said, "try it."

Alligator Boots motioned to the brick. "If you insist."

Taking out a pocket knife, Giulio cut open the package. A tiny amount of white powder fell onto the table. Giulio stepped back and gestured toward what I had to assume was coke.

One of Alligator Boots' associates stepped forward. He dragged his finger through the powder, opened his mouth and placed it on his gums. I couldn't see his face, but I heard him suck in a breath. In Spanish, he said to Alligator Boots, "That is some good shit."

Cosa? How in the fuck would he know that from spreading on his gums? What about a testing kit?

"I told you," Giulio confirmed. "Not only is it better quality, it's cheaper than what you're getting now."

Was Giulio importing drugs into Málaga? Ma sei pazzo? The drug business was dangerous. Though I supposed he was used to it, being Fausto Ravazzani's son.

And it was lucrative. This would explain how Giulio was surviving outside his father's empire.

"Cheaper, how?" Alligator Boots demanded.

"I have contacts," was all Giulio said. "They only work with me. If you want access to this, it has to be through me."

"And I am supposed to believe you? Un niño?" *A boy.* All the men chuckled.

"Do you like money, Señor Martinez? Because I do. And if you aren't interested in making it, there are four other men on my list. I know for certain the Bratva will say yes. Do you know what happens then?" He paused and stared Alligator Boots down. "Me and the Russians run you out of fucking business."

Madre di dio. A dark thrill skated along my spine. Giulio had balls standing up to these men.

I was impressed.

"What if I just kill you and save myself the trouble?" Señor Martinez asked.

"Then my people will go to the Bratva and you'll still be out of business."

"People?" Señor Martinez looked around dramatically, his voice laced with sarcasm. "What other people?"

Now it was Giulio's turn to sneer. "Do you think I have the coca plants in my cellar? That I'm growing them, soaking the leaves and grinding them up myself? My *people* do this—and trust me. You do not want to fuck around with them or me."

Che palle. This display of power, it was astounding. I could feel my groin tighten as lust thickened my dick. I reached down to shift myself in my jeans.

Señor Martinez rubbed his jaw. "How much can you get?"

"Twenty kilos today."

"How cheap?"

"One million Euros."

Señor Martinez cocked his head. "For all of it?"

"Yes. I know you normally pay significantly more. So I'll expect all of it up front in cash. Right now."

Señor Martinez nodded once and beckoned to a man in the back of the group. The associate came forward and put a briefcase on the table next to the coke. Stacks of cash were inside, and Señor Martinez counted out the amount Giulio quoted.

Giulio retrieved a duffle bag off the floor, then stuffed the cash inside. "There's a loose floorboard in the back left corner. Pull up those boards and your coke is all there."

Señor Martinez sent three men over, and they quickly removed the boards. Then they counted the packages. "It's all here," one of them shouted.

Señor Martinez said to Giulio, "If this does well, when can we—"

But Giulio had already disappeared, along with the cash. The package was still on the table.

A smile tugged at my lips. Cazzo, I liked this man. He was crafty and resourceful. Brave. The rumors I heard of his father were much the same, with a touch of a psychotic murderer sprinkled in. But I didn't know Giulio had it in him, too.

I hurried back the way I came. Soon I saw Giulio striding up the walk. I kept my head down and moved to the opposite side of the street. This allowed me to track him in the store windows rather than looking directly at him. He checked over his shoulders several times, but Señor Martinez and his men hadn't trailed him.

Smoothly, he removed his baseball cap and unzipped the duffle bag. Inside was a backpack, which obviously held all the money. He dropped the empty duffle and his cap in a bin, then hefted the backpack over his shoulders. "Idiots," he said with a sly grin.

Fuck me. This twenty-two-year-old was carrying a million Euros on his back.

Colpo di fulmine.

I rubbed my chest and tried to ease the ache there. I hadn't felt this much attraction to another person in a long time. Maybe ever. I didn't understand it. He and I had never met, yet I was drawn to him. I wanted to bite his hard jaw and feel his rough hands on my dick.

He went into his apartment. Currently I was renting the place across the street, but I had no interest in watching him hide the money inside. I'd rather wait here in case he came back out. I hoped he felt the need to celebrate tonight.

Because that I wanted to see.

I'll kill him eventually... but I didn't have to do it *tonight*.

Giulio

I WAS on the search for a distraction.

The bass echoed in my chest as I wound my way through the club. Málaga was very gay friendly and it was easy for me to blend in. Just another man, unattached and searching for a good time. Nothing serious.

I experienced something serious once. Never again.

And blending in was even more important now. Someone out there wanted me dead, but I refused to give them the chance. Until I discovered and destroyed those responsible for that car bomb meant for me —the one that killed Paolo—I had to be careful. So I frequently moved cities and changed my identity.

Which was why I came to places like this. Crowded, anonymous. In and out quickly, just long enough to satisfy this itch.

My phone buzzed in my pocket. I quickly checked the name. *Mimi's Papà*. Mimi was a nickname for Noemi, my half-sister. This was my father calling me.

I declined the call and slipped my phone back in my pocket, but not before noticing there were three other missed calls from him. Cristo. I didn't want to hear whatever Fausto had to say, especially not right now. I'd ring him back when I finished here.

A husky voice with an Andalusian accent said in my ear, "La que tú me haces." A compliment, sort of like, *What you do to me*.

As I turned to see if this might be tonight's choice, my gaze snagged on a different man across the room. To say he was hot didn't do him justice. This man was an inferno, but not in the classic sense. Built and tall, he had jet black hair that was just long enough to show its natural waves. Olive skin that reminded me of home, and a scar running along the cheek of his face. Danger radiated off him in waves and my dick twitched.

His grayish blue eyes were locked on me, tracking me like prey, and I shivered. I recognized a hunter when I saw one.

My heart pounded, the air crackling. He was exactly my type. I liked them menacing and stoic, with enough brawn to make me want to pin them down or shove them up against a wall.

I hadn't seen him here before. This made it even more appealing. If he wasn't a regular, chances were we wouldn't run into each other again after tonight.

I let my gaze wander up and down his body, the message clear.

Shaking off the Andalusian hopeful, I moved toward the back of the club. Toward the dark corners where people like me thrived. In those black recesses where no one could see, I could finally let loose for a few moments.

Anticipation crawled over my skin, through my balls and along my shaft. I knew the man from across the bar was following me. I could feel it through some mafioso sixth sense or something. I was getting more turned on by the second, just imagining grabbing that thick hair while I shoved my dick in his mouth.

I hadn't fucked or been fucked in a long time, not since I left Belgium. Instead, I stuck to hand jobs and blow jobs, which were fast and impersonal. I got what I needed and moved on. It was enough.

Darkness enveloped me as I reached the back of the club. I could hear grunts and groans, see the shape of straining figures, but I didn't stop. I liked this feeling, the buzz that built in my blood right before we got our hands on each other.

A palm landed on my shoulder, spinning me. My back crashed against the wall. *Che cazzo?* Once I recovered from my surprise, I shifted and reversed our positions. We held there for a moment, assessing each other close up, breathing hard. It was the man from across the bar. As I'd hoped, he tracked me to this dark corner, ready for whatever came next. I could feel his dick pressed against my hip through his jeans. I was dying to taste him.

But that wasn't how this worked.

I had a routine. I forced them to their knees, they sucked me off, and I disappeared. No promises, no hard feelings. No reciprocation.

This man, though. I could see myself on my knees for him.

His muscles tightened beneath my fingertips and he readied to move. To leave? To kiss me? I wrapped my fingers around his throat. "*Quédate,*" I growled, telling him to stay.

My dick was stiff and throbbing, eager. I needed this fast and rough, then I had to leave.

With a little pressure I pushed him toward the ground. He resisted for a half second before he sank to the floor, his face in front of my crotch. I unfastened my belt and unzipped, but that was as far as I went. I liked for them to do the rest, to reach inside my clothing and pull out my cock. To prove they were needy little sluts, gagging for it.

He didn't disappoint. Thick fingers dug into my jeans and briefs to find my length and expose it. My skin was hot as he gripped me tight, and I shoved my clothing lower on my hips to make it easier. His light gaze met mine as he parted his lips and sucked me deep inside his mouth.

Wet heat surrounded me and my eyes nearly rolled back in my head. "*Joder*," I gasped, using the Spanish equivalent of cazzo.

He bobbed, his mouth creating ideal suction while one hand remained on the base of my shaft, pulling. There was no teasing, no uncertainty. Just a fast blow job intended to get me off. *Perfetto*.

I let myself sink into the sensation, drifting, turning off my brain. He was good, taking my cock to the entrance of his throat as I thrust my hips. I wished we had time for me to slip inside that tight passage, fuck his throat until he couldn't breathe, but that was too intimate for this. There was no time for training. I didn't do those things anymore.

He relaxed and let me use him. I threaded my fingers through his thick hair and speared his mouth with my cock, the pleasure inside me coiling as I rocked. His tongue slid forward, gliding under my cock, and he gave me the tiniest scrape of his teeth.

Madonna, I never wanted it to end.

All too soon my balls were tingling, my muscles clenching, and my cock swelled against his tongue. With a groan, I began coming, thick jets shooting into his mouth, my hips jerking. He kept sucking, draining me, and it prolonged my orgasm. If I weren't pretending to be someone else, someone Spanish, I would praise him in Italian with all the words I knew. But my Spanish was limited, so I just stroked his hair, petting him, as I tried to catch my breath.

He eased off my cock and looked up at me with an unreadable expression. After a long beat he swallowed, the muscles in his throat working as he drank my load down.

Madre di dio, that was hot.

I sighed, wishing I'd met him in another life. One where I could sink to my knees and pleasure him in return. One where I wasn't on the run from the life I'd left behind. A former soldier for my father, who was one of the most powerful and dangerous men in Europe.

I stepped back, tucked myself away and zipped up. After a nod at the man still on his knees, I turned and went in the opposite direction, intent on getting outside as quickly as possible.

No one stopped me. No one followed me. I was just another body in a sea of bodies. The faded light of an exit door beckoned, so I headed toward it. A minute later I was standing in an alley, the cool night air washing over me.

Walking toward the street, I pulled out my phone and dialed. He answered on the first ring.

"Why the fuck didn't you pick up?" Fausto snarled into my ear.

"*Perdonami*, Papà."

"Would I call you five times if it wasn't a fucking emergency?"

Yes he would. My father didn't like to be ignored. "Is it Frankie or one of the kids?"

He gave a long exhale and I knew the sound well. He was trying to rein in his temper. "It's you, *figlio mio*."

Relief filled me. This was nothing new. I was in constant danger. I started in the direction of my apartment, which was four blocks away. As always, I checked my surroundings. This had been ingrained in me since birth. "Yes?"

"Someone has taken out a hit on you."

I wanted to roll my eyes, but that was disrespectful to my father, even if he couldn't see me. A hit had been out on me for more than four years. But I was smart enough to not let them find me.

"Oh?" I said to my father.

"You sound unsurprised at this news."

Nothing got by Fausto. "Just tell me what you know."

"Have you heard of Alessandro Ricci?"

"I remember the name." Ricci was a sniper, trained by the Italian military. He was rumored to be the best, used by countries to take out heads of state and other politicians. Very high level wet work, not the kind of person normally used by the 'Ndrangheta, who preferred to handle their own murders quietly. An assassin like Ricci was too high-profile.

"Good, then I won't have to explain how dangerous this is for you. I want you to come—"

"No." I shut down that suggestion before he even finished. "I won't, so don't ask."

I was a gay man, the former heir to a mafia empire. No doubt the 'Ndrangheta would prefer to make me disappear. My very existence embarrassed them, and I would never bring that kind of danger near my half-siblings and stepmother. I was better off living far away from them.

I heard a thud and imagined my father pounding a palm on his desk. After a few beats, he said, "Dai, Giulio. This is not like the other."

"The car bomb, you mean?"

"Yes, the one that killed your *ragazzo*. This is very serious."

As if the car bomb hadn't been. Paolo was blown up in front of my eyes, for fuck's sake. With my limited resources over the last four years, I'd been hunting those responsible, digging into everyone I could think of who might've planted that bomb. Fausto was convinced it had been Mommo, one of his rivals, who was now dead.

I wasn't sure. And until I was sure, I wasn't stopping my search.

And this new contract only confirmed my theory. Whoever tried to kill me in Belgium had now gone to Ricci to finish the job. "Who hired Ricci?"

"We are working on finding out."

"Zio Marco?" I said, knowing my father's consigliere would be right there.

"Sì, Giulio?"

"Do you have a photo of Ricci you can send me? I want to know what he looks like."

"Of course."

"Giulio," my father barked. "I do not want you trying to deal with Ricci on your own. You need to be here, at the castello. Where I can protect you. Get on the first flight—"

Was he not listening to me?

Lowering my phone, I disconnected. There. He could stew for a few days.

Five years ago, I never would've hung up on my father. But I was different.

Besides, I wasn't his responsibility any longer. He should be focusing on his other children, his wife. His empire. He didn't need to worry about me, a grown man.

I unlocked the door to the old building where I was renting a room. When I reached my apartment, I went in and shut the door, then engaged all four locks.

Pulling out my phone, I spent a few minutes searching the internet, but failed to uncover a photo of Ricci. Unsurprising. What good was an assassin everyone could recognize?

Marco still hadn't texted the photo, so I began undressing. I was far more tired than I expected. My limbs were loose, the kind of peace only a great orgasm could provide. Today has been a good day. A million Euros and a fantastic blow job. What more did a man need?

I wouldn't mind a repeat performance with the guy tonight from the club. I never hooked up with the same man twice, but I could almost make an exception for another one of those mind-numbing blow jobs.

My phone chimed with a text. Marco.

I opened the message—and all the air left my lungs in a rush.

Dropping onto my bed, I stared at the image. It was blurry and taken from an awkward angle, but there was no mistaking that face.

This . . . couldn't be right. There had to be some mistake. My ears started ringing as I tried to make sense of it.

No, no, no. *Cazzo madre di dio*.

The man from the club? The one who had sucked my brains out through my dick?

It was Alessandro Ricci.

CHAPTER THREE

Alessio

Ten days later
Santorini, Greece

I slipped another slice of tomato in my mouth and walked along the rooftops. This was the part of the job I most liked, if I were being honest. Tracking my target allowed me to disappear, become a ghost. No one knew I was there until I was ready to let them know.

Like the night I let him see me in Málaga.

Giulio disappeared immediately after that blow job. I lost him for a little bit, but caught up with him again here in Greece five days ago.

I'd spent a lot of time researching Giulio Ravazzani since Málaga. After the car bomb in Belgium, he bounced around in the Scandina vian countries. I had to assume his Mediterranean looks made it impossible to blend in there, so he got smarter.

He traveled to places where men looked more like him. Began working with his former contacts to import drugs and undercut the existing local dealers. When the situation turned dangerous—and it always did for a man working alone—he moved to another city and assumed another identity.

He was smart. His money sat in off-shore accounts that were nearly untraceable. He wore caps in public for the CCTV cameras. Switched his phone every few weeks. Never logged into his social media profiles.

He never let down his guard. Except for his late-night visits to clubs.

Giulio couldn't seem to resist the lure of anonymous encounters. Each one was the same as it had been with me. A dark corner, a man on his knees with Giulio's cock in his mouth. Giulio never offered relief in exchange, instead immediately departing after shooting his load and returning to his apartment.

That I was one of many didn't sit well with me.

The hookup in Málaga had been different. Good. Satisfying—though he hadn't touched me. I couldn't explain it.

But to know he did this over and over again, a different man every time? It soured the memory for me.

He's just a job.

I couldn't forget this. Enzo D'Agostino had my balls in a vise and my only priority was to assassinate the Ravazzani heir. Otherwise, my career as an assassin was over. Word would get around that I failed. No one would hire me after that.

Word would also get to Fausto Ravazzani that I pulled the trigger in Siderno four years ago. He would hunt me down with all the resources at his disposal.

So why wasn't Giulio dead already?

Maybe because I found this man fascinating. I knew what it was like to live secretly in a dangerous world. Desperate to leave home, I joined the Italian military when I was seventeen. By that point I knew I was bisexual, and being around so many men meant I had to be extremely careful. Encounters were fleeting and kept very, very quiet.

Giulio turned and entered an open-air food market. My phone buzzed. With Giulio shopping I had a free minute to check who was ringing me. I tapped the glass. "Pronto."

"Where are you?" Former Russian intelligence, Sasha oversaw my business. She was ruthless, cold and methodical. Exactly like me.

"On a rooftop," I answered.

"I was contacted by a Serbian—"

"No."

"Do you not even wish to hear how much?"

"No."

I was not for hire at the moment. When I completed this job I could go to Serbia or Tanzania or New Zealand, wherever the fuck. But for right now I was working on Giulio. "Is that all?"

"*Mudak*!" she swore in Russian. "I am sitting around doing nothing, a waste of my valuable time. You are dragging your feet. Just kill him already and—"

I disconnected. Giulio had paid for his vegetables and was leaving the market. I needed to move.

The rooftops were close together here, which made it easy to travel the city from up above. Giulio had no idea he was being tracked, though he kept his head down and didn't speak to anyone. I admired the shift of his broad shoulders, the smooth muscles under his clothing. My nonna would have called him *un vero fusto*, a real hunk. In her later years she watched a lot of American reality television shows, which had colored her already robust vocabulary.

I still missed her. She'd been the only person I gave a shit about in my entire life.

I popped the last piece of tomato into my mouth and jumped onto the next roof. A couple was making out on the far side, but they didn't notice me as I crept silently along. Giulio walked to his apartment, probably to fix *pranzo*. He favored risotto, usually mushroom, then a frittata. To finish he would slice apricots or peaches. Then he would work on his laptop or watch something on his tablet. Pass the time until he could go out to a nightclub.

The mornings were my favorite, though.

After drinking caffè, he completed a rigorous workout routine while clad only in a pair of tight briefs. There were push-ups and pull-ups, high-intensity jumps and lunges. His cock and balls were on display, and I enjoyed watching them as he moved. Sometimes he would put on clothes and go out for a jog after. I easily trailed him, though I rose before dawn to run ten miles every day.

When he reached his building I stayed on the roof, hidden in the shadows. I rented the apartment directly across from his, but it was a nice afternoon and I liked to be outside.

He started playing music and took out his vaping pen. I never drank or smoked so I didn't understand the appeal, but seeing Giulio sprawled on the couch, his dark hair falling over his brow, as he let his lungs fill was incredibly sexy. He would soon be loose and relaxed, and I wished I could crawl between his legs and lick him all over, suck on him until he came down my throat again.

It would be no effort at all to kill him right now. I had an easy shot, straight through the window and into his forehead. There was no wind today and he'd never spot me up here. But I wouldn't. There was plenty of time to do what needed to be done.

For now, I was curious. Why was I so fascinated with this man?

I cursed myself for ever taking the job to kill Fausto Ravazzani. I normally didn't involve myself in the petty squabbling of the mafia. But I was a hired gun, nothing more. No allegiances, no loyalty except to myself.

If someone had enough money, I was available.

Still, I shouldn't have attempted a job on the seventeenth of the month. It was terrible luck, but D'Agostino's people had pushed, saying this was the only day Ravazzani would be outside the castello. An appointment at his wife's obstetrician. And I had failed.

Giulio's phone buzzed. He checked the caller then tossed the phone onto the table. Ah. His father, most likely. Don Ravazzani was keeping close tabs on his eldest son, now that word about the hit had circulated. No doubt he was pressuring Giulio to return to Siderno. Thankfully Giulio resisted, which was foolish on his part. Other than the Vatican, the castello was the one place in the world where I couldn't get to him. Probably.

The phone buzzed again. With a heavy sigh, Giulio picked it up and read the screen. He grinned and accepted the call. "Ciao, *matrigna*."

Francesca Ravazzani, then. The two of them were close, talking almost every day.

Whatever she said made him chuckle, softening the harsh bitterness normally lurking around his eyes. Or maybe it was the effects of the weed? Mesmerized, I couldn't look away from him, while my dick thickened with the memory of Málaga.

Annoyed with myself, I heaved a small imperceptible sigh.

Giulio's head snapped toward the windows and his gaze locked with mine. I held perfectly still. Had he spotted me?

No, no. It was impossible. I was concealed by the shadows, my clothing blending in with the surroundings.

And besides, no one ever spotted me.

In a blink, he rolled off the sofa and disappeared from sight.

Minchia! He'd spotted me.

———

Giulio

Two months later
Isle of Canna, Scotland, U.K.

My BALLS WOULD SOON FREEZE off.

Growing up in southern Italy, I was used to warm weather. Sunshine. Rolling green hills and wine. This was the exact opposite.

Scotland was fucking cold.

A tiny island in the Inner Hebrides, Canna was four miles long and one mile wide. The population was only sixteen, including me, and these people didn't care for outsiders. Most looked at me like I was a wild animal. I couldn't give a shit. This place was remote as fuck. Only three ferries went in and out during a given week, mostly for supplies.

Let Alessandro Ricci find me here.

How that *coglione* tracked me to Greece was a mystery. Changing countries, phones, and names wasn't enough to elude him, obviously.

I discarded anything that might leave a digital footprint in Santorini. Then I went completely off the grid. I hadn't touched my bank accounts. No calls or messages to anyone I knew. I bought a farm house when I first arrived here and I lived simply. It was lonely, but I was alive.

The lack of devices meant my investigation into Paolo's killers had stalled. That was what bothered me most about being forced to retreat here. Not the lack of movies and television shows, or the absence of a decent bottle of wine. Paolo's killers remained unpunished, while I was stuck here, hiding. I hated Ricci for that alone.

No doubt my father was working to eliminate the hit out on me. But I didn't want to be his responsibility any longer. I was no longer his heir, no longer in the 'ndrina. He needed to focus on my half-siblings and his new wife. This was my problem.

I rolled my shoulders, sinking deeper into my coat, and kept walking. Three sheep lived at the farmhouse and I fed them every day. I grew up with lambs in Siderno, as well as pigs and horses, so I knew a little about taking care of animals. They also kept me company.

My life was a sad fucking state of affairs. But I was alive.

The sheep were eager to see me today, bleating as they rushed over. I knew they were only excited for the bucket in my hand, but I smiled when they nuzzled me. "Ciao, amici!"

I spent a few minutes petting them before pouring some feed into their small container. They dove for the food, ignoring me, their heavy coats keeping them warm in the frigid temperatures. After they finished I talked to them in Italian and gave them more attention. But soon they lost interest in me and wandered away.

Sighing, I started back toward the house and thought about the long night ahead of me. I had nothing to do but read boring poetry books. There was only so much iambic pentameter I could take.

Cazzo. I longed for a proper Italian cocktail or glass of Ravazzani cìro. The farmhouse had only whisky.

I found myself walking in the direction of "town," which consisted of a building with a combined pub, general store and grocery. I went there every week for provisions. But today I felt the need for something other than whisky.

The pub was empty, so I sat on a stool at the bar. "Hello?" I called.

An older woman came out from the store area. Mrs. Campbell, the owner. She reminded me of a younger Zia, and a wave of homesickness settled in my stomach like a stone.

"Mr. Drakos," she said in her thick Scottish brogue. "Didn't expect to see you sitting here."

Everyone believed I was Nick Drakos, a Greek writer who needed the solitude and quiet to work on his next novel. "I decided to get out for a bit today."

"That's good. A young laddie like you needs exercise. How long before that book of yours is finished?"

"It's hard to say. I am not a fast writer." Or a slow one. I wouldn't know the first thing about writing a novel.

"It'll come along. A bevvy for you?"

"Campari and soda."

She began bustling behind the bar. "Of course."

A deep male voice said something in Gaelic as he sat on the stool beside me. Mrs. Campbell smiled at him and nodded, returning in the same language.

I expected to find a local sitting next to me. Who I did not expect to find was Alessandro Ricci.

Madre di dio!

I flew off my stool and faced him warily, my muscles tight in readiness. "Che cazzo?" I barked. "What are you doing here?"

Instead of standing, he pivoted on the stool to face me and propped his arm on the bar. In Italian, he continued, "The same as you, no? Buying a drink."

Was he planning on killing me here? In this pub, in front of a witness? "I know who you are, Ricci."

He appeared unsurprised. "I assumed. Otherwise you would not have disappeared from Santorini."

"I also know why you are following me."

"Again, I assumed."

Mrs. Campbell set two drinks on the bar. Ricci slipped over a large bill and spoke to her in Gaelic. Of course this stronzo spoke Gaelic.

I stood perfectly still, wondering if I could get past him to escape out the door. How the fuck had he found me? He was not a man who could blend in, especially here. Ricci was big and intimidating. Handsome. He would attract attention anywhere.

Mrs. Campbell wandered away, leaving us alone. This was the moment. It was me or him. I took a threatening step in his direction.

"Sit down," he said quietly. "I am not going to kill you right now."

Right now. So he was toying with me? Following me, sucking my dick. Watching me. "I don't give a fuck what you want. We will finish this here."

Sighing, Ricci reached behind his back and took a pistol out from the waistband of his jeans. He put it on the bar. "Is this what you wish? To die in this little shit hole in the middle of nowhere?"

"Fuck off."

"Sit." Ricci kicked my empty stool. "I promise you won't die today."

"The word of a man like you, one who is loyal only to whoever pays him, means nothing to me."

Lifting the gun, he removed the magazine and slid the barrel to expel the bullet from the chamber. It all happened in a blink. He slapped all the pieces on the bar. "There. Now fucking sit."

If he intended to shoot me dead, my blood would already be pooling on the floor. While I hated his cocky display, I had to respect it.

Cautiously, I moved to the stool and sat. I snatched my cocktail and took two long swallows. The familiar flavor reminded me of home and my throat tightened. "What do you want?" I snapped.

He drank from his glass. "I had thought you would beg for your life."

"I never beg."

"Or reciprocate blow jobs, apparently."

I didn't want to think about that night. "I hadn't realized you wanted one."

"You think I wouldn't like for you, the handsome heir to the biggest mafia empire in Europe, to give me a blow job? Ma dai."

It didn't matter what he wanted. I wasn't next in line for the Ravazzani empire any longer. I hadn't been for a long time. "Too bad for you, then."

He sipped his cocktail. "Yes, it is too bad for me."

Now we were discussing blow jobs? "Who hired you to kill me?"

"What sort of man would I be if I revealed my clients?"

"I can offer you more than what they are paying you."

"You assume this is about money."

Wasn't everything? "It must be La Provincia. They want me dead because I'm gay and I left." This was the council of the 'Ndrangheta leaders. My father was a member, and while he swore the other dons weren't after me, I didn't believe it.

Ricci said nothing, merely stared at the bar as he took another drink.

I couldn't help but ask, "How long have you been on this island?"

"Four days."

Cristo. "Watching me, I suppose."

He snorted. "Too fucking boring. Nothing but sheep and poetry."

Of course he knew this. I was getting sloppy—I should've spotted him. He could have killed me at any time. "Forgive me for boring you, Alessandro."

"Alessio. No one calls me Alessandro."

"I hadn't realized we were friends."

"You should hope so, Giulio. You do not want me as your enemy."

"Any man trying to kill me is automatically my enemy."

"It is a job. Nothing more. You should understand that, considering all you've done for your father's 'ndrina."

In a strange way I did understand, but we were not the same. Not even close. "That was in the name of family, of brotherhood. You are in it for only one person—you."

"Yes, this is true. But I work better alone. The 'Ndrangheta is full of jackals, all trying to eat their young."

We were talking about the mafia now? What the fuck was happening here?

I angled toward him, my muscles tight in readiness. "While this existential conversation is riveting, I want to know how long you've been following me. Were you responsible for what happened in Belgium?"

"I am not responsible for the death of your ragazzo."

"And I'm supposed to take your word for it?"

His top lip curled derisively. "I don't use bombs. Too public. Too messy. The work of an amateur."

I actually believed him.

"Many people wish to kill you, it seems," Alessio continued. "You are very popular, no?"

I let that go. "Why haven't you killed me yet?"

"Are you so eager to die?"

I clenched my jaw, anger at both him and myself flooding my veins. "I left the 'Ndrangheta behind. They refuse to let me go because I am gay."

"Not everything is about your sexual preference."

"*Cazzata*. It's the only reason someone would hire you to kill me."

"You are more foolish than I thought if you believe that."

Was he implying another reason? "If it's to strike at my father, they must not have heard he disowned me." This was the public story, the one Fausto spread to keep me safe.

Alessio finished his drink and placed the empty glass on the bar. "Anyone familiar with Ravazzani knows he would never let you go."

"Then they would be wrong. I gave up the right to his throne the minute I left Siderno."

"As you like to say, cazzata." He showed no emotion, his voice remaining flat and even, his face impassive. If there was a heart beating in his chest, I couldn't tell.

Except for the night of the club. From his knees he had glanced up at me with such fire and longing it singed my skin. He'd been anything but cold and remote then.

I didn't want to think about that night. Not now, not ever.

"It's true, whether you want to believe it or not," I snapped.

"We will see, no?"

I threw back the rest of my cocktail. "I suppose we will." I stood and tossed more money on the bar. "I'm walking out. Unless you plan on shooting me in a few seconds, know that I'm coming after you next, Ricci."

A flicker of a smile flashed before he masked it. "I look forward to it, *il bel principe*."

Handsome prince.

Clenching my fists, I hurried out into the cold Scottish wind.

CHAPTER FOUR

Alessio

Mrs. Campbell returned to clean up and offered me another drink, but I declined. I didn't often drink and never excessively. The single cocktail was enough for now.

I didn't move from the bar, staring at the rows of bottles on display. Giulio's reaction, anger and disbelief, had been expected. It was my own reaction to him that troubled me.

It had taken almost six weeks to track Giulio here. In Santorini he ditched his phone and identification, which made it more difficult to find him. He hadn't touched his bank accounts or his email. By pure luck I learned a man fitting his description boarded a plane to Edinburgh. The flight attendant confirmed it, and from there it was easy. A man as good looking as Giulio Ravazzani did not blend into the fair Highlands.

I slapped the pieces of my gun together, so familiar with the procedure that my fingers moved automatically. I didn't like the heat in my belly, the way I couldn't stop thinking about his mouth, his hands. The night in Málaga he was rough with me. Selfish and demanding, exactly what I liked.

But it shouldn't matter. I should have killed him by now.

I lied about being bored while watching him. Nothing could be further from the truth. Giulio fascinated me, even while he was sitting still. He was pretty, like a magazine model, but there was strength and anger inside him. So much anger. I recognized it because I often felt that anger, too.

But he was bad luck for me. I could feel it in my bones.

Giulio would be wary now, on guard at all times, but there was nowhere to go. The ferries ran sporadically and the island was isolated. I actually liked it here, but then I was used to being alone. Canna had to be torture for a man like Giulio, one who craved people and attention. He liked cities and crowds, parties and alcohol.

Mrs. Campbell slid a glass of water over the bar. "Drink," she told me in Gaelic. "You look thin and tired."

I'd been staying in the apartment over the saloon ever since I arrived. The older woman had an air and attitude about her that I recognized as former military. I could spot them wherever I went. Not that I'd asked her about it, but I suspected her time in the service was the reason she was on this remote island in the middle of nowhere.

To please her, I drank the water. "Happy?" I asked in Gaelic.

"What do you want with that poor Mr. Drakos? He keeps to himself, never bothers anybody."

Only because there were no night clubs here. "Maybe I am his boyfriend."

"That would explain why he is angry with you. Did you break his heart?"

"Why do you assume I am in the wrong?"

Leaning on the bar, she gestured to my face. "Because you don't let your feelings show. You are closed up. Locked tight. Anyone who tried to love you would end up frustrated and angry."

I didn't like that she read me so well. "Two men together, this doesn't bother you?"

Mrs. Campbell rolled her eyes. "Och, I have a satellite dish. I'm not ignorant of what goes on in the world. I've seen *Modern Family*."

"What happened to Mr. Campbell?"

"Divorced him thirteen years ago and moved here. Last I heard he was remarried and living in London."

"Regrets?"

"About my divorce?" When I nodded, she straightened and began wiping down the bar. "Not about Hamish, no. We married young and he wasn't a good husband."

"But?"

She considered this for a moment. "I wish I had kids when I had the chance. Now it's too late."

It wasn't what I expected her to say, considering where she lived. The residents of Canna were loners, like me. In Gaelic the Outer Hebrides were called *Na h-Innse Gall*, which meant "islands of the strangers." It sounded like a perfect place.

My phone buzzed. I excused myself and went outside. It was Sasha. "Pronto."

"Is it done yet?"

I didn't answer, instead letting the silence speak for me.

"*Zhizn' ebet meya!*" A Russian expression that meant something similar to, *life is fucking me.*

"Was there anything else? Or did you call just to berate me?"

"Do you know how much money you are losing? How many jobs I have passed up for you?"

I hung up on her. Though Sasha was a great assistant, she was impatient. Some days it felt as if she cared more about my reputation than I did. She remembered every hit I had carried out.

And she didn't understand my obsession with Giulio Ravazzani.

Fair, as I hardly understood it myself. But I would not be rushed. I would complete the job on my terms, when I decided it was time. He wasn't going anywhere, not from here.

Shoving my phone in my pocket, I started walking away from town. Not a soul was around, no car or motorcycle in sight. The wind and the waves were the only sounds, with a chill that sank into your bones. The brisk temperatures didn't bother me in the least. I ran every morning on the western side of the island, up in the freezing hills. It cleared my mind and kept me sane.

I headed toward the dock. If I knew Giulio—and I did—he would try to board the first ferry off the island. Or he would bribe a fisherman to take him out on a boat. I had to prevent both.

I didn't want him to get away.

It took the better part of the day, but I found the three local fishermen and the ferry operator. With a flash of my pistol and some money I had them agreeing to refuse any request from Nick Drakos. Unlike Giulio, I had no need to hide my identity here. So I let them know exactly what would happen to anyone who aided Mr. Drakos off the island.

Satisfied, I headed back to my rooms. Giulio would be armed and waiting for me to show up at his farm, but I wasn't in the mood. I would deal with him another day.

Maybe Mrs. Campbell would let me watch satellite TV with her over dinner.

When I wasn't on a job I spent most of my time training and exercising, keeping my skills sharpened. Excluding my run every morning in the mountains, I hadn't spent much time with my rifle. This would need to change. I would need to learn the wind patterns here.

I already found the perfect vantage point to take out Giulio during my first day on the island, a spot on the outskirts of his farm that would allow me to kill him in a blink. So I needed to start practicing.

The sun was starting to fade as I went up the stairs. I stopped outside my room. The single strand of hair I placed between the door and the doorjamb was still in place, so I unlocked and went in. But as soon as I went in, I felt the change in the surrounding air. Something was off.

Then the faint hint of weed and wool teased my nose.

Giulio.

On instinct I swung my arm out and connected with solid muscle. A gun went off and I felt a burn across my left arm. Then he lunged at me, but I was ready. Though I normally avoided close combat, I remembered how it was done.

I kept my arms close to my frame and used short, powerful strikes toward strategic places on his body. Unfortunately, Giulio was competent, and he blocked most of my attempts while returning a few of his own. Back and forth we punched and twisted, kicked and dodged. Furniture toppled over and a vase crashed to the floor.

He'd been trained well by his father, but he was no match for me, a killer bred by the military. I was barely breathing hard, my heart rate not elevated in the least, and Giulio was panting, using too much energy to fight me. He was starting to tire, his blows not as sharp.

It was only a matter of time.

I landed a jab to his kidney and he stumbled backward. I advanced, sensing his weakness and moving in for the kill. There was no mercy inside me, no restraint. Calm settled inside me. *I will finish this.*

He tried to dodge me, but I was faster. I had him by the throat and slammed him against the wall. My fingers tightened.

Suddenly, a thumping sound broke through the noise in my head. Someone was pounding on the door. Woman. Gaelic words.

"Are you all right," she called. "Young man, answer me."

I blinked as the roaring in my ears eased slightly. Mrs. Campbell.

"I'm fine," I called back in the same language.

"You owe me for that broken vase," she said.

"I know. I'm sorry."

Just then, Giulio used both hands to push my chest hard, shoving me off him. I let him go and dropped back a step.

"Get off me, *stronzo*," Giulio snarled and shouldered me out of the way.

I rolled my neck and leaned my back against the wall, never taking my eyes off the mafia prince. His brow was bleeding, the flesh split open from my knuckles. He was still the most beautiful thing I'd ever seen.

He was wary, his expression like a wild animal that had been cornered. "How did you know I was here?"

Did he think I was stupid enough to give away my advantages? I kept quiet.

"Cazzo, you're like a . . . robot or something," he grumbled, then winced and touched his side. "If I start pissing blood, I am coming back and torching this entire building."

"You would kill Mrs. Campbell?"

He made a noise in his throat, one of disbelief and surprise. "You think I care about that old lady?"

"She is not old—only fifty-three. And she has done nothing to warrant dying."

"Neither have I."

It didn't matter. Not to me. "You are an assignment. One I cannot refuse."

"Why?"

I said nothing. He wouldn't understand, nor would he care. The target never did. Their only concern was over their own miserable life.

"You're bleeding." He nodded toward my arm.

I looked down and saw a tear in my coat, the red stain growing underneath. Pulling off my coat, I examined the wound. It was a scratch. "You're not a very good shot."

He folded his arms across his chest. "You sound disappointed, Alessio. Were you so keen on dying today?"

"To be killed by the Ravazzani heir, it is a privilege, no?"

"Stop calling me that," he snarled through clenched teeth. "I told you, I have nothing to do with my father any longer."

"Your phone records say otherwise."

His eyes widened. That this surprised him said a lot. Giulio had grown cocky in the years since Belgium, believing he was more clever than his enemies. He should've known better.

We stared at one another and I wondered what he would do now. He couldn't kill me and he couldn't get off the island. Even if he did, there was no place on earth he could hide from me.

I held the power over this man, not the other way around.

His gaze traveled the length of my body, almost as if he was assessing me. Just as he did that night in the club. I knew how I looked, a scarred face. Terrifying. Cold. But whatever Giulio saw across the crowded club had appealed to him. He'd chosen me—and I'd let him.

"Are you hoping for another blow job?" I asked softly. "Because you'll be disappointed."

"Va all'inferno, testa di merda." *Go to hell, shit head.* "As if I'd let you near my dick again."

Needing to prove a liar out of him, I licked my lips slowly. "Cazzata. If I dropped to my knees, you'd whip it out—"

"*Vaffanculo!*" Brow pulled low, he stormed toward the door and yanked it open. "Stay away from me, Alessio. Or next time I won't miss."

He slammed the door behind him and I was left alone, the hint of a grin on my face.

CHAPTER FIVE

Giulio

I needed more weapons.

In the early morning dawn, I stared at the supplies spread out on the dining room table. Three old guns, four boxes of bullets and a large hunting knife. It wasn't enough, not for taking out Ricci.

After our encounter in his room yesterday, I tried to buy passage off the island. Except none of the fishermen would take me. They all waved me away with a fearful expression, like I was cursed or something.

Clearly Alessio had threatened all of them to keep me trapped on Canna.

I hardly slept last night, convinced Alessio would come after me in the dark. Yet he hadn't. The evening had passed quietly, with no sign of him anywhere.

So today I arrived at a decision. While I was no longer a member of the 'Ndrangheta, I was still my father's son. A Ravazzani, raised on blood and death. We were survivors, a line of kings born in the dry Siderno soil.

Which meant I would not sit around and wait for Alessio to shoot me.

No more poetry, no more sheep. It was time to go on the offensive.

Alessio thought he had me trapped. But the reverse was also true. If I couldn't find a way off this island, then neither could he.

And only one of us would survive.

"To be killed by the Ravazzani heir, it is almost a privilege, no?"

Alessio would soon find out, because I would not die in the middle of nowhere, on this cold remote island away from my family.

I missed them. Four years ago, I'd distanced myself from everyone in my old life to protect them. And since then I never stayed in one place long enough to make new friends.

I rubbed my chest, wishing away the hollow feeling that was almost always there. It wasn't supposed to happen like this.

When I left the mafia, I thought Paolo and I would live our best lives together, with parties and friends. Dinners and trips, then marriage and maybe a kid or two. I never thought I would get him killed. I never thought I would live my life on the run, in hiding.

But I had no time for regrets. I would kill Ricci, return to Europe and find Paolo's killers. Once they were dead, I could finally go to Siderno for more than just a day or two. I could visit my family—a real visit, for weeks. Maybe a month.

I fucking wanted that. No, I *needed* that.

My last trip had been too short. Rafe turned three in March and I'd gone home for the party. I hadn't stayed for barely forty-eight hours.

I checked my watch. It was five o'clock here, but Siderno was an hour ahead. Should I call? No doubt she was sick with worry after not hearing from me for so long—and I knew she was already awake.

There was another reason to call. A much darker reason. If Alessio got lucky and succeeded in killing me, I wanted to hear her voice just one more time.

I grabbed one of the burner phones I'd purchased before coming to Canna. It was already charged, so I dialed quickly.

"Pronto," the raspy voice said.

"Zia, it's me."

My great-aunt, who was more like my nonna, gasped. "Is it really you? Oh, *ometto*. They said—"

She didn't finish, her voice cracking, and guilt lodged like a bullet under my ribs. Ever since I could remember, she was the only one who ever called me "little man." Swallowing the lump in my throat, I said, "Va bene, va bene. It's okay. *I'm* okay."

She began reciting a prayer in Latin, so I waited for her to finish. Zia was very religious, a devout Catholic woman. I suspected she had to pray harder on account of being related to Fausto. When she quieted, I heard her blow her nose. "Don't cry," I said. "You'll ruin your makeup."

"Makeup." She made a dismissive noise. "You know I never bother."

Yes, I knew. She said God made her this way and why did she need to look like anyone else? "*Come stai?*"

"Worried. I worry every day over you. I prayed so hard. I knew you were not dead. I would feel it, no?"

"Perdonami, but I couldn't call. My phone wasn't safe."

"Your father, he has been beside himself with worry, too. When you disappeared, ma dai . . . . He nearly hopped on a plane for Greece."

Unsurprising, as Fausto was still watching my every move. Or he had been, until I went off the grid here in Canna. "I'm glad someone stopped him."

"His wife reasoned with him. But he was very unhappy, very worried. This will ease his mind, to learn that you are still alive."

I didn't want my father involved. He had two young children now, and Frankie was pregnant with a third. It was better if he stayed in Siderno.

I could handle one assassin—even if he was rumored to be the best. I would outsmart Alessio, beat him at his own game.

I said, "You can't tell him. Or Frankie for that matter. This has to stay between us, Zia."

She didn't respond for a long time, then she sighed. "Why would you keep this a secret from the people who love you best, ometto?"

"It's not safe, and I don't want to put anyone there in danger." I decided to change the subject. "How are the babies? How is Frankie?"

Zia launched into stories about my half-siblings, and I missed them all with a bone-deep ache. Raffaele was a mini-Fausto, already demanding and difficult at three years old, just like the true future leader of the 'ndrina. At almost two, Noemi was quieter, but no less energetic than her brother.

"You must be exhausted," I told Zia.

She grunted to express her displeasure. "They hire nannies. Too many nannies, I think. They don't want to bother me, but I'm not so old that I can't control that devil child. After all, I could control you!"

I smiled. I never truly inherited my father's temper or stubbornness. I took more after my mother, supposedly, who was killed when I was very young. "That's true. I remember the time I was caught eavesdropping."

When I was nine, Zia found me outside Fausto's office, listening to one of the 'ndrina meetings through the door. I was desperate to wrap my head around what it meant to be the Ravazzani heir. What did my father do all day? In these meetings, what did they discuss? What would be required of me when the time came?

My aunt had grabbed me by the ear, made me confess to Fausto. Then I weeded her garden every day for a week, sunup to sundown.

Seeing a weed still made me twitch.

"And you learned, no?" Zia asked.

"I learned I never wanted to garden."

She chuckled. "You always hated the dirt."

True. I glanced out the window. Light was shining on the horizon. "Zia, I should go. I have to go on a run."

"You don't need to run. You're already too skinny."

This was an old argument. She never understood my need to exercise. "To stay alive I need to stay in shape."

"Then go, ometto. When will you call again?"

"I don't know, but don't worry. I'll be fine."

"I'll stop worrying when I'm dead. And it wouldn't hurt for you to step into a church every now and again," she chastised.

I tried not to roll my eyes. The Catholic Church was less than progressive when it came to my community, so that was a hard pass. "I'll try, Zia. *Ti voglio bene.*"

"Ti voglio bene, ometto. Call soon, *per favore.*"

"I will. Ciao." Like ripping off a bandage, I disconnected quickly. Then I destroyed the burner phone.

My chest churned with anger and regret. Whoever planted that car bomb in Belgium was going to suffer. They had destroyed my life, caused my family anguish and worry. But first, I had to deal with Ricci.

Already dressed to run, I pulled on my knit hat and went outside. The wind tore through me, chilling me to my bones, and I cursed. I hated this godforsaken place.

As soon as I killed Alessio I was on the first boat to Portugal. Then I would restart my search for whoever planted that bomb in Belgium.

The cold ground crunched beneath my feet as I ran. The air punched into my lungs like needles, sharp bites of pain that stung. I headed toward the hills. My thighs burned as I charged up the incline. Madre di dio, was I so out of shape? I focused on my breathing and continued climbing. I needed to clear my head and figure out what to do about Alessio. I still ached from our fight yesterday. His blows felt like hammers.

For a split second he'd almost won. When he shoved me against the wall with his hand on my throat, his eyes went flat and lifeless, looking more machine than man. There was no mercy, no kindness in him and I knew he was about to strangle me there in that small apartment.

For a split second I thought I was about to die.

Which only proved I didn't deserve to inherit Fausto's kingdom. I would never be strong enough, resilient enough. Not like him. So it was good he had Raffaele. The boy would make a great don one day.

I shoved all those thoughts aside and kept running, pushing myself harder until there was no room in my head for anything except for my breath. My feet. The swing of my arms. The pounding of my heart.

Minutes later, a noise behind me nearly caused me to trip. Looking over my shoulder, I saw Alessio jogging up the path. He wore a baseball cap and running clothes that looked older than he was. Stopping, I bent over and put my hands on my knees, never taking my eyes off him as he closed the distance between us. Why was he up this fucking early? Was he exercising or following me?

And why hadn't I brought a gun with me?

Stupid, stupid, stupid. I clenched my jaw, grinding my back teeth, and considered my options. I could tackle him, except yesterday proved I couldn't take Alessio in a fight. My options were limited, but I wouldn't make it easy for the bastard.

His lips twitched, like he knew what I was thinking. I straightened as he drew closer, my body tired but ready to take him on. My hands closed into fists.

Except he didn't break stride. "Andiamo, principe," he said as he passed me. *Let's go, prince.* He didn't even sound out of breath, the stronzo.

A wise man would probably go the other way. Keep hiding. Wait for the next attack.

But I was tired of hiding and waiting.

If we were running together, he couldn't take me by surprise. Better yet, an opportunity to kill him might present itself. A rock to the back of the head, maybe?

I made a split decision. Turning up the path, I started after him.

Alessio

WHEN I HEARD him follow I slowed the tiniest bit. Giulio wasn't in terrible shape, but he couldn't keep up with me, not at my normal pace.

I hadn't expected to find him out here. The hills were usually quiet this time of morning, with not a soul around. It was my favorite time of day, after the sun first peeked into the sky and I could be completely alone. No noise, no traffic. Just me and the ground.

"You are up early," I said when he was close enough. I knew his routine. He normally rose around eight or eight-thirty.

"Let me guess? You are always up at this time."

"It is the best part of the day, no?"

"Oh, sure. The rest of your day must be stressful, with all the stalking you need to squeeze in."

He sounded so cranky that I nearly smiled. He was not a morning person, a fact I learned instantly when I started tracking him. Hard to visit nightclubs for anonymous blow jobs and rise early the next day.

We continued to run, neither of us speaking. I preferred the silence, though I was keenly aware of his presence, of his exhales and heavy steps. He was pretty, even with the dark circles under his eyes. His fashionable running outfit was impractical for this weather. But he was still gorgeous. Maybe more so, because he was flushed and sweaty, and it reminded me of sex.

Specifically of what Giulio would look like during sex.

I knew what he looked like when he came, when the hard edges and anger disappeared, leaving just sensation and bliss. Madre di dio, I still thought of his face mid-orgasm when I jerked off. Did he ever think of me on my knees, my mouth around his cock?

Idiota. Of course not. Giulio had been with plenty of men, so why would I stand out? I'd only been with a dozen or so men in my lifetime, and never openly. Each encounter hurried, frantic. Unsatisfying.

He wheezed beside me. I took pity on him and slowed to a stop, trying not to laugh as he collapsed onto a rock. "You need to breathe from your—"

"Fuck. Off," he panted.

I held up my palms and stretched my muscles to keep them warm. This wasn't yet halfway for me, and there was a long way to go. "You can turn back, if you like. No one is forcing you to stay."

"How are you not even breathing hard?" He squinted up at me. "Are you human?"

The words nicked an old wound, one that has never quite healed. *"He's not normal,"* my father used to shout in his drunken rambles. *"What is wrong with that boy?"*

I'd been a disappointment to him, a man who wished for a loud and boisterous son, someone more like himself. Instead, I was quiet and awkward, more inside my head than not. I could sit for long stretches of time and do nothing, which was what made me the best sniper in the world. But a terrible son.

"I am human," I told Giulio. "Just in better shape than you."

He mumbled a string of Italian curses and wiped his face with the sleeve of his shirt.

I was suddenly curious about his former life in Siderno. "Your father, he doesn't force his men to stay in shape?"

"It's not the military, Alessio."

Too bad. With proper training, he might have eluded me. As it was, he left breadcrumbs in his wake everywhere he went. Giulio was like a brilliant sky, full of color and life. He was impossible to miss.

He eyed me suspiciously. "Do you have a gun on you?"

I held out my arms. "No, I don't. Other than puffins and eagles, there isn't anything around at this time of day." I paused mid-stretch. "But I don't need a gun to kill you, Giulio."

It was a fact. His neck still bore faint bruises from my fingers.

"I'm not as weak as you think," he said.

"I don't think you are weak." Far from it. The 'Ndrangheta did not raise weak men, and Ravazzani would have ensured his heir was strong enough to take over when the time came.

But I was a killer, a soulless monster. Trained to take down an enemy quickly and quietly. He was no match for me.

I suddenly had a lot of questions rolling around in my head. "What is your favorite way to kill a man?"

He frowned, his eyebrows lowering. "Ma dai, what the fuck kind of a question is that?"

I lifted a shoulder and concentrated on the ground as I stretched. "It is the one thing we have in common, no?" This, and an intimate knowledge of Giulio's dick.

"Except I'm not an assassin."

I snorted, unable to hold it in. "Cazzata. You were your father's soldato. You carried out murders."

"I didn't do much wet work."

"Much," I repeated. "But you did some. So tell me. What is your favorite way to kill?"

"Why the fuck do you want to know? Wondering how I will kill you?"

As if he could. But it was clear he found offense in my question, so I wouldn't push it. If he could not see who he really was, the man underneath the designer clothes and good looks, then who was I to point it out?

I motioned with my hand. "Andiamo. Break's over."

His lips flattened, wariness and unhappiness etched on his handsome face. "How much farther?"

"We are not yet halfway." He glared at me, and I could see his indecision. For some reason I wanted him to stick it out. "Come. You can keep up."

"Fuck off, Alessio," he grumbled as he stood. "I'm only doing this to get stronger so I can kill you."

"Va bene, *uccisore*. Let's go."

Giulio clearly didn't like being called a killer, but he followed when I set off again, his footfalls crunching behind mine.

We ran for several minutes before he spoke. "What is your favorite way to kill?"

The truth escaped before I could stop it. "With my hands." I grimaced and tried not to think about how crazy that made me sound. It was why I preferred my rifle. The gun was cold and unsatisfying, leaving a distance between me and the victim that made it easier to justify, easier to carry out. Easier to keep my demons at bay.

Killing with my hands was a rush unlike anything else. Intimate, personal. A challenge that felt elemental, more animalistic than human. In the moment I felt nothing other than the desperate need to survive over my opponent. And when I succeeded I felt exhilarated.

"He's not normal."

Sì, certo.

I touched the cornicello on the chain around my neck and kept running.

Giulio mumbled something behind me. I glanced over my shoulder. *"Che cosa?"*

"I said mine is a knife."

Ah. He was finally playing along. "Your father's as well, no?" Fausto's preference for a knife was legendary. It had earned him the nickname Il Diavolo.

"I've never asked him, but I assume so."

"It is too messy for me. The blood, I mean."

"That is the point," Giulio said. "To make a show. To intimidate. Not to mention cause pain."

"No, that is killing to impress others. It is why you mafioso get caught. Because you need to measure your dicks, make sure everyone knows how important, how dangerous you are."

"It is necessary to instill fear, so that others recognize the danger of crossing you. To make people do what you want. It's the only reason to murder, outside of self-defense."

I shook my head. "Murder needs no reason. Sometimes it just needs to be done."

"Is that how you justify carrying out your assassinations? Is that how you sleep at night?"

Irritation swept along my spine like the claws of a cat and I smothered the urge to lash out. I didn't sleep at night, actually. Three or four hours, max.

Still, I needed no justification for who I was and what I did. I was a ghost. My targets never saw me coming. A single bullet to the forehead and I was in the wind.

"What is your rate, by the way?" Giulio asked from behind me. "What does the best assassin in Europe charge?"

"It depends on who is asking."

"Let's say it's me."

"You can't afford me."

"Fuck off," he snapped. "This is hypothetical, because the only person I want dead is you."

Fine. I would play along. "Who am I to kill?"

"A world leader. Pick one."

"I can't. The identity matters. Some are easier to get to than others."

"Who would be the most difficult?"

"Chinese. Russian. Not impossible, but difficult."

The path widened, so I slowed a fraction to allow him to catch up. When we were side-by-side, he asked, "So what would you charge to assassinate the Russian president?"

"Off the top of my head . . . Ten million."

He whistled. "What about another mafia leader? One of the other dons."

I knew how much I received for Fausto's assassination, money I'd returned to Don D'Agostino. "A million, depending on who."

"What if it was Enzo D'Agostino?"

I looked over at him sharply. Had he read my mind? "Because he is your father's enemy?"

He grunted in answer. "I'll never forgive D'Agostino for trying to kill Fausto."

Except it hadn't been D'Agostino looking through the sight on the rifle, squeezing the trigger to take the shot. What would Giulio say if he knew I had almost assassinated his father?

I couldn't think about that now. I had no intention of ever telling him.

"So, tell me," Giulio said. "How much for D'Agostino?"

This was not a line of questioning I wanted to entertain. Soon he would ask if I knew who D'Agostino hired to shoot at Fausto from that rooftop. "He's well fortified in Napoli, from what I understand," I hedged.

"More than the Russian president?"

He looked at me through his lashes, and the impact of his eyes was like a fist to the chest. I nearly tripped. Sweat dripped off the sharp lines of his jaw, and I had the wildest urge to lick the sweat from his skin.

Cazzo, this had to stop.

I didn't wish to discuss assassinations and money and mafia dons. He was my target. I didn't want to grow close to him.

Yet I couldn't stay away.

In other words, I was fucked.

Admit it. You just don't want to kill Giulio.

I didn't like that voice in my head. This was a job, just like any other. Yes, it was taking longer than usual, but I would do what needed to be done when the time came.

"Hurry up," I muttered and picked up the pace, not caring if he kept up or not.

CHAPTER SIX

Giulio

Alessio was a moody motherfucker.

After I asked about how much he charged to kill some-one, he shut down and practically sprinted along the path. I couldn't keep up and his tall form soon disappeared into the twists and turns of the hill.

Slowing, I jogged at my own pace again. Was he planning to jump me? I tensed around every bend, my eyes scanning the landscape, but he wasn't there. His shoe prints were steady and straight, headed down the other side of the mountain toward flat ground.

I didn't understand him. At all.

I'm not supposed to understand him. He's here to kill me.

Well, I wouldn't make it easy. I was tired of running, both literally and figuratively.

Drawing to a stop, I bent over and put my hands on my knees, sucking in great gulps of air. My thighs felt like noodles. Thank God I quit smoking cigarettes at Paolo's insistence. Vaping weed was bad enough on my lungs—not that I ever planned to give that up. Some nights it was the only way to catch a decent sleep.

I walked to the bottom of the hill. Alessio was long gone, not even a speck in the distance. I scanned the surroundings. Was he out there with his rifle, hiding and waiting?

Somehow, I didn't think so.

Heading toward the farm, I considered this. What would I do in Alessio's shoes? The ferries on and off the island ran three times a week, and the next one was soon. If Alessio was smart, his plan would be to kill me then immediately board the ferry and disappear. It made perfect sense.

So I had to strike at him first.

Once at the farmhouse, I showered and dressed. Then I ate break-fast and examined the guns I'd found in the house. They were older, unused for some time. I'd used one in my failed attempt at killing Alessio last night. Had I missed because my aim was rusty, or was the gun faulty?

I needed to find out.

I bundled up with layers upon layers of clothing. Then watched the perimeter of the farm, looking for signs that someone else was out there. From what I could see, it was all clear. I loaded one of the guns just to be safe before heading outside into the cold.

Madre di dio, this weather. My Mediterranean soul weeped.

I kept walking until I found a tree stump. I rested three empty bottles on top and moved back. Then I took aim at the bottles.

Figlio d'un cane! I only hit one out of three.

I grabbed a different pistol, loaded it, and tried to shoot. But this one jammed. I tossed it aside.

The last pistol was older and heavier, like ones from those old Clint Eastwood movies. I liked the weight of it in my palm. I shot four times, but only hit one of the remaining bottles. "Minchia!"

"You need to brace your legs."

The deep voice startled me and I whirled to find Alessio leaning against the sheep pen, his gray eyes watching me. He wore a knit cap, jeans and a hoodie, with an apple in one hand and a knife in the other. It was no kitchen knife, though. It was more like a hunting knife, one used for skinning, not chopping.

Alessio cut off a chunk of apple without looking down, then popped the slice in his mouth. I brought the gun up and pointed it at him. "*Ma che cazzo fai?*"

"I'm out for a walk."

"You're stalking me."

He lifted a shoulder. "If that's what you prefer to call it."

"You don't seem worried that I will shoot you in a few seconds."

"You couldn't hit the bottles from ten feet away. Do you really plan to hit me from all the way over there?"

"Are you willing to take that chance?"

His gaze raked me from head to toe. Though I wore mounds of clothing, I felt exposed. Like he could see the bare skin underneath.

The lines bracketing his mouth deepened. "If you shoot, I will hurl this knife into your throat." He flipped the large knife in his hand a few times without breaking our stare. "And I promise I won't miss."

I hated him so much. I lowered the gun slowly, but didn't take my finger off the trigger. "*Figlio di puttana.*"

This only seemed to amuse him. "You know, for a mafia prince you're not very smart."

My fist tightened around the handle of the gun. Fuck, it would be so satisfying to shoot him. "What does that mean?"

"It means you haven't thought this out. Let's say that by some stroke of luck you are able to kill me and leave this island. What then?"

"You want to know where I'm going next? Is that it?"

"You have some bad men after you, Giulio. If I don't kill you, they will."

"They haven't succeeded in four years."

He threw his head back and laughed. "Cazzo, you are full of yourself."

"Do you want to get shot again?" I snapped.

He sobered and a muscle jumped in his jaw. "Here is my advice: Stop being childish. You're a grown man. So start dealing with your problems instead of running and hiding."

Anger sparked in my veins, bright and hot. Judgmental prick. He had no fucking idea what I'd been doing the last four years. How hard

I'd worked to find Paolo's killers. "Is this where you tell the gay man he's too effeminate? Too weak?"

He shook his head and heaved a sigh. "I am bisexual, Giulio. I like men and I like women. For the last time, this has nothing to do with your sexuality."

My jaw fell open. Alessio was bi? Well, that explained the exemplary blow job in Málaga. "I didn't ask for your advice. And I plan to find and kill them next."

"After you kill me, you mean." He gave me a half smile and I was shocked to see a dimple in his right cheek. Alessio did not seem the sort of man to have dimples.

Paolo had dimples.

"Yes," I growled. "After I kill you."

"Then you had better keep practicing." He pointed at the two remaining bottles on the stump.

"It's the guns. Not my aim."

"It's both. You don't know how to handle those old weapons, especially in this wind."

"And you do?"

"Sì, certo."

Cazzata. He might be good with a long-range rifle, but these were old handguns. Who knew the last time they'd been cleaned and oiled? "I'll take your word for it."

"Would you like for me to show you?"

"And give you a weapon to shoot me with? Ma sei pazzo?"

"Then perhaps, for the sake of the sheep, we call a temporary truce."

A truce? Was he serious? "Why the fuck would I do that?"

"You need my help."

This was unbelievable. My lip curled into a sneer. "Are you really an assassin? Because all you do is talk and follow me—"

The knife whizzed toward me in a blink. The blade sank into the ground a millimeter from my big toe. I hadn't seen the weapon even leave his hand.

I looked back up at him. He was watching me coolly, his expression unreadable.

It was clear he could have killed me, but he hadn't. This was becoming a theme between us. There had been ample opportunity for him to take me out, not only here but elsewhere.

Why was he toying with me? Did he get off on the power?

Fuck this.

I was not some weak, inexperienced politician. Or a delusional world leader surrounded by sycophants. I was raised to kill and hurt people. To make others bend to my will. This assassin would not make a fool of me.

Bending, I removed the knife from the cold ground.

I balanced it in my palm, learning the weight of it. With a flick I sent it flying toward him, but aimed a bit higher.

Directly at his crotch.

He moved aside just before impact. With a *thump,* the tip of the knife embedded in the wooden sheep pen. Right where his dick would've been.

"It would be a shame if you cut it off before you had a chance to see it," he said, smoothly removing the blade from the wood.

"I don't want anything to do with your dick, Alessio."

He pushed off from the wood. With slow, measured steps he came toward me. "Too bad. It's a very nice dick."

I braced my legs. If he wanted a fight, then I'd happily give him one. The pistol in my hand still had two bullets left. I settled the piece deeper in my palm and cocked the hammer.

The air grew thinner as he drew closer. I could barely hear the sheep over the pounding of my heart. He stopped just out of reach and tipped his chin toward my hand. "That is a .44 Magnum Colt Anaconda double-action revolver with an eight-inch barrel. Produced in 1990 in America in Connecticut. The originals aren't easy to find anymore. It's heavy, a hunter's gun."

When he paused, I asked, "Are you trying to impress me?"

"No, I'm trying to tell you why you are missing. The early versions had an accuracy problem, which could explain it. Also, until you're used to it, the double action could give you trouble." He shrugged. "Or you might just be a terrible shot."

Testa di cazzo.

Raising my arm, I took aim once more. Alessio told me to widen my legs even more, so I did and used both hands to steady the gun. The bullet exploded. So did the target. Then I lined up and shot again. *Boom.* The second target disappeared.

I expected him to gloat. But when I looked over, I found him wearing an odd expression, one reminiscent of how he'd stared up at me that night in Málaga.

It stirred something inside me, and I couldn't help but remember Alessio on his knees, the bass rattling in my chest as he took me out of my jeans. The grip of his wet, hot mouth. Holding my gaze as he swallowed my come. Heat rolled through me, a dark craving to have that all just once more.

Disgust quickly followed. What the fuck was wrong with me?

"You look good with that gun in your hand, principe." His voice was deep. A caress I felt all the way in my toes.

I shoved the confusion over my feelings aside. If he wasn't going to kill me, then there wasn't any reason for him to be standing here. "Get off my property, assassino."

The scar on his cheek twisted as he frowned. He opened his mouth to speak, then closed it. Good, because I didn't want to hear whatever he had to say.

Silent, he walked past me. Continued toward the farmhouse and the path that led to town. His movements were fluid and graceful, but economical. The military training was evident in everything he did.

I didn't budge. Instead I watched as his frame grew smaller and smaller. Finally he disappeared down the path.

Then I picked up the guns and went back inside. I had to figure out what to do next.

———

Alessio

I SHOULD HAVE KNOWN he would be waiting.

When I started up the trail for my run the next morning, I found

Giulio leaning against a rock, his arms folded across his chest. I frowned but didn't stop.

His steps began dogging mine.

I didn't say anything, merely pushed harder. I would lose him in the hills.

Sasha had two jobs lined up. The first was next week in Toronto, then another the week after in São Paulo. That meant I had to deal with Giulio before the ferry in two days' time. Once he was dead, I would fly from Edinburgh to London to Canada, changing identities each flight.

My time in Canna was over.

Finally I could get back to normal. I'd allowed myself to *want* and *feel* when it came to this man. He'd become an obsession. It broke every rule I'd established for myself, yet I hadn't been able to prevent it.

Ever since I first saw him on that Siderno street, smiling at his father and stepmother, I hadn't been able to think clearly. And terrible luck had followed.

"Bad mood today, assassino?"

He was closer than I expected. How was he keeping up? I said nothing, just kept running.

"I've been waiting on you for thirty minutes," he continued. "I started to think you were sleeping in."

Ma dai. I never slept in, not since I'd lived with my nonna.

He kept talking. "But maybe you are trying to avoid me. Which would make killing me difficult, no?"

I gritted my back teeth until the pain in my jaw distracted me from my irritation. All my life I'd hidden my feelings, my intentions. This one man saw too much, got under my skin. And I had allowed it, like a fool.

I glanced over my shoulder. "Today is your last day on earth. Strange that you would waste it baiting me into an argument."

"Do you want to know what I think?"

No, I absolutely did not.

The cold stung my lungs as I climbed, my legs burning. I needed this. I needed to punish my body, work myself until exhaustion.

"I think you don't want to kill me. I think you—"

In a flash, I spun around. Then I grabbed him and slammed his back into a rock. I braced an arm across his throat and leaned in. "You have no idea what I want."

"Don't I?"

There were no signs of fear in his expression, the bastard. He stared at me with a challenging glint in his eye, his lips curled into a knowing smirk.

I shoved harder into his windpipe. "Why would I not kill you? Enlighten me, principe."

"You like watching me. You like thinking about what we did in Málaga."

My lungs constricted. It felt like the air was in short supply, even though we were outside with nothing around but grass and dirt and the ocean breeze. I could hear my heartbeat in my ears, the rush of blood thrumming in my veins.

I attempted a sneer. "Málaga doesn't matter. Nothing about you matters to me."

"So why am I still alive?"

"Maybe I am taking my time. You can't escape. What's the rush?"

His stare was unwavering. "You won't murder me."

"I will. But don't worry. You won't see it coming. And it will be painless."

A hand fell onto my waist.

I sucked in a sharp breath. Giulio was *touching* me. His rough grip rested on my hip bone like it had the right to be there. Tiny shocks raced over my skin and my groin tightened with need. I could feel the heat from his body, even under the heavy clothing. It was both not enough and too much.

I wanted to touch him so badly, I shook with it. But I didn't trust myself.

I released him as if he were a live grenade.

He didn't move, his body pressed against the rock. "If you were going to kill me, you would have already done it."

"Delaying the inevitable."

Pushing off the stone, he started toward me. There was no fear, no hesitation. Confidence radiated off every part of him, his muscles loose and relaxed. The exact opposite of me at the moment.

"Cazzata. If my life has taught me anything," he said, "there is no such thing as inevitable."

I said nothing. He was wrong. Me tracking him down was inevitable. His death was inevitable.

He moved around me and sprinted up the trail, his shoes crunching on the frozen ground. I followed him. We started out with a light jog to warm up as we headed toward the hills. The air was cold, the path hard. I focused on my feet, my breath. The surroundings. Anything but the man in front of me.

Ten minutes passed before he spoke. "So are you a top or a bottom? You know, with men."

I knew what he was trying to do. I frowned at his broad back. "Why is it always sex with you?"

"Just making conversation, assassino. I'm curious about the man who wants to kill me."

Was he trying to soften me up in the hopes that I wouldn't carry out the hit? Make us relate on a human level? It was a tactic captives used with their captors. And it wouldn't work. "You're wasting your time."

"Does that mean you won't answer?"

"No, it means I know what you are doing. Also, I don't like labels."

"Well, I hate to tell you, but the *B* in LGBTQIA+ means bi. You are a label."

I supposed. But I didn't try to analyze my sexuality or think about what it meant. I slept with whomever I wanted to at the moment, whoever I was attracted to. And I happened to find both women and men attractive. I hadn't understood it for a long time, especially when I was younger. In the military, a fellow soldier tried to convince me I was gay and covered it up by occasionally sleeping with women. But pussy got my dick hard just as much as cock.

Giulio wasn't letting it drop. "Maybe you're a switch."

"Are these things gay men really discuss?"

"Yes."

"I like to fuck and be fucked. Does that help?"

His feet stumbled slightly before he righted himself. I smothered a satisfied grin. He wasn't as immune to me as he pretended.

Did he often think about that night in Málaga, too?

We didn't speak for a long time, our feet climbing higher on the path, his breath growing labored. I liked watching his muscles shift under his clothing as he ran. The way the sweat gathered between his shoulder blades. This view made up for the slow pace.

"When did you know . . . you were bi?" he panted.

I sighed. He had a one-track mind, apparently. "Around nine or ten, I suppose. My nonna watched a lot of football. I didn't care much about the ball. I was fascinated by the players."

"Was it hard in the military? To find men to sleep with?"

I chuckled. "No, not at all. It was easy, but it had to be quick."

He didn't say anything more. Was he thinking about his upbringing? His lover who'd been killed in Belgium? I found myself curious about him. "And you? When did you know?"

"Always."

"How did you hide it from your father?"

"Looking back, I can't believe Fausto didn't figure it out. I had posters of Gianluigi Buffon all over my bedroom walls."

My eyebrows lifted. Buffon and I were the same height and similar features, both with dark hair. Had Giulio recognized the resemblance? "A fantastic goalkeeper."

"I was obsessed with him. Never even considered a woman in the same way."

"Have you ever slept with a woman?"

"No, never. Paolo and I found each other when I was sixteen. He was my first."

"You must miss him."

He shrugged, as if to say *what-can-you-do*. "Yes, but I've had a long time to come to terms with the guilt. I had no idea someone would try to kill me. I thought I was free from all that. That we would be—"

Safe.

How could he have been so naive? "Your father has made many enemies."

"This isn't about my father. I'm the embarrassment, the gay man who left after pledging my life to them. They can't let me go."

I had no idea who was responsible for the car bomb, but I seriously doubted it was the 'Ndrangheta. "What does your father say?"

"That the man responsible is dead. But I can't take that chance until I know for certain."

"Car bombs haven't been used since the Camorra or the Cosa Nostra in the eighties. I don't think it's the 'Ndrangheta."

"Then who was it? You're an assassin. Who still uses car bombs?"

"A few groups." Factions of al Qaeda and ISIS. The PKK. Russians. "None that would care about you."

"So you think it was, what? Coincidence?" His voice rose in anger. "I've seen the CCTV footage leading up to the blast. There was no hesitation which car was their target."

This surprised me, though it shouldn't have. "You've been investigating the bombing."

"Sì, *certo*. Did you think I have been sitting on my ass for four years?"

"I thought you were trafficking cocaine," I said dryly.

He came to an abrupt halt, his sneakers skidding on the cold ground. Whipping around, he pinned me with narrowed eyes. "You were following me. In Málaga."

"Were you under the impression I first found you in that club? Ma dai, Giulio." He didn't say anything, so I continued. "A million Euros in one day." I whistled. "Nice."

He put his hands on his hips and mumbled something.

"Cosa?"

"I said I can undercut the existing suppliers because it's just me. I have no overhead."

"Smart of you. Does your father know what you're doing?"

"Of course not."

"Because you're worried he'll try to take over?"

Giulio looked at me as if I had two heads. "Because he would worry about my safety. Cristo, Alessio."

I held up my hands in apology. "Aren't you worried about your safety?"

"I'm on a remote Scottish island, jogging with a man hired to kill me. I think we both know the answer to that question."

Turning, he started up the path again. I found myself following once more.

CHAPTER SEVEN

Giulio

I studied the hills as I ran, my head swimming. It wasn't from lack of air, though. No, the more I interacted with Alessio, the more confused I became.

My hand tingled as if I could still feel his body under my palm. Last night I decided to use his attraction for me as a weapon. I would push him, bait him, and cause him to drop his guard. Then I could either kill him or convince him to drop the hit.

I hadn't expected to feel something in return.

"I like to fuck and he fucked."

Cazzo madre di dio, those words.

Now I was picturing it. His long, strong body underneath me, straining and trembling as he let me inside. Was he quiet when being fucked? Alessio didn't strike me as a moaner.

I hadn't been with another man like that since Paolo. And I should be ashamed that I was thinking about it, even briefly, with Alessio. Was I so broken, so twisted after the last four years that I'd stoop so low?

And yet.

If it kept me alive, who cared? Alessio wanted me, so I needed to use that against him. Whatever I felt was immaterial.

Keep him talking. Keep him focused on me. Get inside his head.

I used to be charming and easy to talk to. At least that was what people said back in Siderno. It couldn't be difficult.

And there was no way to kill him. I already tried that and failed. His skills were sharper than mine, his aim more deadly. I had to get creative in order to remain breathing. I needed to use my brains to beat him.

I cast a quick glance over my shoulder. Alessio's head was down as he ran, but I knew he was paying close attention to me. "You said killing me was an assignment you couldn't refuse. Why?"

"Have you been getting high already this morning? You asked me this once before."

"And I never received an answer."

"Because I don't owe you one."

Fine. I'd try another topic. "Why do you like Mrs. Campbell so much?"

"She reminds me of my nonna."

I latched onto this glimpse of his personal life. "The one who liked football?"

"Yes."

"What does your family think of your profession?"

"They're dead."

My mother died when I was young. Murdered on a beach by my father's enemies. I doubted this was the case with Alessio's family, though. "Illness?"

"My father left when I was six. My mother gave me away when I was eight. I never saw either of them again. Both are dead to me."

My jaw fell open. *Eight.* Dio santo. I couldn't help but feel pity. No child should be given away or abandoned by a parent. "You went to live with your nonna."

"Sì. She died almost ten years ago."

"She must have been proud of you."

"She framed my medals and hung them on her walls."

Medals, plural. "I suppose you were well decorated."

"The military appreciates those who kill with efficiency. I am a very efficient killer."

Am, not *was*. I said, "The mafia also appreciates an efficient killer."

"It's much the same, killing in service of another. But when I left the Bersagliere, I decided any killing would benefit only myself."

"Which is why you're the most sought-after assassin in Europe."

He didn't answer. We both knew it was the truth.

We were near the top, with the entire island visible from this vantage point. Ocean waves rippled in the distance as far as one could see. Alessio's steps grew louder. Suddenly, he brushed by me, overtaking the lead.

"Was I boring you, assassino?"

"No, but you are slowing me down."

His powerful leg muscles popped and shifted beneath his running pants. I let myself enjoy the sight as he increased our pace. "If you don't kill me, what happens?"

He shook his head. "Let it go, principe."

"Why? It's not like I need to worry that I'll piss you off. And I'm genuinely curious."

"The people who order these things are generally not forgiving people."

"How do I know unless you give me a name? Maybe it's the Pope."

A deep chuckle floated between us. "You have a high opinion of yourself."

We started down the other side of the hill. This required more concentration to guard against slipping and falling on my ass. For a tall man, Alessio moved like a damn mountain goat. He was pulling away. But I needed to keep him close.

"So the men, the car bomb," I called out. "How would you find them?"

He slowed a bit. "What did the Belgian police say?"

"Nothing. No clues, no leads."

"There had to be something in their reports."

"How do you know I've seen them?"

"If you accessed the CCTV footage, then you were paying either a hacker or someone on the police force. You would have made certain to get the reports, as well."

He was right. I had paid off a police officer. "Bomb was a standard explosive device, five hundred grams of TNT. Placed under the car on the driver's side. Detonated remotely."

"Easier than wiring it to the ignition. Where were you?"

"Across the street. We were leaving a club and Paolo took my keys because I had too many drinks. He was going to come around and pick me up."

"So they knew it was Paolo behind the wheel?"

"My guess is they saw us come out of the club, left, then detonated it a few minutes later."

"How do you know your ragazzo wasn't the target?"

"It was my car," I said. "And Paolo wasn't supposed to join me that night. He surprised me when he got off early from his shift. The bomb was put in place almost as soon as I went inside."

"Who planted it?"

"Two men, average build. They wore hats and dark jackets."

Alessio thought about this for a few moments. "A professional would have cut the CCTV before wiring a car like that. Any of your father's business dealings go south about that time? Low-level associates, I mean."

"I told you, this isn't—"

"About your father," he finished. "Yes, I know. Humor me."

I thought about Enzo D'Agostino, but he was hardly low-level. And a car bomb was definitely not his style. He'd hired an assassin to take my father out in broad daylight. "Not that I know of."

"Hmm."

"What does that mean?" I steadied myself on a rock when my feet slid.

"That you're not thinking hard enough when it comes to your father's enemies."

"I already told you," I snapped. "There's no one."

"Cazzata. *If* you weren't about to die, I would tell you to dig into the Ravazzani empire. It should be easy for you, considering."

"Considering, what? I'm no longer in it."

"You are il bel principe. You'll never be anything else."

Alessio didn't understand. I wasn't that man any longer. And I didn't have access to such information. "You make it sound so easy."

He disappeared around a bend, but I heard him say, "That's because you're making it hard."

I blew out a frustrated breath as I took the corner after him. "What would you do?"

"You mean what would I do if someone was trying to kill me?"

"Yes."

"It's hardly the same. And the car bombers are not the only ones trying to kill you."

"Let's forget about you for a moment."

"As if you could," he threw back, sounding offended.

"I'm serious. Someone is after you. What do you do?"

"I don't know. I've only been on the other side of it and most of what I do is research. I learn everything I can about my target."

I gaped at his back. "This is why you were stalking me in Málaga and Santorini."

"Yes."

I blurted, "What did you learn?"

"Principe." He drew to a halt and shoved his sweaty hair out of his face.

I stopped, rested my hands on my knees, and sucked in air. "I want to know. What did you learn about me?"

"Why? So you can try to change your patterns when I need to kill you?"

"Would that even work?"

"No. So, why do you want to know?"

I couldn't explain it, but I needed to know. I was curious what he'd learned in those months observing me. I lived a lie for so long. Being an openly gay man had only lasted a short time before I was forced to go on the run. All I knew was hiding, pretending to be someone else. Keeping my true self a secret to stay alive. What could this stranger possibly have discovered?

"Humor me, Alessio."

He folded his arms across his chest and braced his feet. Like he was readying himself to report to his superior in the army. "You like people and crowds. You thrive off the energy in a city. I've never seen you drive, but I assume you like speed so you probably drove an expensive sports car. You vape weed whenever you are feeling down and missing your friends and family—especially Frankie. You want to break free of your father's control, but you also miss him. You're slightly jealous of his new children, though you tell yourself it's for the best that he has another son who can assume the Ravazzani legacy."

He drew in a deep breath and kept going, his voice staccato, like reading a list in his head. "You eat healthy and exercise every day. You rise around eight or eight-thirty and surf gay porn on your phone. Usually D/s videos, probably because you prefer being a top. Then you jerk off in bed, easy as you sleep naked. Once you come you clean up quickly, almost like you're embarrassed. I suspect Roman Catholic guilt." He raised one eyebrow. "Should I go on?"

I nodded once, unable to form a single word. I was both fascinated and horrified. But I was also growing aroused, which made no sense whatsoever. He had scrutinized my life and I shouldn't be getting erect —yet I was thickening in my pants.

He kept going. "Then you workout in a pair of briefs. Your female neighbors try not to watch but can't help themselves—and who could blame them? The lunges and push ups . . . madre di dio. You could sell tickets and make a fortune. Anyway, once you finish and shower, you shop for the day's meals. You might make a mushroom risotto or frittata. You like stone fruits as dessert, though you treat yourself to pistachio gelato every now and again. In the afternoon you watch a streaming show on your tablet. The most recent season of *Gomorrah* made you laugh and roll your eyes."

When he paused, I said, "What else?"

"We already talked about the coke, which just leaves the nightclubs."

I leaned slightly forward, dying to hear the rest. After all, our first encounter had been in a nightclub. "What about the nightclubs?"

The skin of his neck turned a dull red, and I realized he was embarrassed. Cazzo, he was adorable. This big, scarred assassin was capable of embarrassment. "Dimmi, assassino," I ordered.

"You go late, after it's crowded. You wear jeans and a tight t-shirt and you wait for someone to approach you, never the other way around. You want someone eager and you don't much care what he looks like. You lead him to a dark corner and never kiss on the mouth. Instead you tell him exactly what you want, and no one ever refuses. They get down on their knees and suck your cock until you come. You never thank them or reciprocate, and you can't get away fast enough."

When Alessio finally fell silent, I couldn't speak. It was all true. Every word. He *knew* me, some ways better than I knew myself. Alessio was smart, smarter than I'd given him credit for. And he'd been following me a long time, watching me. Learning me.

How many men had he seen me with at the clubs? There had been a few in Málaga. Two in Greece. But none of those blow jobs had been as good as Alessio's.

Lust was suddenly a tight fist in my belly, undeniable and urgent. He didn't look away, just continued to watch me with his cool gunmetal gaze. He thought he had me all figured out. So did he know the thoughts currently running through my head?

I doubted it.

Because right now I was angry and turned on. I wanted to both punish him and make him writhe and moan. My body was hyper aware of him, of me. I noted every rise and fall of his chest. The way his lips parted slightly, the ruffle of his hair in the breeze. I was buzzing, my skin crawling with heat and need. And I was remembering Málaga.

I hated us both for it.

Stepping closer, I moved in until only a few centimeters separated us. Our chests were almost touching, and I could feel the heat coming off his big frame. I pitched my voice low and soft. "You're wrong, Alessio. It very much mattered to me that night. I wanted it to be you. And I haven't been able to stop thinking about it since."

I heard his quick intake of breath. I kept talking, curious to see how far this would go. "When you waited to swallow my come? That was the hottest thing I've ever seen."

He licked his lips, but said nothing.

My pulse pounded in every part of my body. He was so close I could count his eyelashes. I cataloged each whisker he'd yet to shave off and dragged my gaze over the jagged edges of his scar. The air between us turned heavy with expectation, like we were both waiting for the other to do something.

Silence stretched. I couldn't tell what he was thinking, so I decided to push him even further.

"Would you like to suck my cock again, Alessio?"

The words were less a question and more an invitation. There was no way he missed it, either. I could see the indecision, the tension inside him, as he contemplated it. Pupils blown with lust, he curled his hands into fists at his side.

Finally, he pressed his lips together and shook his head once.

Satisfaction flooded me. I didn't bother suppressing my smile as I eased past him. "Liar."

CHAPTER EIGHT

Alessio

The cold wind slapped my face as I headed down the mountain. It felt deserved, like nature was punishing me for my stupidity.

"Would you like to suck my cock again, Alessio?"

Worse than being attracted to my target? Having him recognize it and use it against me.

Failure sank in my belly, mixing with the anger to leave a bitter taste in my mouth. I was an idiot. I never should have let Giulio see me in Málaga. He and his whole family were bad luck for me.

This time I didn't try to keep up with him as we ran. Hopefully, he would disappear to the farmhouse and I could get my head on straight.

Two days. The ferry returned the day after tomorrow, by which time Giulio needed to be dead. I had to sort this out quickly. Then I could leave Scotland and keep busy with other jobs.

When I reached the bottom, there was no one around. Only rolling hills and craggy rocks. As I started for town, I dug my phone out of my pocket and dialed.

"Is it done?" Sasha asked instead of a greeting.

"It will be. I'll be on the next ferry in two days."

"Thank fucking God," she said in her heavy Russian accent. "I am so bored."

"I apologize for not providing you with enough entertainment."

"Has been almost three months. Is a long time for you." She paused. "Should I update D'Agostino? I have not talked to his people since Málaga."

"No." The less contact with D'Agostino, the better. "You can update him when it's done and get the rest of the payment."

I disconnected and kept walking. I rolled my shoulders and tried to shake off the portentous feeling clinging to my skin.

By the time I reached Mrs. Campbell's pub I was calmer. Tomorrow, I'd finish what I came here to do and disappear. All of this would be a terrible memory.

The pub sat empty. Not surprising at this early hour. I reached behind the bar for a glass, then poured myself a lager from the tap. Mrs. Campbell could add it to my bill. I sat down on one of the stools and took a long drink.

Mrs. Campbell appeared from the storage room in the back. She had a clipboard in one hand and a pencil in the other. "Och, it's just you."

I lifted my chin in greeting. She went behind the bar and set her things down. Then she eyed my glass. "Bit early in the day, isn't it?"

"It's breakfast."

"I see." Her sharp gaze studied my face. "Anything you want to talk about?"

Frowning, I didn't say anything. Where would I even begin?

"Give me a minute." She disappeared into the kitchen.

I continued to drink my beer, content to sit alone in the silence. I needed a proper shower and a change of clothes, but couldn't bring myself to care at the moment.

"I wanted it to be you. And I haven't been able to stop thinking about it since."

Madre di dio. How I wanted that to be true.

But he was full of shit. Giulio and his runway looks and anonymous blow jobs. He was trying to fuck with my head.

Unfortunately for me, it was working.

I was finishing the last of the beer when Mrs. Campbell returned, a plate in her hands. She set it down in front of me and refilled my empty pint glass. "A bacon sandwich. That's my homemade bread."

I took the beer but didn't touch the plate. "Thank you."

"You'd better eat it. I don't like my food going to waste."

She was still watching, so I put the glass down and took a bite of the sandwich. It was salty and crispy, the bread warm and crusty. All of the sudden I was starving.

She busied herself while I finished eating. It didn't take long, only three or four more bites. She nodded to the plate. "Would you like another?"

"Do you have any soup?"

"The best cock-a-leekie in Scotland. I'll bring you some more bread." She took the pint glass away and replaced it with water. "Does this have anything to do with nice Mr. Drakos?"

Mr. Drakos wasn't so nice. "How did you guess?"

She hooked a thumb toward the beer tap. "I know man troubles when I see them. Are you two still arguing?"

"You know we aren't boyfriends."

"I figured, when I saw you carrying a HK P30L and heard that you threatened all the fishermen on the island."

It was telling that she recognized the type of pistol I carried. "So you also know this isn't going to end well."

Her dark brown gaze was understanding and weary. A woman who'd seen and done a lot in her time. "All of us make our own choices, laddie. And it's never too late to change your direction."

"Sometimes it is."

"No, it's not. Don't live your life with regrets. People like us? We have enough demons as it is."

I twisted the water glass on the bar top, not meeting her eye. "What branch were you in?"

"Well, now. That's a story for another time." She straightened and reached for her clipboard. "I've got more inventory to do. Think about what I said."

After she left, I stared at the water droplets on the glass in my hand. She was wrong. I couldn't make my own choices, not about this job.

It wasn't a question of what. Only a question of when.

———

Giulio

INDECISION ATE at me the rest of the day.

Ax in hand, I continued splitting logs for firewood. The back-breaking work was keeping me occupied. Maybe I'd exhaust myself and stop worrying whether I made a mistake with Alessio earlier.

Had I misread him?

I didn't think so.

He definitely wanted me. Those were signs I definitely recognized. And he'd stalked me for *months*. But maybe he wouldn't act on it if I could get inside his head.

Cazzo. I had to figure out what to do, and jogging with him every morning wasn't the answer. After today I suspected he would become frustrated. He wouldn't want me using his attraction for me against him. That meant he had to decide to either fuck me or kill me. Hard to say which he'd decide on at this point.

I was leaning toward killing.

The ax cracked apart the log and sank into the stump below. I hung my head and panted. My arm muscles ached. I was not cut out for farm living. The men at the castello would laugh their asses off if they could see me right now, playing the part of a lumberjack.

And being stuck in my own head was not helpful. I needed another opinion on Alessio.

Months ago I would've called Frankie. She was my closest friend and confidant. Except she was married to my father and this compli-cated things. I didn't want him to know about my current situation on Canna.

There was Benito, my cousin, but he worked for Fausto. I couldn't ask him to keep this from my father. It wasn't fair.

There was one other person. An Italian friend from when I lived in

Belgium. Theo and Paolo had been close, and Theo and I stayed tight after Paolo's death. He was good at reading other people and he definitely knew a lot about men.

It was what made him a talented fashion designer. Since leaving Bruges, Theo had gone to Paris and worked his way up through the design houses. Now he was the head designer at a world-famous luxury brand.

Deciding I was done with chopping, I carried the split wood into the farmhouse. I took my jacket off and started a fire, then found Theo's number in a small journal I carried with me. The charged burner phone powered up and I began dialing.

"*Allô?*"

"Theo?"

A long pause. "*Qui est à l'appareil?*"

"It's Giulio," I said in Italian.

"Bello! Is it really you? It has been forever since you called me."

I smiled, though he couldn't see. "It's me. How have you been?"

"Is this your new mobile? I tried to call you a few times, but the old number had been disconnected."

"No. I'm without a permanent phone at the moment."

"Oh." I could hear shuffling, like he was moving around. In the background, a deep voice asked, "*Où vas-tu?*"

Theo answered back in French, then I heard him kiss someone quickly. I immediately felt guilty. I said, "I can call you later."

"No, absolutely not. I've been worried about you." A door slid open and I heard street sounds. "Besides, Nic can wait. I just let him fuck me into the mattress."

"How long have you kept this one around?"

"Two weeks. It is a record, bello!"

I grinned, happy for my friend. "Congratulations. Maybe he'll be the one."

He made a noise of disgust. "There is no *one*. This is what I keep trying to tell you."

This had been Theo's way of consoling me when Paolo died. At the time it had felt as if I'd lost the greatest love of my life. Now Paolo was a dull ache in my heart, ever present but not crippling. I might never love someone like that again, so blindly and completely, and I was fine with it. I didn't ever want to experience that pain again. Once was enough.

"But," Theo said in a low, almost hushed tone. "I really, really like this man."

"Good for you. Someday, when we are alone and I have more time, you must tell me all about him."

"I will. Now, tell me how things are with you."

"I need advice."

"Oh. Is it a man?"

"Yes, but I need you to tell me if I'm making a mistake."

"Is he handsome?"

"Yes, but—"

"Then there is no *but*. Sleeping with a handsome man is never a mistake. Even if he is terrible in bed, he looks gorgeous while doing it."

"What if this man has been hired to assassinate me?"

Theo hissed through his teeth. He knew vaguely what Paolo and I had done in our former lives, that my father was someone important. And after the car bomb incident, he'd probably put the pieces together. "Assassinate you?" he whispered. "Is he . . . you know, from Bruges?"

"The car bomb was someone else. This one is a sniper."

There was a long pause. "Bello, just how many people are trying to kill you?"

I closed my eyes and laughed at the incredulity in his voice, because what else could I do? My life was a bad James Bond movie at the moment. "Several, it turns out. But can we get back to the assassin I am trapped with on this island?"

"Oh, tropical paradise. I like the sound of this already."

"Hardly. This place is the opposite of a tropical paradise. It's very small and cold. And I can't avoid him."

"Wait, this assassin isn't trying to kill you?"

"That's just it. He isn't trying very hard. He's procrastinating. Following me around. Watching me."

"Ah, I begin to understand. Tell me everything."

I gave Theo the details of what had happened since Málaga up until today. "So please, tell me. Because I no longer trust my own judgment."

Theo paused. "Bello, stop picking up strange men in nightclubs. *Dio mio*. Use an app, like everyone else."

"Theo, focus. The assassin. I'm not misreading this, am I?"

"No. This man, he wants to fuck you. He's desperate for it, but conflicted. So he will do nothing and wait for you to do something."

"I gave him an opening this morning. He didn't take it."

"He will. But is that really the best plan?"

"What do you mean?"

"Why not kill him first?"

"I'm not sure I can." I dragged a hand down my face and exhaled. "I've tried already and failed. He's former military. Very, very good."

"Better than you?" Theo's voice rose with incredulity. "We have never discussed your background, but Paolo spoke very highly of you. He said you were a badass."

A pang of sorrow echoed in my chest. Paolo was a good man. "I appreciate his faith in my skills, but this assassin is like a machine. There's no sneaking up on him."

"So you are hoping to get him to fall in love with you and keep you alive."

"I think love is a reach. Lust sounds more probable, no?"

"Yes. But if he is a machine, it will be hard to convince him to forget this assignment. Lust or love, it is a gamble, bello."

"So try to kill him again?"

"Sì, I think so. Seducing him only will delay the inevitable."

This made sense.

"Unless," Theo continued, "you can offer him more money than whoever hired him. Pay him not to kill you."

"He said it's not just money. It's a debt he has to repay."

"Then you are in a tough place, amico. Please, do not let him hurt you. I cannot lose another friend."

My throat tightened, emotion welling inside me. "You won't."

"Good. And who knows? If you fuck him, maybe this assassin can help you with the other men trying to kill you."

Doubtful. Alessio didn't seem the type to do favors for anyone, especially a man he was supposed to eliminate. It wasn't like we were friends. Or lovers. Or anything.

"Wait," I said. "Are you saying fuck him or kill him?"

"I don't know." Theo sounded agitated, like he might be pacing. "This is all very difficult for me, bello. I don't wish to give a wrong answer, and I still have post-orgasm fog in my brain."

"I understand. Still, you've made me feel better."

"I am glad, but now I am worried about you all over again."

"Don't worry. It will work out." Possibly.

"I hope so. When will I see you again?"

"Soon, I hope. It's been too long."

"Well, if you kill your assassin and want to come to Nice, ring me. Nic and I are taking his yacht there on holiday next week."

A holiday on a yacht reminded me of home and my family. Fuck, I missed them. "I'll keep it in mind. Ciao, Theo."

"Ciao, bello!"

When the line was dead, I sat up, put the phone under my boot, and destroyed it.

I wasn't sure I knew what to do yet, but I had to decide quickly. I was running out of time.

CHAPTER NINE

Alessio

I decided to kill him the following afternoon.

This allowed me the best light and the most time to set up. Then I had only one night to wait before the ferry arrived. Less time for the body to be discovered and an alarm raised.

I stayed in my room, only leaving for meals. I cleaned my rifle. Exercised. Stayed hydrated. Slept.

The best time to set up would be during *riposo*, shortly after one o'clock. This was when, like every good Italian, Giullo would eat and relax. Probably read, as well, since he'd ditched his electronics in Santorini.

I put on my backpack and hefted my rifle case. No one saw me as I left town.

I took the long way, skirting the area where the farmhouse was located. The woods were thin but provided ample cover as I moved, staying low. There was a slight elevation about sixty meters from the farmhouse. This position offered the perfect angle of the back door, where he would come outside to either vape or feed the sheep.

An easy shot. One I could make with my eyes closed. All I had to do was wait.

I sat behind a shrub, well hidden from the view of the farmhouse. There I assembled and loaded my rifle, each step performed in the same order. I stored everything I didn't need in the brush. Lastly, I pulled on a brown beanie that would help me blend into the woods.

On my belly, I crawled into position, making sure not to disturb the surrounding vegetation. It was slow going but I had infinite patience when it came to carrying out my assignments.

When I was where I wanted, I stabilized the rifle on its bipod legs. I took out my range finder to get the exact distance. Then I adjusted for elevation and windage, and applied it to the sight for the perfect shot. Now all I had to do was wait.

No movement from inside the farmhouse. That wasn't unusual. Most likely he was sprawled on the couch.

The sheep were milling about, bleating, no doubt hungry. That was good. It meant he would come outside soon.

I remained flat, completely still. The only movement was the slight rise and fall of my chest as I took measured breaths. The pad of my finger remained on the trigger, my face resting on the cheek weld. My heart was beating slow and steady as I watched.

It's no different than any other assignment.

I repeated this to myself in my head. I needed to be ready to squeeze off a shot. No hesitation this time.

No thinking of bright blue eyes and blow jobs.

It's no different than any other assignment.

A twig snapped nearby. I shifted in the direction of the noise—and saw Giulio there. He had a gun pointed at me, the same one he'd used the other day to destroy the bottles.

"Don't fucking move," he snarled.

My mind raced with a variety of scenarios. I could risk it, hoping his aim hadn't improved. And if he did hit me, I doubted he would kill me. As long as it wasn't in my chest or belly, I should be able to survive and take him out.

But the best idea was to play along, see what he planned.

"Clever of you," I said as he drew closer. "I thought you were napping."

"I've been waiting for you, hiding out here since daybreak. I knew this was what you were going to do."

"Allora, now what?"

He crept closer, the gun aimed at my chest. "Get on the ground. Hands behind your head."

I did as he asked. With my head turned to the side, I could see him out of my peripheral vision. All I needed was an opening. He couldn't beat me in hand-to-hand combat. Just as soon as he came within reach . . . .

He was several meters away, but I didn't take my eyes off him. "Is this where you have me dig my own grave? Or maybe give me a pair of cement shoes?"

"You watch too many movies."

"So you're not going to put a bullet in the back of my head?"

"Yes, I am."

Steadily, he came up on my right side. His gun remained on me the entire time. My rifle was close, but I wouldn't be able to shift it quickly enough to shoot him. I waited.

Then he made a mistake.

Lifting his foot, Giulio kicked at my rifle to get it out of my reach.

That was when I pounced.

Staying low, I rolled and tackled his legs. One yank and I had him down in the brush. The gun went off at some point and he landed on the ground with a grunt.

"Cazzo!" he barked, but I was already crawling over him. I clamped one hand on his wrist to hold the gun out of the way and wrapped the other around his throat. I squeezed.

He bucked and landed a punch on my temple. A wave of dizziness hit me briefly, and he used the split second to slam the butt of the gun handle into my shoulder. Pain rippled through my torso but I ignored it.

I made another grab for the gun, and we wrestled on the cold ground. Each of us tried to get the upper hand. Snatching his wrist, I banged his arm on a tree branch to dislodge the weapon. The pistol flew out of his grip and landed out of reach in the vegetation.

"Stronzo!" he seethed. He shifted his knee, aiming for a groin shot, so I edged sideways. This gave him just enough leverage to roll me over. Then I was on my back with Giulio on top of me, so I punched his kidney. We went on like this for a minute or two, trading jabs as we tried to gain the advantage. A searing pain tore through my left arm. He had a kitchen knife in his hand. The blade had just torn through my jacket and shirt to the flesh underneath. It wasn't deep, but it was annoying.

He wasn't weak. He was lean and strong and *quick*. Scrappy.

But I was bigger, with bigger hands and better technique. I grabbed his hand that was holding the knife and peeled his pinkie finger back until I nearly broke it. Hissing, he dropped the knife and I tossed it away. Then I got in position and held him down, using my bulk to pin him with his arms over his head. Panting for breath and covered in dirt and grime, we were left to stare at one another.

"Get off me." He strained and bucked, but I was immovable.

I told him calmly, "You should have shot me when you had the chance."

Anger boiled inside him. I could see it in every line of his face, each crease of his narrowed eyes. "I could say the same about you."

I knew why I hadn't killed him before today. Was it possible Giulio felt the same? Had he hesitated today because of the strange attraction between us?

"I wanted it to be you. And I haven't been able to stop thinking about it since."

No, it wasn't possible. Giulio knew what would happen if he didn't kill me first. He wouldn't risk it.

Not easing up my grip in the least, I watched him. His chest rose and fell as he struggled for breath, but he didn't look away. I was stretched out on top of him, so I could feel every bone, every muscle of his long frame. I could detail the chiseled features and angular jaw. The straight nose. Those gorgeous blue eyes framed by long thick lashes. He was devastating this close up.

"Why didn't you kill me?" I asked.

"I was about to." Each word was carefully enunciated through clenched teeth.

"Cazzata. You could have pulled the trigger from over there."

"I was worried I'd miss. Then you would shoot me."

It could be true, I supposed. But he didn't strike me as inept. Not the man who just wrestled with me on the ground for five minutes and tried to filet my arm, and not after our target practice.

I pushed, unwilling to let it go. "Why did you say those things yesterday? About Málaga and the blow job?"

He blinked a few times, like he couldn't believe I'd brought it up. Then he tried to move. "Get off me and I'll tell you."

I didn't want to give up my advantage. "No. Tell me now."

"I'm not saying shit until you let me up, stronzo."

I wished I didn't care. That I could kill him without answers. But I wanted to know every thought in his head. I was fascinated . . . even if he was the cause of my own destruction.

I considered my chances of survival if I let him up. The weapons were far enough away that I wasn't worried. And I could grapple him to the ground again, if necessary. He was tired, where I was not.

Using my arms, I pushed up and eased my body off his. Shifted my feet to stand. I thought Giulio would scramble to his feet and try to run, but he didn't. He remained on the ground, propped on his elbows, and stared up at me.

I offered a hand.

After looking at it for a beat, he clasped my palm in his and I pulled him to his feet.

Then I let him go.

My limbs were loose and relaxed, muscles ready. Giulio seemed on edge, his body locked and anxious to fight. He panted and watched me, dark hair hanging in his face. Neither one of us spoke.

I had infinite patience. And I wasn't the one who needed to explain.

"You've had every chance to kill me," he finally said, his voice a deep rasp. "I didn't even know you were here. It would have been easy to do it and slip away. Two ferries have come and gone since you arrived on this island. Yet you've been watching me, giving me advice on improving my aim. Running with me."

"And?" I prompted when he didn't continue.

"And it's exactly what you did in Málaga and again in Santorini. This is a pattern with you. So I wonder and try to figure out the reason. And there's only one explanation, Alessio."

The air around us shifted. *He knows.*

With my heart now pounding, I felt my senses go into overdrive. I was cognizant of everything around me, each part of my body. The hard ground beneath my boots. The pain in my shoulder, the burn in my arm. The expansion of my lungs with every breath, the blood rushing through my veins.

I didn't want him to say it.

Because it was true and giving voice to it would only bring me shame.

I tried to deflect. "Maybe I don't see you as a threat. I can take my time, knowing you can never get away from me."

His lips curled into a sexy smile. It was the first time he'd looked at me like this—like he wanted to strip me down and fuck me into oblivion—and I didn't know what to do. It disoriented me. Made me want things I couldn't possibly have. My mouth went dry.

"That is not why, assassino, and you know it. When you jerk off, who do you picture? Who are you imagining?"

I didn't want to answer.

"Is it me?" He took three steps closer, putting himself within my reach. "I make your dick hard, no?"

I snorted and tried to make light of it, though my insides were on fire. "So you like that the man who will murder you also wants to fuck you?"

"I do, yes." The truth was there in blue eyes now darkened with lust. "Maybe it's fucked up, but I like knowing that you crave my cock again so much that you're risking your career and your life. And I would be a fool not to use that against you."

"These mind games are a waste of time. In the end, I will do what needs to be done."

"I don't think so." He took another step closer to me. Then

another. We were almost touching now. He let his gaze linger on my mouth. "I think you'd rather blow me again."

I did, yes. Very badly. But I would not admit it to him.

Instead, I lifted one eyebrow and tried to appear unaffected. "I think you miss having a cock in your mouth, principe. I have a very nice one. Maybe if you do a halfway decent job, I'll let you live."

Very slowly, *achingly* slowly, he placed one palm on my chest. I could feel the heat of him through the layers separating us. Then he dragged his hand higher until he reached the bare skin of my throat. Sliding his palm to the side, he clasped my neck, as if holding me still.

Goosebumps raced over me at the feel of his firm grip. I couldn't move, mesmerized by the heat and aggression staring up at me. At the moment, no one else existed. This man was all I could see and feel.

His voice was barely a whisper. "Have you been thinking about it? Remembering the taste of my come?"

The truth tumbled out before I could stop it. "Yes."

Gaze locked on mine, he reached for the zipper of my jacket with his free hand. Then he pulled to lower it, each metal tooth unlocking in a sensual rasp. When the sides were free he pushed the heavy cloth over my right shoulder, then the left. It slid down my arms and dropped to the ground.

I was left in a tight compression shirt, much like the kind I wore when I ran. Giulio looked at my chest and shoulders for a long second, then back to my face. "Take out my cock," he ordered. "And get on your knees."

I could have refused. It was the smart thing to do.

But I was weak when it came to Giulio—and he knew it.

Like in a daze, I reached for the button on his jeans. I flicked it open and unzipped, careful of the thick bulge now pressing against his briefs. He was already hard for me, a fact I liked very much.

Reaching in, I wrapped my hand around his cock. He was hot, the skin stretched tight, and my mouth watered. I jacked him slowly, wanting to prolong this. Wanting to torture him.

He sucked in a quick breath. "Fuck, keep going." He shoved his briefs and jeans lower on his hips, giving more room. "Tighter. That's it."

I stroked faster, harder. We were both looking down at my hand, our heads nearly touching. I thumbed the underside of his shaft, then moved up to the slit. I smeared the precum waiting there over his skin, using it like lube as I continued pumping my fist. His hand suddenly twitched on my neck.

"In your mouth," he growled. "I need to get inside your mouth again."

I lowered myself to my knees. Giulio didn't hesitate in putting his cock to my lips. His blue gaze was feverish, wild, and it made me wonder which one of us wanted this more.

Because if he wanted it even half as much as I did, then we were in trouble.

"Va bene," he crooned as he slipped past my lips and onto my tongue. I sucked hard, drawing him deep. He didn't look away and instead concentrated on my mouth.

His free hand rested on my head, almost petting me. "Dio, your mouth is so hot and wet. I could fuck it for days. That's it. You're so eager, aren't you? You need my come again, no?"

In answer, I flicked and swirled my tongue, giving him extra stimulation. Then I took him to the back of my mouth, while I tried to relax my jaw and my throat. I wanted all of him.

I swallowed around the head of his cock, and his thighs tightened under my palms. "Cazzo! I wish I could fuck your throat. Oh, Alessio. The things I would do to you if I had time."

His hand moved to the top of my head and he began rocking his hips, fucking my mouth. It was similar to Málaga, but better. This time I knew what he liked. I knew he wanted it deep and messy, to overtake me. He got off on the degradation, the control. Of having a man on his knees, servicing him.

But not just any man. Me.

"I wanted it to be you. And I haven't been able to stop thinking about it since."

I stared up at him, his head thrown back, face slack with pleasure. He was using me, but I held all the power. I controlled this, not him.

It was time to prove it.

I moaned around his thick shaft, sending vibrations through his flesh. Then I cupped his balls, rolling them in my fingers. His muscles began to tremble. "So good," he muttered. "It's too good."

I pulled off with a pop. His dick bobbed in front of me while I massaged his balls. Giulio frowned, his breathing uneven. "What are you doing? Make me come, assassino."

"Beg me, principe." Bending, I ran the flat of my tongue over his sac. "Then I'll let you shoot down my throat."

He grabbed his cock and began stroking. "Maybe I'll shoot on your face instead."

"You know that isn't what you want." I held his wrist, making it impossible for him to jack off. "You would much rather fuck my mouth, no?"

A bead of fluid leaked from the head of his dick. I licked it up with the tip of my tongue.

"Figlio d'un cane!" he hissed. "Dai, Alessio. Per favore. *Prendilo in bocca.*"

"Still giving orders. But you did say please."

I swallowed him down, taking even more than before, and sucked hard. I dedicated myself to the task. Bobbed my head. Worked a steady rhythm. Kept my tongue flat and the pressure tight. My own cock throbbed in my pants, but I ignored it.

"Perfetto . . . Ah, sì. *Non smettere.*"

He didn't need to worry, I wasn't stopping.

Seconds later, he shouted and come shot onto my tongue, the salty taste of him flooding my senses. His dick pulsed as his balls emptied into my mouth, while his fingers clutched my hair. It went on and on, like he'd been saving it up for me.

The idea of that got me so fucking hot.

I resisted the urge to open my throat. After Málaga, I knew what he wanted.

Finally, he stopped twitching and tilted his head toward me. His skin was flushed, eyes glazed from his orgasm, but I could see the eagerness, the anticipation. "Are you holding it all in your mouth, like a good slut?"

I jerked my chin once, his semen rolling over my tongue.

"Va bene." He stepped back to put his cock away. When he was zipped and buttoned, he stroked my head, pushing my hair out of my face. "So big and dangerous. But put a cock in your mouth and you're so eager. So needy."

I waited, knees screaming in pain, my cock begging for attention. But there was a reason why we both couldn't forget Málaga. I wouldn't disappoint him.

"Fichissimo." *Crazy hot.* Giulio dragged a finger down my cheek. "Now, swallow."

I let it all go down my throat.

Something dark, almost sinister, flashed in his eyes. "You definitely picked the wrong career, assassino. You could give blow jobs for a living."

I got to my feet. "This is where you tell me you won't reciprocate, no?"

His fingers tangled in the front of my shirt as he jerked me closer. "This is where I tell you to get inside the farmhouse so that I can fuck you in my bed."

CHAPTER TEN

Giulio

I enjoyed the look of surprise on his face.

Alessio had expected me to leave him hard and unsatisfied, as I'd done with countless men over the last four years. Including him. Yet I'd invited him inside, to my bed.

I hadn't planned to when this all started. But we'd firmly established that neither one of us intended to kill the other. At least not today.

And fucking him was exactly what I wanted to do right now.

That blow job only took the edge off. Lust still sat heavy in my groin, my balls tight and full. For whatever reason I was drawn to him. And our fight had only worsened that craving.

Alessio was long and lean, packed with muscle. Strong and deadly. I was a good fighter. I knew how to handle a knife and a gun. I'd tortured and maimed, killed and dismembered. But I couldn't beat this man. He was like a machine, his punches like blows from a sledgehammer. Nothing seemed to hurt him, not even when I sliced his arm.

No one had ever been able to subdue me so quickly. When Alessio held me down? I liked it. Far too much, unfortunately.

To the assassin's credit, he recovered quickly. "You want to fuck?"

"Yes, I do."

"What happened to putting a bullet in the back of my head?"

I gestured to his rifle. "What happened to shooting me in the forehead?"

"You are trying to manipulate me with your dick."

"Just like you manipulated me with blow jobs." He hesitated, so I heaved a sigh and rubbed my jaw. "Dai, Alessio. I don't know what the hell I'm doing anymore. All of this is crazy. But we're attracted to each other and we're trapped on this godforsaken island. Do you really want to spend it hiding in the woods?"

"I can't back out of this contract, Giulio."

I didn't believe him. Whoever hired him wasn't as powerful or rich as my father. Even I had several million Euros in off-shore accounts. No way was his client someone I couldn't either outbid or kill myself. "Why?"

"Because I owe the client. And if I fuck this up, my career—and possibly my life—is over."

"There has to be a way around it. Nothing is inevitable."

He put his hands on his hips and stared off at the farmhouse. "You sound like Mrs. Campbell."

He'd been talking about this with Mrs. Campbell? I set that confusing fact aside for later. "Who is your client?"

"I won't tell you, so stop asking."

"I have a right to know."

"No, you don't. I'm not a negotiator or mediator. I'm an assassin, principe."

"Fine, but how do we know you're not working for the men who killed Paolo?"

"No, definitely not. I told you, car bombs haven't been used since—"

"The Camorra and Cosa Nostra in the eighties. Yes, I remember." I glared at him, irritated. "You will give me the name eventually."

"I was given interrogation and survival training by the army. You think to do worse?"

Yes, I did. I could tie him up and edge him until he talked. Or finger his prostate until he was almost ready to come and then stop. I would wear him down. "No way you trained for the type of techniques I would use."

"I see." The edge of his mouth hitched. "I wouldn't mind that torture, actually."

Now I was thinking about it. My groin tightened as blood rushed to my dick. "Do you want to fuck or not?"

"Are you always this direct?"

"Would you prefer it if I wrote it down in a letter? An official invitation, maybe?"

He cocked his head and stared at me thoughtfully. "You're a smartass. How did I not know this?"

Because I hadn't interacted with anyone on more than a superficial level in . . . a long time. Ages. Maybe not since Paolo. I had to be strong, self-reliant. Even with my family I was guarded. Almost dying and living on the run had done that to me.

I didn't want to think that it might be Alessio causing me to drop my guard.

I snapped, "Just answer the question, assassino."

"You are cranky for a man who just came like a fountain."

"And I'd like to reciprocate, if only you'd answer the damn question."

"So we fuck tonight? Tomorrow? For how long?" He folded his arms across his wide chest, drawing my attention to his muscles. So hot. I really, really needed to see him naked.

"Does it matter?" I would fuck him as long as it took to get the name of whoever hired him.

"Aren't you worried I'll kill you in your sleep?"

No, I wasn't. He didn't *want* to kill me. For some reason he felt he *had* to, but I would get answers regarding that later. "You should be worried I'll kill you first."

He snorted, the bastard.

Anger sparked hot in my chest. That was enough. He could keep his blue balls. I wasn't going to beg.

"Vaffanculo, Alessio." I started through the brush in the direction of the farmhouse. Later, I would return to retrieve the pistol. At the moment I needed to be where he wasn't.

I'd figure out what to do about him once I wasn't so pissed off.

As I passed his rifle, I snatched it up, not slowing down in the least.

"Where do you think you're going with that?" he called.

"Call it insurance," I said over my shoulder. "You want it, you know where to find it."

I heard him muttering behind me, but couldn't make out what he said. I continued toward the farmhouse.

Fuck this. I didn't need this frustration and confusion. My life was complicated enough. I had to get back to civilization, to my electronics. Find whoever was responsible for that car bomb. I would get on that ferry tomorrow and disappear. I didn't care what Alessio did anymore.

And I was definitely going to purge those two blow jobs from my mind by visiting the first nightclub I came across.

Just as I stepped through the door, an arm pushed me inside. I stumbled forward and the rifle clattered to the floor. What the fuck?

Then he was on me, shoving me against the wall and pressing his body against mine. He slammed our mouths together. It took a second for my brain to catch up. I hadn't even heard him approach.

Alessio was kissing me, his tongue already deep in my mouth. Lust exploded inside me, a rush of white-hot need so fierce that I was already panting with it. I grabbed the back of his head with both hands and returned the kiss. It wasn't sweet or gentle. It was like we were trying to devour each other. I took out my anger and irritation on his mouth using my lips, teeth and tongue.

He was hot and wet, the salty taste of my come still lingering. My groin tightened and my dick thickened with each rapid beat of my heart. *More*. That was my only thought as I dragged him closer. I couldn't get enough.

Then his hands were everywhere, removing my jacket, working my shirt off. We broke apart only for a split second as he tore the fabric over my head. In a flash his lips were attached to mine again, our tongues dueling feverishly, while his palms swept over every bit of skin he could reach.

I began grinding our hips together, unable to help myself. Through my jeans I could feel his erection through his thin pants, and each brush of his hardness made me see stars. *Fuck, yes.*

Soon we were building up a rhythm, working together, shifting and rolling hips, our frantic breath mingling. It was so good. If I wasn't careful, I could come like this.

I broke off and held his shoulders. Alessio's flushed olive skin and lust-drunk expression stared down at me. I said, "Bed. Now."

He didn't argue. Bending, he tore at the laces of his boots and removed them. I quickly did the same, but slower because I was distracted by the sight of his ass flexing as he walked down the hallway to the bedroom. Cristo santo, he was perfect.

The bedroom door was half open when I got there, so I pushed it wide.

Madre di dio.

His tall frame was stretched diagonally across the tiny mattress, a sinful slash of bare limbs and dark coarse hair. Lithe and muscular, his frame had no flab, nothing wasted. He was sculpted, but not bulky from a gym.

A cornicello hung around his neck on a gold chain, the amulet nestled below his collar bones. He hadn't struck me as a superstitious man, but so much about him continually surprised me.

He still wore his briefs, but I could see the large bulge behind the cloth. I couldn't wait to get my hands on it.

I stripped my pants off slowly, even though I felt ready to leap out of my skin. I wanted him so badly. His cool eyes burned intensely as he watched. He examined the tattoos, the scars. Signs of my former life. Much of my torso was covered with ink, markings that meant something once upon a time.

Alessio reached for his crotch and stroked his erection over his briefs. "You are a work of art, principe," he said softly.

I didn't like the way those words wrapped around my battered heart.

I focused on his body instead, and the red slash on his arm caught my attention. I knew from experience how bad those wounds could hurt.

Alessio noticed where I was staring and shook his head. "It doesn't hurt. Come here."

"I hope it stings like a bitch."

His lips twisted with amusement. "Bloodthirsty and hot. I like it."

Naked, I crawled onto the bed and dragged my palms up his legs, over his hips. I skimmed his stomach and chest. He was warm skin stretched tight over ropy muscle and strong bone, and I wanted to bite him, mark him. Devour him. "Tell me what you want."

"You said we were going to fuck."

"You ready to bottom for me, assassino?"

"Unless you'd rather bottom for me, yes."

"I don't bottom," I said, bending to drag my tongue over his ribs, along his pecs. Brushed his nipple. Then I stretched out on top of him and sank my teeth into the curve of his neck. He shivered and gasped, his fingers clutching my hips.

"Never?"

"Only once. I didn't enjoy it."

"That's because it wasn't with me."

Arrogant asshole. He thought he could do better than Paolo? Ma dai. I rolled my hips and ground our dicks together. The friction felt amazing. Craving a connection to him, I sealed our lips together and slipped my tongue in my mouth.

We continued to rub against each other, gaining speed, until he tore his lips off mine. "Minchia!" he hissed. "If you keep doing that, I'm going to come."

I pushed up and reached for the nightstand. Digging around, I found what I needed.

"You go on the run with condoms and lube?"

I lifted a brow. "You don't?"

"No. I wasn't thinking about all the dick I was going to get on Canna when I was packing."

"You're not going to get any dick at all if you don't shut up and take your briefs off."

That got a half smile out of him, and one of his dimples popped.

Molto bello. My chest swelled, but I quickly shoved any of those fanciful thoughts away.

He shoved his briefs down his legs and his hard dick slapped against his stomach. I stared, mesmerized. *Madre di dio*. It was picture perfect. The kind of girth and length that landed you in porn. "Fuck, Alessio."

He was already leaking, stretched tight. Eagerly, I reached for him. I stroked a few times, enjoying the sight of my hand on his shaft, until he stopped me, saying, "I'm too close."

"Then turn over."

I rose up and Alessio rolled onto his stomach. I raked my eyes over his broad back and trim waist. The tight ass and long legs. Cazzo, he was beautiful.

Leaning down, I kissed the firm globes of his ass. I moved up his spine, pressing soft kisses as I went, pleased when he trembled. I ground my shaft into the cleft of his ass and he pushed back against me.

I bit the shell of his ear. "Do you need to be fucked, Alessio? Do you need me to fill you up?"

"Yes," he said and let out a long moan as I thrust my hips against him.

"Va bene," I murmured, and trailed my lips along his neck and over his shoulder. He felt so good beneath me, all needy and eager, his strength and brawn mine to use as I wished. His skin was smooth, and I got lost in the exploration of his shoulder blades, the ridges of his spine. My cock throbbed against him, and I had to fight the urge to take him roughly, without any prep.

Finally, I reached for the lube. I flicked open the cap and moved to my haunches between his splayed thighs. "Look at how gorgeous you are." Spreading his cheeks, I drizzled the lube down his crack and over his hole. "Your ass is perfect."

His fingers clenched the sheets when I started to massage him open. Was he nervous? "Relax," I whispered. "I will take good care of you."

"It has been . . . a while for me."

I understood. This wasn't easy, trusting another person intimately.

After a few more circles my thumb slipped into his hot, tight passage and my eyes nearly rolled back in my head. I couldn't wait to feel this ass strangling my cock. "Oh, fuck. That's it. Let me inside."

I stroked his hip and pumped my thumb until he was rocking into the mattress. More lube, then I worked in two fingers. Alessio moved onto his knees and began stroking his cock in time with my hand. A light coating of sweat broke out on his skin and he was so beautiful like this, trusting me. Giving over to me. It felt like a gift I hadn't earned.

"Principe," he pleaded, his voice a deep rumble that tugged at my insides.

"Don't worry. I'm going to give you what you need." With my free hand I reached for a condom. I handed the foil packet to Alessio and, keeping my fingers inside him, shifted to where he could reach my dick. "Get me ready to fuck you."

He opened the package quickly, efficiently. The condom went on and I had to grit my teeth at the rough way he handled me. Exactly as I liked, with big calloused hands that weren't gentle in the least. Then he used lube on me, slicking the latex. "Stop." I jerked out of his grip. "I need to get inside you."

Blood whooshed in my ears, my pulse pounding along the length of my cock, as I moved behind him and withdrew my fingers. I lined up at his tight ring of muscle and pushed slowly. The crown slipped in and I couldn't breathe. Tight. God, so tight.

When Alessio tensed, I smoothed my palms over his hips. "That's it. Just wait," I said. "Let me inside. I need to be deep inside. Relax."

After a few seconds I advanced, sinking further. Invading. He reached to stroke himself, but I smacked his hip. "Not yet. I don't want you coming so soon."

He huffed but placed his palm back on the mattress. I began rolling my hips ever so slightly, pulling back and pushing in a little farther each time. It was easy now, and I lost the ability to think. There was just sensation, the need to ride him, to chase my own orgasm. He surrounded me, a perfect fit. Almost like he'd been made for me.

Our hips met and Alessio writhed restlessly beneath me. Muttering, cursing in a dialect I recognized as Sicilian. He was Sicilian? I wouldn't have guessed.

Though my body was screaming for friction, I couldn't help but order, "Beg me."

He didn't hesitate. "Ti prego. *Scopami forte.*"

The words lit a spark inside me. I grabbed his hips in both hands and began thrusting hard. His body rocked against mine, and I lost myself in the back and forth, the drag of his hot passage along my length. Fuck, he felt so good. "This is what you needed, no? This is why you followed me in that nightclub, because you wanted my dick. You're a slut for it, aren't you?"

He moaned and I changed the angle slightly. He shouted as I found his prostate. I closed my eyes and tried not to come. "That's it, right there. That is the perfect spot."

"Don't stop," he said huskily.

I pounded him, our bodies now slick with sweat. Part of me wished I could see his face while I fucked him, so I could watch as the pleasure overtook him. *Next time.*

He began shaking, his muscles clenching. "My dick. Please."

My lips curled into a cruel smile. I liked him begging and desperate. More than anything I wanted to make him come from my cock alone. Nothing in the world felt better than a prostate orgasm. "No. Don't dare touch it, Alessio. I'm all you need. Only me."

He groaned and I kept at it. If I hadn't come in the assassin's mouth moments ago, I wouldn't have lasted this long. Already I could feel my balls drawing tighter, but I wanted him to come first. No idea why it mattered all of a sudden, but it did.

"Fuck, fuck, fuck," he chanted, his head hanging down. "Fuck, please."

Slick slaps filled the room, our exhales picking up in volume. I grabbed his hair for leverage and yanked him back toward me, riding him properly. Instantly, his muscles contracted and he shouted to the ceiling. His body began milking mine, squeezing me as his climax went on and on.

It was too good. I couldn't take it anymore.

After a few more thrusts, pleasure burst through me, rushing up my legs and out my dick. The orgasm dragged me under, leaving me helpless as jets of come shot into the latex.

As it ebbed, I slumped over him and tried to regain my breath. I was weak and dizzy, like he'd turned me inside out. That had been fucking amazing. A thousand times better than a quick blow job in a club. It felt right in ways I couldn't explain. I already wanted to do it again.

I gripped the base of the condom and pulled out. Alessio hissed when I slipped free, and I patted his hip before departing for the toilet.

At least tonight, the only way one of us would kill the other was with a dick.

CHAPTER ELEVEN

Alessio

My limbs were still shaking when Giulio flopped back down on the bed. Our bodies were close, but not touching. "That was fun," he said.

I shifted to face him. "No regrets?"

The edge of his mouth kicked up. "None."

"You're very good at that."

He dragged a hand down his face. "A bit out of practice."

God help me if this got any better with him. I think he fucked my brains into next week.

"I want to shower," he announced, stretching his long body.

I closed my eyes, exhausted and dick-drunk. "Go ahead, then."

"Come with me."

That caught me by surprise. I cracked one lid to peer at him. "Shower with you?"

"Yes. Do you have something against it?"

"No, I just . . . ."

"Andiamo, assassino." He slapped my hip and rolled off the bed. "Let's get clean and then we can discuss my dick in your mouth again."

I snorted as I slowly sat up. "I need more than a few minutes before my muscles are capable of that."

He disappeared into the washroom. "That's okay," he called. "You can lie there and I'll fuck your mouth."

Unbelievably, my dick twitched. That sounded hot.

The shower started and by the time I entered the room, Giulio was stepping into the small tub. The two of us would be a tight fit.

Still, I opened the curtain and slid into the steamy spray. Giulio was under the water, running his hands through his hair, wetting it. Cristo, he was sexy.

He was truly a work of art. No museum in Florence has anything remotely as beautiful as this man.

I frowned when the water stung my arm. The knife wound. I'd forgotten about it. I pinched the cut, reopening it to flush it out. Red water ran down my arm.

"Here." He handed me the soap.

I cleaned my arm carefully, then used the soap everywhere else.

"Will it need stitches?" he asked, tilting his head toward my arm.

I almost laughed. This was nothing. I'd experienced far worse. "No."

He shook his head. "I don't know why I find that so hot, but I do. Does anything hurt you?"

"There's something wrong with that boy."

Though it had been decades, my father's voice still haunted me. If I had been a better son, maybe he would've stayed. Maybe my mother wouldn't have given me away.

Maybe, maybe, maybe.

But there was no changing the past. Just like I couldn't change the fact that I had just let my target fuck me into oblivion.

He reached for the shampoo and his hip brushed my stomach. "So, now what?"

"What do you mean?" I knew what he meant, but I wanted to hear his thoughts first.

"We had two options, Alessio. Kill each other or fuck each other. We obviously chose option B."

I leaned against the tile and watched him clean his hair. "This doesn't change anything. It only delays it."

"Aren't you getting tired of saying that?" He rinsed and wiped the water out of his eyes. "Stop lying to yourself and to me."

Irritation slid along my skin like needles. "You don't understand how the real world works, principe. You live in a bubble of privilege, where you're protected by your father's name and bank account."

He froze and his eyes went glacial. Stepping closer, he crowded me into the tile. "You condescending prick. I've been living outside the mafia on my own for four years, on the run for my life. Anonymously. No one knows my last name. And I haven't taken a dime from my father since I left."

In a flash, I flipped our positions. His back slammed against the wall. Slick rough skin met mine as I pressed our lower halves together. I used my hand on his throat to keep him pinned there. "Do you think your father isn't having you watched? That he isn't aware of every move you made the last four years? Ma dai, Giulio."

I saw the resentment boiling in his mind. He knew what I was saying was true. And he didn't like it.

"Get off me," he snarled.

"Because you don't like to hear the truth?"

Before I could brace for it, he grabbed my wrist and twisted. At the same time he shifted his body weight, using gravity to pull me off balance. I righted myself, but not before he was behind me, shoving me face first into the tile. His hips met my ass, and I could feel him begin to thicken against me.

"You are getting hard right now?" I asked over my shoulder.

He sank his teeth into my shoulder and rocked his hips. His cock slipped through my cleft. "I can't help it. Fighting with you gets me fucking excited, apparently."

My dick began to respond to this, too, perking up. "You like to hold me down."

"Fuck yes, I do." More grinding. "Let's stop talking. I want to make you come again."

A tremble went through me as blood pooled in my groin. Now it was all I could think about. "I want that, too."

He slapped my ass, then turned off the water. "Go get on the bed. I feel like blowing you."

That was something I was dying to see.

I opened the curtain and stepped out, grabbing a towel to quickly dry off. Giulio watched, his gaze burning my skin, as he waited.

The air was cool on my damp flesh as I settled on the bed. I was half-hard, so I stroked myself while I waited for him. Was he really going to let me fuck his mouth? I'd imagined it so often that I could scarcely believe it might actually happen.

He strode into the bedroom, his muscles shifting under all that inked olive skin. His eyes dragged over my limbs and settled on where I was jacking my cock. "Stop," he ordered.

Biting my lip, I obeyed. I didn't know why, but his dominance and aggression turned me on. Maybe I was a closeted submissive? Or maybe it was just this man?

Giulio settled between my legs and I clenched my muscles, struggling for calm. I couldn't look away. I didn't want to miss a minute of what was about to happen.

He nuzzled my shaft, inhaling me, then he flicked his tongue over my crown. I hissed. I was already impatient. I didn't want to be teased. I needed to get inside his mouth and feel those perfect lips wrapped around me.

"Suck, principe," I ordered, taking his hair in my fist. "Take me deep and make me come."

The head of my cock disappeared inside his mouth—and I lost my train of thought. Wet heat surrounded me, his jaw stretching to accommodate the width. Oh, fuck. I hadn't expected it to feel this good. Or to enjoy the sight this much. This was no gentle wave of pleasure; it was a storm of sensation, all focused in my groin.

He moaned and the vibration sank into my shaft. I thrust up, unable to help myself. "Feels amazing," I gasped. "Keep going."

He began sucking in earnest, his cheeks hollowing with the effort. His mouth, madre di dio. The suction was perfect as he worked the base of my cock with his hand. He didn't try to take me deep, but I didn't need it. Not with whatever he was doing with his lips and tongue. And watching him made it even better. I wanted this to last for days. *Weeks.*

"Fuck, you are good at that," I whispered.

He began working my balls, rolling them in his fingers. But he wasn't gentle, like he was afraid of hurting me. Instead, he squeezed them, pulled on my sac. I was balancing on the edge of pleasure and pain, and soon my legs were clenching, my body on fire.

When he sped up, I knew my orgasm wasn't far off. My skin felt too tight, like I might explode at any moment. Then he scraped the sensitive underside with his teeth and I couldn't hold back any longer. Ropes of come shot out from my cock and into his mouth as my body trembled uncontrollably. My vision blurred, and I shouted to the ceiling.

The room finally stopped spinning and I tried to catch my breath. Quickly, Giulio pushed up to his knees and I saw that he was already jerking himself off. Had blowing me turned him on?

Three more tugs and he clutched my thigh, his eyelids slamming closed. "Alessio, fuck!" Thick spurts began coating my stomach. I watched, transfixed, as his mouth slackened, bliss etched in every one of his features. Absolutely nothing could've dragged my attention away from him as he came.

Bellissimo.

With one final tug he released his cock and flopped onto the bed next to me. I stared at the ceiling, thinking. No question it was the best blow job of my life. Not necessarily because of the technique, but because of the man giving it to me. I'd watched him for so long and wondered what it would be like. Now I knew.

And I would risk almost anything for him to do it again.

"I think you broke my jaw, assassino."

Shifting, I regarded him as he rubbed the lower half of his face. "Such a baby."

"Your dick is massive."

"You'll live, principe."

"Stronzo." Reaching, he dragged a fingertip through his come on my stomach. Then he brought his hand to my mouth. I opened my lips and licked the digit clean. Giulio's nostrils flared as he inhaled sharply. "I like the way you look, drenched in my come."

Grabbing the back of his head, I jerked him forward for a deep kiss with plenty of tongue. He kissed me back, his fingers threading into my hair. When we broke apart, I asked, "How does it taste, the two of us together?"

His lips twisted into a devious smile. "Like bad ideas and imminent danger all rolled into one."

I laughed. "Good. Because we are going to do it again as soon as we both recover."

————

Giulio

WE EVENTUALLY MADE our way to the kitchen. It was the middle of the night and we'd skipped supper in favor of another round of orgasms.

Alessio settled on a bar stool at the island while I found provisions. I was wearing briefs, but Alessio remained completely naked except for the chain around his neck. I set a dish of olives in front of him, then poured him a glass of wine.

"Did you poison it?" he asked, lifting it to his mouth.

"And ruin good wine? Ma dai." I returned to the risotto I was stirring on the stove. "I decided to poison your risotto instead."

"I'm still surprised that you can cook."

Right. He'd been stalking me for months. "I don't have Zia to feed me any more. If I didn't cook I would starve."

"I can't really cook," he admitted. "Eggs and pasta."

"Please tell me you don't use a jarred sauce."

His mouth curved into a small embarrassed smile that showed off his right dimple. Mamma mia, I wanted to bite that dimple. "Jarred is good enough."

"Zia would smack the back of your head if she heard you say that."

"You must miss her."

"I do." I sighed and watched my spoon swirling in the pan. "I spent a lot of time in her kitchen growing up." With my father busy running an empire, most of my well-being had fallen on Zia.

"There weren't other boys on the estate to play with?"

"My father didn't allow it. I had my cousins sometimes, but I was the future heir." Fausto said I would rule over the estate one day. I had to be a strong leader, ready to make the tough decisions, not become friendly with everyone.

"That sounds lonely."

I shrugged and continued stirring. "Almost as lonely as a boy sent to live with his nonna."

"Is this why you like parties and clubs? Because you were denied this as a child?"

"I can lose myself in a crowd. Be anyone I want, do anything I want. Drugs and booze, sex. Whatever. I can step outside of my own skin."

"Did you hate being the heir that much?"

"Hate is the wrong word." I reached for my wine glass and leaned against the counter. "The responsibility was mine for as long as I could remember. And hating the responsibility meant hating myself. So I didn't hate it. There were parts I loved. The way people treated me, accommodated me. Any club, any restaurant. Anything I wanted was available with a snap of my fingers."

"But?"

I took a long swallow of wine and tried to put my feelings into words. "But I resented it, too. Every day was filled with dread. Was this the day I would be forced to marry a woman I cared nothing for? Or when everyone learned I was gay? Worse, was it the day my father would be murdered? There is no way to prepare for a future you don't want."

He plucked an olive out of the dish and slipped it in his mouth. "Still, it's foolish of you to stay away. The castello is the one place you're virtually untouchable."

"Virtually untouchable is not untouchable. And an enemy stormed the estate a few months before I left, so I know it's possible."

"What enemy?"

I resumed stirring the risotto. It was thickening nicely. "The men of another mafia don. You've probably heard of him. Enzo D'Agostino."

"Yes, I've heard the name."

His voice sounded odd, so I glanced over. "What?"

"Nothing. I try to stay out of the local mafia squabbles, but I know the names of the players."

"Does that mean you don't work much in Italy?"

"I work mostly in Eastern Europe and South America. Occasionally in the Middle East."

"What was your last assignment? You know, before me."

The scar on his face twisted as he frowned. "You know I don't talk about my clients."

"I'm not asking who hired you. I'm asking about who you killed."

"A politician in Minsk."

"Do you know why?"

"No."

My eyebrows shot up. He said it so calmly, so matter of fact. Like just another day at the office. I'd done terrible things for my father, for our brotherhood, but I always knew *why*. "And that doesn't bother you? Not knowing why?"

"If they tell me why, then I start to rationalize whether the person deserves to die or not. That is not my job."

I took my eyes off the risotto briefly to glare at him. "So you don't want to know why you've been hired to kill me?"

"What makes you think I don't know?"

The wooden spoon fell out of my hand and into the risotto. "Do you?"

He took a long drink, his throat working as he swallowed. Then he carefully set the wine glass on the island. "I don't want to have this conversation."

Fuck the risotto. I turned off the gas burner and propped my hands on the island. Met his stare. "Alessio, we need to talk about how this is going to work."

"What do you mean?"

"Don't be a dick. You know what I mean. This, here. Us fucking."

He tapped his fingertips on the island while he regarded me thoughtfully. "Can we call a temporary truce?"

"For how long?"

"A month."

The answer came quickly, as if he'd been considering this in his head. A month with him sounded nice after my many fantastic orgasms today. But it was a long time with a man hired to kill me. "Why a month?"

"I don't think a week—or even two weeks—is long enough for all the filthy things I want to do to you."

My dick liked that reason very much. "What happens at the end of thirty days?"

"I give you a head start, then come after you to carry out my assignment."

"Dai, Alessio. You expect me to keep fucking you, knowing this is what awaits?"

He shrugged, like this was no big deal. "You could disappear somewhere I can't find you. Or you could kill me first."

"Do you honestly believe either of those things are possible?"

"No."

Dio santo, this man. "I'll agree on one condition."

"Oh, we are negotiating?" He leaned back and folded his arms across his chest. An annoying smirk spread over his face. "Let's hear what you think a month of fucking me is worth—and it can't be for me to drop the hit."

I knew he wouldn't consider it, which is why I was asking for something different. "Help me figure out who planted that car bomb."

He sat perfectly still, a statue, as he thought this over. "What if I can't help you?"

"I thought you could find anyone."

"No, I can always find *you*."

I went back to the stove and relit the burner. The risotto could probably be saved. "You're saying you can't figure out who was responsible."

"I'm saying it's been four years and if your father believes the party responsible is dead, then I'm inclined to believe it."

"I'm not willing to bet my life on that. I'll sleep easier once I know who did it."

"You think your father would risk your life so casually?"

"No, of course not." I rolled my shoulders. "He wants me back in Siderno, so I think he doesn't care whether the party responsible is dead or not."

"So, go back to Siderno. Have your father help you find these people."

"I won't put my family at risk."

He started chuckling. "Giulio, your father is the risk. The money, the empire. Not you."

Back to this. Alessio believed a low-level associate of my father planted the bomb as a retaliation. I was more inclined to believe it was personal against me.

But it didn't matter. The bastards had killed Paolo and I would make them pay.

"If someone murdered your nonna," I asked him quietly, "would you let it go? Would you assume they were dead, or care whether the target was really you or not?"

He sighed heavily. "No, I wouldn't. I would hunt them down and peel the skin from their bones."

I gestured with my free hand. "Now you understand. Paolo was a good man. I loved him. I wanted to spend my life with him—and he was blown to bits in front of my face. I can't stop until those responsible suffer."

His lips pressed together before he took another sip of wine. I concentrated on the risotto. I hoped Alessio said yes. Because of his job, he had resources I didn't. And maybe he'd notice something new if he looked at the information I had gathered on the bombing.

I had to believe it might help.

"Fine," he said, sounding less than certain. "I'll try to help in exchange for four weeks."

I added butter to the pan to finish the risotto. "Good. Then I'll hold off on adding poison to your dish." Over my shoulder, I added, "At least for today."

He merely sighed. "I need to call Sasha."

"Who is Sasha?"

"My assistant."

"And here I thought you worked alone. I feel disappointed. It's like when they pull back that curtain in *Wizard of Oz*."

His face screwed in confusion. "Cosa?"

"*Wizard of Oz*. Haven't you seen it?"

"When I was a boy, maybe. What does a curtain have to do with my assistant?"

I grabbed bowls out of the cupboard. "Nothing. You are a real ray of sunshine sometimes, no?"

Pain suddenly radiated through my ass cheek as a loud crack sounded. I narrowly avoided dropping the bowls in my hand. He'd slapped my ass? I hadn't even heard him come up behind me. "Ma che cazzo!"

Alessio was practically grinning as he leaned down to kiss my forehead. "That is for the ray of sunshine comment." Then he walked out of the kitchen.

CHAPTER TWELVE

Alessio

A *month*. I would have him to myself for four weeks. I could fuck and kiss him whenever I wished. It was almost too good to be true.

A lightness filled my chest, a happiness I hadn't felt in a long time. I found my pack in the pile of things I'd dropped earlier. Then I dug my phone out and unlocked it. When I found Sasha's contact number, I pressed on it.

She picked up immediately. "About fucking time! Is it done?"

I spoke to her in Russian. "No. And it won't be for at least another month."

There was a long pause over the line. "Tell me you are joking."

"I am not."

Eventually, she sighed. "I'll push off the São Paulo job to someone else. And then I'll start work on my CV."

I knew she wasn't going to leave me. I paid her better than anyone else ever would. "I need a favor."

"You are already trying my patience."

"It's important. I need you to dig around with your contacts. See if anyone else is trying to kill Giulio Ravazzani."

After a weighted pause, she snapped, "Ty s uma soshyol?" *Are you out of your mind?*

"Whatever you are thinking, stop."

"I finally realize the reason you have not killed him. No wonder this assignment never ends."

I ignored that for the time being. "Someone planted a car bomb in Belgium four years ago to kill him. Just see if there is any chatter about it, anyone looking for him."

"And then what? You will kill these people for free?"

"No."

"Why don't I believe you?"

"Sasha," I barked. "Do as I say. I know what I am doing."

"You are thinking with your dick," she told me, disapproval dripping in her voice. "Just like every other man."

"Call me when you have an answer." I disconnected and carried my phone with me to the kitchen.

Two plates of steaming risotto along with slices of crusty bread were placed on the island. Giulio was already sitting in the seat next to mine. "You sounded angry," he said.

"She is busting my balls over you."

His sharp blue eyes locked with mine. "You told her we were fucking?"

"No, but she can surmise. I asked her to dig around, see if anyone is trying to kill you."

"Where, in your assassin group chat?"

I grabbed the nape of his neck and shook him slightly. "Smartass. These things are handled in very secure places on the web. But Sasha also has contacts all over the globe."

Giulio's mouth twisted into a devious smile. "Hearing you speak Russian was hot as fuck, assassino."

"Yeah?"

He ate a bite of risotto. "How many languages do you speak?"

"Seven. Eight, if you count my limited Scotch Gaelic, which I learned when I knew I was coming here." I ate a forkful of the mushroom risotto . . . and almost died, it was so delicious. Creamy, with just the right amount of bite. "Fuck, Giulio. This is good."

"You're welcome."

I elbowed him gently. "Thank you."

"So, Sasha the Assistant. She's . . . a former lover? Current lover? Fuck buddy?"

I focused on my plate and tried not to laugh. "No, nothing like that. Only an assistant. And she'd cut off my balls if I ever made a pass at her."

"How long has she worked for you?"

"Almost three years. She's former Russian intelligence."

"Ah. That explains the Russian."

We ate in companionable silence. I was used to eating alone, sleeping alone. Not since the army had I been around another person so much. Were Giulio and I capable of tolerating each other for four weeks?

Probably not. And there was the matter of his father's assassination attempt. Giulio would resent me the minute he learned who took the shot. Maybe I would confess it at the end of our time together, as a guarantee to earn his hatred. It would make killing him easier.

I finished off another piece of bread. "What do you plan to do once you learn who is responsible for the car bomb? Will you go alone, or will you tell your father?"

"Back to my father," he muttered. "Why are you obsessed with Fausto?"

Obsessed? I'd asked a reasonable question. "Giulio, your father has resources and manpower. Guns. It would be smarter—and safer—for you to ask for his help."

"You are the one who said these were low-level associates at best." He pushed his empty plate away. "Besides, I'm not telling you anything about what I'm planning four weeks from now."

"It won't make a difference," I said quietly. "You can't hide from me."

"You think this month is just about orgasms?" He wrapped an arm around my shoulders and leaned closer. "You spent months studying me. So I will use this time to learn everything about you. Your weaknesses, your habits. I will know you better than you know yourself." Then he nipped my earlobe with his teeth. "And you will never find me."

A shiver went through me, a rush of anticipation that settled in my balls. Cristo, this man. Never had anyone affected me like this.

And he wanted to know my weakness? All he had to do was look in the mirror.

I didn't want him to discover how much I liked this idea of his. So I made a dismissive hand gesture. "All I need to do is follow the trail of cocaine and find the new dealer in each town. Or I could wait in the gay nightclubs for a very good-looking man who doesn't like to give blow jobs."

He shoved me then stood up, and already I missed the warmth of his body. "Oh, yes. I hate giving blow jobs." He went around the island, collected our plates and took them to the sink. "Which is why I've given you two just today."

"And you'll soon give me a third."

Over his shoulder, he gave me a challenging look. "Is that what you think, assassino?"

Rising, I stalked across the old pine floor until I had him backed up against the sink. His fingers were clutching the old porcelain, eyes locked on mine. I could see the amusement dancing in his bright blue depths. He liked goading me. Fighting with me.

An idea occurred. "Do you want me to force you? Hold you down and shove my dick down your throat?"

"Absolutely not."

But I could see the way his pupils dilated, the pounding pulse at the base of his neck. He didn't hate the idea.

In a flash, I spun him around until he faced the sink and I was pressed to his back. I licked his neck, my dick suddenly liking the feel of the firm muscled globes in front of me. "Maybe I will hold you down and fuck you."

"I don't bottom, Alessio."

I began kissing Giulio's nape, down his spine. "I would make it so good for you, principe. Lick you and stretch you. You'd be begging me for it."

"No. And even if I wanted to, your dick would rip me in two."

"That is what plugs are for."

I reached around and shoved my hand into his briefs. My fingers found his semi-hard dick. Warm soft skin stretched over thick steel. Madonna, I loved the feel of him. He kept his hair trimmed, as I did, and even his cock was beautiful—long with a slight curve.

"Faster," he grunted, trying to push up into my grip.

I slowed down, stroking his shaft leisurely. "Still giving me orders?"

"Get me hard. I want to fuck you again."

My skin heated, now buzzing with need. I wanted that, too. But I couldn't give in so easily.

Releasing him, I took a step back. "Get on your knees."

He turned, his mouth tight with irritation. "You are trying to make a point."

I didn't say anything, just faced him squarely. Waited.

Giulio pushed off from the sink and closed the distance between us. He dragged a fingertip along my erection—and I shivered. His lips twisted. "You want to be rough with me?"

"Don't pretend you hate it."

"Oh, Alessio. You think I can't top from the bottom?" He sank to the floor, his eyes never leaving mine. I held my breath as he rubbed his nose and face all over my dick. His warm exhales, the moan he couldn't keep in . . . I had to lock my knees to keep them from buckling.

I expected him to suck me into his mouth, devour me and make me lose my mind. But he didn't. He peppered the shaft with light kisses, up and down, like he was worshiping my dick. It was the hottest thing I'd ever seen.

Then he used his tongue—and my eyes nearly rolled back in my head.

"*Fuck*," I breathed as he licked me like his favorite treat. Sparks raced along my thighs, then up my spine. Each swipe of his wet tongue was better than the last.

Then he looked up at me and sucked the head just past his lips. Heat enveloped me, but he didn't move. He kept perfectly still, like he was waiting for me to give direction. Those blue eyes burned into my soul and dried out my mouth.

"Take me deep. Into your throat," I rasped.

He pushed, drawing me in. Wet warmth bathed my dick as the pressure increased. My crown bumped the entrance to his throat and I expected him to pull off. Instead, he shuffled his knees to get lower and tilted his neck back. Then he swallowed.

His throat muscles squeezed around the head of my cock and I saw stars. "Minchia! Do that again."

He didn't. He pulled back, dragging his lips and tongue along my shaft, then paused to tongue the slit at the tip. I bit my lip to keep from crying out. This had only started and already I was aching with lust.

Threading my hand through his hair, I pulled on the strands until he gasped. "Faster."

Still, he moved at his own pace, the asshole. Suddenly, I shoved in until he gagged. I didn't give him a chance to pull off. I let him recover for a half second and then went deeper, into the muscles of his throat. It was heaven.

Then he started really moving, like he was eager for my come. The sight made me so hot. This beautiful man, taking my cock into his throat again and again.

"Dio, that's it." I gave another rock of my hips. My balls were so heavy. "That's where I want to be. In your throat." It was where I wanted to *stay*. I could happily live out the next years of my life with my dick in this man's mouth.

I wasn't used to having sex with the same person over and over. In the military our "we like cock" circle had been small, and we were often shipped all over Europe in separate units. Encounters had been fleeting and rare. Which had been fine for me, because I liked women just as much. They were easy, willing, and not hard to find.

But I was becoming addicted to Giulio. This was better than anything I'd experienced before, man or woman.

He moaned and the sound vibrated up my shaft. My back bowed, my thighs shaking.

Large fingers slid behind my balls, up my crease. They found my hole and circled, teasing. Sizzles went all through my lower half and I couldn't hold back. "No, too soon. Don't—"

The tip of one finger pushed inside and I couldn't stop it. The orgasm slammed into me, my body no longer in my control. Pleasure rushed up from my toes, euphoria turning my vision white. With a shout, I poured into his mouth. It went on for what felt like forever, my body emptying into his. Giving him everything.

I finished and stumbled backward, slumping against the island. Tried to catch my breath. Giulio stood and smirked at me. His lips were swollen, his face flushed. But the gleam in his eye was pure victory. "Get on the bed, assassino. I'm going to fuck your mouth again."

CHAPTER THIRTEEN

Giulio

Light streamed through the windows, teasing me awake. Awareness trickled into my brain. I was in my bed at the farmhouse. A man was with me, his frame nearly pinning me down. *Alessio*. He was still asleep, the soft, even breaths coasting over the nape of my neck. My cock was hard, my entire body primed for sex.

Considering everything we did yesterday and last night, I was surprised my dick had any energy left.

I hadn't expected to like being with him so much. But I was insatiable for him. I hadn't come this hard or this often in years. And I loved making him come, as well. He was a stoic badass until I started ramming his hole. And then he was a needy little slut. Dio, how it turned me on.

"Good. You're awake." His lips moved over the nape of my neck, sending waves of heat rippling through me.

"I thought you were asleep."

"I've been up for hours." His mouth brushed my jaw, behind my ear, soft kisses that made me hyper aware of every inch of my body. "Roll over, principe."

He shifted to press his lower half against mine, and an erection nudged my ass.

Still, I didn't turn over. "Does your dick need attention, Alessio?"

He thrust his hips, rocking the heavy length between my cheeks. "Very badly. Turn the fuck over, principe. I want to rub us together until we shoot all over each other."

Frotting sounded like a good fucking idea. I rolled to face him, and he pressed our cocks together, holding them in one large hand.

I sucked in a breath at the skin-to-skin contact. "Cazzo, that feels amazing."

We were both leaking, so there was no need for lube. He squeezed tighter and I began rocking, giving us friction. I hooked my leg over Alessio's hip for leverage and thrust into his tight grip.

"Kiss me," he whispered and edged closer. "Fuck, I need . . . . Kiss me, principe."

With a small growl he placed his mouth on mine. His lips were firm but soft. I continued fucking our cocks together and kissing him back, shutting off the rest of my brain. Alessio was rough and eager, exactly what I liked, and the world tunneled to just this room, this bed. Just this man. I let him control the kiss while I worked my hips, and sizzles coasted along my spine. I wouldn't last much longer.

Soon we were panting, our lips nearly touching as we shared the humid air from our lungs. Grinding and grunting. Straining and gasping. This was nice, but I craved more. I wanted to pin him down and devour him. Wreck him. I wanted every sigh, every shiver. I wanted to *own* him.

"Are you sore?" I whispered.

"You want to fuck?"

"Yes, very fucking badly."

He released our erections and rolled onto his back. Then he slid his arms above his head, stretching out and waiting for me like a feast.

I slid over him and began covering his throat in kisses. "I'm going to make it so good for you." His whiskers were longer today and I loved how they scraped against my lips. "Better than last time."

He swallowed. "I can't see how that is possible."

My cock throbbed, my heartbeat pounding along its length. We hadn't fucked again since that first time yesterday and I wanted to do this slow. And from the front so I could see his face as I pounded inside him.

I kissed my way down his chest, licking each nipple, before continuing past his stomach. He was panting by the time I settled between his large thighs, his cock straining against his belly. I kept on, pressing my lips to his hip bones and lower.

I nuzzled his balls, then licked with long swipes of my tongue. He moaned and widened his legs to give me more room. I took each one into my mouth and used gentle suction until he was writhing on the bed.

He grabbed his cock and began lightly stroking. I watched his forearm muscles shift with his movements, the long fingers barely dragging along the sensitive underside. Like he couldn't keep from touching himself, but didn't want to come too soon.

Then I flicked my tongue over his hole—and Alessio cursed. He tensed but didn't stop me. So I continued, using my hands to expose him. I licked and increased the pressure. The nerve endings there were incredibly sensitive, and soon he was moaning and clutching the sheets with both hands, his dick leaking on his belly.

"Principe, per favore." Lust had turned his voice to gravel.

I reached for the lube and a condom in the nightstand. Quickly, I slicked my fingers and began working one inside his hole. It wasn't long before I was easing in another. I pumped two fingers and watched him. His eyes were closed, his bottom lip caught between his teeth. The scar on his cheek was a white slash next to the surrounding flushed skin.

"Molto bell'uomo," I whispered. *Very handsome man.*

Handsome and hard. Alessio was brutal and cold, ruggedly appealing, sort of like these Scottish islands. There was loneliness there, too. A softness he kept buried. But in moments like these he couldn't hide it.

Rising on my knees, I tore open the foil packet and rolled the condom on my dick. Then I drizzled lube on my hand and slicked myself up. "Are you ready?"

"Hurry," he said.

I shoved his knees higher, which tilted his ass enough for me to line up. Then I was pressing in, rubbing and circling, until the crown popped past that tight ring of muscle. He sucked in a breath, but said nothing.

"Va bene?" I asked.

"Please, move."

A light sheen of sweat broke out on my skin. The grip on my cock was unbelievable. I never wanted to pull out. Slowly, I worked my way inside, giving him time to adjust. I stroked his erection, as well, just to balance any discomfort.

When I was fully seated, I had to stop and take a few calming breaths. Madre di dio, it was too good. Alessio shifted to put his legs on my shoulders. I hissed as my cock slid even deeper. It was like being squeezed to death in the best way possible. I couldn't take it any longer.

Clasping his knees, I began thrusting. I withdrew until I was just barely inside, then I plunged all the way in. The friction and heat, even through the condom, was unbelievably good. I tried to maintain a regular pace, but soon I was ramming him with wild abandon. Alessio tilted his head back, the tendons in his throat standing out in sharp relief as I pounded his ass.

I loved watching his reactions, trying to gauge what he liked best. When I dragged over his prostate, he gasped. "There, right there."

I didn't change a thing. I just kept fucking him in that one spot. He needed to come first. I wanted to watch his face as he fell apart.

I started urging him with my words. "Do you like it? Do you like having my cock in your ass?" He moaned in response, so I kept going. "You are so tight, so hot. You are squeezing the life out of my dick. Feels so fucking good."

He was panting now, his eyes screwed tight. "Ti prego," he nearly whimpered.

"That's it. Beg me. Beg for my cock." My muscles shook with the effort but I didn't stop. I hammered his prostate, the bed rocking with each powerful thrust. "Come for me, assassino. Grab your cock and jerk yourself."

As if he'd been waiting for permission, he instantly fisted himself and started pumping, his hand a blur. His body clamped down on mine, every muscle going rigid, then come shot onto his stomach. The pressure was too much and suddenly I was coming, too. The world disappeared for those few seconds as I filled the condom with jet after jet of warm liquid.

"Oh, fuck," I gasped, my limbs twitching.

When the world stopped spinning, I carefully pulled out, holding onto the condom. I cleaned up with the tissues I kept at the bedside. Alessio had an arm thrown over his eyes. He didn't move or speak. We were both sweaty and spent, and his flat belly was covered in come. I liked seeing him like this.

Bending, I used my tongue to swipe up some of his come. "Mmm." Then I licked more, the taste a mixture of sweat and salt.

His arm fell to the mattress and those gunmetal eyes watched me. "You are beautiful," he whispered thickly. "Especially when you come."

A long-dead part of my heart flared to life, like it had been frozen and was now thawing out. I ducked my head, hiding my reaction from him.

Compliments and tender kisses? What were we doing? This was supposed to be four weeks of fucking. Not feelings and sweet-talk.

I shifted until I could stretch out next to him. In a few minutes I would get up and make us a caffè. More than anything, I needed to regain my bearings. To remember who this was and what we were doing here. "Will you give me the name of who hired you to kill me now?" I asked.

"You think I'll say it just because you fucked a great orgasm out of me? Ma dai, Giulio."

Turning, I gave him the simple truth. "I will get that name out of you, even if I die trying."

Then I pushed off the mattress and went to clean up.

———

Alessio

THE NEXT WEEK was a blur of fucking.

The sex was unbelievable. We had a spark—some bone-deep connection—and each time we finished, I was wrung out and wrecked. I swore it couldn't get better. Yet it always did.

It felt like fate. The military, my training. The missed shot on Ravazzani. Blackmailed by D'Agostino into this job. My whole life has been a series of steps leading up to the farmhouse right here. With him.

I knew it wouldn't end well. It couldn't. But I would enjoy whatever time we had together.

At the moment I was sitting at the kitchen island as Giulio made dinner. He was doing most of the talking, but I didn't mind. I tended to be quieter, while Giulio was loud and bright, like the nightclubs he frequented.

I could see why he was always surrounded by friends and family. He was easy to get along with, personable and funny. Self-deprecating and humble. He regaled me with stories about being in his father's 'ndrina, growing up in Siderno. He spoke little of Fausto and Frankie, though. Mostly he talked about his Zia, who I gathered had raised him in the absence of a mother.

We shared that in common. My nonna sounded a lot like his great-aunt. A very old school Italian woman who was devoted to the church and tolerated no nonsense.

"When was the last time you spoke to her?" I asked after he finished telling me another story about his Zia.

"About three weeks ago."

"If someone is trying to find you and kill you, making phone calls isn't very smart."

He drained the wine in his glass, then rolled his eyes. "I have burner phones, assassino. I'm not a complete novice."

"Phones can be tapped on the other end, principe."

"Which wouldn't help them find me unless I gave away my location. Which I didn't. Dio santo, man."

"Who else did you call? Frankie?" I knew from trailing him that he and his stepmother spoke regularly.

"No. I called a friend from Belgium." Reaching for the wine bottle, he refilled his glass.

"Why not? I know how close the two of you are."

"I don't want to tell her what's going on. She can't keep secrets from my father. Even if she tries, he gets it out of her somehow." He set the bottle down and returned to the chicken. "And it's not fair to ask it of her. Fausto and the children are her priorities, not me."

"What about your father? When was the last time you spoke?"

"Málaga."

That was a long time ago. Were they not close? "You don't talk to him much, not as often as his wife."

"It's probably not hard for you to imagine, but my father can be a bit controlling."

"A Ravazzani trait, I'm learning," I said.

He shrugged, as if it wasn't the first time he'd heard it. "I don't want him worrying about me. I'm a grown man."

I let that go. I didn't know what it was like to have a father. "Your mother died when you were young?"

"Yes, the last time Fausto went to war. I was just a baby. I don't remember her at all."

"How did everyone find out you were gay?"

He flicked a glance at me. "You are full of questions tonight."

I couldn't help it. I'd followed him for so long, but that didn't show me inside his mind, or help me understand his history. Those things he had to tell me himself, and I was suddenly greedy to know everything. And there had been a certain distance between us these last few days, as if he were holding parts of himself back from me. I didn't like this. "Does it bother you to talk about it?"

"No, of course not." He put the knife down. The muscles in his arms stretched as he braced his palms on the island. He kept his eyes on the far wall, not on me. "My father caught me on camera. I was blowing Paolo outside one of the exits at a club."

"*Porca dio!* On camera? He must have been furious."

"Furious isn't the word. He was . . . hurt. Disappointed. Livid. Worried. And I honestly thought—"

He snapped his jaw shut, so I prompted, "What?"

A rattled, pained breath left his lungs. "I honestly thought he was going to have me killed."

"That must have been terrifying."

"It was, but then he decided I was just gay for Paolo. That if he got rid of Paolo, I would turn straight."

A bark of laughter escaped my throat before I could stop it. "Scusa," I said, collecting myself. "But that is so stupid."

"It's his generation, I guess." He picked up the knife and continued working on our dinner. "Frankie tried to talk him out of it, but he sent Paolo away. Wouldn't tell me where."

"Then what?"

"He told me I would settle down with a nice Italian woman and make Ravazzani babies."

Now I was beginning to understand why Giulio had distanced himself from Fausto. He had spent a long time in his father's shadow, under his father's thumb. No wonder he craved independence.

"Everything changed when he was shot, though."

My head snapped up at Giulio's words. This was actually one topic from his past that I didn't wish to discuss. Not yet, at least. I had no regrets—killing Fausto Ravazzani had been another job to me. It wasn't personal. None of them were. But I knew Giulio wouldn't be forgiving of the role I'd played in the D'Agostino/Ravazzani war.

"Fausto almost died," Giulio continued. "One of D'Agostino's men tried to take him out from a rooftop in Siderno, and the experience changed my father. When he recovered he let me choose whether I wanted to stay or go be with Paolo."

This was nothing short of astounding. I'd wondered how this all came to pass, because gay men didn't live long in the Italian mafia. The fact that Giulio had been given permission to leave was unheard of. "Did you consider staying?"

"Not even for a minute. I loved Paolo. I wanted to be with him more than anything else." He turned to the range and flicked on the gas burner. "Besides, I had a glimpse of my future as the don when he was in the hospital. It was awful."

Eager for the change in topic, I asked, "Why?"

"I wasn't prepared for the vast number of businesses he's involved in. Like, a horse farm in Kentucky? A hedge fund in Vancouver?" He shook his head. "I was overwhelmed. And everyone panicked over his condition. I had to reassure all these people that he was fine, when he really wasn't."

"Did your enemies try to gain advantage?"

"Yes, every time I turned around. It was like being a CEO and a general at the same time. I think I slept three or four hours a night. It was a nightmare."

"But you must have done a good job, because nothing suffered for it."

"I suppose. Still, I was relieved when he came back."

I hadn't considered how Fausto's injury would've affected Giulio's role as the heir. I was shocked to hear he hadn't been better prepared to step in.

Giulio carried the plate of raw chicken to the stove. "It all worked out for the best. He has Raffaele, who is so like him it's scary. Rafe will make a great don one day."

I scowled at Giulio's back. Would Ravazzani think one son was just as good as another? I doubted it.

"Rafe is better," Giulio continued, like he was trying to convince me. Or himself. "He's exactly what Fausto needs. A son who will marry and have Ravazzani babies and carry on the family tradition."

Again, I wasn't certain his father would agree with this. Giulio seemed convinced that his sexuality made him *less* capable as a leader. But what mattered in the 'Ndrangheta was money. As long as a don continued to bring in millions, no one would dare to cross him—even if he was gay. And children could be adopted.

"Your father could have a stroke or a heart attack tomorrow," I reminded him. "What happens then? Rafe is too young."

"There are others who could step in until Rafe came of age."

But none as qualified as Giulio, the first-born son. I don't know why this bothered me, but I didn't like to see him discount his worth because he slept with men. It was no one's business, and it certainly didn't change his abilities to lead. He'd made millions on his own over the last four years. Didn't that prove he was capable? Who cared whether those old men approved of his lifestyle or not?

But what did I know about family responsibilities and legacies? I had no right to judge Giulio for his choices.

I stared at his naked back, the patterns of ink. Words and symbols drawn over sleek muscles. My mouth watered just looking at him. "I bet you had women throwing themselves at you all the time."

Chuckling, he shifted to give me his profile. "It was wild. Once a woman followed me into a men's room and practically accosted me at a urinal. It used to piss Paolo off."

"Was he worried you'd take one of them up on the offer?"

"No, of course not. But I had to flirt with women. It had to look believable, that I was really attracted to them, so no one would suspect my secret. He hated it."

I could imagine. I didn't care for the idea of Giulio's attention on anyone else, either. I shifted on my stool, uncomfortable that I might be jealous, too.

Three more weeks. Nothing more.

Though it was hard to remember we were temporary when we screwed all the time. Or when he wrapped around me in the middle of the night, holding me like he was worried I might disappear. The lines on where we stood were becoming blurred—for me at least.

I wanted to be near him every second. My skin buzzed with the need to touch him constantly. Even now I was counting down the minutes until after dinner when I could get him naked again.

And I wanted to *talk* to him. To hear his thoughts and his opinions. His laughter. I could happily listen to him tell stories for hours.

Basically, I was fucked.

CHAPTER FOURTEEN

Giulio

We settled into a routine. Wake up and fuck. A run, followed by breakfast and a shower.

Then Alessio would chop wood while I fed the sheep. After, we'd read or talk until lunch and riposo, during which we'd jack each other off or trade blow jobs. Usually we both fell asleep once we came.

Later in the afternoon, I would make dinner while Alessio disappeared with his rifle. He practiced shooting somewhere on the island, though I never asked where. Far enough away that I couldn't hear the shots. More often than not, he came back with provisions from Mrs. Campbell. He liked spending time with that old lady.

We drank wine and ate, then went to bed. In the darkness, we spent hours exploring each other, discovering what drove us wild. Each night I thought it couldn't possibly get better. But it always did.

A shame that our time was more than halfway over. Twelve days remained until he gave me my head start off the island. Then he would come after me.

I had my doubts on whether he would be able to kill me. The man who whispered endearments in my ear? Who clung to me every night as we fell asleep? He liked to touch me all the time, even just simple brushes of his hand across my back.

I was equally as eager for him. Restless when he wasn't right next to me. Alessio had a steady calm presence that I found relaxing. I didn't need to talk a lot or entertain him. He seemed perfectly content to sit in silence as long as we were together.

But this wasn't real. We were hovering in the eye of the storm, just waiting to get drawn in again. Soon I would need money and another fake passport. A city far away. Somewhere in Central America, maybe? Was there any place Alessio couldn't find me?

There hasn't been any word from his assistant on the car bombers. Not that I'd expected Sasha to discover the answer so quickly—I was far too unlucky for that—but I had to find them before they found me.

Which was why I was looking through my notes on the bombing tonight. I'd been studying them this afternoon while Alessio was out. Nothing had changed, though. I still had no clue as to who those men in the parking lot were.

I was in the kitchen, rolling out pasta, when Alessio returned. I heard the door open and close, then the locks clicked back in place. His boots hit the ground and his heavy footsteps grew louder as he headed toward me.

Instantly, gray eyes found mine and his mouth lifted. It was the same every time, like he was relieved to see me again. He closed the distance between us and held my face. "Il bel principe," he whispered before kissing me. The gentle sweep of his lips sent shivers through me.

I loved the way he kissed me. Reverently, with such tenderness. Worshiping me with his mouth. He was bigger than me, yet he made me feel fifty meters tall with his attention. As if I could do anything.

When he pulled back, I was clinging to his jacket, my dick suddenly interested. "Fuck, Alessio." Reaching down, I adjusted myself in my jeans. "Did you have a nice visit with Mrs. Campbell?"

"A Juventus match was on," he said, referring to an Italian football club. "They won."

"That explains why you taste like beer."

He sat on a stool at the island and snagged a piece of prosciutto off a plate. "I don't know what you have against beer."

"That it isn't wine?"

"Not everyone was raised on a vineyard, principe." He tilted his chin toward my notes. "What's this?"

"My notes on the bombing. Feel free to take a look."

After wiping his hands off on a towel, he pulled the papers toward him. He started with the police report. I rolled the pasta dough into a thin sheet as I watched him read. He sat very still, absorbed in his task. Occasionally, he'd flip a page. At one point I set a glass of wine in front of him, but he didn't touch it.

Then he moved on to the photographs I received from my police contact in Bruges. Alessio studied those for a long time, pulling them closer to see the detail. "These other cars, you've had their plates checked, no?"

"Yes, of course."

"And the CCTV footage surrounding the club?"

"Nothing."

"Recent sales of large quantities of TNT?"

"None."

"Hmm." He began reading the notes I made, little things I'd learned or investigated. "What does this mean, 'ED location?'"

"Enzo D'Agostino. This was before we knew where he was."

Alessio grew still. "What do you mean?"

"For four years he hid out on a boat in the middle of the ocean. My father had been searching for him, but no one suspected the water."

"But you know where he is now?"

I frowned at Alessio, unsure why he was so concerned about D'Agostino. "Certo. He's dating Frankie's sister. They're living together in Naples."

Alessio barely reacted, but I knew him well enough by now to see the surprise in his features. "Enzo D'Agostino is dating your stepmother's sister?"

"Crazy, no? But the last time I spoke with Frankie, yes. Apparently Gia and Enzo are madly in love."

"When did this happen?"

"While I was in Santorini. The story is a wild one. It involves a cage and—"

"Scusa." Alessio stood and pulled his phone from his pocket. "I have to make a call."

He started toward the back door. Just before he reached it we heard several bottles crash together. Alessio snapped, "Get down."

The concern in his voice had me immediately kneeling. He did the same, eyes closed while listening.

After a few seconds, I whispered, "What was—"

He held up his hand to quiet me. There it was again, the faint tinkling of glass on glass. "Minchia!" he hissed to himself. To me, he said, "Those are the traps I set around the perimeter. Someone is out there in the woods."

Traps? I hadn't even known.

But who would be out there? It didn't make any sense.

I knew better than to argue. From his military duty, Alessio had more experience with this than I did. If he believed someone was on the property, I trusted him.

Alessio was suddenly in front of me, his expression solemn. "Listen very carefully. As quick as you can, get every gun and bullet you can find. Put on your boots. We can't sit here and wait for them. We need to go out and attack them first."

"Okay."

I kept low to the ground and went to the door for my boots. After tying them on, I began collecting all the old guns and the bullets in the house. I could hear Alessio assembling his rifle, which he did in seconds. Then he was helping me load the guns.

"They're coming over the same ridge where I waited for you," he said softly. "I want you to go out to the sheep enclosure and stay there."

"What are you going to do?"

"Hunt them down."

"In the dark?"

He tilted his chin toward his rifle on the ground. "Night vision scope. Andiamo. Out the front door, principe."

I could see why he'd made such a good soldier. He was calm and cool, in complete control. If I weren't so distracted by impending danger, I might've been impressed.

I gathered the guns and more bullets. "I'm ready."

Alessio went first. When I followed, we stayed close to the edge of the house as we went around it. He moved methodically, making no sound. He'd taken off his jacket at some point. Now he wore dark jeans, a black shirt, and boots. "Stay low," Alessio told me. "Go fast. I'll watch out for you until you're safely there."

Lifting his rifle, he scanned the horizon through his scope. I didn't hesitate. I hurried toward the sheep pen, slipping under the fence posts. The sheep were inside their enclosure, resting. I went in and got into position. The small window allowed me to see the hill where Alessio said he placed the traps. I had my pistol in my palm, ready to fire.

It could be an animal out there, of course. The island had a huge rabbit population. Eagles. Mice. If a bunny had set off one of Alessio's traps, we would have a good chuckle over it later.

I watched but couldn't see anything in the darkness. I couldn't even see Alessio any longer. I had no idea where he went. The night was completely still. No movement, no more sound. The sheep were bleating, probably wondering what the hell I was doing out here.

I was beginning to wonder the same thing.

Eventually one of the sheep moved closer to rub against my leg, begging for attention. I absently scratched it behind the ears as I kept my focus on the darkness.

A pop sounded in the distance. A shot somewhere in the trees. Was that Alessio? Cazzo, I hated not being able to see him. Had he been shot?

If he died on this island . . . .

My heart started kicking harder. I had watched Paolo die. I didn't want to see another man in my life, another lover, murdered. Even if Alessio and I were only temporary.

So, what was I doing about it? Hiding with the sheep?

No, absolutely fucking not.

Carefully, I eased away from the animals, trying not to scare any of them. I pressed tight to the wooden shed as I went around it.

The wind had picked up since nightfall, but I hardly felt the chill. I listened intently. Another pop, off in the trees to my left. I decided to go right and then double back.

Gun in hand, I hurried to the edge of the farm. There wasn't much cover here, so I moved quickly and stayed low. With no moon, I hoped the darkness concealed me enough to reach the trees.

Then I heard a spray of shots, like from an assault rifle. Then three more *pops* sounded. Fuck, fuck, fuck. I started running, not caring if I was low enough or not. I had to get out there and help Alessio.

Alessio

THERE WERE six men converging on the farm. They were well armed, but not military. I knew because they were quiet, but not silent. You could always tell when an enemy had been trained in stealth tactics or not. These men, I could hear their gear, their clothing. The sound of their feet in the brush. They didn't know how to move about undetected.

But me? No one would hear or see a trace.

At the moment I was hidden behind a fallen log, partially covered by the bramble. With my scope, I was staring right at the six shapes as they waited. After the bottles were overturned, they had paused, clearly hoping no one would come to investigate.

Thank God Giulio was tucked away, safe with the sheep. I wouldn't be able to focus if I were worried about him out here. If one of the men somehow got by me, then he could take them out with his pistol.

I rubbed the cornicello around my neck for luck.

When enough time passed, the men began fanning out. They carried assault rifles, the kind you could buy on most street corners in the United States. A weapon meant for shock and awe. Not precision, like mine.

All I had to do was pick my moment.

One man veered off from the pack, headed toward me. I waited until he was far enough away from the others before I squeezed the trigger. A clean, quiet shot through the head before he fell to the ground.

The rest of them were now realizing something was wrong. Still, I waited. The more I could pick off without them finding my location, the better.

Three men went left, while two came in my direction. Most likely coming to look for their missing compatriot. I adjusted my scope. Relaxed. Kept my heart rate steady.

I lined up on the bigger of the two men. When I had the angle right, I shot one then quickly the other. They both went down, but now a man from the other group started firing in my direction. I squeezed the trigger, but my distance was off. I hit him in the shoulder.

I made some adjustments and reloaded. The two uninjured men split up, and one came toward me. Out of my peripheral vision I saw the other head toward the sheep enclosure. Fear gripped my throat. I didn't want him near Giulio.

There wasn't time to debate it. I had to choose where to aim.

Shifting my body, I used the mil dots in my sight to estimate his size and the distance. I did this automatically, without really thinking about it. Lining up, I squeezed off a shot. The man fell about seven meters from the sheep pen.

"Got you, asshole," I heard in Sicilian.

I glanced in the direction of the shooter, but he was already on me. Standing three meters away, his barrel aimed at my head. I rushed to get in position. I knew it was too late, but I had to try.

It happened in a blink.

A loud bang. The Sicilian pitched forward, the rifle dropping from his hands. Red mist exploded from his chest and he went down face first.

Dio santo!

Giulio stepped out, his hands still bracing the pistol. He saw me and his shoulders relaxed. "Thank fuck."

A shape moved in the brush. Twenty meters, eleven o'clock. "Get down," I barked at Giulio as I searched for the fucker in my scope.

A spray of ammunition rained into the area where Giulio had been standing.

I didn't calculate or plan my shot. I just squeezed the trigger, trusting my instincts and my training.

My bullet went straight through the man's forehead.

I jumped up and sprinted toward the spot where I saw Giulio go down. His body was flat on the ground, face first, and I swore my stomach dropped out through my toes. I couldn't see any blood. Hands shaking, I dropped to my knees. Rolled him over.

He blinked up at me. "Are they dead?"

Relief cascaded through me and I sagged, bracing my palms on the ground. Cazzo madre di dio. He was *alive*. I tried to drag in air. "We should check, but I believe they're all dead."

"Are you hurt?"

"No," I croaked.

I didn't know what was wrong with me. I had served many tours, gone on many missions. I'd seen death over and over, been in countless dangerous situations. Never had a panic attack or PTSD. Never lost my shit in the middle of a battle.

But right now, faced with how different tonight may have turned out, my lungs weren't working right.

I was just . . . so fucking glad he was alive.

"Hey." Giulio was there, his hands on my face. "We're okay. I'm okay. Breathe, Alessio."

Soft blue eyes found mine, and I let myself fall into them. I wasn't a weak man by any means, but right now I felt raw and unsure.

"That's it, baby," he said quietly. "Just breathe."

Then he kissed my lips. A simple brush of our mouths, but I could feel that contact sink into my bones. Reassurance. Comfort. Relief.

I exhaled.

My lips sought his for a brief instant. I wanted him to know. He needed to feel how much I cared for him. So I showed him without words, kissing him, pulling on his lips with mine. He was warm and real, solid beneath my fingertips.

Finally, I eased back. "I need to go check the bodies and make sure they're dead."

"I'll come with you."

I shook my head. He would only distract me. "Go find two shovels. We need to bury them."

Rolling to my feet, I offered him a hand and pulled him upright. He tucked his pistol into his waistband. "Shovels? Dead bodies? Now you're just trying to make me homesick."

I laughed.

Unbelievable. We had a farm full of six dead bodies, plus a night of backbreaking work ahead of us to get rid of them. And Giulio could still make me laugh.

"Andiamo, principe. I won't feel better until they're dealt with."

We separated. I slung my rifle over my shoulder and went into the trees. I checked each body, ensured it was dead, then dragged them all to one area. The ground was soft here. It would make for an easier time digging.

Giulio returned with a shovel and a hoe. "It was the best I could do."

"That works."

I put my rifle down and took the shovel. We began digging up the dirt.

"Why the fuck did you leave the sheep enclosure?" I asked as I worked.

"Good thing I did, or else you'd be dead."

"That wasn't the point. You were supposed to stay there and stay safe."

"Were you . . . .?" He blew out an irritated breath. "Dai, Alessio. I don't need you to protect me. I know how to shoot a gun. I've killed before."

I didn't say anything. I knew all this, but it was about more than just his abilities. It was about the way he affected *mine*.

"And," he continued, "you should be glad I didn't listen to you. I know you're a big bad assassin, but it's okay to need help every now and again."

"Big bad assassin?" I pretended to think about this. "Should I put that on my business card?"

A breathtaking smile spread over his face. "You made a joke, assassino. I'm so proud of you."

I ducked my head, hoping he wouldn't notice how pleased I was by this exchange. It was rare for me, this banter. This closeness with another person.

We worked together for a long time. The hole didn't need to be huge. We only needed to hide these six bodies long enough for us to get off the island.

Sweat poured down our bodies as we carried the dead men into the grave. I saw one of them had a familiar tattoo, and it reminded me of the dialect I'd heard. "These men are Sicilian," I said through my heavy breathing.

"How do you know?" Giulio wheezed, his hands on his knees as he tried to catch his breath.

"I heard one of them speak and I could tell by the accent. Also, that tattoo. It's Medusa, a part of their flag."

He straightened and wiped the sweat off his face. "Why would Sicilians come to kill us?"

"Not us. You."

"How do you know they aren't targeting you? After some hit that went bad."

"My hits don't go bad," I lied. "And I don't work with Sicilians."

"Why not?"

Because I grew up in Sicily. My father and mother were still there somewhere. I wanted nothing to do with that entire island. "I just don't."

"I haven't done anything to the Sicilians. And my father has an alliance with them. There's no way they are after me."

"Principe." I swept my hand out toward the dead bodies. "They were after you. The question is, why?"

He frowned at the ground, clearly thinking it over. I left him to his thoughts. Maybe for the first time he would have a new clue as to what happened to Paolo.

Picking up the shovel, I began covering the bodies with dirt.

Eventually, he grabbed the hoe and started helping. Between the two of us, we got the grave filled and then started toward the farmhouse.

"Go inside and start packing," I said. "Only what you can't live without, capisce?"

"Why?"

"Because we must leave, right now. There is no time to lose. They know you are here and when this group doesn't report back . . . ."

More men would follow.

He nodded. "Right. This sucks."

I hated it, too. I wished we could stay in our little Scottish bubble forever, but I had to get him to safety.

Because Giulio was mine. And I wasn't giving him up.

Everything had changed. Enzo D'Agostino was now dating Gianna Mancini, Fausto's sister-in-law. Ravazzani would be heartbroken and furious if Giulio was assassinated, and the entire war would begin once again. D'Agostino would not be so foolish as to risk it, not if he truly cared for Gianna.

This meant the hit on Giulio was no longer needed. Once I spoke to D'Agostino, I'm sure he would agree.

I felt lighter, as if a huge weight had been lifted off my shoulders. I didn't have to kill Giulio. I could be with him, at least for longer than a few weeks. This meant keeping a huge secret from him, but I didn't think anyone would ever find out.

I wouldn't tell. Because Giulio would never stay with the man who almost killed his father.

And if D'Agostino thought to open his mouth, all I had to do was threaten him with the hit he'd ordered on Giulio. Gianna Mancini and Francesca Ravazzani would not like this information one bit. Maybe D'Agostino didn't allow Gianna as much influence as Fausto did with his wife, but I would bet anything the truce between Ravazzani and D'Agostino was a tenuous one. They wouldn't want to risk it.

Once we were inside, we separated to gather our things. I moved out of Mrs. Campbell's days ago, so all of my belongings were at the farmhouse. Not that I traveled with much.

I found my pack and shoved in the essentials. Fake passports and cash. Bullets. A change of clothing, including a cap. My phone and portable battery. I zipped up the sides and threw it over my shoulder. Then I put my rifle back in its case.

Giulio came in as I was finishing. "You don't have to come with me, you know."

"Do not dare suggest that I let you go alone."

"Assassino . . . ." He sighed. "This is my problem."

I was on him in a blink. Cupping the nape of his neck, I put my forehead to his. "Your problems are my problems. You're not getting rid of me, principe. I will fight for you with my dying breath."

His warm exhale gusted over my lips. "Alessio," he whispered. "I can't watch another man I care about die."

He cares about me.

The words filled me with such happiness that I couldn't keep from kissing him. We needed to escape this island, but I needed to take a moment and hold him in my arms. I slipped my tongue into his mouth and we were quickly clinging to each other, our hands roaming. We acted like lovers reunited after a long separation.

He broke off and kissed my jaw. "Baby, we need to go."

I nodded. "Do you have what you need?"

Grabbing my hand, he gave me another brief kiss. "Yes. Come on."

CHAPTER FIFTEEN

Giulio

We jogged toward town. It was almost midnight, and there was no moon. Alessio kept a brisk pace in the darkness, his rifle case slung over one shoulder. On his other shoulder was his backpack. He made it look easy, while I struggled to keep up.

I didn't know what was happening between us. After the gun fight in the woods, I thought he was going to have a panic attack. My only thought was to comfort him. To ensure he was okay.

"You're not getting rid of me, principe."

So, he was on Team Giulio? What happened to the hit he was supposed to carry out? The four-week time limit we'd imposed on ourselves? The whole situation had turned upside down.

Not that I was complaining at the moment. I was grateful for his help tonight. I'd be dead otherwise. Fighting off six assailants with assault rifles was beyond my abilities.

But not Alessio's.

He'd been amazing out there in the woods. Taking out the man headed toward the sheep enclosure was his only mistake.

Then the truth hit me like a hammer. Alessio believed that I was in the sheep enclosure.

"I will fight for you with my dying breath."

Warmth suffused me as I stared at his broad back. Madre di dio, that idiot. He'd risked his life to protect me.

The flutters in my chest multiplied. I didn't know what to say. Thankfully, I hadn't waited with the sheep. Instead, I was able to save him in return.

Thinking back, it would've made sense for me to run while Alessio and the assassins were busy in the woods. But the thought never occurred to me.

Cazzo. I couldn't catch feelings for Alessio. What kind of fool fell in love with the man hired to assassinate them?

I pushed all of this aside for later. The priority was getting to safety. Then I could sort out my head.

When we reached town, he headed for the pub. Were we stopping for a drink? Was the place even open?

Alessio went in.

With no other choice, I followed him. Mrs. Campbell was behind the bar, her expression turning serious as she looked us over. Without missing a beat, she faced the one man drinking and watching the television. "William, get out."

"But—"

"Don't argue with me, you bawbag." She took his beer right out of his hand and dumped it in the sink. "Go home. I'm closed."

William started to dig money out of his pocket, but Mrs. Campbell waved him off. "It's on me, because I cut you short. Good night."

Muttering the whole time, William shuffled outside, leaving us alone with Mrs. Campbell. She focused on Alessio, her demeanor all business. "What do you need?"

Alessio set his rifle case on the bar. "Some men attacked the farm. We need a boat, preferably."

Smart. Hiding on the water had worked for D'Agostino all those years. It could work for us. We could investigate the Sicilians while keeping away from land.

That reminded me of Theo.

I touched Alessio's arm. "I know of someone with a yacht."

"Your father?"

"No, a friend."

"Good. Then we'll find them."

Mrs. Campbell went over to a beer sign on the wall. With a flick of her wrist, she pulled on the edge—and the wood swung open to reveal a safe. In a blur she twisted the knob back and forth, right and left, and the safe unlocked. She grabbed a set of keys, then closed the metal door.

She motioned for us to follow. "Come with me."

As we walked outside, Alessio angled toward me. "Do you know where this friend is at the moment? Even a rough guess?"

"Off the coast of Nice."

Mrs. Campbell strode toward the docks, but kept going around the bend surrounding the inlet. "How'd they find you?"

"I suspect they were tapping phone lines," Alessio answered. "Someone was making calls from here."

"Someone was using burner phones," I grumbled.

"Och, but on the other end," Mrs. Campbell said. "They can still be listening."

"Exactly," Alessio said and I proceeded to ignore them both.

It felt like we walked forever. There were sailboats and fishing boats bobbing in the dark water. I wondered which one was hers.

She headed toward a long pier off on its own. At the end was a fancy cigarette speedboat. The kind used for drug running. I would know. Many of the Colombians I worked with had boats like this.

Stopping, she held the keys up to Alessio. "She's full of fuel. Good luck."

"I'll return this back to you," he said, taking the keys.

"I'm not worried. You'll do your best."

"We need to get to France," I said. "Fast. Any idea where we can stop for fuel?"

"If you need to get to France," Mrs. Campbell said. "You'll need a plane."

"You don't happen to have one?" Alessio asked dryly.

"No, but an old friend of mine on Skye does." She pulled out her mobile. "Let's see if he picks up."

————

Alessio

Nice, France

As Giulio contacted his friend, I went inland to find provisions. Nice was crowded with tourists, the hot Riviera sun encouraging bare skin and good times. I kept my head down and headed to a market. We were exhausted, having traveled by boat and plane to get here.

Mrs. Campbell's friend had been a pilot in the Royal Air Force. He had a small plane that he kept on the Isle of Skye for tours. Thankfully, he'd been willing to accept a large stack of Euros in exchange for a trip to the south of France.

Before I went shopping, though, I had a call to make.

Unlocking my phone, I found the contact I needed and tapped on the glass.

"Pronto," Vito D'Agostino said in my ear.

"I need to speak with your brother."

A voice sounded in the background. They had me on speaker. "You have me, Alessandro. How may I help you?"

"You and Gianna Mancini. Is it true?"

"I hardly see how this is any business of yours."

"Because you contacted me. Months ago. Told me to get to Málaga, remember?"

There was a pause. "You didn't succeed, did you?"

I couldn't tell whether he was hopeful or worried about the outcome. "You should have updated me when the situation changed."

"Are you ringing to *chastise* me? Ma dai, Ricci. I would hope you know better than that."

I ground my back teeth together. "You don't own me, D'Agostino. And you don't want to piss me off, either. Otherwise, I will tell Ravazzani—and his wife—who put the hit out on Giulio. What will that do to your happy little home life?"

The line went very quiet. D'Agostino's voice was low and deep when he finally spoke up. "If you do, coglione, I will have much to say about who sat on that rooftop in Siderno four years ago. I don't think you will be forgiven for it."

I couldn't let Giulio find that out. He would never stay. He might even try to kill me again.

"So we agree," I said, my fingers digging into the sides of the phone. "I'll keep your secret and you keep mine."

"I don't like owing favors to others."

"Too fucking bad. We don't have another choice."

The silence stretched. He and Vito had probably muted the phone to discuss the proposition. I waited, dodging tourists on their way to breakfast.

"Fine," he said. "We take this one to our graves. And lose this number."

He disconnected.

Dio santo, he must love Gianna Mancini a fuck of a lot.

My face broke out in a huge smile. *Free.* I was finally free of D'Agostino and Ravazzani for good. No one would ever learn of my involvement in their feud.

And I could pursue Giulio as a partner . . . lover . . . boyfriend. Whatever he wanted. The label didn't matter to me, as long as we were together.

An ache settled behind my sternum. I suspected it was pure happiness.

In the market I bought as much cheese, meat and bread as I could carry, then headed back toward the docks. Giulio was having caffè and a croissant when I found him. He gestured to the empty seat across from him. A bag with my breakfast waited on the table.

"Grazie, principe." I opened the bag and took out the croissant first. "What did your friend say?"

"They are turning around and heading closer to shore. Forty-five minutes or so. He'll send someone with a boat to pick us up."

In the morning light I couldn't stop staring at him. Unshaven and wearing sunglasses with messy hair, he was gorgeous. He fit in here, in this beautiful city with the most beautiful people. But then, he looked good no matter where he went.

I couldn't help it. I removed his sunglasses off his face and leaned over the table. I heard his intake of breath just before I sealed our mouths together for a kiss. I moved my lips over his slowly, needing a moment of reassurance that he was here. Safe, with me.

Mine.

I pulled back after a few seconds and retook my seat. Giulio's cheeks were flushed. "I hadn't pegged you as an exhibitionist."

"I can't kiss you in public?"

"Of course you can. I didn't think you'd want to. You're a fairly private person."

"You think I'm shy?"

"No." He sipped from his cup. "Private doesn't mean shy. Private means I don't know shit about your life, other than what you do for a living, that you were raised by your nonna, and you have an assistant named Sasha."

I chewed a bite of croissant. "What would you like to know?"

He cocked his head thoughtfully. "Who hired you to kill me?"

I couldn't help it. I laughed. "You are like a dog with a bone."

"Can you blame me? This is my life we're talking about."

He was right. I was being cavalier, only because I knew the issue had been resolved. I sobered, saying, "It doesn't matter, because I no longer need to carry it out."

Giulio's mouth fell open. "You are kidding."

"No. The person who wanted you dead has reconsidered."

"This is a joke. You are . . . ." He huffed angrily, his nostrils flaring. "How could you possibly know this?"

"I rang them just now. It's canceled."

"Madre di dio." He rubbed his face with two hands. "This is unbelievable. Just like that?"

"Well, certain events fell into place. Based on those events, the contract became unwise."

"You're talking in riddles, but I don't care. I'm glad that one less person is trying to kill me."

"One down, one to go." I sipped the hot espresso. It was never as good in France as it was in Italia, but I wasn't complaining.

I let him sit with this news for a few minutes. I knew it came as a shock.

Finally, he leaned in. The look in his eyes was different. Possessive. Aggressive, borderline angry. "And you tell me this now, assassino? When we are in public? When I can't hold you down and fuck you so hard your teeth rattle?"

My insides wound tight and I licked suddenly dry lips. It was safe to say I liked this new side to Giulio. "You will have to wait, principe."

"As soon as I have you alone, I'm going to tear you apart."

Cristo, I couldn't wait.

He put his sunglasses back on and stared at the horizon. I couldn't tear my eyes off him. And I no longer had to hide my thoughts and feelings. I didn't have to pretend that I wasn't half in love with this man.

"You look very sexy right now," I said, as I finished my croissant.

He slid me a crooked grin. "I look sexy everywhere."

We finished our breakfast. Finally, his burner phone rang. Giulio read the number and picked the phone up off the table. "That's Theo."

He answered and I listened to the short exchange. It sounded like they were close to shore already.

I watched the crowd in the the marina. We hadn't been followed, but it was a habit ingrained in me from years in the military. I was constantly searching for danger, vigilant against potential threats. And now I had Giulio to protect.

I wouldn't let anyone hurt this man.

Ten minutes later we were on a tiny speedboat headed out to sea. There weren't many other boats on the water at this time of day. Soon a one-hundred-meter super yacht came into view. It was sleek and white, with five decks and dark windows.

"Mamma mia," I whispered. Whoever owned this boat was *rich*.

Giulio said nothing, his expression unchanged. No doubt he was used to seeing wealth like this, considering his father. Even though I had millions of Euros in the bank, this was not my lifestyle. More like the lifestyle of my clients.

We slowed and docked at the back of the yacht, where the crew were already waiting to help us aboard. Instantly, I noticed the bulges under their jackets. Odd, for a ship's crew. Maybe the owner was a paranoid French billionaire.

A crew member led us to the interior of the ship. A man jumped up from a long sofa and came rushing forward on bare feet. He wore wide-leg purple silk trousers and a tank top, his wrists covered in bracelets. Black eyeliner edged his eyelids. "Bello! There you are!" He embraced Giulio, kissing both his cheeks.

"Bonjour, Theo. You are looking tan and rested."

"That is what good sex on a yacht will do for you," the man said, turning to me. In French, he asked, "And who is this very tall and handsome man?"

I stuck out my hand and answered in French. "Bonjour. I'm Alessio. Thank you for letting us hide out here."

Theo blinked, his brilliant green eyes shocked. "Your French is flawless. Surprising for an Italian assassin."

Ah, so Giulio had told Theo about me. A man came up behind Theo. He had dark hair that was starting to silver at the temples and blue eyes like ice. Tattoos peeked out from under a linen shirt that fit him perfectly. I froze. Recognition washed over me like an ice bath. Now the armed guards and super yacht made sense. Madre di dio. Did Theo have any idea . . . ?

I shifted closer to Giulio.

"And this is Nic." Grinning wide, Theo pulled the larger man forward and linked their arms together.

I pressed my lips tight, not saying anything as *Nic* shook Giulio's hand. "Welcome to my little boat," he said in French, though I heard the true accent underneath.

"Giulio is terrible with French, *mon grand*," Theo said. "English would be better."

Nic spoke again, this time in English. The accent was thicker. "Welcome, and please make yourselves at home here."

When he reached to shake my hand, I let him see exactly what I was thinking. *I know who you are.* His chilly gaze widened slightly, but he recovered quickly. "Welcome, Alessio."

I nodded, unable to speak without giving anything away. We were now trapped on this man's yacht. We needed his hospitality to stay alive. I did *not* wish to piss him off.

A man walked in and beckoned Nic over. Theo and Giulio began chatting about the boat and where we would sleep . . . but I kept my eye on Nic. He nodded at whatever the other man was saying. Then the two of them walked over and Nic thrust his hands in his pockets. "We must search your bags and store any weapons in our gun safe. You understand, I'm sure."

I ran my tongue along the back of my teeth. I didn't wish to give up my rifle. I had others at home, but this was like taking away my right arm.

Sensing my hesitancy, Giulio said in Italian under his breath, "Va bene, we're safe here."

Reluctantly, I handed over my rifle case and my backpack. My bag was quickly returned but the rifle was taken away, along with Giulio's pistol. We were unarmed.

But what choice did I have?

Theo took Giulio's hand and began tugging him toward the back. "Now, let me show you to your staterooms. Or, is it one stateroom, bello?"

I didn't move. I crossed my arms over my chest. "I'll be along shortly," I said in French.

Theo stopped and his eyebrows pulled low. "Mon grand?"

Nic kept his eyes locked on mine. "*Ça va, mon chou.* Get your friend settled and I'll find you on deck later."

Then we were alone. I stared at Nikolai Kuznetsov, the pakhan of one of the most dangerous Bratva criminal syndicates in Germany. "*Nic*," I said flatly.

The other man cocked his head. "Have we met?"

In Russian, I said, "No, but I know who you are."

A muscle jumped in his jaw. He switched to Russian, as well. "I see. And what do you plan to do about it?"

"Does he know?"

"No. It is too dangerous for him."

I knew this. Russia was not known for its acceptance of the

LGBTQ+ community. Even powerful Bratva leaders. "So, what? You will kill him when you are finished fucking him?"

"Don't be ridiculous."

I lifted one eyebrow. "There is a reason this secret has never gotten out."

"Because I am careful," he snapped. "I keep my personal life anonymous and discreet."

The exact opposite, I believed, of Theo.

Nikolai's mouth flattened as he regarded me. "Do you plan to tell him?"

"As long as you don't hurt Giulio, then no." It wasn't my business what went on between Nikolai and Theo. Giulio was my only concern. "I only need a few days here. Giulio is being hunted by some Sicilian assassins. Once I learn who, we will disappear and you'll never see us again."

"Good. Keep your mouth shut and we'll get along just fine."

CHAPTER SIXTEEN

Giulio

Theo dropped onto the bed in my cabin. "He's very handsome, your assassin. In a brooding Heathcliff sort of way."

I frowned at him. "Heathcliff?"

"Bello! Don't you ever read? *Wuthering Heights.* Emily Brontë. It is a classic."

I sat in a chair and rubbed my face. Exhaustion tugged at my brain. "They didn't teach that book at my American all-male boarding school."

"I will buy you a copy when we're back on land. You will love it. Now, you must tell me about this man of yours."

Sighing, I stared at the wall. "I think I'm too tired for this conversation. And I need drinks to be able to tell it properly."

Theo laughed. "I can't wait, then. It must be very good."

It was something, that was for certain. "We appreciate you letting us crash your vacation with your new man. But I didn't know who else to ask."

"If you're in trouble, then I am happy to help."

I hadn't gone into too much detail when I called Theo but his response had been instantaneous. He said to come to the yacht and we could stay as long as we like. "I hope Nic doesn't mind that we're here."

"He said he was happy to help my friends. And he didn't mind the blow job I gave him as a reward, that's for sure."

"Tell me about him."

Theo waggled his brows. "Isn't he delicious? I didn't think an older man would do it for me, but Nic is an absolute beast in bed. I'm having so much fun."

"And what about him?"

"Well, he obviously can't get enough of this." He gestured to his body. "And who can blame him?"

I smiled and shook my head. "I mean what does he do for a living?"

"Oh, that. He's a businessman. Owns some big oil company in Europe."

"You didn't tell him my last name, did you?"

"Of course not, bello! Your secret is safe with me."

I assumed, but it was a relief to hear it. I checked my watch. "I should nap. We can talk over dinner and drinks tonight. I'll catch you up on everything."

Theo pushed up off the bed. "I should nap, as well. Nic kept me up until very late last night. God, his dick. It should be cast in bronze and put in a museum." He stretched his arms over his head. "Then again, maybe not. All other dicks would cry in shame if they could see it."

I chuckled and took off my shoes. "I'm glad to see you are the same, amico."

He came over and grabbed my face in both his hands. "You look much better than the last time I saw you. After, you know." After Paolo's death. "He has brought you back to life. I approve."

After kissing both of my cheeks, Theo left and I was alone. I wasn't certain where Alessio was or what he was doing. His jaw had been hard and angry as he'd lingered behind to talk to Nic. But it didn't make sense. Alessio had no reason to be angry with Theo or his boyfriend.

Just as I stretched out on the bed, the door opened and Alessio walked in. My heart did its weird fluttering thing that was happening more and more when I was around this man.

Instead of joining me on the bed, he began walking around the room. He studied the art, the lamps. Behind the bed.

"Che cosa?" I asked.

He tapped his ear and pointed to his eyes. Ah. He was trying to find listening devices and cameras. Would Nic bother? A rich businessman might be paranoid, but Nic couldn't be *that* paranoid.

I just watched, fully expecting Alessio to give up after a few seconds. I was wrong. He investigated every nook and cranny of our stateroom. There was a fire alarm on the ceiling and he climbed up on a chair to take it apart.

His shoulders immediately tensed. With the cover removed it was easy to see the tiny camera positioned inside the fire alarm. My eyes went wide as I sat up. "Porca puttana!"

Alessio grabbed the device and pulled, yanking it clean out of the base. He tossed it onto the bed and resumed his search. Nothing else was discovered, thankfully.

I studied the camera. It was the kind my father sometimes used. Expensive. Fairly undetectable. How had Alessio known to—

"I am not letting you out of my sight while we are on this ship."

I blinked at his declaration. "Does this have something to do with this camera?"

Coming over, he crawled in behind me and pulled the blankets over us. His arm fell over my waist. "Yes, but let's talk about it later."

A rush of contentment filled me and I closed my eyes. I never wanted to move. "Are we safe?"

"For the moment."

"What does that mean?"

"I don't like being without weapons. I can't protect you."

"I grew up a mafioso. I can take care of myself."

He shifted closer, putting his face in my hair. "If not for me, you would be lying dead in that farmhouse."

"If not for me, you would be lying dead in those woods."

"Next time they will send more."

"There won't be a next time," I said. "They won't find us, not on the open water."

"I hope you are right. Sleep, principe."

"You are bossy today."

Exhaling, he kissed my head. "Don't worry. You will be back to ordering me around soon."

"You like when I order you around."

I could hear the smile in his voice as he said, "Maybe."

His proximity, the simmering attraction between us all night and this morning . . . I suddenly wasn't tired anymore. I pressed back against him, rubbing my ass into his crotch.

Alessio chuckled until I yawned again. He held me still. "Go to bed. We will fuck when we get up. I want you well rested so you can make good on your promise."

To take him apart.

I couldn't hold my eyelids open any longer. "You had better rest up, too. Because I won't go easy on you."

The last thing I remembered was Alessio's deep voice saying, "I can't wait."

Alessio

THE BED SHIFTED and I was instantly awake. On alert. Giulio was easing off the mattress carefully.

"Where are you going?" I asked.

He glanced over his shoulder, his expression apologetic. "I was trying not to wake you."

"It's fine." I rolled onto my back. "You aren't leaving, I hope."

"Only to use the toilet and brush my teeth. Is that okay?"

"Yes. I didn't want you wandering the boat without me."

He pushed off the bed and headed for the washroom. I shamefully admired his body as he went. "Should I be worried?" he asked.

I didn't want to keep secrets from Giulio. I was already keeping a very big one, so I didn't want to add any more. "No. But you should know that Nic is a very dangerous man."

That stopped Giulio in his tracks. "Dangerous, how?"

"He's Russian. A Bratva pakhan."

Being a Ravazzani, he would be well aware of what this meant. "Cazzo madre di dio! Why didn't you tell me this before?"

"Because you needed to rest and I knew this would upset you."

"I don't like secrets, Alessio, even for a short amount of time. I never would have agreed to stay if I'd known this. What is Theo thinking?"

"He doesn't know—and you can't tell him."

Giulio cursed again. "We are discussing this when I get out." He disappeared into the washroom, closing the door with a soft snick.

I didn't want to talk about Nic or Theo or the Bratva. I would much rather spend our time on other more worthwhile activities.

Throwing off the covers, I removed my briefs and tossed them to the floor. I grabbed my dick and slowly stroked, thinking about the man in the other room. How much I needed him. How I craved being underneath him, his body taking up all the space inside mine.

Heat unwound in my belly, sending pulses of pleasure to every part of me. I closed my eyes and sank into the anticipation. The mattress was soft beneath my back, the sheets cool against my warm skin. When was the last time I'd felt so relaxed, so at peace? So happy to simply *be?*

"Look at you," Giulio said softly, now leaning against the door jamb to the washroom. "My needy slut, getting ready for me."

Had he been there long? I could see his erection through his briefs. My mouth watered as he approached the bed.

He put a knee on the mattress and shoved my thighs wide with his big hands. "Oh, Alessio. The things I am going to do to you." He bent to nuzzle my balls, then sucked each orb into his mouth to roll it on his tongue.

Sizzles shot up and down my legs, and I arched my back. "Don't tease me."

"No?" He dragged the flat of his tongue along my shaft, flicking over the head to lick the slit. "Do you need it hard and fast, assassino? Do you need my dick filling you up?"

"Sì. *Sbrigati!*"

"I love when you are desperate," he rasped. His lips pressed along my stomach. "How do you want me to fuck you? On your stomach?"

I knew what I wanted. To see his face as we joined, to ride him until he forgot his own name.

Using a leg for leverage, I flipped our positions. It happened in a blink and Giulio grunted as I landed on him. Our cocks lined up and I rolled my hips, the friction unbelievably good.

"Cazzo," he hissed, grabbing my ass in both his hands. "That's it."

"Where is the lube?"

"In my pack. But you can also check the drawer by the bed. If I know Theo, he's stocked every stateroom on the yacht."

Sure enough, the nightstand contained a bottle of lube. I grabbed Giulio's hand and poured some on his fingers. "When was the last time you were tested?"

"Greece. I'm clean."

I hadn't been with anyone but Giulio since my last test. "I am, too. But if you still want—"

"I don't. I want you bare." His eyes were feverish and wild, like the idea was turning him on. "Come here, *caro*."

I eased lower and propped myself on my forearms, sealing my lips to his. We traded kisses, open-mouthed and hot, as his fingers slid along my crease. Then he was pushing against my hole with a fingertip, breaching me.

His finger sank deeper, deeper, stretching me, until he was all the way inside. It was a necessary burn, one that I relished. *Il mio bel principe.* I would give him anything, let him have any part of me. I was his for the taking.

"More," I gasped against his mouth.

Another finger. More gentle rocking. My body accommodated him, making room, as my cock weeped against his stomach. "Please," I begged.

"Get me ready." He removed his fingers and handed me the lube. "I need to feel you."

I slicked his shaft. The head of his cock was red and angry, oozing with precum. When I had him ready, I pushed up on my knees and lined us up. A twinge of pressure and then he was inside.

Making me his.

Ah, the heat. Madre di dio, such heat. I could feel him without latex between us, his body overtaking mine.

Giulio cursed, his eyelids shut tight. His chest rose and fell, his bottom lip disappearing between his teeth. Impatient, he rocked his hips, sending his cock deeper into my ass. I threw my head back, my breath fast and shallow. I was balancing between pleasure and pain, but I knew it would tip over into bliss soon.

"You can take it," he crooned. "You are being so good for me, no? Giving me your ass whenever I like."

"Fuck, Giulio."

"It's mine, isn't it? Tell me this ass is mine, caro."

He pressed up, advancing, and I sank down. I needed him so badly. "It's yours," I gasped.

"Look at my needy slut," he murmured, his hands running up and down my thighs. "Un *puttano*."

God, the way he talked in bed. It was absolutely filthy and I loved it. Unable to help myself, I reached for my erection. But Giulio's hand slapped my fingers away, preventing it.

"That is my dick, not yours," he said sharply. "When we are fucking, I will touch it, not you."

I moaned, my body on fire. Everything he was doing and saying, dio santo. He was going to make me come before he was even fully inside me.

"Do you need me to touch you? Do you want me to jerk your cock?"

Leaning back, I put my hands on his knees. My dick was so hard, skin stretched tight. My pulse throbbed along the shaft. "Sì!"

"Beg me, puttano."

"Ti prego, Giulio. Ti prego."

He wrapped one hand around my cock at the same time that he drove his hips up, ramming my prostate. It was like an electric shock through my entire system. "Cazzo!" I shouted to the ceiling. I was already so close and we hadn't even started yet.

Except for his breathing, Giulio didn't move. "Hold still. I want to stay here for hours and look at you like this. *Il più grande assassino*, impaled on my cock. How long could you take it, do you think?"

Sweat broke out on my skin. I was trembling, lust clawing in my groin. I needed friction. I needed him to fuck me, to jerk my cock. Something. Anything. "Principe," I whined.

He growled deep in his throat, a possessive sound that I felt in my balls. "Fuck yourself on my dick," he ordered, his fingers tightening on my shaft. "No more teasing. I want to shoot inside you."

Cristo, I wanted that, too.

I began rolling my hips, working him in and out. Nothing compared to the feeling. I wanted to drown in this man and never resurface. The head of his cock brushed my prostate with each thrust, and my skin threatened to split open at any moment from the sensation. Sweat rolled down my temples, but I didn't stop.

His face was slack with pleasure, his muscles taut. I loved seeing him like this. I loved knowing I was the one to drive him out of his skull.

"You like it, no? You like having my dick inside you. Tell me."

"It feels so good," I said through heavy pants.

"You look fucking hot like this." He jerked me harder, faster. "I want you to shoot all over my chest. Show me how much I can make you come."

Minchia! The combination of his hand and his dick was too much. Unable to help myself, I began moving faster, chasing the finish. Goosebumps raced along my skin. The orgasm slammed into me, my hips stuttering as jets of come shot out of my cock.

I moaned, helpless, as streams of fluid streaked across his skin, marking him. My ass clenched around his cock and he pressed up, his body straining. "Ah, sì. *Così va bene. Sto per venire!*"

Three more pumps and he pulsed inside me. I could feel him swell as he came, hot liquid filling me. "Fuck!" he shouted. His fingers dug into my thighs and his back arched.

When he sagged into the mattress I fell forward, trying to catch my breath. My hands rested on the mattress by Giulio's head. "Dio mio," I whispered.

"Fichissimo." He ran his hands over my shoulders and cupped my face. "Come here."

Lowering onto an elbow, I let him take most of my weight as our mouths met. The kiss was light, our lips brushing softly, lingering, with neither one of us in a hurry to pull away. His fingers trailed over my back, stroking my skin lazily.

He dropped kisses along my jaw. It was tender, almost reverent. Worshipful. "Alessione," he breathed into my throat.

My heart turned over at the pet version of my name, one Italians used in fondness. I swallowed hard, suddenly unable to speak. I kept perfectly still, soaking in his attention like a plant starved of rain.

His fingers trailed between my legs, to where we were still joined. He traced the edge of my rim stretched around his half-hard cock. "Such a good slut," he murmured against my collarbone, sucking my gold cornicello into his mouth before letting it fall. "You are mine to fuck and use whenever I want, no? Only mine."

A shiver went through me. I didn't know why this possessive side of him turned me on, but it did. I felt drunk on him, delirious with sensation and satisfaction.

"Sì, il mio bel principe." I rocked my hips again, and we both sucked in air.

He slapped my ass once. "Raise up. I want to watch my come drip out of your hole."

Helpless to deny him anything, I pressed up on my knees. His dick slipped out of me, and I could feel his come dribble out and land on his groin.

He cupped my cock and balls and moved them out of the way so he could see. "Madre di dio. I love the mess we make together." He ran his palms over my thighs, my stomach. "We should get cleaned up and make an appearance on deck."

CHAPTER SEVENTEEN

Giulio

We found Theo and Nic in the dining room. They were at the table with one of Nic's men, the one who took our guns away, eating roasted fish.

Alessio and I had discussed Nic and his position as a Bratva leader at length. We disagreed about whether Theo was in danger or not. I was certain Nic would kill Theo at the conclusion of their affair, but Alessio believed the word of the Russian when he said he wouldn't.

At Alessio's insistence, I agreed not to do anything about the situation until right before we left the yacht. Then I would strongly suggest Theo come with us.

"Bello!" Theo called when Alessio and I entered the dining room. "You are alive!"

"*Buona sera,*" I said. "We apologize for sleeping so long." I didn't look directly at Alessio as I sat, but it was almost like I could still feel the tight clasp of him around my dick.

"Oui, sleeping," Theo said with an exaggerated wink. "That is definitely what it sounded like."

I shrugged. I would not feel ashamed for being loud. A crew member placed a dinner plate in front of me. "Grazie."

Theo gestured toward my plate. "Eat, before it gets cold. I was just telling Nic how we met."

"How you met Paolo, you mean."

"That is a boring story. He worked as a bouncer at the club where I went dancing in Bruges. We became friends. See? Boring." He grinned and pointed at me. "But you . . . I saw you on the street outside the club. I told everyone I found my future husband and he was a tall brown-haired man with bright blue eyes. Imagine my surprise when I learned you were partnered with my friend." He put a hand to his heart. "I was crushed, bello."

I remembered that night well. Paolo had been so jealous. I'd fucked him in a supply closet in the club just to calm him down.

"Did you flirt with Theo?" Paolo growled, his eyes filled with suspicion.

"Che cazzo! Of course not." I moved in closer and put my hand on his hip. "I am in love with you, mia splendida bestia."

"Why? Now that we're both out you can have anyone."

"You think I was with you only because you were in my father's 'ndrina? Because you were convenient?"

This became a recurring argument once Paolo and I left Italy. Frowning, I reached for my wine glass. It felt disloyal to remember these things. Paolo deserved better from me.

Something tapped my foot. Alessio's boot. I glanced up and found him watching me closely. Concern etched his rough features. "Va bene?"

"Sì, certo." I attempted a smile and took a long drink of a crisp Sancerre.

Throughout dinner, Theo told stories about the fashion industry in Paris. This was how he met Nic, who'd attended a runway show of Theo's designs.

Alessio remained quiet, watchful. I knew he hated being unarmed around Nic and his men. He was worried we'd be set upon at any moment.

"I am not letting you out of my sight while we are on this ship."

It was nice having someone worry about me after being alone for so long. Alessio was sweet and thoughtful, but also dangerous. Seeing his long body stretched out with his attention on his target, shooting those men in the woods? Fuck me. It was like assassin porn. My man was the best shot in Europe *and* gave amazing head. What more did I need?

A man came in and whispered to Nic. Bratva business, no doubt. I exchanged a quick glance with Alessio, who was watching this unfold very carefully.

Nic rose from the table and buttoned his suit jacket. He was handsome in a rough, older man sort of way, kind of how Frankie described my father. Then the Russian walked over to Theo's chair and put a hand on my friend's shoulder. "I must make some calls, so please excuse me. I'm sure you all will have fun this evening without me."

Theo looked up at him. "We will certainly try, mon grand."

Nic's lips twisted into a pleased smile as he bent to say something in Theo's ear. Whatever he said made Theo bite his lip and turn slightly pink. I almost couldn't believe my eyes.

Nic and his men walked out, leaving the three of us alone.

The exchange bothered me. I wished I could tell him who Nic really was. "I can see you are smitten, but—"

"Basta!" Theo exclaimed. "I'm smitten with his dick, bello. You know I don't do relationships."

Alessio kicked my leg under the table in warning. I lifted one brow at him. I would stick to the plan. I wouldn't tell Theo. But that didn't mean I couldn't try to warn my friend in other ways.

I pushed away from the table. "Let's go on deck for some air and more wine."

"Excellent idea." Standing, Theo snatched up a bottle and his glass and headed toward the exit.

Alessio took my hand as we left the dining room. He was rumpled and surly, a combination that appealed to me for some reason. "You don't have to come," I told him, "if you'd rather go below."

"I told you, I'm staying with you," he said quietly, his stare intense. Serious. Like I was the only thing that mattered to him in the entire world.

I didn't mind this protective side of him. In fact, it was pretty hot. I leaned over and kissed his cheek.

Outside, we found Theo stretched out on a deck chair. He toasted us with his full glass. "To good friends and good wine."

I sat on the deck chair next to Theo and put my feet up. Then I poured another glass of wine. Alessio stretched out next to me, but didn't take the wine I offered him. He hadn't had any at dinner, either. At least one of us was remaining sober.

I turned toward my friend. He wore a kilt-like skirt paired with a tight black shirt and military boots. His style was cool and edgy, like a mixture of Harry Styles and Keith Richards. "Are these pieces yours?" I asked, gesturing to his clothes.

"Of course. Do you like them?"

"I do. They're very you."

"Thank you. So . . . ." Theo poked my shoulder. "You most definitely have a type." He nodded toward Alessio.

Physically, maybe this was true. But my former boyfriend had been a teddy bear. Alessio was sharp and hard, cold at times. He wasn't afraid to stand up to me. Paolo never would've dared. "Stop. He's right here."

"And he's listening," Alessio muttered.

This caused Theo to laugh. "You two are cute together. Which is surprising, considering he was hired to kill you."

I shrugged and sipped my wine. "It makes for an interesting 'how did you meet' story."

"This is true," Theo said. "You never do things the easy way, bello."

"And Nic? I saw the way you looked at him tonight."

Theo ducked his head and smoothed his already-smooth skirt with one hand. "I think I might like him," he said quietly. "It's disgusting."

"You are allowed to be happy. For longer than two weeks, I mean. But what do you know about him?" I heard Alessio sigh heavily beside me, but I ignored him.

"I'm not sure he is out." Theo looked around, making sure we weren't overhead as he leaned in. "In Paris, we stayed in his hotel room. He never left. No visitors. Then he brings me here to this yacht.

Either he's closeted or he's embarrassed of me. Or married. Maybe all three."

Theo didn't hide. As long as I'd known him, he was proudly gay and wore exactly what he liked, regardless of gender norms. I couldn't imagine him dating a closeted man. "Have you asked him?"

Theo pinched the tips of his fingers with his thumb. "Ma dai. Don't be ridiculous. We've known each other for less than a month. I want to enjoy whatever time we have together and not ruin it with heavy conversation."

"You're afraid of the answer."

"Sì, certo. And this is just temporary."

"You noticed the crew? The guns?"

"Of course." Theo's brows lowered as he frowned at me. "A man as wealthy as this? We would be surprised if there weren't guns aboard, no?"

"I'm worried about your safety," I said quietly.

"Fair, then, because I've spent the last four years worried about yours." His voice was sharp and clearly I'd hit a nerve.

"Forgive me. But you know I didn't have a choice."

"What I know is that you are stubborn. Siderno, your father's estate, is the safest place. Yet you avoid moving back, even at the cost of your own life."

Alessio grunted in agreement. I ignored him and kept my focus on Theo. "And a good thing I did. They sent six men to kill me in Scotland. Do you think I can risk Frankie and the kids? My mother died when she was caught in one of my father's feuds. I won't risk it."

Settling back in his chair, Theo relaxed and grabbed my hand. "I don't wish to argue, bello. It is good to see you. I have been worried these last few months. After Greece I stopped hearing from you and I feared the worst."

"I'm sorry. I should have called sooner."

"Where were you in Scotland?"

"The Upper Hebrides."

"That sounds very cold and so very not-gay."

My lips twitched. "It was cold. But I found it surprisingly gay."

"I bet you did. You are pretty enough to make the straightest of straight ones curious." He sipped his wine, gazing at Alessio over the rim of his glass.

Theo was fishing, but Alessio didn't bite. I answered instead. "He's bi."

"Ah. I can appreciate a man who orders from both sides of the menu."

"There you are," a deep voice said. Nic was now on deck, his face softening when he saw Theo.

I studied Theo's man and it only made me more concerned for Theo. A Russian pakhan would not let anything jeopardize his position. The Bratva was as tolerant of gay men as the 'Ndrangheta—meaning not tolerant in the least. I had to get Theo off this yacht.

"Mon grand!" Theo waved Nic over. "Come watch the stars with us."

Alessio tensed ever so slightly at Nic's appearance, though I was likely the only one to notice. I should put him out of his misery. No doubt he'd feel better once we were locked in our stateroom together.

Rising, I grabbed my bottle of wine and put my free hand on Alessio's shoulder, squeezing. "We should get some sleep."

Nic settled in a chair and patted his large thighs, his eyes locked on Theo. "Come here, *luchik*."

That was our cue to leave. I rose and said, "Good night, amici."

Theo was already settling in Nic's lap as Alessio and I departed. Once below deck, I asked Alessio, "What did that word mean, the one Nic called Theo?"

"Ray of light. An endearment in Russian."

There'd been no hint that Nic meant Theo any harm, but I still didn't trust him. What a mess. We needed to be dealing with the Sicilians, not the Bratva. I asked Alessio, "Did we make a mistake in coming here?"

"Probably. But it's too late now."

Alessio

WE TOOK our time getting up the next day.

After trading blow jobs, we stayed in bed, kissing and touching. There wasn't much talking, but I didn't mind. We were in our own bubble, safe from the outside world. No Sicilians, no Bratva. Just this.

Eventually we grew hungry, so we showered. After we dried off, Giulio leaned against the door. "Hurry up," he said as I pulled my jeans on. "I'm starving."

"Swallowing my dick wasn't enough for you?"

"Terrible. You are lucky you give such good blow jobs."

Luck had nothing to do with it. I loved worshiping him with my mouth, draining him dry.

"Andiamo. Theo will start searching for us soon if we don't appear."

Not bothering with shoes, we went out the door and into the corridor. He walked ahead of me, his shoulders pushed back, confidence in every step. *Il bel principe.* Did he even realize it? How could anyone see him and not instantly recognize the hundreds of years of power and privilege in his bones? He was a fool to let those old men drive him away from his legacy.

Music blared from the back of the yacht. I didn't recognize it, but Giulio began singing along. Full of bass and lyrics I didn't understand, it sounded like one of the songs from the clubs he frequented. He slid me a glance. "Do you like Rihanna?"

"Who?"

He chuckled. "Dio, you are adorable."

Theo was on a deck chair, sipping a tall drink with an umbrella sticking out of it. He wore sunglasses and a tiny black bathing suit. When he saw us, he pushed up his sunglasses. "Oh, look who is finally awake."

A nearby table had pastries, bread and cheese, so I went there first. Instead of joining me, Giulio went to Theo and kissed his cheeks. "We have been awake for some time," Giulio admitted.

"I bet you have, bello. You look very relaxed. Ciao, Alessio!"

I nodded in greeting, then continued to load my plate with food. When I sat, I found both Giulio and Theo watching me carefully.

"Che cosa? Where's mine?" Giulio asked, nodding to my plate.

I frowned. Did he expect me to serve him, like an American house-wife on those old television shows my nonna used to watch?

"Leave him alone," Theo scolded Giulio. "No doubt you made him do all the work this morning. He's built up a voracious appetite."

Theo wasn't altogether wrong.

Giulio pulled off his shirt and tossed it on a deck chair. Tattoos rippled over hard muscles in the sun and I paused mid-chew. Mamma mia, he was gorgeous.

"Bello," Theo said with a chuckle, "your boyfriend is about to choke on his tongue. Maybe you should put your shirt back on."

I waited for Giulio to refute the boyfriend comment, but he said nothing as he went to the food table. Boyfriends. Hmm. I liked that. What did Giulio think?

"I have suits for you," Theo said, pointing at a bench with swim trunks on it. "Well, Nic has suits for you. Mine all look like this." He gestured to the fabric barely covering his dick.

I would love to see Giulio wearing one of Theo's suits. He would look very hot.

Without an ounce of shame, Giulio stripped out of his jeans and briefs. He kept his back to us, but the sight of his luscious ass . . . I longed to bite it. Grind on it. *Fuck* it.

I wasn't the only one admiring Giulio's body. Theo had his glasses pulled down, openly staring at my man. Something dark passed through me. I growled softly in the other man's direction.

He shrugged. "I can't help it. When a gorgeous man takes off his clothes, I have to look."

Giulio carried the extra bathing trunks over to me. "Stop frowning and go change, assassino."

"This isn't a vacation," I said quietly. Earlier, I'd asked Sasha to investigate any Sicilian groups who might have reason to put a hit out on Giulio. I also planned to ask Nic for a laptop so I could do my own digging. But I also didn't want to leave Giulio's side.

"I know." Leaning down, he kissed me, his lips curved into a smile. "But we are allowed to take a break from worrying for a few minutes."

We were so different, he and I. This was what he loved, friends and parties. Drinks and yachts. I didn't fit into this world.

"Per favore, baby." He gave me another kiss. "For me? I just want to relax for one fucking afternoon with you."

I couldn't say no. Not to him.

Without thinking, I stood and held his face with both hands. Then I slammed my mouth on his for a deep kiss with plenty of tongue. Already his skin was warm from the Mediterranean sun and I wanted more.

When we finally parted, he was breathing hard and sagging against me. "Cazzo, baby."

"No flirting," I said in his ear. "And keep your clothes on. I'm the only one who gets to see that now."

Turning on my heel, I went inside to find the lavatory. I would change there.

It didn't take long. I quickly changed into Nikolai's swim trunks and folded my clothes. But when I emerged from the tiny room, I wasn't alone. Nikolai was waiting on the sofa, eyes locked on me. He wore no suit coat, just trousers and a dress shirt. His arms were spread along the back of the sofa, his legs spread wide.

"A word?" he asked in Russian.

I set my clothes on a table and approached him. While I tried to appear relaxed, I was tense. My muscles were on high alert, ready for trouble.

Though there was room on the sofa, I chose to sit across from him. I didn't speak, our gazes locked on one another.

"I did some digging," he said, continuing in Russian.

"Did you?"

"Yes, and I was surprised at what I discovered. Alessandro Ricci." He whistled. "I never would have guessed."

How had he learned my identity? I tried not to let my surprise show. "And?"

"And I would like to know what you are doing on my yacht."

"It has nothing to do with you. I didn't know you were here before I stepped on board."

His expression remained unchanged. "A coincidence. Is that it?"

"I did not choose to come to your yacht."

"And Ravazzani? Does he know who I am?"

So he discovered Giulio's identity, as well. "He knows."

Nikolai tapped his fingers on the wood, restless energy crackling off his large frame. "I could kill you, yes? Put a bullet in your head and let the sharks have you."

It was what I feared he would do. There was nothing stopping him. Except Theo. Hopefully. "And what would your *luchik* say about that?"

A muscle jumped in Nikolai's jaw and I let out a silent breath of relief. Theo *meant* something to this Russian. Which gave me a small bit of leverage.

"My only goal is to keep Giulio safe," I said quietly. "I don't care about your secret or your relationship with Theo. As soon as I discover who tried to kill Giulio in Scotland, I will leave to go kill them."

"And his father?"

"Does not know where we are." I decided to give Nikolai a little peace of mind. "Giulio refuses to involve his father. He doesn't want to put the rest of his family in danger."

"Why should I take your word for it?"

"Because I don't lie. And my business is keeping secrets."

He watched me thoughtfully. "This matches what I have learned about you, that you can be trusted. I spoke to Alexi."

Alexi Zaitsev. A Russian oligarch and former client. I killed his brother-in-law in Warsaw three years ago.

I said nothing. I wasn't going to admit knowing Alexi or give information about the nature of the contract away.

"You will do a favor for me," Nic declared, his jaw firm and unyielding.

I didn't like it. But what could I say? Giulio's well-being depended on this man at the moment. If I said no, what was to stop him from carrying out the shark threat and making up a lie to tell Theo?

I dipped my chin. "You have my word."

"Don't you want to know what it is?"

"Are you giving me a choice?"

"No."

"Then it is pointless to discuss it. I will give you the name and number of my assistant. You schedule it through her. And I have a request of my own."

"You presume to bargain with me?"

I held up my palms apologetically. "The sooner we discover which Sicilians want him dead, the sooner we leave. Do you have an untraceable laptop I can borrow to do some digging?"

He considered this, running a hand over his jaw. "I will do you one better. But you must agree to another favor."

Two assassinations? Madonna, this Russian didn't know when to quit.

Before I could answer, he said, "It's not another job. I don't want —" He glanced toward the deck, where Theo and Giulio were sunbathing. "I don't want him to know. You and Ravazzani can't tell him. Ever."

Merda. Giulio wouldn't like that. He was loyal to his friend. "That is a big favor. How do I know what you offer in exchange is worth it?"

"Trust me, it is worth it. How do you think I found you?"

I didn't know what this meant, but I had to try. Staying on the yacht only kept us in danger. "Agreed."

He stood, so I followed suit. We shook hands and he said, "Meet me back here in one hour and I'll take you to the security room."

"Mon grand!" Theo came in, his skin gleaming from the sun. He hurried over to Nikolai and wrapped around the larger man like a weed. "Were you missing me?"

Nikolai bent and kissed Theo's mouth, his palms finding Theo's ass. "Always, luchik."

Giving them privacy, I went out onto the deck where Giulio was sunbathing. He would not be happy over the deal I just made, but I hoped it paid off.

Giulio looked me over, concern etched in his features. "That took a long time."

"Everything's fine."

"Did Theo find you? We were worried you got lost."

Putting my hand on his sternum, I bent over him. "He's with Nic, which means we're alone."

His fingers trailed up my stomach and through the hair on my chest. Then he fingered the cornicello around my neck. Every place he touched on me sizzled. "You look fucking good out here."

I was scarred, both inside and out. Hardly beautiful like Giulio. "And you look like you belong on the cover of a magazine, amore."

He hooked his finger through my necklace and pulled me closer. "Well Fucked Monthly?"

I laughed as his lips captured mine. His mouth was warm and soft. I angled my head and slipped my tongue in his mouth. I loved kissing him. I hadn't kissed many partners over the years, and rarely the same person twice. But Giulio's kisses felt necessary, like I would starve without them.

Finally, I eased up on Giulio's mouth, but didn't pull away, instead switching to gentle, affectionate kisses. Telling him everything with my lips that I hadn't said out loud.

You're mine, principe.

CHAPTER EIGHTEEN

Giulio

"You did *what?*" I snarled. I kept my voice low, so I wasn't overheard. "*Che cavolo fai*, Alessio!"

His cheeks reddened slightly. "I had no choice. I have to keep you safe. And we need to—"

"Fuck that." I dragged him over to the edge of the deck, farther away from where Nikolai and Theo chatted in the salon. "You had no right to agree to either of those things."

"No right?"

I shoved my finger into his chest. "We decide these things together. Unless . . . ." Had I entirely misread him? I didn't think so, not with everything Alessio had said and done. But I had to be sure. "Are we not together? Is this just temporary for you?"

He grabbed my hips and pressed his forehead to mine. The heat from his large frame wrapped around me. Sank inside my bones. "We are together, principe," he whispered. "I told you, you are mine."

"Good." I slid my hands around his back. "Then we decide together. I don't want you owing the Bratva any favors." Who the fuck knew what Nikolai would demand of Alessio in return? Assassinate the pope? A world leader? A dictator? "And I need to look out for Theo's best interests. He's my friend."

"What else was I supposed to do? I need to keep you safe."

I wanted to sigh. I understood this protective streak of Alessio's, but I wasn't weak. I was a killer, too. Raised to run an empire. I wasn't afraid of the Bratva.

And I was not about to sacrifice Alessio and Theo for my own safety.

I grabbed the back of Alessio's neck. Held tight. "Do you trust me?"

"Of course." He sounded offended that I even asked.

"Va bene. Let's go."

I released him and strode for the salon. This couldn't wait. Nikolai had pushed Alessio . . . but I was about the push the fuck back.

I removed my sunglasses as we entered the salon. Theo and Nikolai were on the sofa, speaking quietly. Theo glanced up at our approach. "Bello? Is everything okay?"

"I need a minute alone with Nic."

Nikolai's mouth tightened, while Theo's head swiveled between Alessio and me. Then over to Nikolai. "Mon grand?"

Nikolai helped Theo to his feet, then pressed a kiss to the top of his head. "It's fine, luchik. Give us a minute."

Theo moved closer to me. I could tell he was worried. "Should I stay?" he asked quietly.

"No. We won't be long."

He transferred his attention to Alessio. "And I assume you're staying, too?"

Alessio nodded. Theo patted his arm and then went out on deck alone.

"My office?" Nikolai asked.

"Yes," I said. I didn't want Theo overhearing any of our conversation.

Nikolai began walking out of the salon. I started to follow, but Alessio put a hand on my arm. "What are you doing?"

I was good at negotiating, at dealing with criminals and thugs. I wasn't worried. "Relax, assassino. You'll see."

The three of us wound through the tight corridors decorated with teak paneling and brass fixtures. Modern abstract artwork decorated the walls, no doubt all original works worth a lot of money.

Nikolai led us to a closed door, which he unlocked and held open. I walked in and immediately went to the sofa against the wall. He strode behind his desk, obviously thinking it a position of power, and Alessio stood somewhere in the middle of the room. The door had barely closed when it opened again, and Nikolai's man appeared. He hovered by the exit, as if blocking it, but I ignored him. Instead, I focused on my opponent.

I had watched my father do this hundreds of times. I myself had done it in the last four years when dealing with dangerous men. The Russians might have us on pure strength, but the Italians couldn't be matched when it came to style.

The first move?

I sat in the center of the sofa and crossed my legs, then draped one arm across the back. I wore no shirt, so my inked skin and various scars would tell another story without me needing to verbalize it.

The second piece was to employ silence. So I twirled my sunglasses and pretended I was totally at ease. No cares, no threat.

Nikolai tapped his fingers on the wooden desk, watching me. His face resembled chiseled granite, cold and remote. His gaze was icy and intense, like good Russian vodka. A man used to getting his way.

But I held off on speaking. We would see who broke first.

"You are Giulio Ravazzani," he said after a long minute, and I could now hear the Russian plainly in the way he spoke.

"You have heard of my family?" I made sure my accent was thick, too, every syllable meant to remind him who he was dealing with.

"I know of your father, yes."

"Good. This saves us some time." I cocked my head. "I was raised by my father to take over his empire. I saw many things in my eighteen years under him. I learned when men were lying, when they were telling the truth. And do you know what else I learned?"

He didn't speak, so I continued. "I learned when I was being taken advantage of."

I let that linger.

"Allora," I said after a long beat. "You told Alessio he owes you a favor. I am revoking that promise. He owes you nothing."

Nikolai's lips curled into almost a sneer. "Are you so eager to become fish food?"

"I'll not allow him to agree to a job for you without knowing the details. If you want to hire him, go through the proper channels. If he says yes, then you'll pay him a fuck lot of money for his services."

"These promises, they were made in good faith. To ensure you remain alive."

"You won't kill either one of us."

"I would not be so sure of that." The words were soft and dangerous.

I kept my tone light. "Did you know I lived in Màlaga a few months ago?"

"Oh?"

"While I was there, I kept very busy. A little of this, a little of that. Capisce?"

"And? What does this have to do with me?"

"The Bratva there. Golubev and his men. Do you know them?"

"Yes, of course."

I had assumed so. If Nikolai was as powerful as Alessio said, he would be like my father, with his fingers in various places all over Europe. "When I was looking for someone to partner with, I found Golubev . . . distasteful. I worked with a local man instead. Martiñez."

"He is also distasteful," Nikolai said dryly.

From what I understood, the Bratva and Martiñez had been fighting for control of Málaga and the Spanish drug market for years. Martiñez had certain Colombian connections that didn't trust the Russians. So this allowed Martiñez to keep a stranglehold on the product. His high demand and insatiable greed were what allowed me to sell him twenty kilos. "Yes, but he has a weakness that can be exploited."

Nikolai eased forward in his chair. "*You* know of Martiñez's weakness?" The thread of disbelief was not lost on me. Nikolai didn't think I was telling the truth.

I gestured to his phone on the desk. "Call Golubev. Ask him if he met with me three months ago. I was using the name Javier Martín."

Nikolai seemed to consider this. He looked at his man by the door. The man must've nodded because Nikolai lifted his phone, unlocked it, and found the contact he was looking for. He held the mobile up to his ear. Golubev picked up immediately, and the two had an exchange in Russian. I heard the name Javier Martín.

When Nikolai hung up, he tossed his phone on the desk and stared at me. I twirled my sunglasses slowly. "I assume Golubev confirmed my story. And keep in mind Alessio is fluent in Russian." I tipped my chin toward my ragazzo.

"*Da*," Nikolai clipped out. "He said Javier Martín offered up a lot of coke for a ridiculous price. He said it had to be shit product."

"It was," I said with a nod. "And that is Martiñez's weakness. His people don't know when they are being sold pure coke or baking soda. But I wasn't lying to Golubev about my ability to bring in whatever he needed there. I could've helped him run Martiñez out of business."

"Golubev does not trust many people. It is what has kept him alive into his sixties."

"My contacts also do not trust many people. But they trust me and they trust my family. And they will trust whoever I tell them to work with in Málaga."

"Golubev, you mean. If I agree to let you live."

"No. Golubev missed his chance." He'd treated me like a coglione, a fool. A boy playing at a man's game. I would not forgive it. "But you, Nikolai, I could get them to work with you."

The lines around his eyes deepened as he squinted at me. "You think I wish to expand into Spain."

"No." I paused, then said clearly, "*We* would expand into Spain."

"I have no intention of going into business with Fausto Ravazzani."

"That is not what I offered. This would be between you and me."

Nikolai's gaze darted to his comrade near the door. "And what of Golubev?"

"He's old. From another era. You and I could make a lot of fucking money there."

The moment stretched. I could tell he was intrigued. "Have you done this before?"

"Of course. Frankfort, Hamburg. Zadar, Tirana. Corfu. I haven't stayed in one place very long as a precaution. Once Alessio and I deal with the Sicilians, though, I will be ready to put down roots. Grow my business." I spun my sunglasses lazily. "Why not Málaga?"

He leaned back, angling his chair to the side. He stared at the far wall. I let it go, not pushing, knowing he needed to think it through. Killing Golubev was risky. It needed to be handled carefully.

"I will think about it," Nikolai finally said, coming to his feet. "I will discuss it with my people." He tipped his chin toward the silent man still blocking the door.

How could he turn this down? I was offering him millions of Euros on a plate.

In the end, I knew he would agree.

Rising, I slipped my sunglasses on my head. "You do that and let us know. Now, I believe Alessio asked about a laptop to do some digging?"

Nikolai came around the desk. "Follow me. I'll take you to the security room."

As he walked by me, I grabbed his arm. The entire room froze, like we were all standing at the edge of a cliff. But I had something else to say, something very important.

"If I think he is in danger," I said quietly. "If I think he should be told, I will do it. He deserves to know the sort of man he is in bed with."

We both knew I was talking about Theo.

"He is in no danger, Ravazzani. Not from me."

"Good. See that it stays that way."

Nikolai shook off my hand. "I am not a fool, nor am I a child. I know the risks and am doing everything to shield him from my life. He will return to Paris next week, none the wiser."

"But perhaps heartbroken."

A hint of guilt—regret?—flashed over Nikolai's face before his usual mask returned. "But he will be alive."

———

Alessio

IF THERE HAD EVER BEEN any doubt of Giulio's lineage or his relationship to Fausto Ravazzani, that meeting completely eradicated it.

Giulio had been fucking brilliant. A master. Cool and calm. Confident but not boastful. He dangled the one thing in front of Nic that no one in this world could resist: money.

But partnering with Nikolai Kuznetsov and the Bratva? This was a risky move. I hadn't realized Giulio wanted to return to Málaga and to begin trafficking cocaine again. Shouldn't he and I have decided this together?

I frowned as we followed Nikolai from his office. While I was relieved to no longer owe Nikolai a favor, I wasn't sure Giulio's plan was any better. It was probably worse. Now we would deal with him for years, instead of for just one short job.

"Stop worrying," Giulio whispered for my ears alone when we were in the corridor.

I kept quiet. We needed to be alone for our conversation.

We passed the bridge. The captain and a crew member were inside at the controls, and they nodded in deference to Nikolai as he passed. Nikolai opened a narrow door and gestured for us to go in. One of his men sat at a desk, typing on a keyboard. Three big monitors faced him, but I couldn't see what he was working on.

He straightened at the appearance of the big boss. Nikolai spoke in Russian, telling the man we were looking for some information and directing him to help us. Then he turned and left.

The silence stretched as the door snicked shut. "Do you speak English?" I asked the man in Russian.

He shook his head. "Nyet."

I walked over. "Do you mind if we sit?"

He gestured to the one empty seat beside him. Giulio and I exchanged a look. "Sit, assassino," Giulio said quietly in Italian. "You speak his language. You can tell him what to do."

I took the only chair and checked the three screens. Two of them had security cameras up. I noticed there was one in every guest stateroom, save ours. That was only because I'd found their camera and destroyed it. The other monitor had computer code on it.

"How may I help you?" the man asked.

"Can you hack into the police records in Bruges?"

"Of course."

"We are looking for material, video on a car bomb attack." I looked over at Giulio. "The date of the car bomb?"

The Russian began typing as Giulio provided the date. I translated, and told him some other basic details. "I assume, because you were able to learn our identities, that you have facial recognition software."

"Da."

That was good. Glancing over my shoulder, I asked, "Have you used facial recognition on the CCTV footage?"

"No. The Belgian police said there weren't enough features to bother. Why? You think he can pull something?"

The technology on facial recognition has improved dramatically in the last few years. "I won't know until we try. But knowing we are looking for a Sicilian could help narrow the field."

"So fucking smart." He bent and kissed the back of my head.

My chest pulled tight, like someone was tugging on a string there. I was probably blushing. "You don't need to stay."

"Are you sure?"

"This could take a while." No doubt he was anxious to reassure Theo. And I no longer needed to worry about Nikolai chopping Giulio up and throwing him overboard. "I don't mind."

Giulio squeezed my shoulder then strode from the room like he owned it. I watched his muscles shift beneath all those tattoos, mesmerized. Fuck me. I never got tired of looking at him.

But I was coming to see he was much more than a beautiful face.

It took some time, but Nikolai's man was talented. I had watched Sasha do this from time to time, when we needed sensitive information not available through the normal channels. But she didn't work as quickly as this man did.

"What is your name?" I asked.

"Andrei."

"I am Alessio," I said, even though he hadn't asked. He didn't react, just continued to type on his keyboard. I didn't bother him again. I wasn't good at small talk, and I sensed he didn't want it, either.

Once he was in the police files, we found the car bombing. There were notes about Paolo, even a passport photo. I stared at his face, this man that Giulio had loved. He was handsome in a bodybuilder sort of way, thick neck and blunt features. A nose that had been broken at some point. Brown hair and brown eyes. He looked kind.

As I expected, the police reports were worthless. They suspected organized crime and didn't bother investigating further. Giulio's name wasn't mentioned, but there were references to ties to an Italian criminal organization.

Andrei pulled up the CCTV archival footage. We went through it slowly. Enhanced, zoomed in. Pulled footage from nearby cameras. Andrei took stills of every face we thought might be related to the explosion.

Other members of Nikolai's crew came in at various points. I suspected they were checking on us at Nikolai's instruction, but they gave Andrei shit, laughing and joking with the security man. Andrei cracked a smile every now and again.

When I checked my phone, I was surprised to see that four hours had gone by.

"Would you like food?" Andrei asked, standing to roll his shoulders. "These images will load into the software. It should take two or three hours to get a hit."

"No, thank you. I will go on deck. You will let me know if you get a hit, yes?"

"Of course."

I shook his hand. "Thank you, Andrei."

Leaving the tiny room, I went toward the deck. I could hear music and laughter. Giulio. My mood lifted, like the mere thought of him filled me with joy. Dio, I was in so much trouble when it came to this man.

I am in love with him.

Did he feel the same? I still didn't like that he had decided to partner with Nikolai without even discussing it with me first. Maybe what we had was temporary in Giulio's mind. Maybe he was using me to find the men after him and then he planned to cut me loose.

Cazzo, I hated all this unknown. It was why I didn't do relationships and feelings.

They were in the pool, arms propped on the edge, talking, when I emerged. Theo excused himself and went in, leaving Giulio and I alone. Giulio peeked at me over the top of his sunglasses. "Find anything?"

I only had eyes for the gorgeous man staring up at me. His hair was wet, slicked back. My fingers itched with the need to run my fingers over his glistening skin.

"The software is running the images now. We should know whether it works or not in a few hours." I crooked a finger at him. "Get out of the pool."

His lips curled into a devastating smile. "Why?"

"Because I said so."

Using the side for leverage, Giulio pushed up on his arms in one fluid motion. Water cascaded down his back and legs, then he was out and striding toward me.

He stopped just out of reach. "Do you want food?"

"No."

"Then what do you want?" He bit his lip, well aware of the answer.

I hooked a finger into his waistband and yanked him closer. "You."

CHAPTER NINETEEN

Giulio

Three steps and I was in front of him. Alessio's eyes were lighter in the sun, like twin pools of silver. He cupped my face in his hands. "We have a lot to discuss. But first we are going below to fuck."

His lips brushed mine and I couldn't help but sag into his touch. "I know you are angry about what I offered Nikolai."

"Yes, very," he said against my mouth. "But we will discuss it later. After."

I dragged my palm down his chest. "I will fuck you and you'll forget you were ever mad at me."

"You think I am that weak when it comes to your dick?"

"I *know* you are weak when it comes to my dick."

He slid his hands lower to wrap around my throat. Then he squeezed. "Do you have a death wish? Partnering with the Bratva? Ma dai, principe."

"You think I can't handle some Russians, assassino?" I shook my head. "I'm not afraid of them. Let's go below. I want to suck you off."

He didn't move, his feet firmly planted on the deck. "You want to get me naked so I'll drop this conversation."

There was no use fighting about it. The offer had been made and I wouldn't renege. Besides, this could make us a lot of money. "Are you complaining?"

The edges of his mouth curled, which was a full-blown smile in Alessio's case. "No."

"Va bene, andiamo." I began guiding him backward.

"This subject is not closed."

I resisted the urge to argue. Instead, I led him below. My skin prickled, anticipation thrumming through my veins. We stepped inside our cabin and he shut the door. I stripped off my suit and tossed it away.

Alessio looked me up and down, his assessing gaze lingering on the tattoos that marked my naked skin. "I never get tired of looking at you," he said quietly.

I felt the same. Alessio was strong and lean. His big thighs stretched the fabric of the trunks, and I could see the outline of his cock through the thin cloth. My mouth watered.

I closed the distance between us and dropped to my knees. I lowered his trunks and his cock bounced in front of my face. Without missing a beat, I took him down. His warm skin was smooth and salty against my tongue. Delicious.

Alessio sucked in a sharp breath. "Minchia!"

His good hand found the back of my head, holding me as he began thrusting into my mouth. "You want to make me come right away. Is that it, principe?"

I moaned around his girth, telling him yes, that was exactly what I wanted.

"Are you going to swallow my cock and suck me dry?"

God, that was hot. Alessio didn't often talk dirty during sex, but I loved when did. I angled my head, trying to take more of him, and the head of his cock bumped the entrance to my throat. I relaxed and he slipped in.

He grunted and rocked his hips once. "Fuck, Giulio."

Then he stepped back. I didn't move, confused. He pushed his trunks off his long legs and pointed to the bed. "Get on the bed."

That curt tone had me obeying. Normally I was the demanding one in bed. But I didn't mind this change of pace, not one bit. He stalked toward me. The gold chain around his neck glinted in the sunlight streaming through the tiny portholes. The hard line of his jaw sent a shiver through me. Was he angry? It reminded me of when he first tracked me to the Isle of Canna.

Reaching the bed, he motioned for me to roll over. I wasn't sure what was happening, but I obeyed. Then the bed dipped under his weight, and his fingers coasted over my back, tracing my tattoos. The largest piece, a heart wrapped in thorns and dripping blood, had been completed after Paolo's death.

A reminder to myself that love had the power to cut deeper than any knife or bullet.

Alessio stretched out until his large frame covered mine. Soft kisses started on my shoulder. They continued downward, his lips brushing, whispering along my nape. He touched me reverently. Carefully. Like he was memorizing my shape with his mouth.

Wasn't this supposed to be angry sex?

"Stop teasing me," I said over my shoulder. "Let me up."

"Just relax. I thought this was about giving me what I want."

I huffed a laugh. "Oh, is that so?"

He nipped my shoulder blade with his teeth. "Yes."

Silent, he continued down my body. By the time he reached my ass I was panting, nearly grinding into the mattress. My skin burned where he'd touched.

Eager for more, I tried to turn over. Alessio's hand held me down. "Stay. You'll take everything I have to give you, principe mio."

"I'd rather fuck you again."

Alessio sank his teeth into one of my ass cheeks. "Maybe I will fuck you instead."

Alessio

He didn't like that idea.

Giulio's body tensed, every muscle now tight with resistance. "You know I don't do that."

"Let me try." I kissed his lower back, the dimple right above his ass. "I will make it good for you, I swear."

"Not everyone likes to bottom."

"I am aware. But your first and only try was not with me. So it can be better."

He buried his face in his arms and laughed. "Your ego is nearly as big as mine."

I sank lower, running my tongue along his crack. "Hold yourself open for me," I whispered into his skin. "Let me see you."

Reaching down, he grasped each cheek and spread himself open. I moved lower, until I was on my knees behind him. I dragged my nose over his balls, letting the musky smell of him fill my lungs.

Already he was panting, his big body trembling. I liked having him at my mercy. Now I wanted to make him feel good.

I swiped my tongue over his hole—and he jolted. "Porca puttana!"

I hummed in satisfaction. There were so many nerve endings back there. I planned to electrify all of them, drive him out of his skull until he was begging me.

My tongue fluttered, long swipes then short ones. Giulio's back bowed and he moaned. "Oh, dio mio. Sì, sì, sì. More, assassino."

I pressed harder, swirling, opening him up with my tongue. He cursed and shook, the sounds from his mouth growing louder. I didn't let up. Instead, I used the tip of my tongue to shove inside him, invading.

"You are killing me."

I kept going. His sounds grew louder, more desperate. He was humping the mattress, rolling his hips, so I had to hold him down. I didn't want him to come before I was ready.

Finally, I couldn't take it anymore. My cock was leaking and I needed to fuck. "Do you want me, amore? Do you want my dick inside you?"

"I don't know if I can, but let's try."

Quickly, I found the lube in the drawer of the nightstand and drizzled the cool liquid down his ass crack. "Keep yourself spread for me."

I used my fingers to slick his skin. Then I slipped my thumb inside him. Tight heat enveloped me and we both exhaled sharply. "I can't wait to put my dick in here," I whispered, twisting my thumb.

As I stretched him open, I studied the tattoos on his broad back, the way his hips and waist tapered in. The firm globes of his ass. My chest squeezed until I could hardly breathe. He was perfect . . . and he was *mine*.

I pulled my thumb out and replaced it with two fingers. His back arched, his body tensing. "Relax," I said. "Give yourself over to me."

I curled my fingers, seeking. When I brushed his prostate, he gasped. "Cazzo! I felt that in my toes."

Humming with satisfaction, I did it again. And again. I wanted to make him feel so good.

I kept going, teasing and rubbing, until a light sheen of sweat coated his skin and he was whining into the pillow. "Do it. Hurry," he panted over his shoulder.

Still giving orders. I purposely slowed my fingers, drawing out his torture. "I won't fuck you until you beg me." I added a third finger. "I'm going to fuck you so hard, principe. And you're going to love every minute of it."

He whimpered. "Please, Alessione."

"That is what I want to hear." I kissed the small of his back as I withdrew my fingers. After slicking my cock, I lined up and slowly pushed against his tight hole. The head slipped in and he sucked in a breath. I ran my palms over his legs and hips, soothing him. "Shh. I'm not going to hurt you. I'll never hurt you. Just breathe."

I held perfectly still, letting him adjust. I knew from experience this wasn't always easy, and I wanted him to enjoy it. I wanted him to feel safe with me.

I dragged in a deep breath to get myself under control. It had been ages since I'd fucked anyone—even longer since it had been a man. I'd forgotten how snug, how hot. It was absolute heaven.

And I've wanted it with this particular man for so long.

"Do you want to stop?" I whispered.

"No." His muscles trembled, his cheeks flushed. "But hurry up." He rocked his hips and tried to bring me deeper.

I held him still. "Wait. Slow down."

I wouldn't rush this and risk causing him pain. Instead, I clutched him and sank in a centimeter at a time. Whenever he tensed, I paused to kiss his back and caress him until he relaxed. Over and over we did this until I was fully seated. Then I was inside him, his channel clamping down on me, and it was like everything I'd ever dreamed.

I closed my eyes and prayed for strength. Cazzo, it was too good. I wouldn't last five minutes.

He shivered and I frowned. "Are you okay? We can stop if it's too much."

"No, don't stop. Fuck! I can feel you everywhere. You have to move."

I gave an experimental roll of my hips. He moaned, which I took as a good sign. "More?"

Giulio's fingers clutched the sheets. "Madre di dio, will you fuck me already?"

Grabbing the plastic bottle, I drizzled some extra lube where we were connected as a precaution. His hole was stretched around me, and I knew I'd never forget this moment, when this brave and beautiful man let me have all of him.

I braced my knees on the mattress and gave a few rough thrusts. His chest heaved as moans fell from his lips. "Yes, Alessio. Let me have it."

"Get up on your knees," I ordered.

He moved to his knees and positioned his ass in the air, but kept his upper half on the mattress. The new angle pulled me deeper, and we both groaned. Then I began really fucking him. My hips slammed against his ass, my balls swinging with each thrust. Every drag of my cock hit his prostate, and I could see goosebumps break out across his skin.

"Cazzo madre di dio!" He threw his head back. "It feels incredible."

I kept pounding, grinding. Sweat coated my body and my heart thumped wildly in my chest, the urge to come rising in my groin. I ignored it. I needed Giulio to enjoy this. Getting him off was all that mattered.

"You are so fucking hot," I said. "Bent over and letting me take your ass. You like it, no? You like being fucked by me."

"Sì, sì. *Mi piace così tanto.*"

I was glad he liked it, but I needed him to finish. I was so close.

Putting a hand on his shoulder, I lifted him upright. I kissed the nape of his neck. "I can't get enough of you. I want you all the fucking time."

His mouth hung open, his skin flushed. I loved seeing him like this, mindless with lust and impaled on my cock. I grabbed his dick and jerked him hard and fast. "I need you to come, principe. Come, so I can shoot inside you. You can feel what it's like to have me dripping out of your hole this time."

"Oh, shit!" He clenched around me as his dick swelled and began pulsing. Thick ropes of come shot out of him, coating the bedsheets, and his fingers dug into the backs of my thighs.

The pressure around my cock was too much. There was no stopping the orgasm that rushed over me. I gave a few pumps and then I was shouting, trembling, hot jets erupting and filling him. The high was unlike any other orgasm in my life, never-ending and soul deep. I wasn't sure I'd ever recover.

Finally, we both collapsed. Lightheaded, I rested on his back and floated. Breath sawed out of my lungs. Madonna, this had wrecked me. *Giulio* wrecked me. Never before had I experienced this desperation, this all-consuming need for another person.

This thing between us wasn't only physical. I felt deeply for him. I wanted his smiles, his laughter. To be close to him at all times. I ached when we weren't in the same room.

"Amore mio," I whispered, shifting to press my lips to his shoulder.

He moaned deep in his throat. "I like that."

"The fucking? Or the endearment?"

"Both." His hand wrapped around to clutch my thigh again, like he needed to touch me in some way.

Eventually my dick was soft enough to slip out of his hole. He winced as I pulled away. "Okay?" I asked.

He nodded. "You were right. It was different."

"Better, I hope?"

The edge of his mouth curled. "Yes, better. I don't know if I'd want to do it often, but occasionally it would be nice." He stretched his arms and legs. "I feel sore, but relaxed. It's strange."

"Good. Stay here."

Pushing up, I went to the washroom. I wet a cloth with warm water and brought it out. Giulio reached for it , but I batted his hand away. "Let me do it. I want to take care of you." I kissed the inside of his thigh.

"You don't need to."

"Yes, I do."

I needed an excuse to keep touching him. I wanted to store up the feel of his skin, the warmth of his smile. The way he looked in bed, with the afternoon sunlight streaming across his chiseled features.

When we were both clean, I curled up next to him. My fingers traced his cheekbone then skimmed his jaw. "Thank you for trusting me."

"You are good at that."

"Fucking?"

He chuckled softly. "Yes, that. But I was speaking of the reassurances, how you put me at ease. There is something about you that makes me feel protected and safe."

Because he mattered to me. I would rather die than hurt him. And I would protect him at the cost of everything else, including my own life. "Speaking of safety . . . are you really going to go back to Málaga to start running drugs again?"

Giulio shrugged. "It's what I know. And I can't go back to Siderno."

"Why not? If we take care of the Sicilians, you're free to do as you like."

"I always thought I'd return home, but maybe being on my own would be better. In Siderno I will always be my father's son. The gay heir who left the 'ndrina. I'll never have anything that belongs to just me."

"And you didn't think to discuss this with me first?"

"I'm sorry. I didn't think you would mind, honestly."

"Because you are planning on leaving me?"

"Alessio, caro." He reached to grip the side of my throat as he stared into my eyes. "Do you think I want to do this without you? It's like you took my frozen, dead heart in your big hands and brought it back to life. I was so lonely and lost until you found me."

My lungs seized as an immense pressure filled my chest. The words were everything I'd ever hoped he'd say. "Ti amo," I forced past the lump in my throat.

"Ti amo, baby." He kissed me softly, sweetly. "Whatever happens next we do it together, no?"

I winced, thinking of the task ahead. I wasn't ready to risk Giulio's life so soon.

"What is it?" he asked, studying my expression.

"Any chance you'll let me go to Sicily to deal with these assassins alone?"

His bright blue eyes filled with amusement. "Ma dai. You should know me better than that."

"I do, which is why we need to come up with a plan." I patted his hip. "First, let's shower. Then I need to get some food."

"You go," he said, waving me toward the bathroom. "I need to gather my strength."

Chuckling, I got up and went to the shower. I turned the water hot and let it beat down on my sore muscles. Soon I got out, wrapped a towel around my waist, and found Giulio wearing a robe and looking over some photos. "What are those?"

"Andrei dropped them off. The results of the facial recognition software." He studied each image then tossed it aside. "I don't recognize any of these people."

"Let me see."

I sat on the mattress and spread out the five or six headshots. Labels were on the back of each with names and cities of last known residence. I picked up my mobile and called up Sasha's contact number. I put her on speaker.

"I don't have an answer for you," she said in Russian, getting straight to the point.

"English, please," I said. "I have Giulio here."

"Oh?" Her voice dropped as she singsonged, "Well, hello, Giulio Ravazzani. Nice to finally meet you. I have heard so very much about you."

His lips curled. "I bet you have. Something tells me you might know more about me than I do."

She laughed. "I definitely do. So why are you two disturbing me?"

I folded my arms across my chest, bracing. "We are on Nikolai Kuznetsov's yacht—"

"Blyad! Are you fucking serious? Do you know how dangerous—?"

"Sasha," I barked. "I know all this and we're handling it. What I need right now is related to the Sicilians out to kill Giulio."

She sounded petulant, like a small child. "I'm working on it."

"I have something that may help. Nikolai's security man ran facial recognition software on the CCTV footage of the car bombing in Bruges—"

"So you are cheating on me with one of *Nikolai's* men."

"And," I continued, "we have some names I want you to reference against what you've found."

She sighed and I could hear her fingers working over her keyboard. "Here's what I know. There are three main Cosa Nostra *cosche* active in Sicily. The Cannavaro in Enna, Zambrotta in Catania, and Buscetta in Palermo. Buscetta is the largest and most powerful family, but the others are equally involved in criminal enterprises all over. I could not find ties to Ravazzani for any of these, though."

"You wouldn't," Giulio said, his eyebrows pinched as he stared hard at the photos. "My father is too smart for that. But he has dealt with Buscetta over the years. The last time was four years ago, that I know of. There was an alliance, so I think they are the least likely."

"What of the others?" I asked him.

"It's been a long time, but from what I remember Cannavaro's in jail. His wife is running things, with his help from prison. Zambrotta I don't know."

"Zambrotta died sixteen months ago," Sasha filled in. "His two sons took over, but they've lost most of their holdings to Buscetta."

"We should call your father," I suggested to Giulio. "And ask his opinion."

"No." His eyes were bright and hard, like chips of diamond. "He gets involved and this becomes a war. And I told you, he thinks it has to do with another don who died around the same time."

"Ah. Because Fausto was responsible."

He didn't answer, but his look said it all. Fausto had killed this other don. "It makes sense. But why the Sicilians? Why not this don's own family?"

"His sons are incompetent junkies. Or at least they were four years ago."

"Maybe the Sicilians came after you in retaliation against your father for this don. The timing is suspicious."

"Why would the Sicilians care about Mommo's death? It didn't involve them." He flipped the photos over and looked at the names. I could see him considering it. "Sasha, I'm going to read out some names. Look for a connection between them and a man from Piedmont, Girolamo Condello. He went by Mommo. He's dead, but maybe he had ties to one of these families."

Giulio gave her the names that resulted from the facial recognition software.

We heard her typing and snapping gum. When she was thinking hard, she always chewed cherry bubble gum. I usually gave her some for Christmas, along with her bonus.

"Did you say Condello?"

"Yes, why?"

"I was researching the Buscetta sons, Nino and Giacomo. Nino, the older one and the underboss, is married to Maria Umberto. Her first cousin, Rina, is the widow of a man named Condello in Peidmont."

"Was her given name Marina?"

"Yes."

"Minchia!"

"So this dead don, his wife was a cousin to Nino Buscetta's wife?"

"Sì." Giulio rubbed his eyes. "Mommo had a lot of wives. Still, how did no one know this before now?"

Sasha's voice came out of the phone. "Rina's last name wasn't Umberto. Her mother is the sister of Maria's father."

Ah, that explained the different surnames.

I looked up at Giulio and raised one eyebrow meaningfully. "Nino Buscetta."

"Nino fucking Buscetta," he repeated. "Let's go and kill that motherfucker."

CHAPTER TWENTY

Alessio

Passo di Rigano, Palermo, Sicily

From the shadows on the rooftop, I watched the Alfa Romeo dealership across the street. Nino Buscetta used the place as a front for his underboss activities, and I was gathering information on him.

I peeled an orange and ate it slowly. Giulio and I arrived in Palermo yesterday, and I insisted he stay hidden during the day. The Cosa Nostra were thick in these parts, and the Buscettas would certainly recognize him. It was too much of a risk.

On the yacht, we learned that Nino's father, Calogero, was the *capofamiglia* of his clan. Don Gero, as he was called, was hardly seen in public and his whereabouts were murky. He left most of the day-to-day business to Nino, a hot-headed coke fiend. With as much coke as I'd seen Nino snort in the last thirty-six hours, no wonder the Buscettas wanted a slice of Fausto Ravazzani's drug trade. Nino probably wanted a bulk discount.

It was believed that Nino was running things these days. Don Gero was in his mid-eighties and most capos that old were just figure heads. The mafia required strong leaders who were constantly putting pressure on those under them.

There was a younger brother, Giacomo, but he was more of an enforcer. A thug in a suit, not the brains. Giulio and I agreed that Nino would've been the one to order the hit four years ago.

My fingers rubbed the smooth cornicello around my neck absently as I chewed on the orange. From what I saw so far, Nino was well guarded and paranoid. He was rarely alone and escorted everywhere in public. The dealership's windows were made of bulletproof glass, and the guards surrounding his estate reminded me of a military base. It wasn't impossible to kill him—hardly anyone was impossible for me— but it would be difficult.

Giulio preferred to kill Nino himself. He wanted the Sicilian to see his face, to know that Giulio had evaded the assassination attempts to enact his revenge for Paolo's death.

I didn't like it. Using my rifle from long range was safer, easier. We could be in and out of Sicily in hours. But Giulio made me promise. He was adamant about doing this, so how could I refuse?

So I focused on Nino, finding out his routine. Looking for the best opportunity to kill him without risk and without being seen. I had to ensure Giulio's safety. This couldn't be traced back to him, and he had to get out of Sicily in one piece.

Nino was on the phone, laughing, his two men reclined in chairs in front of his desk. A woman walked toward the dealership, her body cloaked in a long dark coat. Strange, as it was hot today. Wearing heels more like spikes than shoes, she walked through the front door. A salesman approached and she smiled at him. They talked for a few minutes, then he led her toward Nino's office.

When she entered, Nino froze for half a beat. The men in chairs stood politely, but Nino did not. Instead, he ended his phone call and gestured for the men to leave. Then he was alone with the woman.

She opened her coat. With her back to me, I couldn't see what she wore underneath, but I could guess. Nino's smile turned wolfish and he beckoned her forward. She crawled under his desk and disappeared, just her fingers visible as she unzipped his pants.

He looked around and must have realized the blinds were open. Holding up a remote, he pushed a button and the slats closed, blocking my view.

I finished my orange as I waited. Nino's wife had dark hair. This woman was a blonde. She and Nino were clearly familiar with one another, though the salesman hadn't recognized her. I knew what this meant.

This was the *comare*—the mistress.

I waited. Thirty minutes later, she left the dealership. Nino's blinds opened again and he was back behind his desk, on the phone. I was no longer interested in him at the moment, though.

Instead, I followed her.

I hurried from the rooftop to the street, where I found my motorbike waiting. In seconds I caught up with her. She walked another block and unlocked a fancy red sedan. A gift from Nino's dealership, no doubt.

When she drove off I kept close. She never checked her rear view mirror, never glanced over her shoulder. She had nothing to fear. No worries that she was a target. As Nino's woman, she was untouchable.

Finally, she turned down a side street and parked in front of a small villa. I couldn't risk getting too close, so I stayed at the top of the street and watched as she locked her car and went into the home.

Now that I knew where she lived, this would be easy.

Most mafioso had mistresses, and they often visited them without heavy protection. It would be far easier to get to Nino here than at the dealership or at his home. And I suspected thirty minutes had only whetted Nino's appetite for this woman and he would return tonight for more.

I checked the time. Almost midday, when the entire country would shut down for riposo. I started the motorbike and headed off for our apartment.

When I opened the door I found Giulio prowling the tiny space like a caged lion. "I don't like this," he said as soon as I walked in. "I am doing nothing!"

I set down my things and tried not to smile. "You did this for years," I reminded him. "Vaping and cooking and exercising in your tiny apartments. You can do it for a few more days."

"That was different." He dragged both hands through his hair, leaving the strands messy. "I can actually kill this stronzo and end it today. I don't want to wait."

I unzipped my jacket and threw it over a chair back. "Do I need to calm you down with a blow job?"

"Yes," he said instantly. "But I want to hear what you learned first."

Over lunch I filled him in about Nino, the mistress, and her tiny villa. "Idiota," he sneered. "Thinking with his dick."

"Oh, and you didn't? In nightclubs, risking your safety to get your dick sucked?"

Leaning forward, he slipped an olive into my mouth. "It was worth it just to meet you in Málaga. Dai, I thought you would suck my soul out through the head of my cock."

"No, just your brains."

He chuckled. "Very possibly. So, we are doing this tonight, no? We'll go to the mistress's house and wait for Nino there."

"Yes."

"Thank fuck." Raising his arms over his head, he stretched. The t-shirt he wore, expensive and tight, pulled over his lean muscles. I never got tired of looking at him.

Never had I imagined we would be together, that I would love this man with every molecule in my body. Or that he would love me back. It seemed like a gift I didn't deserve.

I didn't know how to have a boyfriend. Giulio was my first. But I would do anything for him, go anywhere with him. Whatever he needed, I would keep him safe. If he wanted to run drugs in Málaga, then I would be right by his side, making sure no one fucked with him.

And Enzo D'Agostino would keep my secret in exchange for me keeping his.

I would take that to my grave. No one would ever know, especially not Giulio. How could he love the man who almost killed his father?

"What are you thinking about?" Giulio finished his wine and set the glass on the table. "You drifted off somewhere."

I evaded the question. "What will you do if Nikolai says no to Málaga?" The pakhan hadn't given us an answer before we left his yacht. He told Giulio he'd think it over and "be in touch."

"I'm not sure. We can't take on Martiñez and Golubev alone. And the 'Ndrangheta isn't established there, so I can't go to them for help. Maybe choose another city? I can keep going with the low-level sales."

"I thought you wanted to put down roots."

"I do." He leaned back in his chair and crossed his leg. "What do you think we should do? Where do you want to go?"

"Wherever you decide. As long as we're together, I don't care."

"That is a very sweet answer. Will you still accept assassination jobs?"

"Not if you don't want me to."

"You would give that up for me?"

How was he even surprised? "Of course. I'm not going to disappear for a few weeks at a time and leave you unprotected. If you're doing something dangerous, then I'm sticking by your side."

The side of his mouth curled. "You love me."

"I do. Very much."

"Va bene." He checked his wristwatch. "It's time to lay down and fuck, no?"

"You have a one track mind," I said. Then I decided to tease him. "Maybe we should discuss tonight. Make a plan for how we will kill Nino after the sun goes down."

"Wrong." Rising, he came around the table and wrapped a hand around the nape of my neck. He squeezed. "Right now you are going to swallow my dick and see if you can make me come faster than you did in Málaga."

Bossy Giulio never failed to get my cock hard. The warmth spread through me in waves, my skin tightening and pulling, and I was helpless to resist him. Just like from the first moment I saw him on that Siderno street.

We spent the rest of the afternoon in bed, the warm Sicilian breeze blowing in through the windows while we explored each other's bodies. I never wanted it to end.

———

THE CLUB WAS CROWDED and too loud. I covered my mouth as I yawned. It was late, and I would much rather be back in the apartment with Giulio.

Instead, I was still trailing Nino Buscetta around Palermo.

Nino was smarter than I thought. I expected him to visit his mistress, but he hadn't. He was never alone, well guarded. If I didn't find a weakness soon, I'd have to get creative. That could have serious consequences for Giulio, and I was trying to avoid it. I needed to do this carefully, quietly. Then I could get Giulio safely out of the country.

Right now, Nino and his crew were up in the VIP area above the dance floor. He was snorting coke off a mirror on the table, surrounded by several women. Giacomo, his younger brother, was also there, looking annoyed. Armed guards kept watch over the group, which meant I was in the shadows, trying to blend in.

Nino leaned back and wiped his nose, beckoning a woman to crawl onto his lap. Obeying, she started kissing him, their mouths attacking one another.

Movement near the entrance caught my eye. A man wearing a baseball cap and a messenger bag over his shoulder was walking in. My muscles locked in pure shock.

Fuck! What was he doing here?

I surged forward. Wrapping my arm around Giulio, I began towing him toward the shadows. He was stiff in my arms, but didn't fight.

When we reached the wall, I shoved him against it. "Che cazzo?" I snarled over the beat of the thumping music. "We agreed you would stay in the apartment."

"I can't wait any longer. It's driving me crazy. Besides, I can help you."

"Have you forgotten? Your face, the cameras. You'll be recognized and they'll come after you for the rest of your life."

He pointed to the cap on his head. "Don't worry so much, assassino. No one will recognize me."

My hands curled into fists. "I have it under control."

"You're exhausted and Nino is running you ragged all over Palermo. And I'm not the type of man to sit at home and let someone else handle my problems. No, we do this together. Tonight."

"Cristo santo," I muttered and rubbed my eyes. "I am trying to do this carefully. I don't want it traced back to you. I want you to finally be free."

"I know." He grabbed my face in his palms. "And I appreciate it. But let me worry about that. You don't have to do this alone anymore."

I rolled my shoulders. I heard the words, but they still didn't seem real. For so long I'd been on my own. I indulged in the occasional hookup here and there, but there hadn't been a boyfriend or girlfriend. No partners of any kind. It was strange to consider myself as part of a couple now.

But Giulio was here. It *was* real.

And I would do anything to keep him.

"Fine," I said. "But don't let the cameras catch your face. Look relaxed, like we are talking."

"We are talking," Giulio said, sliding closer and rubbing his hands on my chest. "You watch Nino and I'll watch you."

I shifted closer, needing more of his hands, more of his heat, as I kept my attention on the VIP area. "I thought you came to help."

"What is he doing up there?"

"Coke and pussy."

"What about the father?"

Sasha has been trying to find Don Buscetta, but he was like a ghost. "Sasha isn't sure he's even in Sicily."

"He must talk to Nino."

"Nino goes through burner phones like tissues."

"I see Nino's brother is here tonight."

Nino was the one in charge, but Giacomo was the enforcer. All reports were that he carried out Nino's orders, kept the others in line. "He looks bored. And angry."

We stood in silence for a few minutes. "Did you at least bring a gun in that bag?" I asked.

"Ma dai." He sounded annoyed, so I took it to mean that he did have a gun on him.

"Stay where you are," I murmured. "They're all leaving."

Giulio moved in and began kissing my throat. While this succeeded in hiding his face from the Buscettas, it distracted the shit out of me. "Stop that."

"I can't. Being in this club makes me want you on your knees again."

A smile tugged at my lips as I watched Nino and his crew head toward the door. I didn't want to lose them.

"Come on," I told Giulio. "Pull your hat low and keep your head down."

We left the club to find Nino and Giacomo facing off on the sidewalk. I quickly dragged Giulio against the side of the building, making sure to keep his back to the brothers, and began nuzzling his throat. "Listen," I mumbled against his skin, watching Nino from under my lashes.

" . . . am I supposed to do about this meeting?" Giacomo snarled.

"You'll be fine, fratello." Nino was bouncing on his feet, unable to keep still from all the coke in his system. "Use your head for once. I know there's a brain in there somewhere." Nino pressed his finger against his brother's forehead.

Giacomo shoved Nino's hand aside. "Fuck off. This is your deal, not mine. You can't leave."

"You are so needy," Nino said with a roll of his eyes. "Maybe it's time I give you more responsibility. Then we'll see if you sink or swim."

"You're thinking with your dick."

"You should try it sometime. That is, if your dick still works." Nino and his men laughed like this was hilarious.

Giacomo said nothing, just glared as Nino got into the back seat of his car. Two of Nino's men got in the front. When Nino's car pulled away, Giacomo stormed back into the club.

"They're gone," I said. "This way."

When we found my motorbike, I tossed Giulio the helmet. "Hop on." I didn't wait for him to argue or complain. I got on the bike and started it up. "Hurry."

When Giulio climbed on behind me, I zoomed off. I knew where Nino was going. At least, I suspected based on his conversation with

Giacomo. And Giulio and I had camped out at the mistress's house for three nights now, so I was well familiar with the route.

Soon I could see Nino's car. We stopped at a traffic light and Giulio rubbed my stomach absently. Almost caressing me. I reached back to clutch his hip, needing to feel him. I couldn't ever get enough. He was my greatest weakness and my greatest strength.

The light changed color and we started up. Eventually Nino's car turned down his mistress's street. I kept going, not wanting to alert his guards that we were following.

I turned down the next side street, then cut off the engine. Giulio took off the helmet and replaced it with his cap. "What's the plan?" he asked.

"We'll wait ten minutes. By then, Nino should be distracted and his men bored."

"Or he could be finished in ten minutes."

"Not with all the coke in his system," I said. I opened the bike's storage compartment and took out two pistols, silencers, masks, and a few magazines. "Let's get closer. We'll deal with his guards first. Then we go inside."

"How do you want to do this? You said the car windows were bullet proof. We have to get them out of the car to kill them."

I took two lemons out of my coat.

His brows shot up. "Are you serious? In the exhaust pipes?" He pressed his lips together, eyes now filled with laughter. "Are we teenage boys again?"

"Laugh if you want, but it works. And when the car stalls they will get out to investigate."

"I am beginning to see the assassin's tricks." He closed the distance between us to press a kiss to my mouth. "I like them."

I shook my head at his foolishness. "Andiamo, principe."

Our steps were silent as we wound our way onto the mistress's street. The villas here were small, but nice. Private. They weren't piled on top of one another. Lights were on in most of them, but we finally came across a home that was completely dark. So we slipped around the side of it and crept through the gardens.

The mistress's street was quiet. I put out my hand, telling Giulio to stop. Then I slipped on my mask and watched as he did the same. We pulled on latex gloves. Guns were checked and loaded. My heart rate was steady and slow, my breathing even. I was as calm as could be expected with Giulio by my side.

I touched the cornicello around my neck for luck, then started forward. As I suspected, Nino's guards were waiting in his car with the engine on. A foolish mistake. But no doubt Nino didn't want his men listening to him as he fucked his comare.

Like we'd been carrying out hits together our entire lives, Giulio and I were in perfect sync as we approached the car. We stayed low, kept out of sight of the mirrors. Giulio waited, hidden behind a parked car, as I moved toward the back of Nino's sedan.

I slipped a lemon in the left exhaust pipe. It was a tight fit, but I got it in. Then I quickly moved to the right and shoved the other lemon in.

Then I just paused, listening.

The car engine sputtered and died.

Talking inside the car. Bodies shifting. They tried in vain to restart the car a couple of times, but the engine would die soon after coming to life. I gripped the pistol loosely, my breathing steady. I was cool and clear headed. I knew exactly how this would go down. I could see it in my head.

One car door opened. The driver's side. A man got out. Before he could close the door, a puff of air went by and the man fell to the ground. The other guard in the car would now know something was wrong. He would be armed and expecting trouble.

The door opened. I looked under the car, waiting to see his feet. Instead, a pistol appeared. I rolled just as a pop sounded. The bullet missed me by centimeters. Gun braced in my palm, I surged to my feet and raced around the side of the car. Toward the open door.

The guard was just sitting up, trying to get around for a second shot. It was too late. I was there, right in position. I squeezed the trigger. The bullet entered his forehead square between the eyes. He fell back, dead.

Giulio was on the other side of the car. I couldn't see anything but his eyes, which were glittering in delight. "Fuck yes, assassino."

I shook my head. Only the son of il Diavolo would get excited at murder.

We met up in front of the car. "The front door. Me first. Let's go."

CHAPTER TWENTY-ONE

Giulio

Alessio was fucking impressive. I'd seen it before with the Sicilians, but my man was cool and collected. Dangerous. Not to be fucked with. I couldn't see his face, but I knew he was wearing that stern expression he got when he concentrated intently on something.

I was going to fuck him so hard as soon we finished with Nino.

First, we shoved the guards back in the car and closed the doors. There was blood on the street, but that couldn't be helped. At least there weren't dead bodies on the ground to draw attention while we were dealing with Nino.

The street was quiet as we crept toward the front of the mistress's villa. There was a wall surrounding the front, which would provide cover for whatever happened inside.

Alessio didn't know it, but I didn't intend for this to be quick. No, I had a different plan in mind for Nino.

I followed Alessio up the walk. He moved carefully, silently. My heart was pounding, but I bet Alessio's wasn't even beating fast. Each step was smooth and precise, his body on alert.

He tried the knob. Unsurprisingly, it was locked. I was ready to kick the door in, but Alessio put up a hand. He removed a tension tool and pick from the pocket of his cargos and bent in front of the lock. Within thirty seconds, the deadbolt unlatched.

Madonna. He could pick locks, too?

Lifting his pistol, he very slowly turned the latch and opened the door. He angled to each side, left and right, to check that it was clear. Then he crept into the house.

I was right behind him.

Our shoes made no sound on the tile floor. We could easily hear the rhythmic pounding coming from upstairs.

Alessio motioned me left and then he went right. I checked each room, making sure Nino didn't have anyone in the house. There could be kids or another relative. Who the fuck knew?

We rejoined each other in the kitchen. The bottom floor was clear. Alessio pointed upstairs. I nodded.

I stayed behind him as we took the stairs, going slow. At the landing, we paused. The bedroom door was ajar.

"Scopami forte, Nino!"

Deep grunts grew louder, the headboard rocking, hitting the wall. The sound told me the position of the bed in the room.

She moaned. "Sì, il grosso toro!" *Big bull.*

Alessio paused by the door and gestured for me to go right. I assumed he meant that he would then go left. I didn't like catching him by surprise, but I would handle this my way. My need for revenge demanded it.

I held up my hand and pointed to myself. Alessio's gray gaze went wide and he shook his head. He now knew I was about to go rogue.

When he tried to grab my arm, I evaded him and strode inside the bedroom. Nino was on top, still in his dress shirt with his pants around his thighs. The woman was completely naked. "Nino! How is that cocaine dick working out for you? Looks like it's a lot of work."

The woman screamed and Nino scrambled off her, about to lunge for his gun. I was by his side in an instant, pressing the barrel of my pistol into his head. "Don't fucking move, stronzo."

His mistress kept screaming. But she couldn't leave because Alessio was blocking her side of the bed. "Lock her in the bathroom," I told him without looking away from Nino. "And tell her to shut the fuck up."

Alessio didn't question it. He got the mistress off the bed and led her to the bathroom. I no longer paid attention. My focus was entirely on Nino.

He glared at me. "Who the fuck are you and what do you want?"

With my free hand, I reached and pulled the mask off my face. Nino didn't immediately react. He was panting, his dick still out. His pupils were huge, the black nearly swallowing up his whole iris. Still high as shit, then.

"Don't recognize me, coglione?" I asked. "You've been looking for me. You sent six of your friends to Scotland to visit me."

His nostrils flared. "Ravazzani. You little shit."

Out of the corner of my eye I saw Alessio there. "Find me a chair," I called out. "I want Nino to have a seat for our chat."

Nino sneered at me. "What are you planning? To call your father and have him come help you?"

He was either incredibly stupid or trying to rattle me into making a mistake. I smirked at him. "If my father were here, you'd already be dead. Are you so anxious to die, Nino?"

His skin flushed and his chest heaved with the force of his breaths. "You won't kill me. It will start a war if you do."

A chair hit the carpet with a thump. I motioned with the pistol. "Get up. Get in the chair."

I eased back but kept the gun trained on him. He slowly rose from the bed, hitched up his pants, and walked to the chair. Alessio was right there, his pistol on Nino, as well.

"Is this your boyfriend, *finocchio*?" Nino asked, using a slur for a gay man. I hated that word.

"He's the man who will put a bullet in your head if you don't do what I say. Sit the fuck down," I snapped.

Nino threw himself into the chair, his expression belligerent. "This is unwise. You don't want to piss me off, cucciolo." *Puppy.*

I reached into my pocket. "Here." I held out a bunch of zip ties to Alessio. "Strap him to the chair."

"Che cazzo—" Nino stood up, his face now showing signs of concern.

With a palm on his chest, I shoved him back down. "Don't move or I'll shoot you in the fucking face."

I could almost hear Alessio's disapproval as he took the restraints from me, but he said nothing. With efficiency, he began securing Nino's wrists and ankles to the wooden chair. Nino threatened me the entire time, telling me what a mistake I was making. How his men would come after me if I hurt him, blah blah blah. I didn't pay him any attention.

I finally had the man responsible for Paolo's death in front of me.

And I was going to make him suffer.

When he finished with the restraints, Alessio leaned against the wall and folded his arms. Though his body appeared relaxed, his gaze was alert. Hyper-vigilant.

"How long do I have?" I asked him as Nino continued to rant.

"Five minutes," Alessio said. "Maybe one or two more."

I would need to be quick, then.

From another pocket I retrieved a switchblade. Flicked it open. "You took something from me four years ago. Something very valuable."

Nino's chest heaved as he struggled in his bindings. "I don't know what you're talking about. I've only ever dealt with your father."

Ice settled in my chest, a cold resolve to do what needed to be done. I felt no sympathy, no kindness for this piece of shit. "You tried to kill me in Belgium. Your men planted that car bomb."

The reality began to sink into Nino's coke-addled brain. I could see the surprise and guilt in his expression. Yet he still lied. "I don't know anything about a bomb. Ma dai, why would I try to kill you?"

"Because you're a stupid, greedy motherfucker, I assume. Did you think killing me would weaken my father? That you'd be able to take over some of his business?"

"Don Ravazzani is an ally, a friend. There is no animosity between us."

I held the knife up to his cheek. "Cazzata. I want the truth, Nino. Tell me the truth and I'll let you and your woman live. We'll leave and you can go back to fucking her with that pathetic dick of yours. Just tell me why you did it."

"I already told you—"

I swiped the blade across his cheek, causing him to hiss. A trail of red ran down the side of his face. "I don't want to hear lies." I moved the blade to the other side of his face. "The truth, or you'll have a matching scar on this cheek."

"You have to believe me." He tried to edge away from the knife. "I am not responsible for what happened in Bruges."

I cut his other cheek, deeper this time. The coppery scent of blood perfumed the air. "I never said it was in Bruges. Sloppy, Nino. Very sloppy."

Shifting, I pointed the tip of the switchblade at his crotch. "Last chance, Nino. Or this *finocchio* is going to take your dick off."

He began struggling in earnest now. "Don't fucking touch me, you *frocio*!" Another slur, equally offensive.

I honestly didn't want anything to do with Nino's dick, but his repeated insults were making me think I should cut it off while he was still breathing.

I sliced the tops of each thigh, then I pressed the knife into his balls. He squeaked and writhed in the chair. "Tell me," I shouted in his face. "Or I will take off your balls and shove them in your mouth."

"Your father," he panted. "We had a deal. He reneged."

"When?"

"After the business with D'Agostino in Napoli. To rescue his wife."

I nodded and eased the knife away from his balls. "Va bene. See? It is good to tell these things, no?"

He slumped in the chair, no doubt thinking this was over.

In a blink, I lunged and rammed the knife into his side. Nino sucked in a sharp breath, his body going stiff. Putting my mouth near his ear, I said, "I watched as someone I cared about blew up in front of my eyes. So now I'm going to make you scream, testa di cazzo."

I jammed the blade deeper and he howled. Then I yanked it out of his flesh, only to shove it in again, slightly higher. Nino shouted to the ceiling, while blood dripped all over my hand.

"I'm going to poke so many holes in you," I told him, "that you will bleed out slowly on the floor."

"Please. I can give you money. Cars. Whatever you want."

"I come from the most powerful family in Italia, and you think to buy me off?" I grabbed his hair, slammed his head back, and snarled, "I'm a fucking Ravazzani. And you're about to learn what happens to the men who cross us."

I went to work with the blade and the screams echoed off the walls. Then Nino was incapable of any coherent noise at all because I'd removed his tongue.

By the time we left a few minutes later, Nino was slumped in the chair, eyes vacant, his body lifeless. Blood formed a dark ring on the carpet beneath him.

And I felt as if a chapter in my life had finally closed.

———

Alessio

WE LEFT the villa and hurried into the night. Once we reached the other street, we removed our masks and gloves, then walked to the motor bike. No one was around. No one sounded an alarm. Still, I wouldn't breathe easy until I had Giulio safely away.

At the bike, we stashed the guns and then sped off into traffic. Giulio held on to my waist, his fingers digging in tight. Was he alright? I couldn't tell. I'd tried not to intervene as he sliced Nino, knowing Giulio needed to purge his own demons.

He had to be shaken after learning his father's business dealings had caused Paolo's death. That was not an easy pill to swallow. I hoped carrying out his revenge eased some of his grief and guilt.

But I wasn't happy that he hadn't confided in me earlier. It would've been nice to know that torturing and killing Nino slowly was on the agenda.

"Here," he suddenly yelled in my ear. "Turn in!"

It was a small park surrounded by trees. Che cazzo?

I did as he asked, even though I didn't understand. Maybe he was sick? Some soldiers puked after causing a gruesome death. Not me, but I had seen it happen with others.

I pulled toward the back of the parking lot and let the engine idle, my feet flat on the ground. There were four other cars in the lot.

Giulio swung his leg off the bike. "Turn it off and lock it. Then come on."

Without waiting, he strode down the path. I locked the bike and started after him. What were we doing? Again, he had an agenda that he wasn't sharing with me. We needed to have a serious conversation about that.

He veered off the path, toward the trees. I followed, checking our surroundings. No one else was here, despite the cars in the lot. Where was he going?

Hands closed over my shoulders and I was shoved into a tree trunk. I grunted as my back met bark. "What is happening?"

His fingers were already unbuttoning my cargos. "I'm fucking you. What does it look like?"

My dick was not complaining. Suddenly, I was thickening, desire unfurling inside me. "Here?"

He pressed in close, his voice thick with lust. His trousers were covered with dried blood and it was not a turn off. Not in the least.

"Here," he said. "I can't wait any longer."

My pants were around my hips and his hand captured my shaft. He squeezed and I grunted, pleasure streaking through me.

"There's that big dick I love," he murmured against my throat.

"God, principe."

"You are so fucking hot, Alessione. You don't even know." He spun me around, and I put my palms on the tree to keep from falling. He worked my cargos lower, then I heard him dig in his pockets.

"You don't need a condom," I said over my shoulder.

"I'm not. I'm getting lube."

He brought lube? Before I could ask about it, cold dribbled over the crack of my ass, distracting me.

I heard slick sounds as he readied his cock. Then he was there, against my hole. Grabbing my hips, he angled me lower and the pressure increased. I took a deep breath, pushed out, and his crown slipped inside.

My vision went white for a few seconds, pain stealing through me. I didn't care. I knew what would soon follow, and the discomfort was worth it.

"Shhh. Let me in, mio bello assassino. That's it." He rocked his hips, sliding deeper each time. "I'll give you what you need."

I shoved back, taking more of him. "Scopami forte, il grosso toro."

He groaned and rested his forehead against my back. "Stronzo. Do not make me laugh right now."

With three thrusts he was all the way inside. I braced myself against the tree. He began fucking me then, long strokes of his perfect dick that rattled my teeth. Each brush over my prostate had me seeing stars, like an electric charge to my balls.

"So. Fucking. Hot." He punctuated each word with a thrust. "Watching you back there made my dick *so hard*."

Leaves suddenly crunched and I looked over. A stranger was there, lurking. He had his dick in his hand, watching Giulio and I fuck while he masturbated. It became clear why there were cars in the parking lot at this hour. This was *that* sort of public park.

His gaze locked on to where Giulio was ramming my ass, the stranger pulled and twisted his fat cock. I hadn't been watched before. I wasn't sure how I felt about it.

What did Giulio and I look like to this man? Rutting animals in heat? Desperate and wild to fuck? I arched to take more, encouraging Giulio to go faster.

"He's watching you take my cock like a good slut," Giulio crooned, apparently unconcerned about our audience. Hardly surprising, as he'd racked up an astonishing number of public blow jobs in nightclubs. But for me, this was a first.

"You like it, don't you?" he said and continued those long strokes. "You like being watched. Admit it."

At the words my body clenched, balls drawing tight. No one had ever gotten me off faster than this man. My dick hung down between my legs, waving wildly as Giulio pounded me. And the angle of his thrusts was pure heaven, my prostate lighting up with each drag. Tiny explosions rippled through me from head to toe.

"Tell me," Giulio barked. "Admit it and I'll let you come."

"Minchia!" I sucked in air, gasping and writhing against the bark. I was so close. My fingertips dug into the tree.

"*Un puttano*, no? Dimmi, amore."

Whether it was the dirty name or the endearment, I couldn't hold back. Come shot out my dick, my muscles locking, and I clung to the tree like a life preserver. The edges of my vision blacked out, helpless as I trembled and shook.

Giulio thickened and I could feel him shoot inside me. Warm jets filled me, so much that I could feel it already running down my inner thighs. He shouted up to the sky.

When I could focus again, the man in the bushes was gone, but there was a wet spot on the ground where he'd been standing.

Panting, Giulio rested on my back, his cock still buried inside me. "Cristo. So fucking good, assassino."

Yes, it had been. I wished it wasn't over.

He pulled out and I winced. I would definitely feel it tomorrow. Straightening, I started to take off my boot to get to my sock—an old trick from the military days. A way to clean up quickly when a cloth wasn't available.

"What are you doing?" Giulio asked as he hitched up his jeans.

"Wiping up with my sock."

"The fuck you are." He grabbed my hands. "I want you sticky with my come the entire ride back to our apartment."

"Giulio," I sighed.

He cupped my cheek. "Do not argue." Then he kissed me softly, sweetly. If only I could stop time, I would have this moment right here, forever. Sore from his dick, filled with his come, his mouth on mine. It was perfect.

When we broke apart, he held something up. "Look at what I have."

A phone. I didn't understand. "Whose is it?"

"Nino's."

"You stole his phone?"

"Yes, and we're going to take it to someone who can crack it."

I buttoned my cargos, wincing at the wet mess in my briefs.

He reached back and squeezed my ass. "That's fucking hot. I like the idea of you sitting in my come."

Of course he did. But I needed to talk about what happened with Nino. I was still angry.

I grabbed the nape of Giulio's neck and held him tight. "Do not ever surprise me like that again. I didn't know what you were planning back there. It is dangerous for one member of a team to work alone, capisce? We stick together."

He pressed his forehead to my chin and let me take his weight. "Perdonami, assassino. I won't ever do it again."

"Why didn't you tell me?"

"I didn't want you to talk me out of it. And it was something I had to do."

For Paolo. I understood. And I wasn't jealous. But I didn't like surprises. I liked plans and sticking to those plans.

I kissed the top of his head. "I will never try to stop you from doing what you feel is necessary. My only purpose in life is to keep you safe. Do not make that more difficult. If something happened to you . . . ." I let out a shuddering breath. "I could not handle it, principe."

"I won't. Te lo prometto, amore."

As we walked back to the bike, I studied him. "You're okay?"

One eyebrow shot up. "What do you mean? I got my revenge and you gave me an amazing fuck in the woods. Why wouldn't I be okay?"

A smile tugged at my lips. So much for worrying about him. I should've known the former mafioso prince could handle violence.

"You were worried about me," he said, bumping his shoulder against mine. "That's cute."

He slung a leg over the bike, looking like the hottest advertisement for designer cologne or clothing. Fuck, I would buy anything this man tried to sell.

He waved his hand to hurry me along. "Andiamo. We have places to go, Alessione."

I got on and started the engine. The wet come in my pants was uncomfortable, but a reminder of what we'd just done in the woods. I didn't hate it. "Where are we going?"

"You'll see."

CHAPTER TWENTY-TWO

Giulio

Ravazzani Estate, Siderno

I didn't warn them I was coming.

I wanted it to be a surprise. I hadn't been home in almost six months and that visit lasted less than two days. Now I could stay as long as I wanted. The feeling was surreal.

Alessio and I slowly approached the massive gate. I was behind the wheel of our rented car, which would allow the guards to see me first.

Four men surrounded the car, guns drawn, and I recognized only one. "Cugino!" I called out to Benito. "They still have you out here?"

My cousin's eyes went wide as he hurried over. "Madre di dio! I didn't know you were coming."

We slapped hands. "How have you been?"

"Good, good. You going up to the castello?" He pulled out his phone.

"Yes. Is he there?"

"I'll find out. He'll want to know who you brought."

Right. "Bennie, meet Alessandro Ricci. Alessio, this is my cousin, Benito."

Alessio gave a terse nod, his hands on his knees. To anyone else, he might appear relaxed. But I could see the tension in his shoulders, the way his fingertips pressed into his jeans. Was he nervous?

"Ricci," Benito greeted, his phone up to his ear. Turning away, he started speaking a rapid string of information to whoever was on the other end of the line. Zio Marco, most likely. He was the head of security for my father. At least, he was the last time I was here.

Benito motioned to the guard house and the gate creaked open. "Marco will meet you at the door," he told us.

"Grazie. We'll hang later?"

Benito slapped my shoulder through the car window. "Definitely."

We drove through the gate and started up the long drive. The place hadn't changed much since the last time I was here. Olive and bergamot trees. Rolling hills. Bright sunshine and crumbling stone. Such was the beauty of a four-hundred-year-old estate.

The castello loomed in the distance. As it grew closer, the hollow empty feeling in my chest disappeared. This was home, no matter where I traveled to. The dirt and gravel were part of me. I hadn't realized how much I'd missed it.

Alessio whistled as he stared out the car window. "And you gave this up, principe? Ma dai."

To live the life I wanted? Without having to hide or pretend? It had been an easy decision.

Though it hadn't worked out the way I intended. Paolo was dead and now I was planning on throwing my hat in with the Bratva. Fausto would have a thing or two to say about that, no doubt. But I didn't want to live in my father's shadow. I wanted to build something of my own.

Something with Alessio. Something that was *ours*.

The front door swung open as I shut off the engine. Zio Marco walked out onto the steps. His arms were at his sides, but I knew he was armed. He didn't take any chances with security at the castello. Not since my father was almost killed.

I got out and walked over to him. "You put on weight?" I asked, even though he appeared the exact same size as he always did. Zio Marco prided himself on his physical condition. "You look heavier than the last time I saw you."

His gaze narrowed on me. Then his face broke out into a wide grin. "Still pushing my buttons, you little shit." He pulled me into a fierce hug. "It is good to see you, Giulio."

I returned the hug. "And you, Zio."

We broke apart and Zio Marco was watching Alessio, who was getting our bags out of the car. I motioned my man forward. When he reached me, I placed my hand on the small of his back. "Zio Marco, this is Alessio."

Marco nodded once, then shifted to stare at me. "He's been sick with worry."

Guilt arrowed through my chest. "He'll understand once I explain."

"Doubtful. Come on. Let's get this over with." He tilted his chin toward the car. "Sniper, grab the bags."

It shouldn't have surprised me that Zio Marco knew of Alessio's occupation. But it did.

Alessio grabbed our small bags off the ground and brought them inside. Marco pointed near the stairs. "Leave them there. He's outside at the paddock."

At this time of day? I was surprised Fausto wasn't in his office.

Alessio's head swiveled as he took in the inside of the castello. I was used to it, the old tapestries, dark furniture and priceless paintings. It was a mixture of both old and new, a symbol of the Ravazzani tradition, but also of my father's wealth and power.

We stepped out onto the terrace, then started up the path. We passed Zia's vegetable garden, which was thriving thanks to her green thumb. The winery and vineyards were off to the left, but we veered to the right, toward the farm. My half brother loved riding horses. No doubt Fausto was overseeing Rafe's instruction, molding Rafe into the perfect successor.

"We heard you were in Greece, then nothing," Zio Marco remarked. "Where did you go?"

"Isle of Canna. It's in the Scottish Hebrides."

"Sounds fucking cold."

I chuckled. "It was."

Alessio said nothing, just walked alongside me. I had the strangest urge to hold his hand, but this boyfriend thing was new. I wasn't sure yet how he would feel about public displays of affection. Unable to help myself, I brushed the back of my hand along his arm.

He gave me a strained smile.

Marco pointed at the paddock. "There you go." As I passed, he grabbed my arm. "After you finish here, go and apologize to Zia."

"I will." I didn't want to mention that I'd spoken to Zia from Scotland. She wouldn't be angry with me.

Unlike Frankie. My father's wife was going to be furious.

Fausto was leaning on the fence, watching Rafe's pony walk around the paddock with the trainer. My half brother was in the saddle, looking like a professional rider, even at the age of three. Fausto's back was to us, so he didn't see me approach. But Marco would've already told him I was at the gate. Nothing happened on the estate without Fausto's knowledge.

Rafe noticed me first. "Fratello!" he shouted, startling his pony, who began dancing sideways. Instantly, the trainer grabbed the reins.

Fausto turned, his gaze sweeping over Alessio before landing on me. He frowned.

Rafe was through the fence and sprinting toward us. I bent down to capture him and swung him up by his legs, holding him upside down. "Signorino! Come stai?"

He laughed as I let his arms dangle toward the ground. "Did you come to watch me ride, Giulio? Everyone says I'm very good."

"Then I look forward to seeing it." I held him up in front of Alessio's face. "Say hello to Alessio, Rafe."

"Hello," Rafe said, laughing.

"Basta, Raffaele," Fausto called. "Get back to your lesson and let me speak with your brother."

"He's in a bad mood," Rafe stage-whispered as I put him down. When his feet hit the dirt, he ran back inside the fence to his pony.

My father strolled over, his brows pulled low. "You can't call to let us know you are coming?"

"Mi dispiace, Papà," I said.

Moving in, he kissed both my cheeks, then enveloped me in a strong hug. He smelled the same, like my childhood, and I sank into his embrace. My father was unbreakable, a force of nature. To the rest of the world he was a terrifying mafia don, il Diavolo, but to me he was the man who'd raised me since my mother's death. The man who inducted me into the 'ndrina. The man who'd cried when I left.

"I thought you were dead," he whispered. "Don't ever do that to me again. Ti amo, figlio."

"Ti amo, Papà. I'll explain, I promise. I had my reasons. Here, I want you to meet someone."

He sighed and released me. "You and I will have a long talk later." He shifted to glare at Alessio. It wasn't a welcoming expression on his face. "And who is this?"

"Papà, meet il mio ragazzo, Alessio Ricci."

Fausto didn't smile or twitch. Just stared. "The sniper."

Alessio didn't move, his body unnaturally still. "Sì."

My father extended a hand to Alessio. "Alessandro. Your reputation precedes you."

Alessio shook my father's hand. "Alessio, please. It's an honor, Don Ravazzani."

Fausto glanced over his shoulder. "Raffaele, I'm going inside. I need to speak with your brother."

"You already spoke to him!" Rafe shouted. "Stay and watch me ride, Papà."

"I need to work. Be good for Bruno," my father said, referring to the groom giving the lesson.

"I'll bring him in once we finish, Don Ravazzani!" Bruno called.

My father raised his hand in acknowledgment, then turned and began leading us toward the castello. The three of us walked side by side on the path, with me in the middle. My father clasped his hands behind his back, his stride slow. I knew he was gathering his thoughts.

"After Santorini," he started. "What happened?"

"I went to Scotland. A small island in the north."

"And you couldn't call?"

"No. It wasn't safe."

He made a dismissive noise in his throat. "Have I taught you nothing?"

"I wanted to be careful. And then . . . ."

"And then?" he prompted when I didn't finish.

And then we tracked the Sicilians and went after Nino. "Can we discuss this later?"

"You and I will speak shortly. I expect answers."

We came up the path. The castello was bathed in a golden yellow, casting the stone in almost an orange color. It was stunningly beautiful, and my chest expanded with pride. Though it wasn't my legacy any longer, it was still in my blood.

The terrace door opened and a woman stepped out into the sun.

An obviously pregnant Frankie. And she was glaring at me.

"She's very pissed at you," my father said quietly. "Be prepared to grovel."

He strode onto the terrace to meet her, bending to kiss her mouth. "Dolcezza, go easy on him," I heard him say. Looking over his shoulder, Fausto said, "Sniper, with me."

Wait, why did he wish to speak to Alessio? Alarm bells began going off in my brain. "Papà, wait. I will come with you."

"No. Speak with Francesca first. I will speak with your ragazzo."

"Ragazzo!" Frankie's eyes filled with disbelief and hurt. "What the fuck, G?"

"Grovel, figlio mio," my father called from inside the castello.

Alessio

MY MOUTH WAS DRIER than the Kandahar desert as I followed Fausto Ravazzani into his home. Did he know? I could hardly breathe through the panic twisting in my throat.

Was I about to die?

I tried to distract myself with the surroundings. The castello was beautiful, exactly what one would expect for old world royalty like

Ravazzani. And Giulio gave all this up? He must've loved Paolo very much to leave.

"In here." Ravazzani held open a door for me.

I went in and found Marco Ravazzani sitting in a chair beside a large desk. I waited, unsure where to go. Was I allowed to sit? Was he going to shoot me here on the Persian carpet?

Ravazzani walked behind his desk and sat down. "Take a seat."

I lowered myself into one of the armchairs facing the desk. I kept quiet, waiting, as Ravazzani leaned back in his chair. He steepled his fingers and rested them against his lips. His ice blue gaze never left my face. The color was exactly like Giulio's, but these eyes held no warmth or sparkle. No hint of welcome.

I focused on keeping my heart rate low, as I did when I was on a job. Something told me this man would smell nervousness a kilometer away. But the longer the silence went on, the more worried I became.

"Do you think I don't know who you are?" Ravazzani finally said.

I didn't speak, unsure where this was going. Trepidation crawled across my neck, spiders of apprehension, but I held onto the hope that this wasn't about the assassination attempt.

That hope withered as Ravazzani continued. "You see, I have learned a lot about Enzo D'Agostino since he began dating my sister-in-law. And Enzo, he likes the best. He has the money to afford it."

I focused on pulling air into my lungs. *In and out. In and out.*

"For a long time I didn't believe it was you," Fausto said. "After all, you *missed*."

The last word sliced through the room. My stomach plummeted. He *knew*. Fuck.

But could he prove it?

"But to whom else would D'Agostino entrust such an important job?" Ravazzani asked. "There is no one. So we searched for you. A ghost, impossible to find, they said. So I used the one clue I had at my disposal."

Fausto slowly opened his desk drawer and set a glass vial on the desk. Inside was a bullet. My *specially made* bullet.

No, it was impossible.

I could feel everything I'd hoped for, everything I'd dreamed of, disappearing like tendrils of smoke. I couldn't breathe. Blood rushed in my ears as I quietly waited for the blade to drop and chop off my head.

He gestured to the vial. "One man knew that bullet. Crafted by hand in Germany to exact specifications. Your specifications, Alessandro."

I stared at him, barely blinking. Why had I come here with Giulio? I should've known this secret wouldn't stay buried.

Now I would lose him.

But Ravazzani wasn't finished. Leaning forward, his voice turned soft, threaded with violence. "I also know you were hired to assassinate Guilio. So tell me how a man who nearly killed me and accepted a hit on my son is welcome in my home? Around my fucking family?"

He was shouting by the time he finished speaking, his fury a terrifying thing.

With the rope tightening around my neck, I had nothing to lose. I needed to plead my case. "I saved your son's life. I helped him kill the Sicilians responsible for the car bomb. They came to Scotland to kill him."

"Are you honestly so stupid as to think this balances the scales, stronzo?"

No. I knew it was unforgivable, and I would lose Giulio the instant he learned of it. Which would be soon.

"I'm an assassin for hire. You were just a job, just a target," I said. "Nothing more, nothing less. And I can't change what happened."

"So why accept the job to assassinate my son?"

I couldn't answer. D'Agostino had forced me into the hit on Giulio, but I would honor our agreement. Even if it no longer benefitted me.

And it didn't matter why. I'd gone after Giulio with the intention of killing him. Hunted him through various cities, watched his every move. I couldn't deny it.

"I had my reasons," I said.

Fausto exchanged an undecipherable look with Marco. The consigliere turned to me, his eyes hard with loathing. "It would be wise for you to tell us everything, sniper. Including who you were working for."

I didn't back down. "I never reveal the identity of a client."

The moment stretched. Fausto and Marco didn't speak, just continued to watch me. It was an old interrogation tactic, sweating out your opponent, but I wouldn't break.

I focused on Ravazzani and counted my breaths. Squeezed the armrests of the chair. Pressed my toes into the carpet. Concentrating on these small details kept me grounded and calm.

Finally, Ravazzani spoke. "We searched for you for years. But you were gone. *Poof.* Then you trail my son from Málaga to Santorini to Scotland. Now you're here. In my home. And I am supposed to believe you no longer wish to kill him, that you no longer wish to kill me? Do you take us for fools?"

"I love Giulio. I would rather cut off my arm than hurt him."

"Careful, sniper," Marco said. "You might be asked to undergo just such a test."

I didn't take my eyes off Giulio's father. "I love him, Don Ravazzani. More than anything."

"I have no doubt. He is the heir to a great fortune, no? An empire worthy of a king."

He thought I was after Giulio because of his money? I couldn't help it, I laughed. "I have more money than I could spend in ten lifetimes. I don't want Giulio's money."

"And I should believe anything you say? A man with no allegiances, no loyalty to anyone but himself."

"I am loyal to your son."

"Oh? Then have you told him you almost killed me on the street, while he was standing a few meters away?" When I remained silent, he asked, "Have you at least told *him* who hired you to kill him?"

"No, but he knows the hit was canceled."

"Canceled, because you canceled it? Or because whoever hired you no longer wished for my son to be murdered?"

I answered in my own way. "I didn't want to kill him, and then it was no longer required."

His palm slapped the desk, the loud crack echoing like a gunshot. "I've granted you entrance into my home with my wife and children. And in return I receive nothing but lies and evasions."

"Mi dispiace, Don Ravazzani, but I can't tell you anything about my clients. My life depends on my discretion."

"Right now your life depends on me."

The threat was clear in every syllable. I didn't know what to do or say to change his mind. I had dreaded this information getting out.

Ravazzani gestured to Marco. "Get him in here."

My insides clenched, dread sitting like a stone in my chest. I would like to hope that Giulio would understand, that he would be forgiving of my past. But I was a realist. I dealt in cold practicalities, not rainbows and wishes. This would destroy whatever Giulio and I had together.

While Marco texted Giulio, I kept my attention on Ravazzani. "This will only hurt your son. I love him. We're happy together. I will pledge myself to him until my dying breath."

Fausto's chest expanded, his expression darkening. "I have no intention of keeping secrets from my son. He deserves to know what kind of man you are. Then we will decide your fate together."

With those ominous words hanging in the air, we fell silent. There was nothing to do now but wait.

CHAPTER TWENTY-THREE

Giulio

My father's wife—and my close friend—glared at me. We were still outside, standing on the patio. "Seriously, what the fuck, G?"

I put my palms up. "I had a very good reason why I couldn't call you."

She moved in closer. "You called Zia," she hissed quietly. "He doesn't know, but she told me. She didn't want me to worry because of the baby."

Damn it. I wished Zia hadn't told Frankie about that phone call. "I didn't want to put you in that position. He is your husband and I didn't want him to know where I was."

"And now you have a *boyfriend?*"

I dragged a hair through my hair. "Come, walk with me and I'll explain all of it. I've missed you."

She gave me a small smile. "I've missed you, too." Then she was hugging me, her arms tight around my waist. I held her for a long moment, so damn happy to see her again.

"I thought you were dead." She spoke into my chest. "After you hung up with me in Santorini, Fausto couldn't find you. Jesus, Giulio. I was out of my mind with worry."

"I'm sorry. Really, Frankie. I never wanted to hurt you."

She let me go, but wrapped our arms together. "Come on. Let's check on Rafe before he drives Bruno insane."

We began walking toward the stables. Her blond hair was pulled up into a messy bun on the top of her head and she wore no makeup. Even like this, she was a bombshell. No wonder my father lost his mind when he met her. "You look good," I said. "This pregnancy agrees with you."

"Thank you. I'm so tired all the time with this one. It must be another boy."

"What does Zia say?"

"Twins." I let out a bark of laughter, and she elbowed me in the ribs. "Stop laughing, stronzo. I cannot handle twin babies. Like, I will legit lose it."

"You'll be fine, matrigna. My father will take care of you. Get you whatever help you need."

"Yeah, I know how he'll take care of me," she said dryly. "That's what got me into this mess in the first place."

"He loves you." I waved to one of the estate workers who called out my name in greeting. "Which is why I couldn't tell you, Frankie. I couldn't put all of this in jeopardy. I couldn't risk you or the kids."

"Risk us, how?"

I explained about the Sicilians, Alessio finding me in Málaga. Everything that had happened until today.

"Fucking hell. You had two contracts out on you?"

"Yes."

"Weren't you worried Alessio was going to kill you?"

"At first. But then . . . we fell in love."

"You fell in love with the man sent to kill you. Jesus. I don't even know how to wrap my head around that."

"Dai, you fell in love with the man who kidnapped you to marry me. So at least my story is as fucked up as yours."

She chuckled and laid her head on my shoulder. "Who hired him?"

"He won't tell me."

"And you're okay with that?"

I trusted Alessio with my whole being. It was hard to explain, but I didn't care about the past anymore. For the first time in years, I was contemplating my future. And I had Alessio to thank for it. "I'm sure he'll tell me eventually, but I'm not worried."

"Fausto won't like that answer."

"Well, this isn't Fausto's business."

"Everything is Fausto's business. You should know that by now."

I did know this, which was why I planned to move to Málaga and start my own empire. With Alessio. Then I could come back to Siderno and visit whenever I liked, however long I liked.

A small smile twisted my lips. I never thought I'd get my life back, or find another man to love. But I'd gained both those things in the last few weeks.

"It's good to see that goofy, love-struck look on your face again," Frankie said as we strolled along the path. "It's been a long-ass time, you know?"

"You will like him. He's part Adam Driver, part Gianluigi Buffon."

"Who is Gianluigi Buffon?"

I shook my head like I was deeply disappointed in her. "Haven't you researched the great heroes of your adopted country? Ma dai, Frankie."

"It must be a footballer, then. And honestly? You had me at Adam Driver."

Leaning over, I kissed the top of her head. "I'm so glad to see you haven't changed."

"Well, I'm glad to see that you have. You're happier. Lighter. The circles under your eyes are gone. You look like the man I first met way back when."

"You mean when you thought you were going to have to marry me?"

"Thank God that never happened." The paddock came into view and she waved when Rafe saw her. "We would have made each other miserable."

I honestly couldn't imagine. I loved her like a sister. Anything more than that would've been impossible.

My mobile buzzed in my pocket. I pulled it out and saw a text from Zio Marco.

Come to the office. Now.

Minchia! Has something gone wrong with my father and Alessio?

"I have to go," I told Frankie. "Are you okay out here, or do you want to come back to the castello with me?"

"I'll stay here. Now that Rafe has seen me, he'll have a complete meltdown if I try to leave."

Bending, I kissed her cheek. "See you in a bit. Come find me when you're back in the house."

She promised she would, and then I hurried toward the castello. I should've stayed in their meeting. I never should've left Alessio alone with Fausto. My father was probably grilling Alessio about his previous jobs, including the hit on me.

I had to get in there and explain the situation to Fausto. Alessio never had any plans to kill me. Not really. I hadn't been in any danger, and then we couldn't keep our hands off one another in Scotland. My father would understand. It all sounded much worse than it played out.

And I needed to tell him about what happened in Palermo. Nino Buscetta and the broken truce.

I jogged up the small rise that led to the house. Across the patio. Then I was inside. My shoes thumped on the old tile, a floor I'd run up and down as a boy.

I didn't bother knocking. Instead, I threw open the door and went in. The room was deathly quiet, the kind of silence after an argument. "*Che c'è?*" I immediately asked. Someone needed to fill me in right the fuck now.

"Sit down, *figlio*," my father said. He leaned back in his chair, the angles of his face sharper than usual. Marco looked on edge, watchful.

Alessio wouldn't meet my eye.

I sat down in the empty chair next to Alessio. I noticed he was gripping the armrests tightly, his knuckles white. I knew my father could be scary as shit sometimes, but I could handle him.

Reaching out, I touched Alessio's arm, trying to reassure him. He just sat perfectly still, frozen, so I faced my father. "Pàpa, let me explain."

"I will go first, please." Fausto slid a glass vial across the desk toward me. "Do you know what this is?"

I peered closer. Metal fragments. "A bullet."

"Yes. Specifically, the bullet they removed from me four years ago."

"Grim. Okay, what does that have to do with me?"

"It has to do with your ragazzo."

I glanced at Alessio, but received only his profile in return. "I don't understand."

Fausto turned his attention to Alessio. "Would you like to tell him, or should I?"

A muscle popped in Alessio's jaw and I lost my patience. "Madre di dio! Someone tell me what the fuck is going on in here."

Alessio's voice wasn't loud but it was clear. "The contract on your father? The shot from the Siderno rooftop? That was me."

A huff of disbelief left my lips. "You? On the rooftop? That would mean . . . ." The truth snapped into place. It was like all the puzzle pieces instantly aligned inside my brain, the whole picture slapping me in the face.

My fingers slid off Alessio's arm.

Pain lanced though my chest. My breath left my lungs as my spine straightened. Alessio had shot my father. No, Alessio had almost *killed* my father.

But this couldn't be true. Alessio would have told me. We'd even talked about the assassination attempt. I slept with this man. Kissed him, fucked him. I'd trusted him.

I gave him *everything*.

Wait. There had to be something missing. Some reason, some explanation. This was too big of a secret, too important, for him not to share with me.

I curled my fingers into fists, my nails digging into my skin. "I want to speak with Alessio alone."

"No fucking chance," Fausto snapped. "I am not leaving you alone with him."

"He won't hurt me. Go, Pàpa."

"You may feel confident regarding your safety, but I don't. I won't leave you alone with this piece of shit."

The pressure built behind my eyes, and my control slipped. I folded my hands together and banged my knuckles against my forehead. "For the love of God, Fausto. Give me the motherfucking room!"

I'd never spoken to my father like this. He would've punished me for any hint of disrespect before I left home. But respect was the last thing on my mind. I was about to unravel. I had to get answers from Alessio. Alone.

Fausto pushed back from his desk and stood. He pulled his suit coat off the back of his chair and slipped it on. Straightened his cuffs. "Marco and I will be right outside."

They left and the door closed softly.

My ears started ringing as memories assaulted me. Alessio trailing me in Santorini, standing on the roof of the building across and looking down at me. Exactly the same position as my father's assassination. Cazzo, why hadn't I put it together before now?

Because I didn't think he'd hide something like this from me.

I knew my father had been just a job to Alessio. A big paycheck. He hadn't known me at the time. So I didn't fault him for accepting the contract.

But I did fault him for not telling me about it.

My chest drew tight, like a ball of string being wound together, and each breath became more painful than the last. I almost didn't want to have this conversation. I didn't want it to be real.

How the fuck was this happening? Only this morning Alessio and I were laughing and kissing, stopping for caffè on the way here. Holding hands as I drove through the Siderno hills.

He knew and didn't say anything.

He spoke first. "I should have told you."

"So it's true," I snapped, hurt and anger deepening my voice.

"Yes."

"Why didn't you fucking tell me?"

"Because you would've left."

"Instead you lied and let me fuck you. Sleep with you. Share my life with you. You made me—" *Fall in love with you.*

I bit back the words. He didn't deserve them.

"I didn't lie," he said.

"You selfish piece of shit." Standing, I strode around the desk to face him. "You know not telling me is the same as lying. We even talked about the assassination! You had plenty of opportunities to confess it to me."

"I couldn't." His eyebrows slammed together, the scar on his face twisted. "I couldn't lose you."

"And you hoped I'd never find out."

It was clear by the set of his jaw that I was right. He had buried this secret, intending never for it to see the light of day.

I had trusted this man. After having my heart broken by Paolo's death, I'd given the bruised and battered organ to Alessio for safekeeping. I thought we would move to Spain and start an empire together.

All the while he'd been withholding this from me.

I pierced him with a harsh glare. "I was there that day. I watched you shoot him." Fausto had nearly died. If not for Zio Marco's combat medical training, Fausto would've bled out in the car on the way to the hospital.

"I know. I saw you."

"I have no doubt. Up on your rooftop," I sneered. "Alone. Eyes locked on your target, a cold-blooded sniper collecting a paycheck."

Alessio flinched. "No, I *saw* you. The instant you got out of the car. You were—are—gorgeous. This beautiful man with thick dark hair and light eyes. I was distracted. Awestruck." He lifted one shoulder. "And I missed."

"Am I supposed to feel flattered?"

He rubbed his chest, touching the cornicello he always wore around his neck. "I know you won't believe me, but I'm sorry, Giulio."

Sorry? He was only sorry he was caught, that I'd discovered his secret. "Give me the rest of it. Who hired you to kill me? And you'd better not tell me you can't reveal your clients again."

"Enzo D'Agostino," he said quietly. "Because I missed your father."

I braced my palms on my father's desk, my head hanging down in defeat. This was why he couldn't tell me, and why the contract disappeared once Gia and Enzo fell in love. Gia and Frankie would lose their minds if Enzo had me killed, and both of their men wanted to keep their women happy.

Cazzo, how had I not put all this together?

I was a fool. I had loved this man and I was a fool for it.

My muscles shook with rage and agony. I was cursed. The first man I loved had blown up before my eyes, his flesh and bone raining down on a parking lot like confetti. The second man I loved had lied to me, kept a secret so big that I couldn't forgive it.

Now my father knew. Zio Marco. Soon everyone would know what an idiot I was.

I slapped the desk with my palms. "And I fucking brought you here! To meet my family. I was so proud, so excited for them to meet you." Red coated my brain, the anger filling my veins, carrying down to my bones. I barely knew what I was doing as I picked up an empty glass on my father's desk and hurled it against the wall.

Shards of glass exploded and fell to the ground.

The door instantly opened and my father appeared in the doorway. His sharp gaze swept over me, ensuring I was alright.

Cristo santo, he must be so horrified by my choices. Would I ever not disappoint him?

I needed to be alone. I couldn't take the pity in my father's expression. Couldn't handle the realization that I had failed *again*. That I wasn't the perfect son and heir he'd dreamed of.

That I had loved a man who didn't respect me enough for the truth.

Like I was in a daze, I started out of the room. There were decisions to be made, though, and I was a Ravazzani to my core. We always did what needed to be done, no matter how difficult.

Pausing by my father, I said, "I want him gone. Have him taken to the airport and put on a plane. I don't care where."

Alessio was suddenly on his feet. "Giulio, please. Give me time to explain."

I ignored him. My chest had frozen over, a numb expanse that had no sympathy. No forgiveness.

I met my father's gaze, so like my own. And I read his intentions there as clear as day. My stomach twisted at the possibility, and I said, "Do not have him killed."

The lines surrounding Fausto's mouth deepened with his frown. "Figlio, it's the only—."

"Do *not* have him killed, Papà," I repeated. "He leaves, but he lives. Promise me. On the lives of your children."

Oh, Fausto didn't like that. Jaw stiff, he nodded once. "Te lo prometto."

"Here is Nino Buscetta's mobile." I handed over the phone to my father. "Maybe your men can find something useful on it."

Then I drew in a breath and faced the man I had loved for the last time. Alessio's eyes begged me to reconsider, his expression pleading with me to talk this out. I ignored all of it. "Stay gone, sniper. Because if I see you, even suspect a hint of you in the breeze, I will find you and put a bullet between your eyes."

"Giulio— "

"Save your excuses. You are dead to me, Alessandro Ricci."

———

Alessio

I KNEW THIS WAS COMING. As soon as they escorted me into the dungeon, I braced for the worst.

Three of Ravazzani's men, overseen by Marco, took turns hitting me. It started with fists, and when I could no longer stand they switched to kicks. I curled up into a ball and tried to protect my head, but it was pointless. There was pain everywhere, each breath agony. Definitely some of my ribs were broken.

And I had no one to blame but myself. I ruined the only good thing in my life, the only person I'd ever wanted. The greatest love I had experienced. A beating was the least of what I deserved.

"What is wrong with that boy?"

My father's voice echoed as I retreated inside my head. He was always there, ready and waiting to remind me of how broken I was, how no one —except for my nonna—had ever loved me. I prayed for the blackness to overtake me, longed for the oblivion I knew would eventually come.

Maybe then I could forget.

I could forget his smiles and lingering touches. The promises and the kisses. The sweet words he gave me, the plans we made. It was all gone, and I never, ever wanted to remember.

Dizzy, I barely noticed when they strung me up from a hook in the ceiling. I was limp, panting, the room tilting around me. For a second, I thought I would be sick. But then Marco Ravazzani grabbed my face. I gasped through the blistering agony, nearly positive my jaw was broken.

"He saved your miserable life. If it were up to us, you'd be dead on this cold stone floor right now."

I lost track of time after that, drifting through a haze of pain as I dangled, my toes barely scraping the floor. I couldn't focus or hold my eyes open. Blood streaked down my face. My shoulders were on fire.

I came to as I crashed into a heap on the floor, pain robbing me of the ability to breathe. I whimpered. Blood rushed back into my arms, the feeling like needles being shoved under my skin.

I heard Marco's voice as if from a great distance. "Get him into the car."

Hands lifted me and the edges of my vision swam. I didn't know where they were taking me and I didn't care. I just wanted the unconsciousness back.

My wishes were answered, because the next thing I knew I was on the floor of a private plane. The engines rumbled beneath me, the vibrations absolute hell on my injured body. I panted through the pain. My right arm was laying underneath me at an unnatural angle, and I knew it had been broken. A gift from Ravazzani's men, no doubt.

Did Giulio know what they did to me in that dungeon? Would he even care?

"You are dead to me, Alessandro Ricci."

Not Alessio. Not amore. Not even assassino.

I floated in and out, the misery in my chest far worse than any physical aches. How was I supposed to not follow him? Try not to explain? I wasn't sure I could bear a future without him in it. I would rather he killed me.

I woke up with a start when the plane touched down. The wheels bounced along the runway, each hitch and dip like a knife in my joints. Sweat broke out on my skin, my broken arm throbbing under my weight.

We came to a stop. Minutes later, I heard the plane's door depressurize and open. Footsteps drew closer, then I was being carried. More like dragged, actually. I heard my shout as my broken arm twisted, and I grabbed it with my good hand, cradling the limb close to my body.

Many hands got me to the bottom of the stairs, then released me. I couldn't open my eyes, my full concentration on not throwing up at the moment. When the nausea passed I peeked through swollen lids to see Ravazzani's plane slowly rolling away from me. Blue skies soared overhead, the asphalt hot beneath me.

I didn't know how long I was there, but it felt like eons before someone approached me. I recognized the Arabic exclamation right away.

A man leaned over me and asked. "Do you need a doctor?"

I licked my dry lips. I answered back in his native language. "Please. A phone."

CHAPTER TWENTY-FOUR

Giulio

I wasn't proud of the way I handled the next few days.

The Ravazzani estate was vast and full of places to hide. I knew this from my childhood, when I wished to escape from my responsibilities. My favorite place had always been in the winery, a room the vintner used as living quarters way back in the day. Our current vintner had his own home, and so this tiny space hadn't been occupied in a long time.

It wasn't fancy, but I had access to wine and solitude. That was all I needed.

Frankie tried to see me once, but I sent her away. I told her I wasn't ready. Instead I spent the better part of two days drunk and feeling sorry for myself. Anger and bitterness were my constant companions. The third day arrived with a terrible hangover, and I swore off Ravazzani cirò for the rest of my life.

I knew I had to get back to the real world. I had to face whatever awaited me with my family. As soon as I could, I would go somewhere far away and begin a future of my own. Alone.

Hands deep in my pockets, I strode toward the castello. I kept my head down, not wishing to engage in conversation with any of the estate workers, most of whom I'd known my whole life. I couldn't pretend to be polite or give them the impression that everything was okay. It wasn't.

I slipped into the back door and Zia's kitchen. She was there, of course, stirring something at the stove. Her gray hair was pulled up and she wore a black dress, as usual. The eternal widow, like so many of her generation. I didn't say anything, just went to the counter and sat on a stool.

Without turning around, she took a bowl out of the cupboard and began spooning things in it. Then she set the bowl in front of me. "Mangia, ometto."

How had she known it was me?

I stared at the food. Pastina with egg and crispy prosciutto. The ultimate comfort food, one of my favorite dishes as a child. "Grazie, Zia."

She poured me some sparkling water. Two tablets of pain reliever magically appeared, as well. A lump formed in my throat. I didn't need Zia to fuss over me, but I was deeply grateful. I took the pills and started eating.

She didn't make conversation. Instead she worked at the stove and left me with my food. The warm pastina drove away the nausea and eased my headache. When I finished the first bowl, another full one replaced it. I didn't argue. It was pointless, anyway. Food was Zia's love language, and she wouldn't allow me to refuse it.

"I can't eat any more," I said at the end of the second bowl. "I'm stuffed."

She began clearing my dirty dishes. "You were always a good boy." Reaching over, she placed her bony palm on my cheek. "Now you are a good man."

The lump returned to my throat and I shook my head. "No, Zia. I'm really not."

She made a sound of disapproval. "What happened with your ragazzo was not your fault. Your father, he is not perfect. He has made mistakes, too. Do not let this drive you away from your home again."

Figured she had read my mind. Zia had always known me better than anyone. "I can't stay. Especially after this."

"Dai, do not make decisions until you are thinking straight."

Rising, I went around the counter and pulled her into a fierce hug. She was a little thinner and shorter since the last time I held her. "Ti voglio bene, Zia."

"Ti voglio bene, ometto." She clung to me for another long second, then pushed me back. "Now go and shower. You smell."

A smile tugged at my lips as I went upstairs. Today I needed to sit down and have a serious conversation with Fausto. For that, I needed to be properly put together.

I showered, then toweled off, avoiding my reflection in the mirror. I hated myself. Both for falling in love with the wrong man and for the way I disappeared three days ago, retreating like a coward. I needed to be stronger. It was time for me to stand on my own two feet. Come out of the shadows, out from underneath the Ravazzani empire.

Dressed and looking as best as I could reasonably manage, I went downstairs to his office. At my knock, he yelled, "Entri!"

He was sitting at his desk alone, working on his laptop. When he saw me, he removed his glasses and leaned back. "Figlio. Come stai?"

I couldn't read anything in his expression except concern. "May I sit?"

He gestured toward an empty seat. "Did you eat?"

I nodded. "Zia fed me."

"Good. She's been worried sick about you starving out there."

I dragged a hand down my face. "Perdonami, Papà."

"Why are you apologizing to me?"

I let out a dry laugh that held no amusement. "Where to start? The list is too long."

He pushed back from his desk, stood, and shrugged out of his suit coat. Then he hung it on the back of his chair. "Come. Walk with me. My back is killing me from sitting for too long."

I didn't know whether his back truly hurt, or if he was saying it so I wouldn't argue. Either way, I grabbed onto the opportunity. It was far less intimidating to confess my sins to my father if we weren't face to face in his office.

I followed him through the patio doors and into the Calabrian sunshine. The scent of bergamot, olives and dirt filled my nostrils. The air had a salty tang from the ocean breeze. It always smelled like home.

He tilted his face toward the sun and let out a deep breath. "How is your hangover?"

"Nearly gone."

"Good."

We started off, but he headed toward the vineyards, not the farm. It was the quieter part of the estate at this time of year, which probably meant he didn't want to be interrupted or overheard.

He clasped his hands behind his back as we walked. "Tell me what happened after you visited for Raffaele's birthday. I want to hear everything."

So I did. I told him of leaving Amsterdam, going to Màlaga. Meeting a man in a nightclub—sans blowjob, of course. Santorini, then Scotland. The fact that Alessio had chances to kill me and didn't, the way we were drawn to one another. Then I told him of the Sicilians, the search for who had planted the car bomb. The yacht and going to Palermo to deal with Nino. He asked simple questions when he wanted more elaboration, but for the most part just let me speak.

"Buscetta," he sneered. "*Brutto figlio di puttana bastardo.*"

"He said you reneged on your agreement."

Fausto waved his hand dismissively. "They broke it first. Working with Mommo behind my back." He placed his palm on my shoulder, stopping us both. "But I am sorry this led to the car bomb and Paolo's death. I didn't think they would go after you, not after we'd made it clear you were out."

I nodded. There was no changing the past. "I brought your assassin here, so I think we are even."

"Not even close, figlio mio. It's my job to protect you, and I failed."

"You don't need to protect me. I can do it myself."

He let me go and we set off toward the vineyards once more. "This yacht, who did it belong to?"

"Nikolai Kuznetsov."

Fausto's head whipped toward mine. "Che cazzo? Bratva?"

I held up my palms. "I didn't know before we went on board. And my friend Theo didn't know this about his boyfriend." Deceit was going around, apparently.

"This man is dangerous. Did he know who you were?"

"Yes."

"Madre di dio!"

"Don't worry. He tried to use the information against us, but I made him a proposition instead."

"Oh?" My father, the businessman. I knew I had his attention now.

"There is a lot of money to be made in Màlaga." I explained about Martiñez, the product I sold him, as well as Golubev and his hold on the city.

"And how does this involve Kuznetsov?"

"I told him he should take out Golubev, then partner with me to take over the trafficking and run Martiñez out of business."

"No." Fausto said it with such finality, like someone had asked for his opinion. Like it was his decision to make.

"What do you mean, no?"

"You are not doing this. You are not helping the Bratva line their pockets with more money."

"It's a smart business decision, Papà."

He snorted. "The Bratva, they are uncivilized animals. They do not have honor, not like we do."

"I can trust this man." I didn't want to say the reason for that trust was because I knew Nikolai's secret. I could destroy him with one call.

"No man in the Bratva is trustworthy. Maybe to their own, but not to us. I forbid this."

I tried not to get angry. My father was used to being the first and last word on a topic. But this wasn't Ravazzani business. And this was my decision. "You are aware that I don't work for you any longer. I don't even live here."

"I wish to speak with you about this. I think you should come back. Permanently."

It shouldn't have surprised me, but it did. I blinked a few times and thought of what to say. "No," was the best I could come up with.

"Do not be foolish, figlio. You are doing the same as you did for me in these smaller countries. Using my contacts to make money. Why not do it here, where you are safe?"

"You know why."

"Things have changed, become more progressive. That you are gay does not matter as much anymore. And I'm tired of wondering whether you are dead or alive. I'd like you here."

I rolled my shoulders, trying to work out the sudden tension in my neck. I'd been on my own for the last four years. How could I go back to answering to my father for every little thing?

I couldn't. I couldn't stay here, trying to fill shoes that no longer fit.

"Papà, no. I can't."

He sighed heavily and walked to the fence that surrounded the entrance to the vineyard. We both leaned against the wood and stared out at the rolling hills, at the rows of vines that produced some of Italy's best wine.

"I have worked my whole life to turn this over to you," he said quietly. "And you would make an excellent don. Yet, you don't want it."

"I can't say what the future might bring, but right now I need something that is just mine. I need to find my own path, not walk yours."

"Mine is not so bad. All the wealth and power of your dreams, figlio. Yet you want to go and struggle instead. Make these low-level deals."

"Hardly low level. I have almost five million Euros stored away."

"As I said, low-level."

I dropped my forehead onto my arms on the fence. "Papà . . . ."

He put a hand on my shoulder. "I do not mean to diminish what you have done. You have thrived on your own, stayed alive by using your wits. You killed Nino Buscetta, for fuck's sake. I'm very, very proud of you. Never for one second think I am not."

My chest ached at his words. But I also knew he had to be disappointed in me. Cazzo, I was disappointed in myself. "I don't know how you could say that after the past few days."

Using a hand under my arm, he guided me up from the fence so we were looking at one another. He rested one palm against my cheek.

"You are not at fault for what happened with the sniper. He lied to you. That is the beginning and the end. It is on him, not you."

"It's humiliating."

"No one knows of this but Marco and myself. The men in the dungeon were told he was caught stealing from us."

I felt as though the earth stopped spinning for a brief second. "The dungeon?"

Fausto released me and went back to leaning on the fence. "You think someone hurts my child and I don't make them pay in blood? Ma dai, figlio mio."

"I told you to let him live."

"And we did. He breathes, Giulio. He breathes."

"Where did you take him?"

"Tunisia."

Cristo santo. I exhaled, an unwelcome sense of relief coasting through me. I shouldn't care whether Alessio lived or died . . . and yet I did. "I know you also told Zia and Frankie what happened."

"You wish to hide these things from your family? The people who love you the most, unconditionally?"

"I want to pretend it never happened, to be honest."

"No, never do this. You have always been very hard on yourself, even as a boy. But none of us go through life unscathed, nor should we want to. It's in the hottest fire that the strongest of us are forged."

I thought over his words as we stood next to one another, the insects buzzing around our heads. Fausto was wise, and I often forgot how much. But it didn't lessen my pain or humiliation. I wasn't certain I'd ever recover from Alessio's betrayal.

"You know who hired him to kill you, no?" my father asked.

"Yes. D'Agostino."

My father nodded. "That testa di cazzo. I should have killed him when I had the chance."

"To be fair, it happened before D'Agostino and Gia started dating."

"I don't give a fuck about fair, not when it comes to that man." He blew out a breath, like he was trying to stay calm. "Lucky for us Ricci was so incompetent that day in Siderno."

"It wasn't incompetence that caused him to miss."

"What does that mean?"

"Forget it. It was something he said, but it doesn't matter now."

My father angled toward me, leaning on the fence with one hand. "Dimmi."

"He saw me on the street with you that day. He said he was awestruck and flustered, and it caused him to miss."

"Awestruck?"

My father sounded like this was the most ridiculous thing he'd ever heard. Maybe it was. Who the fuck even knew anymore? But I couldn't talk about Alessio. It was too painful to think about. "I don't wish to discuss this anymore. I'd rather circle back to Màlaga and Nikolai Kuznetsov."

"We decided that wasn't going to happen."

"No, you decided that. I am very much in favor of it happening."

"Why?"

"What do you mean? To make a lot of money."

He didn't believe me. He stared intently into my eyes, like he was trying to solve a puzzle. "I can give you a lot of money and you won't have to work for it. Tell me the real reason."

"I told you, I want something that is mine."

"A business? Or an empire?"

If I was going to aim, why not aim high? I had nothing to lose anymore. "An empire."

"Va bene. An empire. I understand this need. But why would we make the Bratva money? They use it to traffic women and fund child pornography. You should make money for our 'ndrina. Our family."

That made sense, I supposed. But I had to do this my way. "I need muscle in Màlaga. You don't have any men in Spain."

He slid a hand over his jaw and rubbed. "That doesn't mean I couldn't get some there."

This was quickly sounding like my father planned on taking over. "I want to do this, Papà. If you do it for me, how will anything ever be mine?"

"Do not be so stubborn. They would be your men. You would lead them and be responsible for them. But you need men loyal to *us*."

"So what are you suggesting?"

"Let me discuss it with Marco. But I'm thinking we send you to Màlaga with some men and a fuckload of guns to see what happens. You want to build an empire there, figlio mio? Then you will need to work your ass off to do it."

I was more than ready. I needed work to stay busy, to distract me from the hole in my chest and from the guilt I carried.

I needed to forget ever knowing Alessandro Ricci.

"Come." He slapped my back. "Let us return to the castello. Nothing will be decided today and your siblings are anxious to see you."

CHAPTER TWENTY-FIVE

Alessio

Shoreditch, East London

"You still look like shit."

I blinked and found Sasha leaning over me. I must've fallen asleep on her couch. Again. "Spasiba." *Thank you.*

She slipped a lollipop in her mouth and walked away. "Don't mention it."

I'd been living here for three weeks, healing. After Sasha flew to Tunisia to pick me up, she insisted on bringing me to her London flat instead of letting me stay alone in one of my homes. I was grateful for her stubbornness. At the time, I hadn't realized just how hurt I was.

I closed my eyes. Most of my physical injuries had healed. The arm was still in a cast, but the bruises were fading. And my ribs only ached when I drew in a really deep breath.

My heart? That was another matter entirely. I would never recover from losing Giulio. There was a crater in my chest, a missing piece of me. I was miserable without him, and I had nothing to do but sit here and think.

I needed work to keep me busy.

"Look for a job," I yelled out to Sasha.

"When your arm is healed, yes."

I would go crazy if I sat around here any longer. "No, now."

"Alessio." I heard her sit in the chair across from me. Then she took the lollipop out of her mouth with a smack. "You are not ready. If you go now, you will get killed."

"Then you can go live on a beach somewhere and hire a handsome pool boy."

"I'd prefer an older businessman, actually. In a suit. Maybe a little gray at his temples."

I cracked my lids to see her. "Do you have a daddy fetish, Sasha?"

Her fair skin colored slightly. "Shut up, *mudak*. We are discussing *you*."

"I definitely do not have a daddy fetish." I let my eyes close and folded my hands on my stomach.

"No, you have a Giulio Ravazzani fetish. I just wish I knew how to cure you."

Same. I'd give everything I owned for a pill or shot to get him out of my system. I was desperate. My headaches were getting worse and I think I had an ulcer. I slept in fits and starts, never getting any meaningful rest.

Every time I slept, he was there. Angry and hateful. Chasing me through the streets of Palermo or Santorini. Taunting me as he promised to kill me. Worse were the dreams when he loved me and looked at me with adoring, kind eyes.

Because I always woke up. I remembered he was gone and my heart broke all over again.

"Find another job," I blurted. "Who is waiting in your email?"

"No and no one."

I scowled at her. "I don't believe you."

"Why don't you go to your house in France, eat some cheese, and wait for me to call you? In the meantime, your arm can heal properly."

"I can't." My words were quiet, laced with the anguish I kept trying to bury. "Please, Sasha."

With her dirty blonde hair pulled into a severe ponytail there was nothing to soften the disapproval on her face. She twisted the lollipop in her mouth. "I am starting to worry about you."

"Because I pay you to worry about me."

"No, this has nothing to do with my position. As a friend—perhaps your only friend—I am worried."

"Noted. Find me a job."

"No."

I glared at her. "No?"

She jumped to her feet and pointed at me. "This is ridiculous. Go to Siderno and apologize. Kiss and make up!"

Was she trying to piss me off? "There is no making up from this, Sasha! I almost murdered his father."

Waving the lollipop in her hand, she made a dismissive noise through her teeth. "In Russia, this is foreplay. Go and apologize, Alessio."

She didn't understand. I lost Giulio, because I hadn't told him about shooting his father. He would never forgive me. And it was *killing* me to sit and think about him all the time. I couldn't take any more.

I had fucked up and there was no *fixing* this. I was broken, just like my father said. Undeserving of love. And work was the escape I needed.

I sat up and dragged my good hand through my hair. "Find me a job *right now*."

"Or?"

"Or I'll find a new assistant," I growled.

She sneered, looking me up and down. "You would fire me? Just because I am telling you to rest and take care of yourself?"

"Yes, that is exactly what I am saying."

We didn't look away from one another. Sasha was stubborn, but so was I. And I couldn't keep laying around, thinking about Giulio. It was killing me.

"Fine," she threw up her hands. "You want to work? We will work!" She stomped over to her computer and threw herself in the chair. Her fingers flew over the keyboard. "We will find you a nice fat contract so you can go and kill someone to make yourself feel better."

"Just do it quietly." I rubbed my temples, my sleep-deprived headache returning with renewed vigor.

"Go and get some pain reliever in my medicine cabinet. Then pour us both a drink."

I wasn't sure I needed alcohol, but I left her to work. The bathroom was tiny. I swallowed two pills and used the toilet. Then I washed my hands and came back out to her living room.

The mood had definitely shifted. She was twirling the lollipop in her mouth almost nervously. "I need you to sit," she told me.

"Why?"

"Just sit down."

I put my hands on my hips. "Spit it out, Sasha."

"There's a hit out on Giulio Ravazzani."

I blinked. No, that couldn't be right. "You mean Fausto, his father."

"No, I mean Giulio. Come and look."

"It has to be old. Or a mistake." I hurried over to her monitors.

"It's no mistake." She pointed to a chat message. "This is the space on the dark web where jobs are posted. I rarely go here, because people usually come to us. See, there he is."

I could see it, as plain as day. Someone had offered a million euros to kill Giulio. "Accept. Tell them I will do it, just to get it down."

"It's already been accepted. Last week. See this reply here?"

"Minchia!" I kicked her trash bin.

"Hey! Do not break my stuff."

Last week. There was no time to lose. "Can we see who posted or accepted the request?"

"I don't know who posted it, but let me see if I can do some digging on the responder." The keys on her keyboard clacked. "I feel like I recognize the user."

"Just message the account. Tell them I will offer them double not to complete the job. And I want to know who hired them."

"I can ask, but they might not answer right away."

"Do it." I grabbed my phone and dialed the first person I thought might have put a hit out on Giulio.

Vito D'Agostino answered on the second ring. "Pronto."

"I need to speak with your brother."

"You have him, Alessandro Ricci." This was Don D'Agostino. "And I thought we agreed last time we spoke to pretend we didn't know one another."

"Did you hire another one?"

"Cosa?"

"Another one, after me. For Giulio." I didn't want to say it over the phone.

"No."

I stared out the window, unseeing. "No?"

"Do you doubt my word?"

"Of course not."

"Smart of you. By the way, I heard you made quite the entrance in Siderno. Meeting the in-laws went well, no?"

I could hear Vito snickering in the background. Fucking mafioso.

I hung up on them.

I was pacing a few minutes later when Sasha said, "I just got a response. Look!"

On her monitor, I could see him. The assassin was German. He was more than happy to take my money for doing nothing. Even better, he gave up the name of the client.

Don Buscetta, father of Nino Buscetta.

I slapped the wall behind me. That old stronzo. So Buscetta knew that Giulio was responsible for the murder of Nino in Palermo. Then I remembered Giulio had been the only one to remove his mask that night. Did Nino have cameras in his bedroom?

Cazzo. Why hadn't I checked? Of course that coke fiend had cameras recording him fucking his mistress.

I had to take care of this. Giulio hated me, but I would not let Don Buscetta kill him. Giulio deserved a life free of car bombs and snipers. Even if I died trying, I would give it to him.

It was the very least I could do.

Sasha leaned back to see my face. "Do you know who that is?"

I nodded. "Book me on the first flight to Palermo."

———

Giulio

"Giulio, did you hear me?"

I pulled my attention back to where I was, which was in the passenger seat of Benito's SUV. I was going on little to no sleep and hadn't eaten much, either. *Three weeks*. It felt like a fucking eternity. The only thing keeping me sane was making preparations for Màlaga. "Hmm?"

"I asked if you're going to let me come with you. To Spain."

I took a drag off the lit cigarette in my hand. The dark streets of Siderno flew by as we drove through town to our meeting, and I let the nicotine relax me. "Of course. Fausto said I could choose. Are you sure you want to go?"

When I shifted to blow the smoke out the window, Benito leaned over to ruffle my hair. "And miss out on all the fun? Ma dai!"

I pushed him away and told him to fuck off. He laughed, but I heard the serious concern when he asked, "You sure you're okay? You haven't said much."

"I'm fine." I have been saying this so often lately, I should make it my newest tattoo.

When I finished my cigarette, I immediately lit another. The buzz distracted me from the mess in my head. I was exhausted and angry. The only person in a good mood these days was my father. He liked having me home. Frankie watched me warily, and Zia kept leaving me church schedules. Worse, I couldn't talk to anyone about it. Other than my close family, no one else knew the true reason why Alessio left.

No one knew that he'd betrayed me.

I took another drag to erase the bitterness out of my mouth. Loyalty was everything to me, the concept instilled in me from birth. Ravazzani men didn't forgive *or* forget. My father's truce with D'Agostino was the only exception I could think of, and that was a testament to how much he loved Frankie.

Benito turned a sharp corner. "So, Spain. Tell me about it."

There was so much to like about Màlaga. It reminded me of

Siderno, actually. "Good food, good wine. The beaches, *madonna*. You will love the women there."

"Good, because I have fucked all the most beautiful Calabrian women already. I need new pussy, cugino."

"Is that the only reason you want to come with me?"

"Of course not." He shoved my shoulder. "I miss you, idiota."

An idea had been in the back of my mind ever since I learned that Benito was coming to Spain. "I think you should be my consigliere."

His head whipped toward me. "Are you serious?"

"Who else can I trust more than you?" Though he was a few years older, Benito and I had grown up together. We were family.

"It would be my honor."

"Thank you." I put my hand on his shoulder. "You'll make a good one, Benito."

He raised his eyebrows. "So you are, what? Don Ravazzani now?"

"Fuck, no." That title was taken until my father died. "I'm just me."

"Don't worry, I will come up with something to call you."

That was a terrifying prospect. We both fell silent as he pulled around to the back of a warehouse. It looked empty, deserted, but that wasn't surprising. Our Turkish contacts were paranoid, and we were about to purchase a lot of illegal guns. Over the last two weeks I'd been amassing a stockpile of weapons, one large enough to start a war in Màlaga.

My mobile rang just as Benito shut off the engine. I hated to take a call right now, but it could be the contact we were meeting here. I glanced at my phone.

Fausto. And he'd sent a text, as well

Call me right the fuck now.

Sighing, I answered. "Pronto."

"We have a problem."

"Can this wait?" I said into the phone.

Benito's eyes went huge. No one asked Fausto to wait.

"No, it can't fucking wait," my father said. "Come home so we can discuss it."

Fausto didn't like to use the phone for 'Ndrangheta business, so this meant it was something related to illegal activities.

"I'm busy at the moment. As soon as I'm done here, I'll come back."

"Now, figlio. Where you are might not be safe."

Ah. I checked around. It was quiet. "I'll ring you back," I said and hung up. Fausto wouldn't like that. But if this was about to turn to shit, I needed all my attention on my surroundings. "Guns," I told Benito, opening the glove box. "Be prepared."

Headlights appeared at the other end of the warehouse. The car slowly came closer to our SUV.

"Should we be worried?" Benito asked. "What did your father say?"

"This might not be safe. Stay inside the car and let me handle it."

"Giulio—"

I held up my hand. I heard his concern, but I was capable of doing this. And I wouldn't willingly put him in danger. "Don't worry. Stay in the car and you'll be fine." The SUV had bulletproof glass. "If it goes to shit, then get out of here."

"And leave you?"

My contacts were getting out of their car, so I opened my door. "Yes, Bennie. If I'm dead, then it doesn't matter."

"Your father—"

I shut the door before he could finish that sentence.

I walked over and shook hands with the two men from Izmir. We hadn't met before, but they sold military-grade weapons stolen from Syria, Armenia and Georgia. It went off smoothly. They explained what they had, I turned over a duffle full of Euros, and then I loaded the weapons into the trunk of the SUV.

Within ten minutes we were done and driving toward the storage unit I was using to keep my supplies. Benito helped me stow the weapons and then we headed back toward the estate. I lit another cigarette and stared out the window, feeling nothing. No relief that Fausto's warning proved unnecessary. No pleasure in the successful transaction. No anticipation of starting an empire of my own.

Nothing.

I was numb, focusing on the small tasks to get me through each day.

My father was waiting for me in the entryway at the castello when

I walked inside. Frankie was there, too, standing close to him, her fingers threading lovingly through his hair. They both turned at the sound of the door. Frankie visibly relaxed when she saw me. "See, baby?" she whispered to my father. "I told you he'd be okay."

He kissed her forehead, then focused on me. His expression was cold and angry. "My office. Now." Without waiting for my response, he strode off into the castello.

Frankie came over and gave me a hug. "He worries about you. And he's paranoid. Go easy on him."

"I'll try, matrigna." I kissed her cheeks. When I started to walk away, she grabbed my arm, stopping me.

"I'm also worried about you."

"I'm fine."

"Yes, that is what you keep saying. G, no one hates what Alessio did more than me—"

I tried to step back. I didn't want to hear his name. I didn't want to discuss this. Ever.

Frankie's grip tightened. "Stop. I have the right to say it. For fuck's sake, I was there when Fausto almost died, too. And I will never forgive Enzo D'Agostino for putting those wheels into motion. But I also know who I married, the world I have stepped into here. I have to accept Enzo for the sake of Gia's happiness. I need to put the past aside."

"It's not the same," I said. "He lied to me."

"You have to realize why he didn't tell you." She searched my face. "Come on, G. It would've been suicide to confess it."

"Giulio!" Fausto bellowed from his office.

"I have to go," I told her.

Frankie's fingers didn't leave my arm. "I forgave your father," she said quietly. "We are capable of forgiveness, G. And sometimes it's the most human, most beautiful thing we can do. Please, just think about it. I don't want to see you unhappy."

I kissed her cheek again. "Ti voglio bene."

"Ti voglio bene." Uncurling her fingers, she patted my arm. "Hurry, before he loses his mind."

I went to my father's office. The door was open and he was

standing behind his chair, gripping the top of it so hard that his knuckles were white. Marco was scrolling his phone in his usual chair. I hadn't expected him to be here this late. I closed the door and came inside.

"I told you," Fausto started softly, his face taut with anger, "to come straight back. I told you it might not be safe."

"I assessed the situation carefully. Everything checked out." I held out my arms. "As you can see."

"Do *not* be flippant. I expect you to follow orders, Giulio."

This was why I didn't want to live in Siderno. After being on my own for so long, I couldn't go back to being his soldato. But I knew better than to argue with him. "Tell me what you've heard."

Fausto gestured to Zio Marco and then gave me his back to stare out the window. Marco said, "There is another hit out on you. Don Buscetta."

I dropped my head and stared at the floor. Figlio d'un cane. When would it end? I was fucking tired of being chased and hunted like a dog.

"Apparently," Marco continued, "Nino had a camera in his bedroom. You took off your mask."

Minchia! I remember Alessio's surprise when I removed my mask that night. But I never considered that Nino had a camera in there to record him fucking. "How did you find all this out?"

"Your assassin."

My spine shot straight, every muscle in my body tightening. "Che cazzo?"

"This was also our reaction."

My skin heated, a burn in my chest that spread to every part of my body. I didn't need—or want—Alessio looking after me. He had no business interfering in my life, even if it was to warn me. "What did he say?"

"It wasn't a long conversation," Zio Marco drawled. "He rang my phone, told me of Buscetta's hit, and hung up. I didn't call him back."

"This isn't important," Fausto said, still looking through the window. "We have to deal with Buscetta. Immediately."

I nodded, in complete agreement. "I'll go to Palermo."

"Not a good idea," Marco said. "You'll be spotted, especially after killing Nino."

"The old man isn't in Palermo," Fausto said. "He's in the hills somewhere. Hiding. No one has seen or heard from him in decades. Not sure how we can even find him."

"What about Nino's phone?" I had turned this over weeks ago, but hadn't given it much thought since.

Marco shook his head. "There's nothing useful there. He was too smart to use it for anything other than to send pictures of his dick to various women."

I considered this. "What about his suppliers? Maybe they've dealt with the old man in Nino's absence."

"They would work through Giacomo, the younger son, no?"

"I don't think so," I said. "I get the sense the family doesn't think much of Giacomo. Nino called his brother stupid. Irresponsible. Buscetta no doubt feels the same."

"Do we know who they use?" Fausto asked, meaning who supplied the Buscettas with their product.

There weren't a plethora of suppliers to choose from. And when Fausto took the drug trade away from the Cosa Nostra, the Sicilians had been forced to get creative. Just as I had over the last few years.

Marco answered first. "It's not our people."

"No, but I'm pretty sure I know who it is," I said. "If not, I can quickly find out."

"Good." My father retook his seat, settling in. "Once we know, we'll send in a team to take him out."

And start a war in the process?

I thought of Frankie and the kids upstairs. Zia. Zio Marco and his family. I didn't want this to become Fausto's problem. It was mine.

This had to be handled quickly and quietly.

"No, I'll go. I can find Buscetta and kill him. No one will ever know I'm there."

Fausto and Marco exchanged a long glance. There was a silent communication happening between them, one born of their long standing relationship. Finally, Fausto said, "Absolutely not."

"Rav," Marco said, his voice soft but admonishing. "You have to let the boy be who he is."

"No, I have to keep him safe."

Alessio's words from that night in the park came back to me.

"My only purpose in life is to keep you safe."

A rush of fresh misery went through me, one that shredded my insides. I wasn't weak. I didn't need protection. I had survived for four years on my own.

I didn't need anyone ever again.

My tone was sharp as I said, "I don't need you to protect me. I'm fine on my own."

Fausto folded his hands and rested his forefingers against his lips. He did this when he needed to break bad news and was thinking of how best to phrase it.

But I didn't want to hear it. I blurted, "I'm going. I'll deal with Buscetta. It's exactly what you would've done at my age."

"He's right," Marco said when Fausto remained quiet.

My father didn't like this. He scowled first at Marco, then at me. "I would have listened to my elders and taken their advice into consideration."

Possibly. But Fausto wouldn't have stopped there. I knew how he'd earned the nickname Il Diavolo. "And then you would've gone to Palermo, hunted down Buscetta, and sliced him to ribbons."

Zio Marco's lips twitched, but he remained silent.

"Take Benito," Fausto growled. "Do not go alone."

I waved this off with one hand. "If I have to go into the mountains, it'll be easier if I'm by myself. Less chance of being discovered that way. I'm not bringing anyone else."

Fausto drummed his fingers on the desk. "If I tell you no, you are going to disobey me and go anyway."

"Sì, certo."

"Cazzo madre di dio!" He slapped the top of his desk. "This is the problem with sons. They always think they know better."

"Papà, I can do this. Tell him, Zio."

Marco's face twisted into a grimace, like he didn't want to come between Fausto and me. "I know the desire for a father to protect his children," he said slowly. "And I also remember what Fausto was like at twenty-four years old."

"You are not being helpful," Fausto said to his cousin.

Marco shrugged. "Tale padre, tale figlio." *Like father, like son.*

Fausto dragged a hand down his face. "I want updates. Do not go days without checking in with me again. Every day, capicse?"

I nodded, smothering the smile tugging at my lips. I could count the number of times my father had changed his mind on something. This felt like a major victory. "I will. Te lo prometto."

Fausto closed his eyes and let out a heavy sigh. "Marco, tell them to ready the jet."

CHAPTER TWENTY-SIX

Giulio

Somewhere in the hills outside of Palermo, Sicily
Five days later

I fucking hated the outdoors.

I wasn't meant to be tramping around in the brush, climbing mountains, and sleeping on the ground. I liked nightclubs and cars and a soft bed. Streaming services and hot food. Pillows and warm showers. This entire journey had been miserable.

I'd been right, though. Buscetta didn't trust his youngest son and had taken control back once Nino died. This meant my supplier network knew the general location of where Buscetta was living. And according to my intel, Buscetta was holed up in a tiny farmhouse tucked away in these godforsaken hills.

Climbing a ridge, I took out my binoculars and scanned the surrounding area. No wonder Don Buscetta remained a ghost. There was nothing around here. I had a ten mile radius to explore, peaks and valleys filled with nearly invisible hiding places. But I would find him eventually.

I took an energy bar from my pack and ate it slowly. I had to make my food reserves last, at least until I could find the next town or village.

"I have the caramel and chocolate flavor, if you want it. Tastes much better."

The voice behind me was familiar. And definitely unwelcome.

Flying to my feet, I spun around to find Alessio standing there. I already had my pistol in my hand, pointing it at him. "Do you have a fucking death wish?"

He was leaning against a tree, hands at his sides. His pack was on the ground at his feet. He looked thinner than the last time I saw him, with several days of whiskers covering his face. A cast covered his right hand and forearm.

How long had he been watching me?

"Three hours," he answered, reading my mind. "You aren't as good at this as you think you are."

"What the fuck is that supposed to mean?" I snarled.

"Tracking Buscetta, being quiet. You aren't very good at it."

"What did I tell you about following me, coglione? You must really want to die today."

"You won't kill me."

Alessio had no right to sound so certain about that. It pissed me off. "You would be wrong."

"If you shoot, they will hear and know trouble is nearby."

Damn it, he was right. I hated that. "Maybe killing you is worth it to me."

"Don't be ridiculous. Besides, I can help you find Buscetta."

"I don't need your help."

"Stubborn principe." He shook his head and reached down to lift his pack. "Good luck, then. You're headed the wrong way." He shrugged the pack onto his back and started to walk away.

Fury lit my blood like a fuse and suddenly I was rushing toward him, pushing him against the tree with one hand. My right hand kept the gun in his face. "Why are you here? Why are you following me again?"

"I only started following you three hours ago. I've been here for a week."

"Why?"

His gray eyes searched my gaze. "To find Buscetta. To kill him before he killed you."

I released him like he was on fire. I took a step back. "I don't need your help," I repeated, slipping the gun into my waistband at the small of my back. "I don't want you involved in my life."

"That is too bad. Because I'm not leaving Sicily until Buscetta is dead."

"This is not your concern, Alessandro."

His expression turned solemn, intent. Like he was about to swear his fealty to me. "You are my concern, Giulio. Always and forever, no matter how much you hate me."

My heart twisted at the words—and the reaction enraged me. How dare he say such things to me when he was the one who ruined what was between us? I pushed aside any kindness or tenderness I had toward this man. I wanted to hurt him, to make him bleed. "It won't change anything. I don't need you and I don't love you. Just like your parents."

His nostrils flared on a quick ragged inhale, pain etched in the harsh lines of his face. The words didn't make me feel better. In fact, I felt worse as he blinked several times, like he was in shock. Then his chest rose and fell before he spun and walked away.

Disappointment filled me. It wasn't enough.

I craved a reaction. I deserved it. My muscles were clenched, demanding a knock-down, drag-out fight. "Is that it?" I called to his back. "Nothing to say, Ricci?"

He didn't turn around. His long legs carried him along the ridge, leading him in the opposite direction. I couldn't stand his silence. This was too easy for him.

"I want you out of Sicily," I said, trailing him. "I don't want to see you anywhere near me or my family."

Nothing. Not a twitch or a flinch. He kept going.

I knew it was immature, but I was too angry to be ignored. He should be groveling at my feet, begging eternal forgiveness. Crying and pleading for me not to kill him. He nearly murdered my father in broad daylight and hadn't bothered to fucking tell me about it.

Before I was aware of what I was doing, I tackled him to the ground. He landed with a grunt, barely able to brace his fall. I punched him in the kidney, pleased when he wheezed in response. "Pezzo di merda! I should break your other arm!"

Pushing up, he bucked me off his back. I fell into the dirt as he rolled over. We'd done this once before in Scotland, and I knew Alessio would try to pin me down with his bulkier frame. I wouldn't give him the chance. And with only one good arm, he was at a distinct disadvantage.

I lunged and got on top of him. When I hit him in the ribs, he hissed, his lids screwing shut as if he were in extreme pain. "Cazzo!" he groaned. "Principe, per favore. My ribs are still broken."

Broken ribs?

I slid to sit atop his thighs and shoved up his shirt. Fading yellowish-brown spots coated his torso, leaving barely any skin unbruised. This horrific tapestry was the result of the dungeon, when my father's men had beaten the shit out of Alessio.

I got off him and stood. I didn't want to feel badly for the sniper's suffering. And yet I did.

Grimacing, he sat up and pulled his shirt down. He was breathing heavily. Even when running, I'd never heard him sound so winded.

The words tumbled out of my mouth before I could stop them. "Are you alright?"

He gave me a stiff nod, then slowly got to his feet. He couldn't bend because of the ribs, so he kept his back straight and stumbled toward a tree. Looking a little gray, he sagged against the trunk.

I squinted at him. "How do you plan on killing Buscetta if you can't shoot and barely move?"

"I can shoot left-handed."

"Accurately?" He didn't answer, so I stated the obvious. "They broke your arm and your ribs."

He just stood there, breathing. Madre di dio. I didn't know how badly he had been injured. I hadn't asked, either. "I didn't think they would hurt you like that."

A tiny shake of his head. "I would endure a hundred beatings—a thousand—for you. There is no amount of pain or suffering I wouldn't take in your name."

Cristo. I didn't want to feel anything at his declaration, but I softened the tiniest bit. "Damn it, Alessio."

"It's true. I'm sorry, principe."

Alone in the hills, we stood in the Sicilian sun and tried to catch our breath. I was angry, but I was also sad, too. I missed him. I missed what we had, the heat and explosive chemistry, before he ruined it.

I gave him the truth. "I can't forgive you."

"Can't—or won't?"

"Both. So if you came here hoping to win me over, it's a waste of time."

"I didn't know you were coming." Wincing, he straightened and stretched his obliques. "I called Marco Ravazzani and told him so they would keep you *home*. Not send you here."

"My father was against me coming to Palermo."

"He was right. It's foolish of you."

"I can look out for myself. I don't need you—or him—protecting me."

"It's not a bad thing to let others help you. Are you so proud and stubborn that you risk your own safety?"

"Says the man who always works alone."

"Not always," he said quietly. "I miss working with you. We made a good team with Nino."

Cazzo, these things coming out of Alessio's mouth. "Stop talking like this. I don't want to hear it. You made a fool of me, lying to me the whole time."

"Giulio," he said with a long-suffering sigh. "I agreed to kill you and that didn't bother you. Yet you can't forgive me for not telling you about your father?"

"I don't like secrets, Alessio. And do not pretend like what you did was no big deal."

"I know it is a big deal. I just hoped that you loved me enough to get past it. But you don't even want to try. You won't even hear me out."

"Do not put this on me, stronzo. It's your fuck up."

"And so that's it? I'm dead to you?"

I snorted, shocked that he even had to ask. "Do you think I will keep fucking the man who almost murdered my father and lied to me about it? Ma dai, sniper."

The misery and pain in his gray eyes doubled, a haunted look I would never forget. We stood there for a long moment, neither of us saying anything. Finally, he reached for his pack. Gingerly, he eased it over his shoulders. "Let's go kill Don Buscetta. Then you never have to see me again."

Without waiting to see what I would do, he began walking down the ridge to the other side.

———

Alessio

THE HOPE in my chest withered and died as I hiked down the ridge. When I first saw him today I thought it was a sign. The saints were looking out for me, giving me another chance with the man I loved.

But the hate, the revulsion in his expression . . . . It was clear that hope had been wishful thinking on my part. I'd lost him for good. Somehow I had to accept it. I had to let go of these stupid feelings. Go back to how things were before.

Except my former existence seemed so pathetic now. I hadn't realized how lonely, how lost in my own head I was until Giulio came along. I wasn't certain I could go back to being that same person again.

How could I have everything I wanted, then be happy when it was taken away?

"I don't need you and I don't love you. Just like your parents."

I rubbed the cornicello around my neck. I wished I could stop hurting. I was a fool to think I could have something lasting, a real relationship with another person. And Giulio deserved better than me. He would've come to that realization eventually. I just hurried the matter along by lying to him.

I heard his footsteps behind me, but didn't turn around. Don

Buscetta was holed up in a farmhouse about a fifteen minute walk from here. Giulio was just due east of the location before climbing the ridge. I'd found the farmhouse during the night, confirmed Buscetta was living inside it. As soon as daylight broke I went into a small nearby village market, which was where I saw Giulio.

The thunderbolt hit me as soon as I recognized that profile, those shoulders. *Colpo di fulmine.* And I couldn't help but follow him.

Stupid, stupid, stupid.

I kept quiet as we walked. What else more could I say? I focused on my feet. I kept my breathing shallow to spare my ribs. I didn't bother with slowing down or wondering if Giulio could keep up. Killing Buscetta would be easy for me, even with a broken hand. I didn't need Giulio's help.

The farmhouse was well-situated. It was tucked into the side of the hill, surrounded by trees and vegetation. Chickens roamed the property, and a small vegetable garden sat off to the west. The house wasn't visible from the nearby one-lane road, so someone would need to be searching diligently to find it.

I moved into the trees on the southern side, well out of sight from the farmhouse, and put down my pack. My ribs ached like a son of a bitch. For a brief second I thought I might pass out when Giulio punched me there earlier.

"You don't need to stay," he said behind me. "I see the farmhouse now. You can go."

Anyone with good sense would probably listen and immediately leave. But I never had any sense when it came to this man. And I still loved him. I needed for him to be safe, even if he hated me. That meant staying here until the job was done. "I will set up." I gestured to the ground. "I'll shoot him as soon as he appears."

"Did you hear me? I said you can leave."

I knelt, wincing at the dull ache in my side, and began unpacking my rifle. There was no use arguing with him. I wasn't leaving and he couldn't force me to go. I was going to kill Don Buscetta and then return to London.

"Alessio? Are you listening to me, stronzo? I don't fucking need you here."

"Talk a little louder, no? Make sure he knows we've arrived."

He lowered his voice to hiss, "What is wrong with you? Why are you being so fucking difficult?"

A question I'd been trying to answer my whole life. "Don't worry, principe. As soon as I kill him, I'll disappear and you'll never see me again."

Out of the corner of my eye, I saw him drag a hand through his hair. "Do you think I'm so incompetent that I need you to kill him for me?"

I slid the pieces of my rifle together, thinking about this. Was this why he believed I was here? Yes, part of me hoped if I killed Buscetta, it might help win Giulio back. That he would see me as his hero instead of a villain. Clearly, this had been foolish—and not something I would ever admit to him.

I went with a simpler, less embarrassing honest answer. "I don't think you're incompetent. But I've killed hundreds of men. What's one more dark spot on my soul? Better mine than yours."

His expression turned into one of pure bafflement. "You're doing this to save me from eternal damnation? You know I don't believe in that shit."

Yes, I knew his feelings on the church and religion. I tightened the scope into the proper position and stood. "But I believe in those things. And if I can spare you from an eternity in flames, then I will do it. With pleasure."

Giulio put his hands on his hips and glared at the ground, his mouth flat with anger. "Porca puttana! Stop saying these things to me."

"Why? They're true." I would shoulder any of his burdens, handle any of his problems, if it helped him sleep easier. "Even though you hate me, I still love you."

I should quit talking, but this might be the last time I had the chance to say it. So I added softly, "I will love you until I draw my last breath, mio bel principe."

"Cazzo," he sighed. His shoulders drooped. "I very badly want to hate you and you are making it so hard."

A tiny flare of hope sparked in my chest. Had I caused a crack in the wall of his animosity and anger?

I had to find out. With my rifle in my good hand, I eased toward him. One slow step at a time, like one might approach a wild animal. I half expected him to dart away or punch me again. But he stood still and watched my approach with those brilliant blue eyes, their color like the Mediterranean waters on a sunny day.

When I was within reach, I stopped. My heart thundered in my chest, and it felt like my lungs were squeezing all the air out of my body. I stood there, unsure what I was doing but unable to stop. He was like a magnet, pulling me closer whether I liked it or not.

I knew what I wanted. My ribs were begging me to reconsider, but I knew this opportunity might not ever come around again. I needed to try. Every cell in my body was straining toward this man, aching for him. Desperate. Hungry.

Mouth dry with nerves, I licked my lips. "If I kiss you, will you punch me again?"

"Honestly, I'm not sure."

"Then I'll just have to risk it."

I dropped my rifle on the ground and moved in to cup his jaw with my good hand. My injured hand rested on his hip. He was warm and solid and *right here*. Fuck, I'd missed him. I moved my face closer, giving him plenty of time to stop me.

He didn't.

My stomach was in my throat, nerves popping and fizzing in my veins, as I gently brushed my mouth over his. He didn't move, but his breath gusted over my skin. I couldn't decipher the swirling emotion in his gaze, so I closed my eyes and let myself sink into the joy of kissing him once again.

I increased the pressure, molding our lips together. I went carefully, slowly, needing to soak in every moment. Every second. If this was truly the last time, then I wanted to make this kiss a memorable one.

And then . . . he began to kiss me back. The tiniest bit at first, his lips shifting, testing, like he was still deciding what to do. My world tilted. I pressed in, encouraging him with my mouth, sealing us together more tightly. *More, principe. Keep going.*

His fingers wrapped around the nape of my neck, holding me, before he inched closer and tilted his head, angling us to fit better. The kiss turned deeper, urgent. Our lips pulled and sucked, and then his tongue was in my mouth. I groaned, my entire body going up in flames. I could taste the aggression in him, and I drank it in like a fine wine.

"Goddamn it, assassino," he broke off to whisper before attacking my mouth again. This time I shoved inside his mouth and got a hint of the familiar toothpaste, but also something new.

I eased back. "You're smoking again."

With a huff, he pulled me back toward his lips. "Shut up."

I didn't like this, but I couldn't complain. And honestly? I didn't care what he tasted like as long as he kept tongue fucking my mouth.

We kept going, waging our own battle for dominance in the Sicilian woods. Then I lost track of time altogether when he brought his hips flush with mine. He was hard for me, and my knees actually trembled. "Giulio," I breathed against his lips.

And then it was over. He shoved me away and stumbled back. "Figlio di puttana!" He turned away like he couldn't stand to see me. "This wasn't supposed to happen."

My mouth felt swollen from his kisses, the best kind of souvenir. I didn't regret it at all. "I am glad it did."

"Minchia!" He threaded his fingers through his hair and grabbed onto the strands. "You're a pain in my ass, sniper."

Back to "sniper" instead of "assassino." My stomach twisted up like a pretzel. "It can be good between us again. We can work through this, amore."

"Do not call me that." He spun toward me, and his eyes were wild as he grabbed my rifle off the ground. "Give me this fucking gun."

I was too shocked to react at first. "What are you doing?" I asked as he got into position on his stomach near the edge of the woods.

"What does it look like? I'm going to end all of this right now."

"Do you know how to use a rifle like this?" Not everyone did, and I wasn't sure how familiar Giulio was with any firearm other than a pistol.

"I'll be fine. How hard can it be?" He put his cheek in the well, spreading his legs to stabilize his body. Keeping both eyes open, he adjusted the scope toward the farmhouse. It showed a basic level of knowledge, and I was relieved.

"I can do it," I said. I wasn't as accurate left handed, but I could still kill a slow old man like Buscetta.

Giulio picked up a bullet and loaded the rifle. "I want this done now."

And he thought I would, what? Procrastinate?

Like I did before, when I was supposed to kill him.

Nothing had changed. He still hated me and wanted to get away from me as quickly as possible.

As I stood there, numb with my failure, Giulio murmured, "There you are, stronzo."

He squeezed. A pop echoed through the woods, the birds in the nearby area scattering and flying away.

"Got him in the chest." Giulio stood and brushed off his pants.

We were too far away from the farmhouse to see whether Buscetta was dead or not. I would need to get closer and make sure.

Giulio grabbed his pack and paused. His face was taut, the olive skin flushed. I didn't want this to be it, but what else could I say? He knew how I felt. And it was clear he'd never forgive me.

He opened his mouth, then shut it. What had he been about to say? Was he willing to give us another chance?

Then he gave a small shake of his stubborn head. "Have a nice life, Alessandro."

And he started out of the woods.

All I could do was stand and watch.

CHAPTER TWENTY-SEVEN

Giulio

Málaga, Spain
Four weeks later

The nightclub pulsed and flashed, the base thumping in my chest. Bodies writhed and swayed on the dance floor, as couples embraced in dark corners. It reminded me of the one person I was desperately trying to forget. Even all this time later I still ached for him.

But I wasn't on the floor, searching for a distraction. Instead I was in the VIP area above, looking down at the sweaty sea of people.

I lit another cigarette and leaned back. The man across from me, Ilya, worked for Nikolai Kuznetsov, who was currently busy with Theo in Paris. But Nikolai had agreed to take care of my Golubev problem for a large payout.

After I filled Ilya in on all I knew about Golubev's operation, I asked, "Do I need to worry about someone else trying to step in once he is gone?"

Ilya finished his drink and set the glass on the table. "Is hard to say.

I think you have many challengers in the future. Spain is a long way from Italy, yes? Are you ready to fight?"

I looked at Benito. We'd arrived in Spain last week and were quietly getting settled. Organized. Finding storage places, houses. Secret holes and untraceable bank accounts. It was a lot of fucking work and I was exhausted.

But were we ready to fight? Fuck, yes. The challenge of it, the possibility of what could be here, was the only thing keeping me going.

Still, it felt like something was missing.

One of my father's men—now mine—walked toward us, his phone up to his ear. At the table he leaned down to speak quietly with Benito. My cousin frowned.

"G," Benito said. "There's a blond Russian woman at the door asking to see you."

Che cazzo? I glanced at Ilya. "Yours?"

"No, but maybe she will be?" He rubbed his hands together."I have not found a woman to take home yet tonight."

"Send her up," I told them. "Let's try to get Ilya laid."

While we waited I ordered another round of drinks. Then I stared out at the men on the dance floor. Not once had I been tempted to go find someone here and take the edge off. My dick had practically stopped working after Palermo, except for when I fantasized about a certain gray-eyed assassin.

Pathetic.

Our guard led a young woman toward the table. She wore a long fluffy tulle skirt and a t-shirt that said something in Russian. On her feet were a pair of new Converse, and her blond hair was pulled into a high ponytail.

She looked directly at me. "Giulio Ravazzani."

I cocked my head. "Do we know each other?"

"I know you." She spoke in English with a heavy Russian accent. "You are even more handsome in person. Now I begin to understand."

"Understand?"

"What he saw in you."

The pieces fell into place. Russian woman. Sasha. "You're his assistant."

"You got it on the first guess. Impressive." She turned to Ilya and said something in Russian. From the way Ilya frowned, I suspected it wasn't friendly.

"What did you say to him?" I asked her.

It was Ilya that spoke up. "She says the Bratva killed her family and she hopes mine meets the same fate."

Cristo santo. I didn't want to piss off Nikolai's man. I needed him. "Sasha, why are you here?"

"To see you, the Ravazzani *principe*."

Only Alessio called me that. The back of my neck turned hot at the reminder. I snapped, "He did not need to bother. It's a waste of your time."

"He didn't send me. I haven't talked to him. I don't even know where he is."

Was this true? I studied her face. "He didn't tell you where he was going? And you haven't tried to find him?"

"I'm not stupid. Of course I have tried to find him. But Alessio is the only person who can evade me. He is like a ghost. *Poof*."

"When was the last time you saw him or spoke to him?"

"Why do you care?"

"I don't," I lied.

She reached into her bag—and Benito shot to his feet, his hand now inside his jacket and grabbing for his pistol. Sasha's gaze flicked to him. "Do not worry, big man. I bring only harmless papers. No weapons."

Slowly, she eased a stack of papers out of the bag. "For you, Ravazzani." She dropped the thick pack on the glass table in front of me. "And I have not seen or heard from him in three weeks, when he asked me to do this."

"Three weeks!" I reached for the papers but didn't look at them yet. "Have you checked his passport, his accounts? He has to be using money."

"He is too smart to use his passport. And he doesn't have access to his money."

What did that mean? He was resourceful—perhaps the most

resourceful man I'd ever met—but why go underground? This worried me. And Sasha was entirely too blasé for my liking.

She pointed at the stack in my hands. "You need to read that."

"Sit down." I extinguished my cigarette and gestured to Benito's empty seat. I wasn't done interrogating her. "Have a drink while I look this over."

Ilya took that as his cue to move in and chat up Sasha. I ignored them and began reading. My alarm mounted with each sentence. Alessio had transferred all of his holdings—bank accounts, investments, even his properties—over to me. He'd given me *everything*. It made no sense. I left him in Sicily, our status very clear. Despite his apologies, I had rejected him. I couldn't get past the lying.

In return he'd given me everything he owned and disappeared.

"Che cazzo?" I looked up at Sasha helplessly.

"I don't know much Italian," Sasha said. "But your face tells me you are as confused as I am."

I switched to English. "Did he leave a note? What did he say?"

"He gave me those instructions," Sasha gestured to the paperwork. "Told me to see it carried through. Once I'm finished, he said I should look for a new job."

"New job?" I threw the papers on the glass. "Fuck, I don't want it. I don't want any of it." Then a horrible thought hit me. I had to grab the armrest to steady myself. "Was this . . . was this meant to serve as a will?"

Sasha shrugged. "A year ago I would have said absolutely not. But he hasn't been the same since Málaga."

I could easily say the same. My whole life had been turned upside down. But then it reset in a new direction, one Alessio had helped me navigate before everything went to shit.

"I don't need you and I don't love you. Just like your parents."

I regretted saying it. I lost my cool and wanted to hurt him. Walking away from him in Sicily had been hard, but I forced myself to do it. Even if I could forgive him for lying, how could I be with him after all that happened? Would I bring him to Siderno for dinners with my family, knowing that he almost killed my father? The idea was ludicrous.

I rubbed my eyes and Frankie's words from a few weeks ago bounced into my head.

"We are capable of forgiveness. And sometimes it's the most human, most beautiful thing we can do."

I didn't know if I could. I was out of my depth, swimming in uncertainty. Paolo had never betrayed or lied to me. Neither had any of my father's men. If so, they would've been killed. Was I weak if I forgave Alessio? Would anyone ever respect me? Could I respect myself?

But Sasha's news had me worried. This wasn't like Alessio. He was a loner, but giving me his money? That was alarming. Was he trying to get my attention? Or was this a penance?

Fuck, I didn't know. But I needed to find him and learn the truth.

I rose and touched the cuff links on my wrists. A gift from my father, the links had belonged to my grandfather and they reminded me of the Ravazzani blood running through my veins. We were strong. Fearless and smart. I hoped to do everything here that my father accomplished in Siderno.

And I would—just as soon as I cleared up my past.

"Sasha," I said, interrupting the arguing she was doing with Ilya. "Where was the last place you saw him?"

"London. But this was before he left for Sicily."

So, where would he go after Sicily without money or a passport? "Is he still in Sicily?"

"No. He boarded a flight for London, but never arrived."

Interesting. "He said he has properties all over Europe."

Sasha gestured to the papers on the table. "Not any longer."

"But he could be hiding in one." While he waited for me to come find him.

"All the houses have been checked. Even the outsides, the cellars. The attics. The mouse holes. Nothing. He is in the wind."

"Are you thinking of searching for him, principe?" Benito was by my side, and I scowled at the use of the nickname. He chuckled. "I like it. Until you give me a better name, that is what I'm calling you."

"Then I will shoot you and feed you to the pigs I clearly need to buy." I inhaled a deep breath and let it out slowly. "And yes, I am thinking of searching for him."

"We don't have much time. How long do you think you'll be gone?"

Alessio could be anywhere in the world. Mexico, South America. Antarctica—

Oh, of course. It made perfect sense. A small smile tugged at my lips. There was only one place he would go, one place so deeply off the grid. No wonder Sasha couldn't find him.

But I could.

I grabbed the papers off the counter. I would go there and force him to explain this nonsense. "I have to go."

Sasha peered at my face. "You know where he is, don't you?"

"I do—and I need to pack a fucking sweater."

————

Alessio

Isle of Canna, Scotland, U.K.

I BROUGHT the ax over my head and swung down. The log split in two perfect halves. I threw each half onto the pile and grabbed another one. When it was in place, I braced my feet and swung. The blade slid through the wood, breaking it apart.

Sweat rolled along my temples, even in the cold afternoon air. I liked chopping wood. I liked the repetitive motion, the mindless task, and the never-ending supply of logs. And it would help strengthen my right arm, which had come out of the cast only last week.

I stopped to drink some water, while the sheep bleated softly in the distance. There were no other sounds. Stretches of days went by where I didn't speak to another human being. It was perfect.

There were the memories, of course. He was everywhere here, from the bedsheets I couldn't bring myself to change, to the pans he cooked with to make us dinner. The poetry he read at night. Those were the hardest, the little things that constantly reminded me of him.

But they were soothing in a strange way, too. Like I still had a small piece of him here with me.

It was pathetic. He didn't want me. I wasn't sure why I was clinging to the idea of him. I needed to let him go.

Mrs. Campbell said it would eventually get easier. That one day I would wake up and not be haunted by him. I couldn't wait. Someday I'd hardly remember him at all.

Shutting off my brain, I went back to chopping wood. I focused on the ax in my hand, the screaming muscles in my arms. Log after log split apart. The stack grew higher.

The hairs on the back of my neck suddenly stood up. Out of the corner of my eye I saw a lone figure walking around the side of the farmhouse. A man with his head down. His coat was too thin for this sort of weather, which meant he wasn't a local.

Then he looked up. *That face.* I knew that face. I dreamt about it every night.

Was he really here? Wait, *why* was he here?

Panting, I set the ax down and wiped my forehead with my sleeve. I hadn't expected to ever see him again, let alone here. How had he known where to find me? I'd been careful to cover my tracks and Mrs. Campbell wouldn't have mentioned it to a soul.

I waited as he approached. I soaked in the familiar shift of his shoulders. And the way the light brought out the flecks of gold in his dark hair. His straight nose, his rugged chin. He was perfect, a gorgeous angel, and I ached from missing him.

It made me angry. I was tired of feeling this way. Tired of wanting someone I couldn't have. Tired of the guilt. I had bared my heart and soul to this man and he'd rejected me. So, what was this? He needed to beat up on me some more?

Giulio stopped and leaned against the side of the house, well out of reach. He stared at me. "I don't want it."

I frowned. What was he talking about? Maybe this was a dream. Or a nightmare.

When I didn't respond, his eyebrows pulled together. "Did you hear me?"

"Why the fuck are you here?"

He blinked twice, probably surprised by my tone, but I didn't care. I'd come to this island to be alone.

"Hello to you, too, Alessio."

"Answer the question."

Straightening, he folded his arms across his chest. I tried not to notice how good he looked. "I don't want your money."

Ah. So that was why he was here. Of course. My stomach sank as if I'd swallowed a stone. "That is too bad, because I am not taking it back."

"Well, I don't want it. If you are trying to buy your way back into my life, you're wasting your time."

I shifted the ax handle to my other hand and ground my molars together. Why was he telling me things I already knew? "I am not trying to buy anything. I am trying to help you, stronzo. Make amends."

"Amends? It's millions of Euros. Ma che cazzo, Alessio?"

That money represented something terrible to me. Until Giulio came along, I had no allegiances, no ties. I'd been selfish, offering myself up to the highest bidder and that money was the result. And earning it had cost me the one person I'd cared about most. "It's nothing."

"It's more than nothing," Giulio said. "And I don't need it."

"Then give it away."

"You are being a fucking dick." He took a threatening step toward me, his mouth flat and tight. "You broke what was between us, not me."

He wanted a fight? I was more than ready.

I threw the ax down and snarled, "And I have apologized and begged your forgiveness for it. Yet you are determined to hold onto your anger like a badge of honor. Too proud to forgive because of how it might look to your stupid mafia and precious father. Too scared to be your own man."

"Oh, *fuck you*," he shouted.

"No, fuck you, Giulio. I'm tired of doing this with you. Either leave me alone or forgive me. Stop kissing me one minute then telling me how much you don't want me the next."

"You have no right to be angry with me. You almost killed my father—and then *lied* to me about it!"

"He was a fucking job, no different than the countless other jobs I've carried out in my career. I didn't know you when I accepted it. I certainly never knew I'd fall in love with you later. People make mistakes, principe. Maybe not *you*, because you are perfect, no? But us regular people do."

"I have made mistakes," he said defensively, "but this is not about me. It's about you. Quit trying to turn it around."

I scowled at the ground. I was too exhausted, too heartsick for this any longer. I'd taken a beating in that dungeon for him, gone to Palermo to kill Buscetta to keep him safe. Turned over all my money. I couldn't prove myself anymore.

I needed him gone.

Picking up the ax, I placed a fresh log on the stump. "You've said what you came to say. You can go now." I held the ax over my head and swung it down. My hands howled in pain, my barely-healed arm throbbing with each movement. I hardly noticed.

"Madre di dio, you are stubborn."

That was funny, coming from him.

I didn't speak. My chest was on fire, misery strangling my heart, and I was afraid I might start begging in a moment. I pressed my lips together, trying to not make more of a fool of myself with this man.

Several minutes passed where the only sound was the blade slicing through wood. The thump of the logs when I threw them onto the pile. Sheep moving in the background. I didn't check to see if he'd left. I told myself I didn't care.

Then he appeared, walking over to examine the woodpile. "Is all this just from today?"

I split another log in answer.

"You're bleeding, Alessio."

I looked down. The ax handle was red with blood, the blisters on my palms cracked open.

Giulio was suddenly in front of me, taking the ax away and grabbing my wrists. I tried to pull away, but he held tight, examining my hands. "Come inside. Let me bandage them."

"It doesn't hurt."

"They will. I don't know why you aren't wearing gloves." He

snatched my wrist and began tugging me toward the farmhouse. His grip was strong.

He's touching me.

My muscles relaxed and I allowed him to bring me inside. "Sit on a stool," he said. "Let me get the supplies."

I did as ordered and rested my throbbing hands on the counter. The marble was cool against my overheated skin. Seconds later, he returned carrying the medical supplies. Then he went to the sink and flicked on the water. "Let's wash them first."

I came around and stood next to him at the sink. After he tested the water temperature, he motioned for my hands. I placed them in his palms and he gently moved them under the water. I hissed and tried to pull away, but he held fast. "Why did you do this to yourself?"

There was no good answer for that, so I stayed quiet. He took the soap and began cleaning my hands. His touch was light and careful. We were so close that our shoulders were pressed together, and I could see every rise and fall of his chest. The sweep of his lashes as he blinked. The kiss of whiskers on his jaw and the slight bow of his upper lip.

"Stop staring at me," he said quietly, still concentrating on my hands.

"I can't help it," I admitted. "*Sei bello.*"

He moved my hands under the water to rinse the soap off. "Giving me the money won't bring me back."

"I know." And I did. What happened between us couldn't be fixed. He'd been very clear about that.

He shut off the water and took a clean towel out of a drawer. Then he patted my hands off gingerly. "*Allora*, do you plan on living on this farm for the rest of your life?"

"I like it here. What's wrong with it?"

"Everything is wrong with it. Sit down and let me put on the bandages."

We didn't speak as he put ointment on my cuts and then wrapped my hands in bandages. When he finished, he shoved aside the box of supplies and braced his hands on the counter. Tormented blue eyes locked with mine. "My whole life has been nothing but secrets,

Alessio. It felt like you were the one thing I had that was true and honest. Except even that was a lie."

Not breaking his stare, I gave him the truth for the last time. "I'm sorry. If I could go back and change it, I would."

He reached into the pocket of his jacket and took out a pack of cigarettes. I watched his long fingers pull one out and put it to his lips. A flick of a lighter later and his cheeks hollowed, inhaling the nicotine and chemicals. White smoke filled the space between us. "I apologize for what I said in the hills that morning," he said quietly. "About your parents."

I don't need you and I don't love you. Just like your parents.

I lifted one shoulder. "It is true, no?"

"I shouldn't have said it. I was trying to hurt you and I was angry."

He stared out the farmhouse window and continued to smoke. Finally, he asked, "How are the sheep? Do they miss me?"

"I've been bulking them up. They were underfed. Too skinny."

He flicked me a glance. "I could say the same about you."

I didn't respond. I knew I looked terrible. That was what misery and regret did to a person. Giulio was still gorgeous, though. Other than the smoking habit, he appeared exactly the same.

We sat in silence for what felt like eons as he finished his cigarette. There was a wall between us and I wasn't sure how to tear it down. Or if I even could. I watched as the paper burned on his cigarette. What happened when he finished smoking? Would he leave?

The words tumbled out of my mouth. "Have dinner with me."

Light blue eyes pinned me to the spot. "Here?"

"Sì, certo."

"You cook?"

We both knew I wasn't competent in the kitchen. Giulio had been the one to prepare most of our meals. "I can make scrambled eggs," I said.

"With your bandaged hands?" He shook his head and the hint of a smile ghosted across his face. "And is this what you have been surviving on? Mamma mia. No wonder you are so skinny."

Turning, he strode to the refrigerator and opened it. He pulled out eggs, butter and a hunk of Parmesan. A lemon that was starting to turn brown. "Garlic?"

"No."

"What kind of red-blooded Sicilian doesn't keep garlic in the house?" He rummaged through the cupboards and found a few seasonings. Flour. Jarred anchovies and a bottle of olive oil.

"Someone cleaned out the refrigerator and pantry after we left," I offered as an explanation as he set everything on the island between us. "You are lucky I have even that."

"If I am cooking for you, then open a bottle of wine."

I scratched my jaw and wondered how to break the news. When I didn't move, he stopped what he was doing. His expression turned wary. "Are you telling me there is no wine in this house?"

"Whoever came in . . . ."

"Took all my good wine? Ma dai, these Scots. Go." He waved me away. "Go and find some wine, assassino. And tell Mrs. Campbell I want *Italian* wine, not French."

CHAPTER TWENTY-EIGHT

Giulio

As I mixed dough for the pasta, I shook my head at myself. What was I doing here? Making dinner, like we were a couple?

I should leave. I didn't owe him anything, and I would find a way to return his money. We'd said everything that needed saying.

So, why was I rolling out pasta and playing house?

Because he looks terrible. Because I'm a fool. Because I miss him.

My phone buzzed in my pocket. Wiping my hands on a towel, I checked the caller. It could be Benito with an update on things in Málaga.

Frankie's name appeared on the screen.

I considered not answering, but maybe she could talk some sense into me since I'd clearly lost my mind. "Pronto."

"Well?" Her voice was breathless, excited. "How did Scotland go?"

Now that I was no longer on the run, Frankie and I talked every day. Often more than once. So she knew of my plans to confront Alessio about the money. "I am in Scotland and it is still going."

"What does that mean, still going? Are you with him right now?"

"Do you think I would answer if he was here?"

"So tell me what happened so far."

As I finished the dough, I filled her in with a brief version of events since I arrived in Canna. "He's gone to find wine and I'm making spaghetti for supper like a . . ."

"Like a man in love?"

"*Stai zitto!*" I snapped, telling her to shut up. "I was going to say like an idiot."

"Stop. Zia has rubbed off on you. It's sweet that you like to feed people. How does he look?"

I rolled my eyes, though she couldn't see me. "I haven't noticed."

She laughed. "Oh, bullshit. You know you checked out every inch of that tall dark snack when you first saw him today."

I had, but I'd never admit it. "He's thin."

"Which is why you're feeding him. God, you're adorable."

"I am hanging up."

"Don't you dare! I told your father where you were going, by the way."

Oh, shit. "Why? For fuck's sake, Frankie—"

"You weren't returning his calls. He rang Benito, who lied and said you had the flu and couldn't pick up. Fausto wasn't buying it, so I came clean. I'm sorry, G."

I scowled at the phone. "Damn it, matrigna."

"I know, I know. I swear, I don't tell him everything. But I hate when he gets worried and he gets that little wrinkle between his brows. Then he paces and sulks. I usually have to distract him with sex, but because of the pregnancy—"

"Basta!" The last thing I wished to hear about was her sex life with my father. "What did he say about me coming to see Alessio."

"Nothing."

That was bad. My father had something to say on nearly every subject, especially when it pertained to me. "Nothing?"

"He said to tell you to ring him when you're back in Málaga."

Strange. "He wasn't angry about Alessio?"

"I told you, he'll respect whatever you decide. It's your life, and he knows the blame for the shooting lies with Enzo. Not Alessio."

I wasn't so sure. But Fausto rarely said anything he didn't mean. "He actually said this?"

"Not in so many words," she hedged. "Anyway, we both just want you to be happy. And I want you to come visit more often."

"That I can do, matrigna. That I can do."

"Ti voglio bene, G. Be happy. And forgive him."

Shaking my head, I said, "Ti voglio bene. I'll ring you later."

"You better. I'm dying to know what happens."

Me too. We disconnected and I went back to making the pasta and sauce. I put a pot of water to boil on the stove. Salted it. The dough was ready to cut, so I sliced the noodles and let them sit. I poured some anchovies and oil into a pan with butter and let it cook on a low heat.

I heard the front door open and close. Heavy boots hit the floor. He was back already?

He strode into the kitchen, a bottle of wine in each hand. His face was flushed. When he set the wine on the island, I asked, "Did you run the entire way there and back?"

"Of course." He said it was no big deal. "You wanted wine, so . . . ."

I didn't want him to see how pleased I felt, so I grabbed the opener out of the drawer and tossed it to him. "Pour us two glasses."

"Oh!" He fished into his pocket and rolled a head of garlic over to me. "From Mrs. Campbell. She says hello."

"Perfect timing." Using the zester, I added two garlic cloves into my anchovy sauce. Zia said this was the best way to put a hint of garlic to a dish. Next were the cooked noodles, then some lemon zest. I tossed it all together then plated it up with more zest and parmesan.

Alessio had two glasses of chianti waiting. I sat on the stool next to him and we started eating.

"È delizioso, principe," Alessio said after a big bite. "Grazie."

I lifted my glass, drank my wine and watched him eat. I wasn't terribly hungry, and he seemed ravenous. How long had he been out there chopping wood today? His hands looked like raw ground meat.

When he finished he checked out my plate. "You are not eating?"

I slid my plate over to him. "I ate a big lunch," I lied. "You take it."

He didn't argue. I refilled our wine and focused on the moment. I didn't want to think about the past or the future. I concentrated on right now, how I felt sitting next to him in this cozy little farmhouse in the middle of nowhere.

I didn't hate it.

I could relax with Alessio. He didn't judge and he was easy to be around. No forced conversation, no awkward silences. I also felt safe, as if nothing bad would happen when he was in the vicinity.

After the last few weeks in Málaga without him, I hadn't realized how much I'd missed this. How much I'd missed his steadiness, his quiet fortitude. Being in a room with him felt familiar and right. Like home.

I lit a cigarette, needing something to do with my hands. I was suddenly nervous, but I couldn't say why. My skin hummed, an electric charge building in my blood. I could count my heartbeats. Each inhale and exhale echoed in my ears. *In and out. In and out.* The sound of Alessio's fork on the plate wasn't half as loud as the riot inside my body.

There was no use denying it. I wanted him. My dick no longer cared about anything other than getting close to this man. And I was losing the battle to resist.

Alessio groaned as he pushed his empty plate away, and the sound was so sexual, so primal that my groin tightened. Had he even realized? Doubtful. As far as he knew, I still hated him.

But I didn't. I was hurt, but the animosity was gone. Left in its place was an ache, a weariness from missing him.

"You are determined to hold onto your anger like a badge of honor. Too proud to forgive because of how it might look to your stupid mafia and precious father."

Why was I torturing myself by holding onto this grudge? He'd apologized, and I believed him when he said he would go back and do things differently. Was it pride holding us back from seeing where this went?

"More wine?" He held the bottle up to me.

"Are you trying to get me drunk, *assassino*?"

His nostrils flared at the nickname. "If it gets you to stay the night, then maybe."

My lips twitched. "At least you are honest."

I hadn't realized what I was saying until it was too late. But now the words were out there, hanging in the air like rotten food. Alessio looked away and set the bottle on the island.

I sighed and stubbed my cigarette out. Would I always be reminded of the past with him? "This is awkward."

"It doesn't have to be." He fiddled with his wine glass, moving it in circles on the marble counter. "I don't want to pretend or be careful with you. I can take whatever you throw at me, principe."

I knew this was true. Our fights were well-matched. I didn't have to hold back with him, and he certainly never went easy on me.

He got up and took our plates to the sink. I stared at his broad back as he began to clean up our supper. The cloth of his t-shirt stretched over his lean muscles. His jeans were looser than I remembered, but they still hugged his ass in the best way. My tongue swept along the backside of my teeth as I stared, wanting. Craving. Wrestling with the memories.

Without realizing it, I started moving across the floor and closing in on the sink. He paused. I knew he was aware of where I was at all times, his keen senses on high alert, but he didn't turn around.

I pressed in, flattening my front against his larger frame, and braced my palms on the cabinets beside his head. Heat wrapped around me, the hard angles of his body fitting so perfectly into mine. I ran my nose along the back of his neck. The smell of his skin—soap, the outdoors, and a little sweat—filled my lungs. My cock began lengthening, and I ground it into the crease of his ass. I had missed this.

The water shut off. Now the only sound in the kitchen was our breath, the rough exhales filled with anticipation. Dio, I wanted him so badly. I couldn't focus on anything else.

"What are you doing?" he asked.

I wish I knew. "Are you saying no?"

"Of course not."

"Thank fuck."

I kissed his neck with light brushes of my lips. He shivered, so I worshiped all the skin I could reach on both sides of his throat. Then I bit down on the meaty part, where it joined with his shoulder. He grunted and rocked his hips, banging into the counter.

"Are you hard for me?" I whispered.

His head bobbed with a nod. Had I robbed him of the ability to speak already? Good. We'd done this so often that I knew his body, his reactions. I knew what he needed. "Then take your cock out."

"You take it out," he threw back.

There were times when Alessio was more submissive, and others when he asserted himself. Both sides had always turned me on. But when he was feeling assertive, I knew we were in for a wild ride.

I didn't hesitate. Shifting, I unbuttoned his jeans and lowered the zipper. Then I worked them down his hips, along with his briefs. His impressive length bobbed out, ready and waiting for me. I angled to the right and caged him in with my legs. "Hands up." When he braced his hands on the cupboard, I reached around for him.

Light as a feather, I trailed my fingers down his stomach, through the coarse hair surrounding his erection. Then I gave the lightest caress along the length of his dick, teasing. I traced the vein that ran along the side, the wide crown. He was biting his lip, watching my hand intently. I asked, "Have you been thinking about me? Thinking about me fucking you?"

"Maybe I have been thinking about fucking you."

"Liar. You have been craving my dick in your ass again."

"I have missed everything about you."

He said it simply, solemnly. I believed him, but I wasn't ready to open my heart to him again. Not yet. I needed time to wrap my head around what was happening between us.

But our physical connection? I had no problem understanding this.

"Do you think you've earned that, Alessione? Have you earned a fucking from me?" I nipped his earlobe and pumped his cock with my hand.

His mouth was slack with pleasure, his expression a portrait of lust and desperation. I loved watching him like this. Driving him out of his mind was a high like nothing else.

I stroked his crown, rubbing the underside, and he tensed. "Giulio," he gasped.

My mobile rang over on the island. I let it go unanswered as I bit Alessio's shoulder, my hand continuing to work him slowly.

"Cristo santo," he whispered. "Just like that, principe."

My phone sounded again. I glanced at it, considering whether I should answer.

"Do not fucking dare," Alessio growled.

Because I was a sadistic bastard, I released Alessio's dick. "Stay here. Don't move and don't touch yourself."

"I am going to punch you," he grumbled as I went to see who was calling.

"I look forward to it." I checked the name on my phone. Benito. I touched the glass to accept the call. "Pronto."

"G, you need to come back. Immediately. We have a problem."

I didn't want details over the phone, and Benito knew better than to offer them up. So I asked, "Can't it wait?"

"No. I need you here. Things haven't gone as planned."

I stared at Alessio, waiting for me by the sink. Shit. Disappointment crashed through me, but I said into the phone, "I'll get on the boat and come back as quickly as I can."

"I'll send a car to the airport. Just let me know when you're arriving."

We rang off and I returned to Alessio's side. He'd followed my orders, which was so hot. I moved in, but didn't grab his cock. "I have to go."

"Fuck, no. Not yet. Let me touch you." He hitched his jeans up over his erection and turned to me. His eyes were blown with lust, the lids heavy. It was all I could do not to push him to the floor.

I held his face in my palm. "There's something wrong in Málaga. I have to leave immediately." With a heavy dose of regret, I stepped away. "Maybe we can revisit this some other time." I had no idea when, but maybe I could return in the next few weeks, after this emergency was handled.

Alessio buttoned his pants. "I'm coming with you."

"That's not necessary. We'll figure all of this out later." I was already texting the captain of the boat I'd hired to bring me here. Then I pulled up the contact information for the pilot at the airport on the Isle of Barra.

My phone disappeared from my hand. "Che cazzo?"

Alessio's fingers wrapped loosely around my throat as he leaned into my face. "Here me now, Giulio. I. Am. Coming. With. You."

My heart kicked in my chest at his deep growl. I wished I had time for us to work all this anger out in the bedroom, but I didn't. And I wasn't sure bringing him with me was wise. "Why?"

"I'm not letting you out of my sight, not until we figure out whatever is happening between us." He released me and stalked across the floor toward the hall. "And I won't allow you to get hurt in Málaga. So wherever you go, I go."

CHAPTER TWENTY-NINE

Alessio

Málaga, Spain

I followed Giulio down the steps of the private plane and onto the tarmac. It was the middle of the night. I slept in my seat during the flight, while Giulio spent the time on his phone, working. In the military we learned to sleep anywhere, anytime, and that had served me well over the years as I trailed my targets.

An SUV waited for us, two men standing guard by the doors. Both of them were wearing guns. One of the men came forward to shake Giulio's hand. "Sorry to ruin your little vacation, G. I see you brought back a souvenir."

Giulio gestured to me. "Benito, you remember Alessio."

I dipped my chin in acknowledgement. Benito did the same. Giulio had already explained Benito's role here and what the two of them planned to do. I couldn't believe they had Don Ravazzani's blessing, but Giulio said his father refused to get involved with the Bratva. So it was decided Giulio would start a mini-Ravazzani empire in Spain.

We began walking to the car. Giulio got in the back, as did Benito.

The message was clear, but I didn't mind. I would happily ride in the front. Giulio and I weren't a couple at the moment. So if Benito wanted to play this game for now, I'd let him.

The streets were quiet and dark as we set off. Giulio lit a cigarette and cracked a window. "Tell me, Bennie."

"It's Golubev. Somehow the word got out. He raided two of the storage units today. I'm waiting for word about the others."

"Motherfucker!" Giulio slapped the headrest of the seat in front of him. "How did he find out?"

"We don't know yet. My guess is he has someone watching us closely."

"Or someone on our team has betrayed us," Giulio said.

"Could be. There are some new men who didn't come with us from Siderno."

"Cristo." Giulio sighed. "I leave for one fucking day . . . ."

"How do you want to handle it?"

"Go find Golubev, obviously. I'm going to kill that Russian asshole."

In the front seat, I bit my lip and tried to stem my smile. Killing Golubev was the right move, and I was glad to see Giulio making strong decisions to assert himself here. It was like watching him step into his father's shoes.

"Do we know where he is?" Giulio asked.

"Probably celebrating," I muttered.

"What was that, assassino?"

I looked over my shoulder at Giulio. "Golubev is probably out celebrating. Does he own any strip clubs?"

Benito said, "That's too public."

"That's why he wouldn't go to a nightclub," I said. "But a strip club, likely in a back room."

Giulio and Benito exchanged a look. "Alessio is very good at tracking people, Bennie. He's probably right."

Benito pulled out his phone. "Let me call one of our contacts. He might know which clubs Golubev owns."

In a few minutes Benito had the name of Golubev's biggest strip club and the one he visited the most often. We stopped to pick up more men and a fuck lot of guns. Giulio watched as I selected a few pistols and an automatic rifle. "How is your aim?" he asked quietly as we stood off to the side, away from everyone else.

"Better than yours, principe."

He laughed and bumped our shoulders together. "Oh, fuck off." Then he turned serious. "You know, you don't have to come. I don't want you to risk your life for this."

I put my hand on his shoulder. "I have risked my life for far less worthy causes. And I told you, I'm not letting you out of my sight until you finish what you started in the farmhouse."

"You just want to get laid."

We both knew it was far more than that. But this was too fragile, too private to discuss here. "You gave me blue balls," I said with a smirk. "You owe me."

"Then I'll just say thank you. This means a lot."

I swallowed the emotions bubbling up in my chest and nodded once.

We piled into two cars and set off into the streets. I slowed my breathing and heart rate, focused entirely on what needed to be done. I wasn't worried. I wasn't kidding when I said I wouldn't allow anything to happen to Giulio.

Once parked we all got out. I followed Giulio and Benito into an alley. There was a camera positioned on a steel door near some dumpsters. I held onto Giulio's arm, then pointed at the camera. He motioned for everyone to stop. Taking out a switchblade, I climbed onto a dumpster, reached over and cut the camera wire.

I hopped down and said, "Now someone will come out to investigate. That's when we go in."

Giulio's mouth curved as he ordered everyone to keep out of sight, behind the door. A few minutes later, the metal creaked open and a guy with a gun emerged. Benito pounced. He yanked the Russian out into the alley, snapped his neck, and dropped him. Giulio was already through the door and into the strip club. Cursing, I followed, wishing he'd let me go first.

Music from the front echoed in the hall. A half-naked woman appeared and she squeaked when she saw us. Giulio put his finger to his lips and held out a stack of money. In Spanish, he asked if Golubev was here. She pointed to a hallway on the other side and held up three fingers. Third door.

Giulio thanked her and told her to stay hidden. We made our way to the correct door. Benito kicked it in and again I was forced to follow. I didn't like it, but this wasn't the time to argue.

The room was a private VIP suite, the kind with long leather benches and soft couches. The lighting was dark, but there was no problem seeing Golubev fucking some girl on one of the couches. Three of his men were there, too, each with a woman. Drugs, money and booze were scattered on the tables. As I predicted, they were celebrating.

The girls began screaming as shots rang out. Two of Golubev's men went down quickly, and the third was just reaching for his weapon when I shot him between the eyes. Benito went to shoot Golubev and Giulio stopped him, shouting in Italian, "*Aspetta!*"

The girl scrambled off Golubev's dick and hurried out of the room. I approached the Russian, gun drawn to keep him in place. Giulio probably wanted to question Golubev on how he'd learned of the storage units. Smart.

Giulio ordered the rest of the men to deal with any of Golubev's soldiers. This left Benito, Giulio and me alone with Golubev. I remained perfectly still, my aim steady.

"You stupid fuck," Giulio said as he stepped forward. "Did you think I wouldn't find you?"

Golubev sneered and said in Russian, "Have you come to see a real dick?" He tacked on a slur for a gay man, one that made me clutch my pistol tighter. Obviously he thought Giulio wouldn't understand.

"What did he say, Alessio?"

Never taking my gun off Golubev's head, I translated into Italian— including the slur. Giulio shook his head at the Russian man and repeated, "You stupid fuck."

Golubev hid his surprise well. "You have started a war by coming here."

"No, I haven't." Giulio lowered himself onto one of the leather benches. He appeared totally at ease, much as he had with Nikolai. "You don't have as many friends in Moscow as you think you do."

A crack broke through Golubev's smug expression. "You know nothing of this, Italian."

"I know that you fucked Volkov's sister, and that's why you were sent to Spain ten years ago. He doesn't have very nice things to say about you, by the way."

Yuri Volkov was the head of the Bratva back in the motherland. I wondered when Giulio had learned all of this.

"Put your dick away," Giulio ordered with a wave of his fingers. "It's making me sick just looking at it."

Golubev tucked his cock back in his pants but didn't button them. "That isn't what I hear."

A violent hatred flared in my belly. I wanted to hurt this man badly. I could do it so easily, too.

It must've shown on my face, because in Italian, Giulio said, "Patience, assassino."

I forced myself to relax.

"Now," Giulio said. "Tell me how you found out about my storage locations."

"I don't know what you're talking about," Golubev said.

"Wrong answer. Trust me, you are going to want to tell me."

"Do you think I am scared of you? A man that has been run out of Italy because he likes to take it up the ass?"

"Ma dai, you are a fool," Benito said.

Giulio didn't flinch. "If you don't tell me, I am going to ask Alessio to hurt you. He's dying to make you suffer. Can't you see it on his face? I wonder what he will do first . . . "

"Is he a fairy, too?"

"Last chance, Golubev. Tell me how you found out."

"Fuck you," the Russian spat, adding on the gay slur once more.

"Alessio," Giulio said with a dramatic sigh, but I was already moving.

I flicked open my switchblade and drove it into the muscle of Golubev's thigh. With my other hand, I cupped the back of his head and drove it down onto my raised knee. I heard the satisfying snap of cartilage as his nose broke. Golubev howled.

It was over in a blink.

Not feeling the least bit satisfied, I leaned down and grabbed his hair, yanking him back so I could see his face. Blood poured out of his nose and his eyes were glassy with pain. I snarled, "That is Signore motherfucking Ravazzani to you."

Then I twisted the knife in his leg—and yanked it out slowly. I could feel the muscle tearing.

Golubev clutched his thigh and screamed. Red welled from between his fingers. We all watched as he writhed on the couch.

"Did I forget to tell you?" Giulio asked calmly. "Alessio was a member of an elite force in the Italian military. He's also very protective of me. If you don't give me what I want, he's only going to keep hurting you."

Golubev panted, his eyes screwed shut. "You are a dead man," he wheezed.

Giulio stretched his arm along the back of the sofa, as if settling in. "Alessio, take him apart."

He didn't have to tell me twice. My hands were eager to inflict pain on this piece of shit. Golubev tried to fight me, but I put my foot on his injured thigh and pushed down. When he sagged in pain, I got him on his feet and marched him to the middle of the room. I had at least four inches and thirty pounds on him, so he was no match for me. I kicked the backs of his knees, forcing him to kneel on the carpet.

Then I punched him. Repeatedly. Benito helped by keeping Golubev upright, until the Russian went boneless and sagged on the floor. I'd broken his jaw and his cheekbone. Dislocated his shoulder. Several of his teeth were now on the carpet. It was reminiscent of what Ravazzani's men did to me in the dungeon.

Giulio appeared by my side. He bent and peered into Golubev's swollen eyes. "Tell me or we start taking fingers. When we run out of fingers, I'm taking your dick."

Golubev said nothing, just panted heavily. I knew the pain he was in. It was excruciating.

Giulio glanced up at me. "Alessio, a knife."

Before I could do it, Benito presented one. "I took this off one of his men," he explained.

Giulio grabbed Golubev's hand and spread the fingers out on the carpet. There was a silver tray on the table, so I grabbed it and slid it under the Russian's palm. Golubev started fighting then.

"Hold him down," Giulio said, and I pressed my knee into Golubev's dislocated shoulder, pinning him to the floor.

With a clean chop Giulio removed half of Golubev's pinky, right at the joint. The big Russian howled, spit trailing from his mouth onto the floor.

When Giulio grabbed the next finger, Golubev said, "No, don't. I'll tell you."

In his next breath, Golubev gave up the name of his informant. We cut off another finger and he told us where to find the product he'd stolen.

Standing, Giulio nodded at Benito, who put a bullet in Golubev's head. The Russian stared, lifeless, at the ceiling. Giulio clapped Benito on the shoulder. "You'll oversee the cleanup?"

"Sure, G."

Giulio strode for the exit. "Assassino, with me."

I nodded once at Benito and followed the love of my life out of the room. He strode to the alley and kept going until we reached the cars. He was quiet, which was strange.

He got behind the wheel of one of the SUVs. I went around to the passenger side and climbed in. Giulio didn't say anything, his eyes fixed on the road as he turned the engine over.

"Where are we—"

"Don't talk," he snapped and pulled into traffic.

Che cazzo? I didn't understand. Was he angry with me? Horrified by what I'd done? Confused and anxious, I rubbed the cornicello around my neck and watched the hint of morning arrive on the horizon. Where were we going? What was Giulio planning?

He came to an abrupt halt behind an empty burned building. "Get out." Throwing open his door, he left the SUV and then came around the hood toward my side. Slowly, I slid from the car.

His face was taut, his eyes glowing bright. If I didn't know better, I would say—

With one hand, he pushed on my chest and shoved me against the door. Before I could blink he was on me, his mouth attacking mine.

Oh. *Oh.* I kissed him back as his hands ran all over my chest and hips. Again and again his mouth slanted, lips pulling and sucking, his tongue sliding past my lips. I couldn't breathe, dizzy, and I held onto his shoulders to steady myself.

He broke off and yanked at my jeans. "This has to be fast, assassino. We don't have much time."

"We are doing this here?"

"If I don't get my hands on you right now, I'm going to explode." He shoved my zipper down. "That was the hottest fucking thing I've ever seen."

I watched as his hand disappeared inside my briefs. "Thank fuck. I thought you were pissed at me."

His fingers formed a tight clasp around my shaft and he rested his forehead against my chin. "Absolutely not. I've never been so turned on in my entire life."

"Then take out your cock. Let's make this good."

He didn't hesitate. In seconds our bare shafts were lined up, and I clasped them together tightly. "That's it," he hissed. "More."

I pumped once, then thrust my hips. It was like being plugged into an electric outlet. My skin broke out in goosebumps, my toes curling in my boots.

Giulio gasped. "Fuck, keep going."

He let me do the work. I rocked my hips, shoving our dicks through the snug grip of my fingers. He held onto my upper arms, moaning. Precum leaked from us both, slicking our skin, and we slid perfectly against one another. Minutes ticked by as our bodies moved in sync.

"Tighter," he murmured, closing his eyes. "That's it. God, I wish I could bend you over. Take your ass and fuck you so hard."

I grunted, my hips moving faster. I wanted that so badly. I could top or bottom, but something about Giulio always had me craving being underneath him. I kept going, our dicks rubbing like they had been created just for this purpose.

He threw his head back as his hands wandered to my chest. "So sexy. So hot. The way you drove that knife into his leg and broke his nose. Jesus *fuck*, Alessio."

His fingers brushed my nipples and pinched. Hard. Pain punched through me and I couldn't hold back any longer. The orgasm ripped through me, my back bowing as my muscles locked, and jets of come spurted from the head of my cock to coat my hands. I nearly lost my grip, but Giulio's fingers closed around mine, and I shouted to the dark sky overhead. Waves of pleasure went through me, on and on, until I thought I might crumple.

Then Giulio was coming, his beautiful face twisting in pure bliss as his hot jets erupted between us. When it was over, we sagged together like a couple of drunk sailors.

"You are staying here, no? With me?" Giulio said through heaving breaths.

Hope filled my chest, expanding until I thought the bones might split apart. "Do you want me to stay?"

"Yes, I definitely do."

I needed to know what this meant. "As what? Your soldier?"

He frowned. "No. You don't have to work for me. I thought . . . We will be together, Alessio. As partners."

"Boyfriends?"

"Yes." He gave me a soft smile, the one that always melted my heart. "Boyfriends."

My throat grew tight, and I wished we were alone in bed so that I could show him how happy this made me. For now I had to settle with digging my fingers into his sides and holding him close. "Fair warning: I will never give you up, principe. Even if your father hates me."

"Let me worry about my father." He rested his forehead on my jaw and let out a sigh. "I can't do this without you."

"Of course you can," I corrected. He'd been doing fine in Málaga for weeks without me.

"Not the crew and the drugs. I meant that I can't live without you. I can't fucking breathe when you're not with me. I've been a wreck."

I hated that he'd suffered, but I liked hearing how much he needed me. "It is the same for me."

He eased back slightly to look into my eyes. "I'm not keeping your fucking money."

"Yes, you will. Consider it an investment in our empire. You will quit smoking, though."

I stared at him and he huffed. "You're going to be a pain in my ass, I can tell. You are lucky I love you."

He still loved me?

Ignoring the sticky mess between us, I yanked him toward me and kissed him hard. My head was spinning. This was all I'd ever wanted, and I couldn't believe it was actually happening. I would happily stand by this man's side for the rest of my life. Whether that was here, Italy, Canna . . . I didn't care as long as we were together.

When we broke apart, he wore a sex-drunk smile on his face. "Ti amo, assassino."

Bending, I pressed a soft kiss to his swollen lips. "Ti amo, Don Ravazzani."

CHAPTER THIRTY

Giulio

Ravazzani Estate, Siderno
One week later

This time I told them we were coming.

This meant when Alessio and I stepped out onto the patio behind the castello, no one was surprised. Wary, but not surprised.

I ignored the stares of my family and focused on my half sister, Noemi. "*Principessa!*" I called out. "*Buon compleanno!*"

Her eyes went wide. "Lio!" She slid off Frankie's lap and took a step toward me, but paused when her gaze landed on Alessio. She wasn't comfortable with strangers, so I wasn't worried. Soon she would love my ragazzo as much as I did.

They all would.

Rafe had no such reservations. My half brother launched himself toward me. I passed Noemi's gift to Alessio to hold and lifted three-year-old Rafe off his feet. He liked when I flipped him upside down, so

I held him by his ankles and let him dangle. "Signorino! You are so much bigger than the last time I saw you."

Frankie scooped up Noemi and brought her over to say hello. I released Rafe and bent to kiss my little sister's cheek. "There she is," I said softly. "Ciao, Mimi."

She reached for me and I took her into my arms for a hug. Mimi was a snuggler. "Are you having a good birthday?" I asked her.

She nodded against my throat. I shifted and pointed to Alessio. "Mimi, this is il mio ragazzo, Alessio."

Alessio gave her a tiny smile and held out the present. "Tanti auguri a te." *Many good wishes to you.*

She perked up and accepted the present. "What do you say, Noemi?" Frankie urged.

"Grazie," Noemi said.

"Don't I even get a hello anymore?" Frankie muttered as we kissed cheeks.

"Hello, matrigna. You look even more pregnant than the last time I saw you." She was in her seventh month, but still appeared as beautiful as ever.

"Fuck off. And it's your father's fault." She moved to Alessio. "Ciao, Alessio. Welcome to our home."

He bent and kissed both her cheeks. "Buongiorno, Frankie. It is nice to properly meet you."

Frankie took Noemi out of my arms, whispering, "He is in a mood. Be careful."

I knew who she meant and I wasn't worried. I had plenty of experience handling my father.

I greeted Zia next, who held my cheeks and declared that I was too thin. Then she spoke quietly to Alessio, his big frame nearly folded in half so he could hear her better. While they were busy talking, I looked over to the head of the table.

Fausto was busy glaring at me, his fingers drumming impatiently on the wood. Marco was at his side, also unhappy. My father and I had business to attend to. Some of that was related to what I was doing in Málaga, but mostly it had to do with Alessio.

I walked over. Fausto unfolded and rose from his chair. When I was within reach he clasped my shoulders and kissed my cheeks. Then he pulled me in for a hug, clapping me on the back. "Figlio mio," he said, his tone tight. "I thought we discussed this."

When I announced I was bringing Alessio with me, my father had forbidden it. I'd chosen to ignore him. Quietly, I said, "No, you refused to discuss it. And I'm not coming here without him. So it's either the both of us or neither of us."

The lines in his forehead deepened. "I am uncertain I like this independence of yours. This is my home and I decide—"

A feminine throat cleared nearby. "*Our* home, you mean." Frankie lifted a single brow in her husband's direction. "And I told Giulio his boyfriend was always welcome at the castello."

A muscle jumped in Fausto's jaw as the two of them stared at each other, but he said nothing. Frankie was a badass, meeting my father's hard stare with one of her own. Marco broke the tension by standing, exclaiming, "Giulio Ravazzani, the king of Málaga!"

Chuckling, I kissed Marco's cheeks. "A slight exaggeration. Ciao, Zio."

"Presents, mamma!" This was from Noemi, who was eating tiny grape pieces at one end of the table.

"Okay, baby girl." Frankie gestured with her hands. "Everyone sit. Let's do cake and then she can open presents."

A large cake was brought out, and it was decorated with characters from a television show I didn't recognize. Noemi loved it and we all sang to her. After everyone finished eating, Frankie handed my little sister presents to open. Paper started flying. It was mostly boring kid stuff, toys and coloring supplies. Clothes and jewelry.

When Noemi finished, I said, "Wait! You didn't open my present!"

"Or mine," Alessio added.

"Whose present do you want first?" I asked Noemi. "Mine or Alessio's?"

"Yours," she told me, as I'd known she would.

I got up from the table and jogged around to the side of the castello, where her present was hidden. Grabbing the remote, I pressed a button, starting my present up and maneuvering it around the corner.

Frankie gasped, while Rafe yelled, "*Che figata!*" Yes, I knew my present was cool.

Noemi's eyes were the size of saucers. She eased down to the ground and came closer to stare at my gift.

I guided the child-sized pink electric convertible Lamborghini onto the patio. "What do you think, Mimi?"

"Giulio, what the hell? Are you trying to kill her?" Frankie said sharply, slapping her palm on the table. "Fausto. Do something before I strangle your oldest son."

I beckoned Mimi over. "It is perfectly safe. Lamborghini made it especially for her. It has seat belts and can't go over ten miles per hour." The door slid up toward the sky, like a real Lamborghini. "And it has parental controls that can override the driver at any point."

As I helped my little sister inside, Rafe appeared. "I want one, too! Papà, can I have a car?"

"Absolutely not," Frankie answered. "And we're not keeping this one."

"Dolcezza," Fausto said, rising to inspect the car. "You cannot take away the girl's present. Let me see it." He took the remote from my hand and studied it, then examined the car itself.

"They assured me it was safe for her," I said just for him. "I told them who it was for."

"And you went through my contact there?"

"Sì, certo."

Bending, he asked Noemi, "Do you want to take a very short drive to see if you like it?"

She nodded her head and gripped the tiny steering wheel. "Per favore, Papà!"

"Fausto, I swear to God," Frankie said. "If something happens to that child, I will make you regret it."

Fausto closed the door of the tiny car. Noemi waved and he gave her a thumbs up. Then he started it forward. She laughed, her smile the widest I'd ever seen it. After a few seconds my father stopped and Noemi protested. "Again, Papà!"

"Later, *polpetta*," he said and helped her out of the toy car. "What do you say to your brother for your present?"

"Grazie, Lio!" She hugged me and we all went back to the table to sit down.

"There's one more present," I told my younger sister. "Alessio brought you something."

With a sheepish smile, my man handed over the wrapped box to Noemi. As she accepted it, Frankie muttered, "At least one of you has sense."

I winked at her—and she kicked me under the table. "Stop spoiling my kids."

I shrugged. "I can't help it."

Noemi opened Alessio's box and pulled out a tiny leather circle. It had a metal tag hanging from a loop.

"Oh, my God," Frankie said. "Is that—?"

"Oh, shit," Marco muttered under his breath.

Alessio was already up and out of his chair, walking inside the castello where we'd left Noemi's present.

My sister shook the collar in her hand. "Mamma, what is it? A bracelet?"

Frankie was shooting daggers at me. "*What the fuck?*" she mouthed.

Alessio returned, a squirming puppy in his arms. There were gasps all around the table. Rafe came running over first, reaching up. "A dog! Let me see! I want to hold it."

"Raffaele," Fausto snapped. "Calm down. It belongs to your sister."

"We thought the children could share the dog, Don Ravazzani," Alessio said as he brought the animal closer to Noemi. "That is, if Noemi doesn't mind."

"A puppy," my little sister whispered. She reached a small hand out, then snatched it back, her expression fearful.

"Here," Alessio said, kneeling by Noemi's chair. "I'll hold her and you can pet her. Feel how soft she is."

Noemi stroked the dog's fur. "She is soft. What's her name?"

"That is for you to decide, principessa," I said.

"Is she nice?" Noemi asked Alessio.

"Very," he promised.

He was gentle, helping her and Rafe get used to the puppy, and I had a flash of someday doing this with our own kids. Alessio would make a great father. Did he even want children? We hadn't broached the topic yet.

Speaking of broaching topics, I needed to clear the air with my father. "Papà, a word in private?"

"Don't be surprised if you're locked out when you return," Frankie said to me.

I chuckled and kissed the top of her head. "Then you won't see what I brought you from Spain."

"I hate you."

"No, you don't." I walked over and joined up with my father. He began walking toward the farm.

When we were away from the others, I said, "You have to forgive him. I have."

"A perk of being the don is that I don't *have* to do anything."

"You do if you want to keep your oldest son in your life."

He clasped his hands behind his back. "Are you choosing him over your family?"

I answered without hesitation. "I did it once, with Paolo, and I will do it again."

"Ma dai, this man—this *assassin*—means that much to you? A man who tried to kill me, who was hired to kill you, and lied to you?"

"You have hired assassins before. You know it isn't personal. D'Agostino is to blame for both of those contracts, not Alessio." I let out a breath. "And yes, he means that much to me. I love him."

Fausto made a dismissive sound in his throat, one I knew well. I had to tell him the rest. "Do you know who bought out Buscetta's contract on my life?"

My father said nothing, so I continued. "Alessio found the German assassin and paid him off not to kill me. This was before he went to Sicily to kill Don Gero for me."

"Which you managed to do by yourself."

"Not quite by myself. I needed Alessio's help to find Don Gero." I clasped his shoulder, stopping him. "Do you know what he did after that?"

My father's expression was bland. "What?"

"He gave me all of his money. His houses and investments. Everything. He said his career had cost him the one thing he'd ever cared about—me. And so he couldn't keep the profits from that career any longer."

"So he bought your forgiveness."

Annoyed, I ground my back teeth together and struggled for calm. "And you giving Frankie your credit card in Rome was, what? Or when you let her work at the company before Rafe was born? Or when you paid for her to get her MBA? Or—"

"Basta," he snapped. "She didn't try to kill me or my father."

"You need to let it go. I am going to marry him, Papà. He will be my husband, my family. Whether we stay part of this family is up to you."

"This is blackmail." I started to argue, but he held up a hand. "But I can see that he cares about you. And I have heard the tales of Málaga."

Benito. That rat. "Yes, he does. Since we've met, he's saved my life countless times, and he's instrumental in helping to establish our 'ndrina there."

"Countless times?"

Of course my father latched onto this. He was worried about my safety so far away from Italy and the castello. "A few times," I amended.

He stared out at the vast estate, his eyes unseeing. "I will be watching, figlio mio. Keeping track of what he's doing. And if I need him, he will work for me at a moment's notice, no questions asked."

"Having Europe's best assassin as a son-in-law could have its perks."

"Believe me, I am aware."

"He's a good man, Papà."

"He had better be, Giulio. Because I will skin him alive if he ever hurts you again."

"After the beating in the dungeon, I am certain he knows it."

My father inhaled deeply, then let it out slowly. "All of my children are so stubborn. I don't know what I ever did to deserve this."

I couldn't help it—I laughed. "That's because we take after you."

We chatted a bit more about Málaga. I updated him on my progress there and the aftermath of Golubev's death. Then we headed back toward the castello.

I nearly stumbled when we came upon the patio. Noemi was curled up on Alessio's lap, along with the puppy. They were quietly talking and petting the small dog. My heart flipped over in my chest. Cristo santo, I loved this man.

Fausto walked over to Alessio's chair. He lifted Noemi into his arms. "Do you like your puppy, polpetta?"

"We named her Bolla." *Bubble.* "Do you like that name?"

"I love it." He kissed her neck, tickling her, and she giggled. "Almost as much as I love you."

He set her on the ground and she ran back over to the puppy. Grabbing Alessio's arm, she tried to pull him up. "Let's show her around inside, Alessio."

Alessio glanced at me and then my father, the question in his eyes. Was he allowed?

Fausto gave a brisk nod to Alessio. "You and the dog are welcome to come inside, Alessandro."

Alessio stood. "Thank you, Don Ravazzani."

Thank Christ. Relief poured through me. It wasn't much, but for my father this was a huge step toward accepting my future husband.

And guess what? Gay marriage just happened to be legal in Spain.

EPILOGUE

Giulio

Four months later
An undisclosed address somewhere in Italy

The venue had been changed three times, with the last location coming only fifteen minutes ago. When we arrived, everyone was searched for wires and weapons, and the room swept for listening devices. Guards were stationed outside the building and on the surrounding streets. If you didn't know better, you'd think a president or prime minister had come to visit.

On one side of the table sat Fausto, along with Zio Marco and me. Alessio and Benito were also both here, leaning against the wall. Giacomo Buscetta, now the head of the Buscetta family, sat opposite us, along with three of his men.

Pasquale Borghese, *capo crimine* and head of the 'Ndrangheta, had demanded this tête-à-tête with Fausto and me. He now sat at the head of the table, while Bernardo Virga, the most powerful *capomandamento* in the Cosa Nostra, took the chair at the other end.

After the death of his father and brother, Giacomo had taken over as don in Palermo. With his reputation as a thug, there'd been some concern in our circles that retaliation was imminent. Everyone was on edge.

Introductions were made. When Fausto came to me, he said, "And this is my oldest son, Giulio. He runs our 'ndrina in Málaga now."

I waited for Don Buscetta to sneer or roll his eyes. Yet I was greeted just as the others had been, with the utmost respect. Perhaps he didn't know I was gay?

"And this is your ragazzo, no?" Giacomo gestured to Alessio. "The famous sniper."

So he did know I was gay and that Alessio was mine. Hmm. When Alessio didn't react, I said, "Yes."

"I am a big fan of your work," Giacomo said to Alessio.

Alessio dipped his chin in acknowledgement but didn't speak. He preferred to let others do the talking at these things. Since coming to Málaga, he'd become my enforcer, spreading terror throughout the city as we solidified control of the criminal underground there. He was brutal and fearless, and I loved that he was mine.

Fausto opened the discussions by speaking first, which was done purposefully to show dominance. "My condolences," he said to Giacomo, "on the death of your father and brother."

Giacomo folded his big meaty hands on the table. I heard he'd been a great boxer back in his teens, and I believed it. His nose was crooked, like it had been broken one too many times, and he was huge, with a thick neck and a dark beard. "They were both pricks. I hated them," he returned casually.

There was really nothing to say in return to such a thing, so my father gestured to Borghese. "Let us get started?"

Borghese smiled like a kindly grandfather, surveying his naughty grandchildren. "The ugliness between your two families has dragged on far too long. We are here today to settle it."

"Ugliness?" Fausto tapped his fingertips on the table. "You mean how the late Don Buscetta pretended to be my ally while working with Mommo and D'Agostino to take me down? Or how Nino Buscetta sent men around Europe to hunt and kill my son like a dog? Is this the ugliness of which you speak?"

"You have repeatedly cut down our profits from the product coming in from the south." Giacomo gestured to Alessio. "And your men killed my father and my brother."

Fausto's expression revealed nothing. "This does not make us even. At all."

Virga cleared his throat. He was younger than I expected, for a man in such a prominent position, but he came from a powerful Sicilian family. "We must settle this discord because it is bad for business."

"We can't have more dead bodies in the streets," Borghese said. "Car bombs and shootings. This brings unwanted attention to everyone."

A muscle in my father's jaw jumped. He didn't like being told things he already knew.

"The Sicilian police," Virga added, "are agitated over these murders, making arrests. Looking for people to blame."

"That is a shame," Fausto said, not sounding sympathetic in the least. I could see the edges of Zio Marco's mouth twitching like he wanted to smile.

"It makes problems for me," Buscetta said. "Which in turn could make problems for you."

Fausto's gaze was cold and flat. "Is this a threat?"

"Signori," Borghese said. "Let us remain calm."

"Why are we here?" Buscetta snapped. "This is a waste of everyone's time."

"We must settle this," Virga said. "Make peace. Otherwise, we are in the newspapers with the Guardia di Finanza crawling up all our asses."

"And what do you propose?" Fausto leaned back in his chair. "Because I am not changing the way I do business." Meaning, he wouldn't cut the Sicilians into the Ravazzani drug trade.

"Don Virga and I have discussed this," Borghese said. "We would like to join the two families in marriage."

Everyone froze. My mind started spinning. They couldn't mean me. I was marrying Alessio. So, who were they talking about?

Fausto barked, "Absolutely not," while at the same time Buscetta growled, "Fuck no."

"We are not asking," Borghese said, his voice as brittle as ice. "It is our job to see it settled and this is what we have decided. Neither of you have a choice. There will be a wedding between your two families. And we have just the bride in mind . . . ."

———

Thank you for reading!

Ready for more??
Announcing
The Kings of Italy Book #5
with
Emma Mancini & Giacomo Buscetta

For release dates and updates, sign up for Mila's newsletter. When you do, you'll get a FREE bonus Fausto & Frankie short story!

ACKNOWLEDGMENTS

Finally! Giulio's story! I hope you enjoyed it.

Thank you to Jennifer Prokop for her amazing editing and help with this book. (I'm sorry about the timeline issues!) You can listen to Jen every week on the Fated Mates podcast, along with co-host Sarah MacLean.

All my love to my amazing writer pals who beta read this one, especially Diana Quincy.

A huge thank you to Letitia Hasser at RBA Designs, who rocks every single one of these covers.

Thank you, thank you, thank you to all the romance readers who have supported this series. I'm eternally grateful!

I would be nothing without my very own Paparino, Mr. Finelli, who helps me with these books and dinner and laundry and a thousand other things that make it possible for me to write. Ti amo, baby.

ABOUT THE AUTHOR

Though she is a *USA Today* bestselling author in another genre, Mila finally decided to write the filthy mafia kings she's been dreaming about for years. She's addicted to coffee, travel and Roy Kent.

For signed books, news & more, visit Mila's website at milafinelli.com.

Join Mila's Famiglia on Facebook!

Want more Fausto?
Sign up for Mila's newsletter and get a FREE Fausto &
Frankie bonus story!

ALSO BY MILA FINELLI

The Kings of Italy Series
MAFIA MISTRESS
MAFIA DARLING
MAFIA MADMAN
MAFIA TARGET

———

Start at the beginning with Mafia Mistress

Book 1 in the Kings of Italy series!

MAFIA MISTRESS

FAUSTO

I am the darkness, the man whose illicit empire stretches around the globe.
Not many have the courage for what needs to be done to maintain power . . .
but I do.

And I always get what I want.

Including my son's fiancée.

She's mine now, and I'll use Francesca any way I see fit. She's the perfect match to my twisted desires, and I'll keep her close, ready and waiting at my disposal.

Even if she fights me at every turn.

FRANCESCA

I was stolen away and held prisoner in Italy, a bride for a mafia king's only heir.

Except I'm no innocent, and it's the king himself—the man called il Diavolo—who appeals to me in sinful ways I never dreamed. Fausto's wickedness draws me in, his power like a drug. And when the devil decides he wants me, I'm helpless to resist him—even if it means giving myself to him, body and soul.

He may think he can control me, but this king is about to find out who's really the boss.

MAFIA MISTRESS is available in eBook, Print and Audio.